# SECOND EDEN

CARLTON W. AUSTIN

**Second Eden**



ISBN: 979-8895311172 (hc)
ISBN: 979-8895311158 (sc)
ISBN: 979-8895311158 (e)

Writers' Branding
(877) 608-6550
www.writersbranding.com
media@writersbranding.com

## Table of Contents

**We shall not cease from exploration**

**And the end of all our exploring**

**Will be to arrive where we started**

**And know the place for the first time**

*—T. S. Eliot*

**We approach a condition in which**

**we shall be amoral without the capacity**

**to perceive it and degraded without**

**the means to measure our decent.**

—Richard Weaver

**Any sufficiently advanced technology**

**is indistinguishable from magic.**

—Arthur C. Clark

# PROLOGUE

Washington, D.C. The near future...

Peter MacKenzie knew Bo Randall would try to kill him. Wouldn't he do the same, if their situations were reversed? They were both warriors, after all. The only question now was, did Bo, who sat beside him, stage-side at the Good 'n' Plenty, already know? Already have a plan? So far there were no certain indications, but for the fact that they were here, at Bo's urgent request.

Peter leaned back on his stool and fished another five-dollar bill from his jeans. As he did, he glanced at Bo, straining to detect any inkling of his hidden intentions. He knew Bo all too well—his explosive temper, quick as a struck match. And now he was sure that Bo knew about him and Beth. Why else would he have insisted they get together right away? And why here, at a seedy Georgetown strip joint? On Christmas Eve? Something was up, and it had stalked the recesses of his mind for the hour or so they'd talked and toasted and bought each other lap dances and reminisced about their days together as "Black Aces" in the elite VF-41 squadron aboard the aircraft carrier USS *Nimitz.* He'd flown his F-14 Tomcat fighter to the edge and back again and again, mostly as Bo's wingman, in the third Persian Gulf War against the Saudis and later against the Chinese in the Taiwan Straits. He remembered how they'd been in and out of scuffles then, both on deck and in the air. Invincible. Inseparable. Like brothers. *Not after tonight,* he thought. *Yeah, he'll try to kill me, all right. Like she just did.*

He rubbed his cheek, which still smarted, and winked at the lap dancer. Only moments before she'd slapped him hard against his face. He felt the marks of her studded ring outlined in pain at the corner of his grin, just next to a sensitive scar from a past encounter with another young woman of equally unsavory disposition. Now she ignored him, gliding to the other side of the stage, her lissome form caressing the dance pole like a scowling spent. He leaned slightly forward. "So, tell me again, Bo. What's this *Areopagus* gig all about?"

"Just a cargo run, really," Bo said. "We'll pick up the probe right after it injects into Earth orbit near the end of June. Should be back to Canaveral around the Fourth of July, give or take. But the freight goes right over there." He pointed over his shoulder. "To Goddard and Herr Professor Miles Lavisch, The Most High and God Almighty Arrogant Prick I've ever encountered."

Peter laughed. "*Intimate* friend, eh?"

"No, *all* my friends are pricks." Bo's eyebrow went up. "Let's just say I know him enough not to like him. Met him when we toured Goddard. He'll be in charge of the samples."

"Neat trick, that. The Mars shot, I mean." And truly he thought it was: Shoot a probe to Mars, have it land, pick up soil samples, then fly itself back home. He felt his body tense. "There's something I've got to tell you—"

Bo took a slug of beer. "*Areopagus* will pick up where the *Vikings* left off in seventy-six. Nothing else we've done since has been as good. Not the *Global Surveyor*. Not the *Odyssey*. Not *Spirit* or the any of the Rovers. Oh, we got nice pictures, all right. But only actual soil samples will tell us for sure if there's life on Mars—or ever was. What did you want to tell me?"

"Ahh, it's not important," Peter lied, hoping he wasn't losing his nerve. He didn't know where the words came from, but somehow there they were, falling on his ears in his own voice: "When's the baby due?" He forced himself to look Bo in the eyes.

Bo stared at him for what seemed an eternity. "July. Right after the mission. Funny you ask. Beth thinks that getting married and having some kids is just what you need."

"What?" Peter felt sweat trickle down the back of his neck.

"Look how happy it made ol' George Bailey, there," Bo said, inclining his head in the direction of a TV that hung behind the bar, where *It's a Wonderful Life* played silently in the background.

"Kids?" Peter snarled insincerely. "Hell, they're the reason *'Ol George'* tried to kill himself in the first place! He'd of been better off if Clarence the angel hadn't saved him."

"Nothing changes your perspective like kids, Pete." Bo slapped Peter's thigh hard. "Nothing makes you want your wife more, want to protect her.... Know what I mean?"

"Why would I?" He cringed and felt suddenly weak, suddenly unwarriorlike, as he glanced down into the white foam of his beer, noticing how the bubbles kept popping away, like the ticking of a clock. "You know what I've always said about women—"

" 'If they didn't have a pussy, men would never talk to them.' Yeah, yeah, I've heard it all before."

Then Peter thought of Beth—and all the others. A stab of guilt surprised him, caused his stomach to knot fiercely. "You know, the guy who wrote that book was right. Men really *are* from Mars. Women may as well be a different species."

Bo shook his head and looked up. "Mars? Venus? Damned if I know. Or care. What I do know is, I couldn't live without Beth and the kids."

"Speaking of our fair alien friends." Peter rubbed the scar on his chin, which still smarted, and nodded his head toward the stage, where his dancer was making her way back toward them. Earlier she'd brushed her taut breast against his cheek, lolling her nipple on his upper lip, just beneath his nose, her hair falling on his face as she nibbled his ear. She smelled of lilacs. He'd rewarded her appropriately enough, or so he thought. Now he couldn't resist one further taunt and waggled his finger for her to approach, but her glare turned meaner. She gave him the finger and jerked her head away, her body following quickly to face the opposite direction.

"Let's get out of here," Bo said. "I think you've worn out our welcome."

Peter zipped his brown leather flight jacket and pushed open the door with his shoulder. A gust of snow-laced wind cooled his still stinging face. He looked up at the full moon, which broke in and out of racing clouds, causing everything to flicker weirdly. Walking fast along the slushy sidewalk, he tried to maintain his well-studied, cocksure swagger, tried to muster his courage, and stayed just far enough ahead of Bo so as not to have to look at him. His stomach floated curiously about, it was a queasiness he'd not felt since having pre-launch jitters before a combat mission. And the more he thought about it, the more he didn't want this to be his last mission. "Could you believe the tits on that babe?" he said finally, forcing a grin as he glanced back at Bo.

"Tucking a five-spot in her Gee-string is one thing," Bo laughed, catching up to him. "But you're not supposed to touch her there, remember?" He popped a mint in his mouth. "Want one?"

"Don't have any Cracker Jacks, do you?" Peter managed to keep Bo in his peripheral vision.

"You and your Cracker Jacks," Bo snorted. "It's a wonder you've still got teeth, boy!" He ran his hand over his balding head, brushing the snow from the horseshoe-shaped rim of hair that circled his skull from sideburn to sideburn before putting on a black, wool-knit stocking cap. His eyebrows bent closer, darkening his already tanned face. "It was good seeing you again, Pete." "Yeah. Same here. Guess it'll be the last time...." The words caught in his throat. "For a while, I meant. Till after your mission."

"Probably so.... I'll be in Houston right up to launch."

They walked faster now, bobbing and weaving through harried crowds of pedestrians loaded with last-minute Christmas gifts, faces bent down against snow that came in blustery squalls. Revelers in the restaurants and bars that lined the sidewalks sang fractured, besotted versions of carols; laughter poured from every open door. But as they turned the corner, the holiday sounds quieted.

For a moment Peter thought they were alone. But then, halfway down the block, he spotted a lone figure wearing a Santa hat and ringing a bell. Beside him a small donation pail hung beneath a tripod. It seemed an odd place to set up shop if you wanted much in the way of donations. He stopped, picked up a handful of snow and made a ball. The ragged scar on his chin tingled, began to itch, as it had an uncanny way of doing whenever there was about to be trouble. He brushed the frozen ball against the old wound. Now was the time to come clean, to tell Bo the truth, but again he hesitated. "You know, I wish I'd gone to NASA when you did."

Bo shrugged. "What? Intelligence work can't be that boring."

"You'd be surprised."

"Well, piloting CEVs—"

"CEVs?"

"Yeah, Crew Exploration Vehicles. That's what we call the new space shuttles, which is still all they are—shuttles. Anyway, it's not as sexy as tooling around in an armed Tomcat; I can tell you that—and it's more dangerous. Wanna tell me what's eating you?"

Peter threw his snowball at a passing cab, the icy sphere gliding harmlessly past the rear bumper. How could he have missed such an easy target? As he watched the cab's taillights recede, something in their red aura caught his eye. Ahead, three men had circled the bellringer. One grabbed the handle to the money pail, but Santa would not give it up. They spun around each other like kids playing London Bridges until the other two thugs tackled him, bringing him down into the street, pounding him with their fists and what looked like a length of pipe. "Hey! Let him go!" Without further thought, he charged after them.

"Wait, Pete!"

The attackers looked up but didn't stop. There was a bright orange flash. A loud *pop!* Like a bursting party balloon. The impact slammed the bellringer to the ground, and the shooter yanked the money pail free. As he did, his gun fired again, wildly, knocking out the street lamp.

Peter had seen the flashes a seeming eternity before the shots boomed in his ears. Everything had slowed down. He felt his legs uncontrollably back peddle, but he couldn't stop. He slid into the lamppost. Close to the gunman. Only steps away. He watched as if in a dream while the gunman turned with a smooth, almost casual motion, and pointed the pistol's dark barrel at him.

*Click!...Click! Click! Click!* The man flung the weapon at a storefront, shattering the glass. Flying shards stung Peter's cheek, snapping his paralysis. He bolted after them. Slipping in the accumulating snow, he chased the thugs to the end of the block, where they ran without stopping through traffic across M Street, then down the steep hill toward K Street, deftly using their shoes like skis as they slid into the shadows beneath the Whitehurst Freeway overpass. Just before they disappeared, one of them dropped something.

Deciding that three against one in the darkness was too great a risk, Peter skidded to a stop where a glint of gold shone through a thin veil of snow. He dug out what looked to him to be something like an Egyptian ankh.

"Those bastards! For a few stinkin' bucks and *this?"* He looked around to find the streets, which moments before had been crowded with blaring horns, blinking lights and scurrying pedestrians, strangely deserted and silent. He trudged back up the hill, panting clouds of steam, where Bo was pulling the wounded man out of the street. Without the streetlight it was dark, but then, with an explosion of light, the moon broke through and he could see the bellringer's long blond hair was matted with blood, which surged through a tattered hole in his greatcoat, dribbling onto the virgin snow in dusky pools.

Bo hoisted the man to a sitting position on the curb. "What's your name, fellow?"

"Apollyon," the bellringer said with the air of a stunned animal. "I'm an angel."

"Sure, Clarence," Peter said derisively, thinking of Bo's earlier comment, "and I'm George Bailey." He nodded his head toward Bo. "This here's Ernie, the cab driver."

"You mock me? I'm *Apollyon!*" the man insisted. "Don't you know it's time?"

"What?" Peter decided not to try to talk logic. "Look, we've got to get you to a hospital. You're bleeding pretty badly." He looked at the dark, accumulating pools of blood and thought the man would never make it.

"Ohhh..." the bellringer groaned. A strong gust of wind swirled into a mini tornado, sprinkling his blond hair with snowflakes that glittered like sequins in the moonlight. Then he began to shudder. He heaved and bucked, as if having a seizure, before quieting down. "Peter!" he blurted, grabbing his arm.

Peter felt the blood go out of his face. "How'd he know my name?" He looked at Bo, who stared back, glassy-eyed and silent.

"To everything there is a season. A time to be born, a time to die. A time—" The bellringer coughed. "I'm cold."

Peter took off his flight jacket and draped it over the wounded man.

"And death and hell delivered up the dead, which were in them: and they were judged every man according to his works. Don't you remember? Help me, Bo!"

"Who are you?" Bo demanded, his voice a mixture of anger and fear.

"Got your cell phone, Bo?"

"No, damnit, it's in the car."

"Well, go call nine one one."

"No! Wait!" the bellringer gasped. "You think I'm crazy, but you're wrong."

Peter knelt beside the man, holding his head up. Then he caught the man's sorrowful eyes. For a split second he thought he was losing his mind as strange images flashed before him, images of mayhem, chaos, death. He shook his head, trying to clear it, but had to look away.

"And I saw a new heaven and a new earth, for the first heaven and the first earth were passed away." The bellringer seemed to be in a trancelike state for just a moment, far away, but then he was all too present. "But it won't be like you think it will," he said with a queer grin.

"What the hell's he saying, Bo?"

"He thinks he's Apollyon. One of the angels in the Bible. In *Revelations*."

"You, Beauregard Randall," the bellringer choked, his head shaking, "you will begin it. You will find our chalice." Then he turned his head. His eyes grew luminous with moonlight. "And you, Peter MacKenzie, you will witness the end as you drink the last measure of its bittersweet portion. For I have seen it!"

"He's nuts," Bo said, voice rattling. His face shone a spectral white from the cold and the snow that mounded on the ridges of his cheeks.

They tried to move the man up against the wall, but the bellringer winced. "My wing!" he complained. "You're hurting my wing...." His voice trailed off to a mere whisper.

"Okay, Clarence," Peter soothed, and tilted his head toward the street where an ambulance had just pulled up. A man wearing a police uniform got out.

"He's shot," Bo told the man. "Talking crazy too. Must've wandered away from a mental hospital or something."

"Yeah, a real nutcase," Peter heard himself say uneasily as he reached for his jacket.

But the bellringer yanked it back, "Look to the moon! Look to the moon!" Then he laughed weirdly and began to sing: "When the moon hits your eye like a big pizza pie, that's the *ennnd….*"

"Burt the cop is here to help you," Bo said, picking up on the Christmas-story charade.

"We'll take him," the police officer replied, handing Peter his jacket. A second uniformed man joined him. They quickly lifted the bellringer onto a gurney, jumped in the ambulance, and sped away without any lights.

Peter shivered, and he knew it wasn't just from the cold. "Something's wrong here. They didn't even question us."

"How'd they even get here?" Bo said. "I never called."

"Someone must have seen what happened." Peter looked around, but the streets were still vacant and dark.

"Let's get out of here," Bo said through chattering teeth.

They walked on towards their cars, parked several blocks away, hunched over in silence against the driving snow, which seemed to reappear in spurts every time the moon went away.

Peter glanced at Bo, who, clothes now completely whitened with snow, reminded him of an altar boy, a ghost—or an angel. "That guy really spooked me." He bent over and scooped up enough snow for another ball.

"Come on, Pete. 'My wing,' for Christ's sake? Remember Y2K? A bust. Nothin's gonna happen. Nothing like *that* anyway—"

He fingered the snowball absently, waiting for a target. "That's what they said about *Titanic,* 'Nothin's gonna happen'... That's what we all thought about terrorism, too. Not here, not on our front porch. That was before New York postcards without the World Trade Centers."

"Maybe you *don't* belong in Intelligence work," Bo said with a laugh that seemed to have a bitter edge. "Besides we do know he wasn't really *Clarence*."

"What the hell do you mean?"

"Clarence didn't have his wings, remember?"

"Very funny. But how'd he know our names? And what was that stuff about you and me and the beginning and the end and all that?"

Bo drew the front of his coat collar up around his throat and said nothing.

"And besides, you're forgetting the end of the movie," Peter said archly. "Clarence *did* win his wings." With all the commotion, he'd almost forgotten his planned confession. He decided if Bo did nothing, he'd let it ride for now. He'd had enough excitement for one night. He felt wet with sweat. Still, his hands were cold and he almost couldn't get his key into the door. He took off his leather flight jacket and was about to fling it into the car when he noticed something odd. "Hey, look at this." He held up the satin lining.

Bo picked a small white feather off the inside of the jacket Peter had just used to warm the wounded bellringer. "Maybe he *was* Clarence after all," he chuckled.

Fingers numb from the cold, Peter took the slender plume from Bo. A shiver shook his hand. Suddenly a raw gust of wind snatched the feather into the hollow darkness.

# CHAPTER 1

The space CEV *Discovery II,* in high Earth orbit...23:30 Hours, June 28...

"Jesus, i'—" a crackle of transient static garbled Bo Randall's transmission, then "—'s here!"

Floating lazily in the blackness of space near the aft end of the *Discovery II's* cargo bay, Bo could just make out the surprised expression on Carla Pascal's face as her lips formed the words.

"What did you say?" she asked in her post-feminist take-charge way. "'Jesus is here'? Maybe you can get him to fix that snare for you, 'cause we're gonna need it in about two minutes."

Bo shook his head, slightly annoyed at his smart-aleck mission specialist's tone. "What I meant was, *it's here,* it's early, and it looks to be about five klicks too high and a couple back. We'll have to reposition to capture it." He pointed back over his shoulder where the ship had just traced its invisible path six hundred and twenty five miles above a nearly cloudless, cornflower blue Pacific and where the *Areopagus* now lay silently against a star-studded field of black. "Grapple's fixed now, anyway. I'm heading in."

As he clambered along the sill of the cargo bay, heading for the airlock in the forward bulkhead, Earth rose over the edge of the bay door, completely filling his visual field. Its stark beauty nearly took his breath away. It appeared so close he felt he could reach out and touch it. With no intervening atmosphere in space, everything at a distance looked closer and clearer. For an instant, he dreamily forgot what he was doing. His foot slipped on the frozen edge of the sill, causing him to float into a sharp-edged bolt before he could recover his balance. *That's all I need,* he thought. *Rip my suit and have my blood boil away.*

In his mind's eye he saw Beth at the door hearing the news. "We regret to inform you...." *I wonder if she'd care?*

But magnetically, the vision of Earth pulled him back out of himself. He looked homeward again, spellbound. Below, the blue Pacific met the yellow margins of the Yucatan peninsula with stark relief. A brilliant white cloud deck covered half its length. Farther down he saw the deep greens of the Amazon rainforest, with its stunning array of life, now partially obscured by the smoke from hundreds of fires, intentionally set by jungle nomads, which would eventually destroy thousands of square miles of precious habitat, eating away at the planet's irreplaceable core of life.

Watching the smoke drift in waves and curls across the continent, he was reminded again just how thin the atmosphere looked from up here, how thin it really was. He remembered an article he'd read concerning a six-mile-diameter asteroid that had collided with the Earth near a small Mexican town somewhere just down below. What was its name? *Chixulub? Yeah.* Mayan for "tail of the Devil," or so he remembered. According to the article, this event, some 65 million years ago, had signaled the end for half the species on Earth—including the dinosaurs.

He wondered how long it would be before another, perhaps larger, asteroid came to rip that thin atmosphere—our world, our lives—away. He thought how easy it would be for the Earth to become like the moon. It was just a matter of time. But this was the pristine present, and he would not spoil it with embarrassment over some stray vocalization. He hit the mute switch on his communicator.

"Mighty moon," he then said aloud. The moon, half bathed in the sun's yellow glow, craters clearly visible, testifying to thousands of battles with giant asteroids and comets over the eons, glowered back at him. "Yeah, old fella, it would be all too easy for us all to go the way of the dinosaurs and have the Earth end up like you, a lifeless, lonely chunk of space rock." He thought of Beth again—and Peter—and was glad he hadn't confronted them about the affair. Somehow his family, bound together, even if imperfectly, was paramount to him now, as was, inexplicably, forgiveness. *Guess we all have our dark side. Just like the moon.*

For he knew, as most people outside NASA didn't, that except for data from the *Clementine* probe in 1994, little was known about the dark side of the moon. Because of its peculiar orbit, which caused it to rotate three hundred and sixty degrees in the same amount of time it took to orbit the Earth, one side of the moon—the dark side—forever lay hidden from the Earth's prying eyes.

"At least Mars has an atmosphere," he said absently, "and maybe life. That's what the *Areopagus* should tell us—if we can just get it aboard in one piece." With one last look back at Earth, then the moon and then the *Areopagus,* which hovered above him like a sullen witness, he headed for the airlock.

* * *

"Well, our Martian package is safely in the vault," Bo said with relief, as he floated up through the inter-deck access portal to the main deck.

"Party time," Carla Pascal said. She winked and did a half somersault, catching an errant penlight that drifted aimlessly about the cabin before stabilizing herself on the back of the pilot's seat. She brushed a wisp of blond hair off her tanned face. The just-visible crow's feet around her bunny-blue eyes deepened in a smile. "Boss, anybody ever tell you that you look like the guy who used to play Captain Piccard on Star Trek?"

Bo gave a halfhearted laugh and winked back, not failing to notice how nicely her cobalt blue mission suit highlighted her slender waist and dainty breasts. If it weren't for Beth, he'd often thought... "No, he was *bald!*"

"Remember Seinfeld?" Mission Specialist Bill Quincy countered. "More like a Kramer and George combination. But you're right about the hair." His close-cropped reddish beard, contrasted sharply with his brown crew cut, which rimmed his baby-moon face like a halo.

"You mean Kramer without the Osama bin Laden nose, don't you?" co-pilot Max Hudson added, smiling.

"All right, all right," Bo relented. "Have your fun at the old man's expense." Then he looked at Max. "What's the status, Number One?"

"Aye, aye, Captain," Max saluted and continued. "All's well and buttoned down at the helm."

"I always wondered how Data's link measured," Carla joked. "C'mon, Captain Jean Luke, let's celebrate—"

*"What the—?"*

Suddenly, utter blackness engulfed them. Bo had never experienced a complete power failure. He couldn't even think how it was possible. There were no alarms, no flashing lights. The only sounds were the whirring of gyros and electric motors as they spun down, bleeding off rpms, on their way to a useless mechanical death.

"Complete power failures ain't supposed to be possible," Max Hudson said, his voice strained but even. "What's goin' on?"

"Certainly not something you see every day," Bo affirmed, directing his voice toward where he thought Max should be.

"Right now I can't see anything," Carla stammered.

"And to answer your question," Bo said with determined calmness, even as a trickle of sweat make its way down his back, "I don't know. Any ideas? Carla? Bill? Anything to do with the special hookups to the sample cases?"

"Don't think so," Bill answered. "But I do know this, without power to suck this dirty air through the lithium hydroxide canisters—"

"We could use the portable oxygen units...and the suits," Carla blurted.

"Yeah, right," Bill argued. "But this isn't *Alien*, and you aren't Rippley. And without power we're just four space road kills."

"Road kills? That's quaint." Bo forced a small chuckle. "Hit by what? A space gremlin? There's always an explanation. We've just got to find it—and pronto!"

"Bo's right," Max said. "We've all just got to calm down. Think this through."

"That's bizarre," Carla declared too loudly, as if they'd all been removed to a distance because of the darkness. "Even the flashlight doesn't work! Can anyone explain that?"

Bo could hear her rapidly click the small penlight switch on and off, on and off. "Let's get back to protocol. Start the checklists."

"With no light, it's going to be tough," Max complained.

"We'll have to do it by feel," Bo ordered, a little annoyed at Max's whining. "As for explanations, they'll just have to wait. Let's get started, shall we?" Then something drew his attention to the windows, where moments before he'd marveled at the spectacular view of the Arabian Peninsula outside. Slowly, he drifted toward the cockpit side window. "My God! Where'd the Earth go—?"

Like a silent bolt of lightning, a searing blue radiance exploded into the orbiter, momentarily blinding him. Reflexively he jerked back, covering his eyes, which screeched with pain.

Then it began.

"Hear it?" Carla whispered.

Bo felt the sound before he heard it. Starting low on the frequency scale, the warbling vibration rumbled through his internal organs like gas, and then shifted several octaves higher, to a more piercing frequency, then lower again. It was a queer, living sound with an eerie intelligence about it. It investigated, probed, and searched; it stole innermost secrets and all sense of control. For an instant, he thought he'd lose consciousness, but then—abruptly—there was silence...*and light*. "Is everyone okay?" he asked hopefully, but thinking it unlikely.

With a flurry of hands, they patted themselves down, as if to make sure all the parts were still there.

"What the hell's that?" Carla cried, pointing to the starboard window.

Bo had noticed movement outside the window an instant before Carla spoke. It pulled his head as if on a string up against the glass. There it was! Moving deliberately and unhurriedly off into the distance, devoid of exterior lights or discernible markings, a hulking metallic shape, which moments before had totally eclipsed their view of Earth, was now clearly outlined against the canvas of the placid, blue ocean. Familiar with at least the rumors of any new aerospace technology, he knew instantly this was a craft of alien origin. *My God! They do exist!* He was instantly glad he'd only thought it, not said it.

*"Discovery!* This is mission control, over! *Discovery!* This is Houston, do you read?" The frantic calls repeated.

Somehow Bo hadn't even noticed the power was back. Mission control wanted to know why they had been incommunicado for the better part of a quarter-hour. *It couldn't have been that long!*

"Houston, this is Commander Bo Randall aboard *Discovery.*" He paused, intentionally deepening his voice, fully aware that what he was about to say could very easily be misconstrued, could very easily end his career. "We—that is, the entire crew—have just made a sighting...."

# CHAPTER 2

Miles Lavisch sat in his office at NASA's Goddard Space Flight Center in Greenbelt, Maryland, picked up the front section of the *Washington Post,* and reached for his glasses.

"Damnit! Where the hell are they?"

He threw the newspaper to the floor and, for the third time this day, frisked himself in vain. No glasses. Resigned, he decided to use his pearl-handled magnifying glass that his own mother had used for needlepoint in her declining years, which he kept in his desk for occasions just such as this. He retrieved it from his top drawer along with a hand-wrapped Cuban Partagas double-corona cigar from a plain brown box, nestled secretly in the far corner. Biting off the tip, he savored the bitter tobacco taste for a moment before spitting the residue on the floor. With the care of a surgeon, he dipped the corner of his handerkerchief into his tea, then gently wiped down the brown tobacco-leaf wrapping of the big cigar. The tea, he'd found, imparted an added hint of piquant flavoring to his favorite smoke. He reached for the Bunsen burner he kept going at all times to heat his tea water and light his tobacco. Using its pale blue flame, he caused the cigar's tip to glow bright orange before mouthing the tip and puffing gales of silver-blue smoke across the room.

Mildly satisfied, he spread the newspaper across his desk. He'd just begun reading through the magnifier when a front-page headline caught his eye:

CIA DIRECTOR TO TESTIFY AT *DISCOVERY II* INQUEST

Today CIA Director Carl Snow will explain to a special Senate investigative committee why he ordered the spacecraft *Discovery II* to land at Edwards AFB instead of at Cape Canaveral as scheduled and why the crew was quarantined until their deaths in a mysterious fire just hours later.

"I want to know why the CIA was involved in a NASA flight that had no defense-related mission," said Michael Tomlinson, Senate minority leader and committee chairman.

The spacecraft's objective was to retrieve the Mars probe *Areopagus,* which had returned to Earth after a two-year journey.

Also at issue are unconfirmed reports that *Discovery II*'s Commander, Beauregard "Bo" Randall, had reported sighting a UFO just before the disputed change of landing orders. Admiral Snow has denied any knowledge of these reports and the existence of Majestic Twelve, a rumored UFO research group of which he is said to be a member.

A former Joint Chiefs of Staff Chairman and decorated veteran of three wars, Admiral Snow has often been mentioned as a probable presidential candidate...

"Lying bastard," Miles grumbled. "Just what we need, another Bill Clinton. But then, maybe Snow will tell us what the meaning of *is* is."

Just then his office door creaked opened. He looked up to see his reading glasses dangling from a hand that snaked inside, soon followed by his daughter Molly's smiling face. Her smile, however, quickly faded as she wagged her finger at his cigar.

"You don't mention the cigar, I won't call you gimp," he said, crushing the butt into an ashtray. He planted a fatherly kiss on her cheek, as she tucked the glasses into the breast pocket of his tweed jacket. "Where'd you find them?"

"In the hallway."

"Well, well," he said with mild annoyance, "to what do I owe this rare pleasure?"

Molly picked up his newspaper and quickly began to riffle through it. "Uncle Malcolm said it was time I paid you a visit."

"Don't mess up my paper! And Malcolm should mind his own business. I'm surprised AJ didn't talk you out of it."

"Allison Jamison may be my best friend, but she doesn't set my social schedule. Besides, I think she's rather fond of you." Molly kept flipping through the paper.

What are you looking for, anyway?" He reached for his cigar, held its tip over the Bunsen burner's flame.

"Comics," she said flatly. "Blondie, to be specific. I'm not surprised you don't remember?"

"Blondie? Huh, didn't even know they were still around."

"Because you don't read comics." She bobbed her head from side to side, leafing through page after page, a delighted look on her fresh freckled face. "I'm a diehard Blondie lover. She's a rock. She's never changed. Not in more than fifty years. And even by today's standards, she's *all* woman."

"So long as it's not Dagwood you admire," he said, exhaling a torrent of smoke. "I don't suppose you have time for a tour?" She looked sternly at his cigar, but he stared her down. He wouldn't be cowed by her, especially not on his own turf.

"Can we?" she asked, waving the smoke from away from her face. "The way I was treated in the lobby, you'd have thought I was with al Qaeda. Why the tight security?"

"High-containment procedures: BL-four protocol. And, yes, we can. It's still *my* lab."

"Long as I don't have to salute you."

Miles shrugged, got up and headed for a side door, waggling his finger for her to follow. "Tight security might be a pain in the ass, but it's necessary. A Martian microbe newly introduced to the human population would be devastating."

"I know. Like Native Americans and smallpox. Or Polynesians and syphilis."

"A lot of people vehemently opposed this project for that very reason," he said. "They wanted a manned probe to do the experiments on Mars while we observed the results remotely."

"I thought that's what you always wanted," Molly said.

"At first, I did. Because no containment protocol is perfect. But economics won out. Sending men is too ex*pen*sive."

"Too expensive?" Molly asked, shaking her head slowly. "Depends what you think the human race is worth, I suppose."

"To be honest," Miles admitted, "I'm glad as hell it worked out this way. Otherwise I'd have died waiting."

"Oh, come on, Dad."

He felt her touch his shoulder and pulled away. It made him feel an uncertain discomfort. And in her little-girl green eyes he saw sadness—and the ever-present fear. Still, he could recall no remorse—and felt none now.

He led her down the hallway, her high-heels echoing smartly in an off-beat rhythm against the old but highly polished green and muted-gray vinyl tile floor, through a series of windowless doors, which, every so often, broke the boring expanse of sterile white walls. Finally, he reached the changing room of the pre-containment area, which was adjacent to the main containment area where the rock samples from Mars were stored, and shouldered the door open.

"Here," he said, handing her a disposable sterile lab coat, cap and booties, the kind used in hospitals for patients in quarantine, "get into these." He began dressing himself. "Need any help?"

Molly's face reddened. "No, I'm fine. Really."

An automatic set of doors shushed open. A familiar rush of air told him the area was under the normal negative pressure required to keep alien microbes from escaping.

Molly knocked on the containment lab's transparent enclosure. "Three-inch?"

"Uh-huh. Standard Plexiglas. But you knew that. Inside is sterilized and completely robotic. Everything's operated from the control room." He pointed at an elevated platform enclosed in another wall of Plexiglas that looked like the bridge of the starship *Enterprise.*

"If someone wants to work with a sample," he said, stepping in front of her, "a conveyor belt moves the containers to specific experimental stations, where automated protocols can be performed." He swept his arm around the entire inner perimeter, pointing at the individual stations. Beside each one, special gloves protruded through the Plexiglas, so a worker could manipulate the samples without venturing inside the tightly controlled room.

"Are those the actual sample cases?" Molly asked, inclining her head toward two shiny stainless-steel boxes in the corner.

"Those are them," he said with sweet self-satisfaction. "The one that's about a meter square is the surface-sample container. It's supposed to have the larger pieces. The box that's about half as big has one hundred forty-four separate compartments, each with a sample taken from about eighteen inches below the surface, every ten degrees of arc, four samples per arc, at half-meter intervals, starting at the base of the *Areopagus.*"

She shook her head. "Seems like a long way to go for so little."

"Not if we find what we're looking for."

"And have you?"

"Not yet. We got the samples from the West Coast just yesterday. Then there was a little excitement when the larger box was dropped off the back of the delivery truck." He saw the shock in her wide green eyes. "Our paleontologist, Paul Blalock, was responsible for that little fiasco. Luckily nothing came undone." He guided her through another steel door, which set off a symphony of animal chatter.

"Animals from Mars?" Molly asked, pointing at cages in a smaller room at the far end of the lab.

"If that was a joke, it was pretty lame," he said derisively. "No, there's a communicating air shaft to the area with the samples you just saw. The Macaques, chimps, and smaller mammals—rabbits and such—are being exposed to—" He shrugged, palms up. "Who knows what?"

Entering the control room, they had a commanding view of the entire automated laboratory area. He drew up a couple of swivel chairs. "We can get out of these things," he said, doffing his cap and booties. "Really don't need the damned things anyway, since we're not going into the main containment area. Not for now at least."

Molly ditched her sterile cloths and sat down with her left leg stretched out, her hands clasped together, resting on her lap. "What's the paleontologist for, anyway?"

Miles knew he made his daughter nervous, and not without reason. He liked it that way. He looked at the no-smoking sign and began fumbling around the desk drawers in search of one of the many half-smoked cigars he kept hidden around lab, but found none. "A very vocal minority in the scientific community thinks the probabilities favor past life rather than current life on Mars, so we had to be prepared to look for fossil remains. At the last minute Blalock was sent—"

"I thought *you* handpicked the team."

"I did. All except him." Finding a loose pack of matches, he tore off one and began to chew on it. "He's trained to find small fossilized pieces of bones or teeth and such—stuff we'd overlook. What he can find in a pile of dirt really is amazing. Too bad I hate his guts."

"You're not serious?"

"As a heart attack, my dear."

Molly frowned. "I wish you wouldn't put it like that. Given your own medical condition."

He snorted, took out some pictures showing the surface of Mars taken from space and spread them on the desk. "See here? Mars *Odyssey* took these. And the British spacecraft *Express* took these." He ran his finger over an area with lighter formations that looked just like dry riverbeds. "Those are clearly erosion patterns. And here, look here. That would have made great ocean-front property—a few hundred million years ago."

"So Mars did have water in the past?"

"Still does," he said confidently. "No doubt about it. A series of rover vehicles proved it over the past few years. Because of that, we fully expect to find microbial life in our samples, at the very least."

"I thought the last Mars Lander—what was it called?"

"There have been a lot of them." He spit out a lump of masticated match. "The *Pathfinder* and *Sojourner* probes a few years back. And not too long ago the *Spirit,* the *Opportunity,* and others. But they didn't have any life experiments on board. The last one that did was the British *Beagle 2*, and it failed to work after landing. No, only our *Viking*s One and Two, back in the seventies, had the right experiments on board."

"I thought they didn't find anything," Molly said.

He shook his head. “That’s what most people think. But in fact, the evidence for life was quite strong, just not conclusive.”

“Like that rock from Antarctica a while back?”

He watched her twist the locket that hung from a long gold chain around her neck, just like her mother used to. It was an irritating habit. He exhaled loudly. “We have to be sure. This time we will be.”

Around them an array of video screens and monitor lights blinked furiously, like a Christmas display gone wild; digital readouts, toggle switches, dials and buttons encircled the room in colorful belts. An atmosphere of pure technology. And he inhaled it like oxygen. He gestured with a broad sweep of his hand. “What do you think?”

“*Very* impressive.”

“I call it Fortress Lavisch,” he said proudly. “We’re making history here, Molly.”

“No doubt about that.” Molly rubbed her arms as if she were cold.

“Want to be a part of it? It’s the best gift I could ever give you. Something to tell your grandchildren about it.” He snorted a laugh. “Well...maybe not.”

Molly looked away. He noticed the back of her neck turn red and smiled with silent satisfaction.

“I-I’m still not—”

“Stupid girl! I see you haven’t changed.”

“Th-th-that’s not f-fair!”

“I won’t ask you again. And stop that stuttering! It’s annoying.”

She swung around in the chair so fast he thought she would lunge at him, but she just glared, almost as if in a state of catatonia. What he saw now was new to him. Not fear, not even just anger. This was hate.

Molly’s whole body shook as she spoke. “Wha-Wha-Why do you al-al—?”

“Calm down,” he said, cutting off the stutter. He hated the sound of it. “Your mother never knew what she caused by dying.”

“That was when I was seven,” Molly said icily. “I didn’t start stuttering until much later. And you know why—”

"Not that again! I never touched you—not in that way. Goddamned psychobabblists gave you that idea. Never should've taken you."

She seemed to struggle to puff out the words. "Y-You did-did more than t-t-that—"

"Oh, get a grip. No one ever believed that—no one's going to." A chirping warning tone sounded. A red light blinked on the console just below a small TV monitor that showed three men in sterile garments walking briskly down the brightly lit corridor. A moment later they entered the control room.

"Molly," Miles began, "uh, *Doctor* Molly Lavisch, I'd like you to meet Doctor James Haverhills, Kim Lee, and Doctor Paul Blalock. Gentlemen, my daughter."

"It's a pleasure to meet you," Molly said, offering her hand with what seemed near-complete composure.

Relieved she'd calmed herself, Miles continued the introductions. "Doctor Haverhills is the team mineralogist. Paul, here, is the gentleman I mentioned earlier, the one who—"

"It was an accident," Paul Blalock said dismissively, extending his hand to Molly. "Pleasure's all mine, Molly."

Miles glared at Blalock, before moving on with the introductions. "Kim, here, is our chief technical wizard. He operates the scanning electron microscope, the X-ray crystallography gear, the robotics—"

"And everything else around here that moves, blinks, or whistles," Lee added.

Dr. Haverhills rocked from one leg to the other, putting his hands in and out of his pockets like a nervous groom. "Miles," he said, looking at Molly, "if it's all right with you, I'd like to go ahead and open the first case. It's next, according to the protocol."

"By all means, Jim."

"I'll help you," Lee said.

"Are they going inside?" Molly asked.

Miles saw Blalock open his mouth to answer, but quickly cut him off. "No, we keep the inside of the main room as near as possible to the real Martian atmosphere—the same pressure and the same temperature. Except for the UV light—"

Blalock sliced into his oration. "All experiments are automated, Molly. If we find a life form, we'll grow more of it, then do animal tests before we risk human exposure."

Miles felt a squeezing sensation grip his chest. "Well, daughter, how would you like to be among the first humans to view rocks from the Red Planet?"

Her eyes lit up. "Of course, but—"

"Jim," Miles said, trying to toughen his tone. "Are you and Kim ready?"

"Chafing at the bit," Haverhills answered.

Miles turned to Blalock and tried hard not to smile. "Paul, I'm afraid you're the odd man out today."

"What do you mean—?"

"I mean you'll stay in the control room," Miles said firmly.

"I will not!" Blalock moved toward the containment area.

Heart pounding against the too-tight collar of his shirt, Miles blocked the door.

"I really should be going, Dad—"

"Stay!" Miles commanded, while he did his best to stare down the defiant paleontologist.

"It's all right, Miles," Haverhills said. "Paul can go. I'll recheck the baseline readings on the animals. We'll see if there's any reaction."

"All right then," Miles relented, stepping aside.

Lee quickly punched a series of buttons, actuating a chain of electrical signals that released all the latches on the largest sample case.

"Where are the other team members?" Molly asked. "I would think everyone would want to be here for this."

Miles made hard fists and never took his eyes off the sample case. "We *are* the team. Fewer people, smaller risk of exposure. You're here only because it's *my* lab and you're *my* daughter." He glanced quickly left and right, at Blalock and Lee.

Lee worked deftly with the controls, and one by one the Martian rocks emerged from the case. The rocks were from the size of pebbles to fist-size pieces, mostly rust brown or reddish yellow.

"Look!" Lee blurted excitedly. "There's the greenish tinge from the *Viking* pictures! The colors that changed over time."

"Yeah," Miles said, unconsciously trying to rub away a twinge of pain in his chest. "The ones we thought might indicate some life process. Looks similar to our lichens."

"This is weird," Lee said. "I can't seem to—" He appeared to struggle to position the robot arms and hands, seemed to find it difficult to get a grip on something inside the large steel case. "Got it now! This one's heavy."

"Gauge says almost three kilos," Blalock reported.

Looking again at the sample box, Miles surveyed the emerging treasure with delight, but he was stunned when Kim lifted out a bluish-black rock about the size of a basketball. Slightly oblong, with a slick, shiny, glasslike appearance, it was unlike anything else in the case.

Suddenly Molly's cell phone sounded, screeching bizarrely. "Sorry."

"Have to go?" Miles said, half hoping she would say no; he needed her as buffer to keep him from strangling Blalock.

Molly shook her head. She squinted at the message window. "That's weird—says I've got a text message, but it's just a jumble of letters and numbers. Never done that before."

"Why don't you just shut it off then?" Miles growled.

"Looks very much like obsidian," Lee nodded toward the sample case, his hands a flurry of activity, twisting dials and flipping switches. "Volcanic glass."

Miles turned to Blalock. "Not unexpected. Wouldn't you say, Paul?"

Blalock glanced sideways but said nothing.

"Wonder why it's so totally different from the others?" Lee said.

"Strange," Blalock finally said, "since it came from the same area."

"A real wing-nut," Haverhills joked. "Can't wait to break into that one."

"It's beautiful," Molly breathed.

"I counted Twenty-nine pieces," Blalock said flatly.

"Good!" Miles said, mildly pleased.

"Dad, I've really got to be going—"

"All right, all right," he grumbled, not wanting to be pulled out of the moment. "I'll walk you out."

"Just to the elevators."

"Bye, Molly," Blalock said with a wink.

Miles jammed his clenched fists into the pockets of his lab coat. "Let's go!"

"Dad...I'm sorry for upsetting you. Let's not fight, okay?"

His heart double beat at the thought of her, so young, so many years ago.

"Blalock didn't seem like the research type," Molly remarked casually as they walked along.

"I'm going to get rid of that bastard, one way or another."

"Oh, don't let him upset you. It's not worth it." She arched her red brow. "Remember your heart?"

"Don't mother me." He kissed the air near her cheek, then turned and hurried back toward the lab.

"Thanks for the tour," Molly called after him.

He didn't bother to turn around, only waved his hand in the air. He walked quickly. His lab coat fluttered in his wake, his mind aflame with questions, not only about the Martian samples but also about how he could rid himself of Blalock.

* * *

*He doesn't look well,* Molly thought as she watched her father round the corner. The elevator doors swished open. She stepped in, pressed the button for lobby, and waited for the cranky World War Two-era lift to respond. The doors clattered closed. Echoing with the closing door, a chill rattled through her. Was it the ugly memories that being in her father's presence always evoked? Or was it her genuine concern for his health. She had to admit her heart was stretched in both directions.

Before she knew it, the elevator doors banged open, and she headed swiftly for the bright sunshine beyond the glass doors when she heard the guard call.

"You've got to sign out, Miss Lavisch."

She turned quickly, too eager to leave behind the bad feelings, and bumped into a man solid enough that she bounced off him.

"Excuse me!" she said. "I should watch where I'm going."

"Oh, but *I'd* rather watch where you're going." He thrust out his hand. "Peter MacKenzie," he said with a canny politeness.

"Molly Lavisch. Pleased to meet you." Her face flushed hot, but she managed to take his large, warm hand before glancing away. Still, in that sliver of a glance, she'd felt something elemental pass between them, and its magnetism drew her back to his delicious smile. His black hair, sprinkled with light gray around the ears, turned up into a slight cowlick in the front. A shadow of a beard was flecked with red and gray. And those hazel eyes, which seemed full of stories, spoke silently to her on some unconscious level. She realized she was starring and gave her head a tiny shake. "Sorry."

"Believe it or not, you're just who I was looking for. Or, rather, your father is. Professor Miles Lavisch is your father, isn't he?"

"Yes. But why?"

"You heard about the astronauts?"

"I saw the papers."

"The commander was my best friend."

"I'm sorry. My father knew some of them too."

"I think there's something fishy about how he and the others died," Peter said. "I thought your father might be able to help. But Genghis Khan over there wouldn't let me up to see him."

"What makes you think something's fishy?"

"They were diverted to Edwards. Bo—my friend—always said that if they were ever diverted to Edwards for no apparent reason, like weather or mechanical problems, it meant they'd seen something. Something with possible national defense implications."

"A UFO?" she sniffed.

"It was part of their flight plan," he said flatly. "But dying wasn't."

"I'm sorry I can't help you right now. I'm late for a meeting."

"How about tomorrow?" Peter handed her two tickets.

"What's this?"

"Tickets to a flying circus. It's called Cilly's Aerial Carnival. At Bealeton, not far from Fredericksburg. You know it?"

"Yes, I've been there."

"Come watch me fly. It's a good show. Bring a friend."

She was just about to say yes when the elevator doors opened and an ashen-faced Haverhills stumbled out. There was blood on his white lab coat.

"Call nine one one!" Haverhills shouted to the guard in the lobby as he fell up against the wall.

"What's wrong?" Molly asked, startled by the trembling man's appearance.

"I don't know," Haverhills said, his voice shaking. "Kim's just collapsed!"

Leaving Peter MacKenzie behind, she followed Haverhills up the four flights of stairs to the lab, where Miles met them at the entrance to the control center.

"Good thing we caught you," Miles said. "Something's wrong with Kim."

As she passed through the inner doors, her cell phone again went wild. "Crazy thing," she said and handed the warbling device to her father before kneeling at Lee's side.

"Tell me!" Miles commanded Blalock. "What did you do?"

"He seemed perfectly fine. Then boom! He collapsed." Blalock appeared bewildered, but managed to support the man's head as blood spewed from his nose in powerful, rhythmic surges. Already the front of his lab coat was drenched with blood.

"There's got to be more to it than that, Paul," Miles growled.

"I'm telling you," Blalock repeated. "I don't know. He was trying to put the black rock back into the case, and he collapsed without a word."

The cell phone continued with its weird, shrill noises, which grew louder and more erratic as Miles moved closer to the containment area wall, near the black rock. "How do you shut this damned thing—?" Dropping the bleating device to the floor, he stomped it into silence. "Where were *you,* Jim?"

"In the animal room."

She'd just begun her examination when the man began to shake, and blood gushed from his nose and eyes and ears. She didn't have a clue as to why, but it was clear the man was near death. "M-My G-God!" she blurted. "D-D-Did he fall? Or h-hit his head?" She took a deep breath, held it, trying to stave off the tremors in her speech.

Blalock shrugged.

She brushed her hands through Lee's hair a section at a time, looking for evidence of a blow. She pulled his eyelids open. Both pupils were widely dilated. She waved her hand in front of his eyes. "Pupils unresponsive...I'm afraid...."

"You're hiding something, Paul," Miles accused. "Now tell us what happened?"

"Just what I said, damnit! Nothing!"

"Contamination?" Haverhills suggested in a quavering voice.

She thought Haverhills looked nearly as bad as Lee—and her father. "Onset was too sudden for any infectious agent," she said, exhaling hard against her palate as she spoke to smooth out the words. "Looks like trauma." She glanced at her father, then Blalock.

Abruptly Lee stopped convulsing; blood stopped spurting and instead flowed like a river. She gently lowered Lee's head onto her folded jacket.

Her father stared at her, red-faced. *"Well?"*

She knew that daunting, demanding tone all too well. She looked at her bloodied hands, then up to meet her father's glare. "I-I g-guess we'll have to wait for the au-autopsy."

# CHAPTER 3

ELMER P. CILLY'S AERIAL CARNIVAL, Bealeton, Virginia...

Molly Lavisch stood with hands on hips and watched the lemon yellow Stearman PT-17 biplane bounce and jiggle over the uneven turf, wings rocking jauntily, engine barking and popping, until it rolled to a breezy stop in front of her.

As soon as the plane's engine stopped, her friend, Allison Jamison, AJ for short, stood unsteadily in the front cockpit, fiddling with the parachute harness, grinning stoically, her blue eyes like cutouts of the perfect blue of the sky above, her blond hair lifting in the wind from the dying propeller. She gave Molly a thumbs-up, and then triumphantly displayed a little white airsick bag, which appeared to have been used, before clambering with halting steps onto the wing.

The stunt pilot's helper, a sturdy teenager with a small gold earring and his shorts showing behind his sagging jeans, reached up and helped her down onto the dry July grass, where as soon as he let go of her arm, she fell down.

"Let me help you," Molly called, moving toward her. But Peter MacKenzie, who jumped out of the rear cockpit right behind AJ, pulled her to her feet and with obvious relish, brushed the dust off the backside of her khaki riding pants with slow, deliberate strokes.

*"Whooo,"* her friend panted, "that's the most fun I've had—" She rocked unsteadily, wiped her sweating face with the back of her hand.

*Please don't say, With my pants on,* Molly said to herself.

"You're next, Molly," AJ beamed.

"How 'bout a loop and a roll?" Peter said, not taking his eyes off AJ's backside.

"No thanks," Molly said sternly, tightening her arms, which she cordoned across her breasts. "I'm sick just thinking about it. Besides, someone's got to drive home."

"Oh, my!" AJ wobbled, bracing herself on the man.

Molly noticed she went out of her way to rub her breast against the Peter's arm, and she thought she detected more than mere pleasure in Peter's face as well.

"Sure you're going to be okay?" Peter asked.

"Yes, Peter," AJ said compliantly. "Thank you."

Molly marveled as AJ worked her womanly way. She smiled up at the man, batted her eyes saucily, her lips in a pouty, star-struck smile. What Molly couldn't figure was why she felt the need; AJ never had a problem luring men. What she was doing was like dumping sugar on Frosted Flakes. Molly sputtered a laugh.

"He's a great stunt pilot, Molly."

"Airshow pilot," he corrected. "We fly planned maneuvers. Stunts imply recklessness."

Molly wanted to go with him, but didn't think her stomach could take it. But before she could speak, his attention had already passed back to AJ.

"Want to go again?" he asked, grinning like a prankster.

AJ hesitated, then spouted bravely: "To the moon, as long as you are flying. But could we rest awhile first?"

Peter chuckled and shook his head. A wisp of his almost blue-black hair curled limply onto his forehead. "Jimmy, why don't you take Miss Jamison to the first-aid station so she can lie down?"

"Oh, no," AJ said, again laughing gaily. "I'm all right. And call me AJ" She rubbed his arm. He put his arm around her waist. "Anyway," she added, "my friend here is a doctor."

"I know," he said. "We've met, remember?" A sprinkling of oil outlined the pilot's hazel eyes where his goggles had been. He wiped the residue from his forehead with the sleeve of his shirt and looked at AJ. "My solo act is up next, so I've got to change planes. Why don't you two meet me afterwards by the big hangar? I'll buy you a drink, and we can have that talk, all right, Molly?"

"Sounds great," AJ gushed, as he winked at her and trudged off.

For a moment, Molly stared at her friend, frozen in amazement. She had to admit, AJ's appeal for men was obvious. Her plaid Western shirt had ruffles, studs, and embroidery; she wore it with flare, unbuttoned to reveal more than a hint of cleavage. Molly glanced down at her own conservative white collarless blouse, jeans that maybe were a bit too baggy, and sneakers that weren't all the rage. The fact that she was only four-eleven didn't help. AJ had a model's statuesque frame. Then she thought, *Everyone tells me I've got Bette Davis eyes? But were* her *eyes even green?* That for a redhead she was pretty? Isn't that what Glen had said? *What does that mean, "for a redhead"?* She stepped back and felt the all too familiar jar her short right leg made against her pelvis, reminding her of her limp, slight though it was, the result of a freak case of childhood polio from bad vaccine. What was worse, because of Peter MacKenzie, she sensed another looming contest with her childhood friend that she feared she wouldn't win.

"Cute, isn't he?" AJ said with a cock of her head, as they headed for the carnival midway.

"I suppose."

"You *suppose*? And I'm a blond unicorn. Some doctor, too, laughing at the wretched ill." She wiped her still damp brow with a pink handkerchief that had little brown horse heads along its border.

"Maybe it serves you right," Molly said, feeling a bit of resentment. "For introducing me to Glen."

"That prick," AJ said, rolling her eyes. "Not telling you he was married. Damnit, girl, every time I try to get you laid..."

"Go ahead. Live your *Sex and the City* life. It's not who I am. A man's marital status is no trivial detail to me."

"Oh, and what makes your hymen so holy? Remember, Good girls go to heaven, but bad girls go *everywhere.*" She opened her arms in a display like a strutting bird and cackled. "Really, Molly, you should—"

She drew her finger across her throat and arched her eyebrows. She hated how AJ always knew what buttons to push. "Let's just say you and I have different tastes when it comes to men and leave it at that."

"Speaking of men, how're Frick and Frack?"

"Who?"

"Your father and your uncle Malcolm?"

"Oh, they're fine. Uncle Malcolm's still teaching comparative religion at Hopkins. Sweet as ever."

"And your father?"

She felt her face burn, and swallowed hard when she thought of him, standing there over Lee's lifeless body, the way he used to stand over her— "Just saw him in his lab at Goddard yesterday. It was very strange. One of his lab technicians died while I was there."

"When I tell people you've got killer looks, I'm only kidding, ya know. What happened?"

Molly had to raise her voice to be heard over the heavy-metal music blaring from the carnival rides as they drew near. "Don't know. It was crazy. One minute the guy was the picture of health—young too. The next, he was unconscious and streaming blood from ever orifice. Then he was dead."

"Bizarre." AJ disposed of her airsick bag in the first trash receptacle they passed. "What's this Mars project anyway?"

"Dad's analyzing the first soil samples brought back from Mars."

AJ looked confused.

"The Mars probe? Don't you read the papers?

"Not if I can help it."

"The *Areopagus?*" Molly urged with exasperation.

"What's that supposed to mean?"

"Actually, it's Greek and it means final judgment. That's the name of the spacecraft. Let's get a hot dog and some popcorn."

"Food? Ugh!" AJ fluttered her hanky about her green-tinged face like a butterfly about to land on a leaf and put her hand over her mouth. "God, girl, what's with you and hot dogs, anyway?"

"Sorry," Molly said, with more than a twinge of satisfaction.

The crowds seemed to suddenly thicken. Concessionaires with greedy eyes barked their husky-throated come-ons. Children and adults alike screamed with delight from the Ferris wheel behind the big hangar and the Madmouse and the Octopus rides, as overhead Peter's airplane twisted through the clear summer air, painting figures with a stream of bluish-white smoke that now settled over the field like a pungent fog.

Molly glanced up as Peter's plane passed low and fast before pulling up sharply in front of the crowd. She followed its upward arc, squinting into a fierce summer sun and wishing she hadn't forgotten her sunglasses and sunscreen. Her fair skin would be bright pink by the end of the day, with a few dozen extra freckles. Just what she needed.

As they made their way along the midway, a small boy with a candy apple in one hand and a mound of cotton candy in the other raced by. A little girl of about the same age in hot pursuit misjudged her turn and banged into Molly with a thump, spun off, then kept running without uttering a word. She watched them disappear into the crowd and sighed.

AJ shook her head. "I know, Molly. But to breed rug rats, first you need a man. Oh! Looky here, old gal." She pointed to a tent like kiosk in the space between two large oaks seemed to pop up from nowhere. Its brown sides were accented with wide, blood red vertical stripes bordered with smaller gold ones. An ice-cream-cone roof supported a long, golden minaret with three bulbs at mid-length, reminiscent of a Turkish mosque. A banner across the entrance read: Madame Lilah Blackwell—Gypsy Princess. Futures Foretold, Mysteries Unveiled, Life Readings. Good Fun. Only $5.

"Just what we need," Molly said with little enthusiasm.

"Indeed it is," AJ affirmed. "A little levity. She'll tell you that you'll meet the man of your dreams, and I'll find out how I'm going to avoid losing my farm to the bank."

Abruptly the deep purple flap of a door flew open. Like an apparition, a slight, colorfully attired woman appeared. She looked directly at Molly. Her piercing eyes were fathomless, lightless hollows that nonetheless seemed to hold a strange and powerful intelligence, which seemed to suck the very air out of her. She felt suddenly faint.

"Come in, please," the slender woman said.

"Let's go Mol. This sounds like a blast."

"You wait!" the tiny woman ordered, stepping in front of AJ

Molly shrugged a smile and went inside, warming to the idea of a harmless lark with a good crystal ball and, as AJ had said, a little levity.

At first blinded by the dark interior, she stumbled in until the Gypsy took her arm. With improving sight, she marveled at the array of occult effects: a small ebony table, intricately inlaid with ivory figures of animals, nymphs, serpents, and strange glyphs. On the table, beside a deck of tarot cards, sat a sculpted crystal human skull. A few paces away, a Ouija board leaned against the wall.

"Sit," the Gypsy said, pointing to a purple pillow with gold stitching beside the stub-legged, black table.

Molly watched as the Gypsy approached a narrow altar against the wall, where she lit two spires of incense that sent up tiny sparks, and along with them, the comforting aroma that reminded her of church when she was a little girl. The Gypsy's gaze lingered over a faded oval portrait of Christ, which hung beside a picture of Satan's temptation of Eve in the Garden of Eden. She made the sign of the cross and mumbled a prayer.

When the Gypsy turned toward her, a gold talisman slung about her neck on a long gold chain amidst a bundle of colorful scarves caught Molly's eye. It looked like an Egyptian ankh with a splayed extremity. She loved jewelry, collected it, had even made some for friends, though she herself wore only a single gold locket; and she could not recall ever having seen anything quite like it. The Gypsy fingered it lovingly, presently sitting on a pillow across from her.

"We won't need these," the dark-eyed woman said, and with one startling sweep of her arm, she cleared the table. "Those are mere props for the uninitiated, not for those whose souls speak freely about destiny and purpose. Give me your hand, Molly."

Fearfully, she jerked her hand away. "How did you know my name?"

The Gypsy eased back, one corner of her mouth drawn up in contrition. A candle in the corner of the room reflected in her large, emphatic eyes. "Your friend said it, no? Cast aside your doubts and suspicions. I want to help you."

"I wasn't aware I needed any help."

"We all need help from time to time. Hear my words. Individual lives intersect for a reason. Our world is randomness, but it wasn't chance that brought you here. And you need my guidance. Now, give me your hand."

Haltingly, Molly offered her hand, palm up. Before she knew it, the Gypsy pulled it to her breast, enfolding it within her own flesh. Again, Molly's breath left her, as what seemed an energetic, living fluid surged up her arm, filled her chest, and spread throughout her body. She was both warmed and frightened by it. "Who? What are you—?"

"You are sad now," the Gypsy declared. "You have lost a lover, no?"

A blush spread like wildfire across Molly's cheeks and forehead. "You tell me," she challenged.

The Gypsy's eyebrow lifted. "So suspicious! Do not respond as you think your father would."

Molly tried to pull away but could not.

"Relax, my dear. Relax." The Gypsy's words flowed slowly, sweetly, like cool molasses, all the while holding Molly's gaze—and her hand—firmly. "Fighting is no good. I see love and a family as your heart's desire, but you must forget Glen. He—"

Molly gasped, her pounding heart fluttered. "How—?" She tried to get up, but the Gypsy pulled her down.

"Love in this world is but a faint trick of the eye. The world itself a shadowland. Many are fooled. There is another for you, but you must wait. Patience is the token that buys your journey." The Gypsy's eyes dropped. "But your journey is fraught with danger."

An uncontrollable shudder reverberated through her body as the Gypsy released her grip, dropping her hand. Her black eyes turned sad.

"Your heart is too big for this life, my sweet one. And soon you will pass from it—"

*"What?"* It was as if she'd taken a physical blow. The room seemed to swirl. She felt faint and braced herself from falling over. But the voice rose again.

"Passing will not be easy, but your death is only one whimper among the wailings of a world in rebirth. Trust your own heart and your own will, for soon you will be reborn with the Earth. But first—"

Abruptly, a radiant burst of sun cleared the darkness. AJ jerked Molly to her feet and began dragging her toward the light. "I heard what the little bitch said."

"Molly, you must listen to me," the Gypsy begged, dropping for just a moment the haunting accent and pointing to the picture of Satan's Temptation of Eve. "A new Eden is upon us. And *you* are the new Eve! *Yes, you!"*

"No, no more!" AJ shouted. "She won't hear anymore."

Numb, Molly stumbled toward the doorway, AJ both holding her up and pushing her.

"Listen to me!" the Gypsy cried out. "Your father—"

"Shut up, you creepy bitch."

AJ picked up the crystal skull and raised her arm as if to throw it, but Molly grabbed her wrist. Compelled by she knew not what, she heard herself ask, "What about my father?"

The words ran together, blurred by the returning accent. She thought she heard: "Tell him bellancarla say beware...."

"Are you all right?" AJ asked as they cleared the door.

Outside, in the bright light of the July sun, Molly's panting breaths subsided. She felt silly, as if the whole incident was but a vulgar fabrication of her imagination. "Whew! That was one good act." Then she coughed a small, hesitant cough, testing to see if the strange warmth was still there. It was not. She noticed AJ looked a bit unglued too.

"Of course it was!" AJ said with quivering voice. "Just an act, I mean." Her hand trembled as she lit a cigarette.

"You know what's funny?"

"No, what?"

"As scared as I was—still *am*—I didn't stutter." An unexpected laugh erupted from her, as if from a stranger. "But why do I still feel so spooked?"

"Come on, you're a scientist. No one can tell the future."

"I know, I know," she said without a bit of conviction. "It's just that...well, she didn't seem quite, quite—"

"Human?" AJ blurted.

# CHAPTER 4

With a feeling of anxious excitement, Miles entered the outer chamber of the containment area where only yesterday Lee had died.

Lee's replacement, Vishnu Chandra, was already at work. East Indian, with characteristic raven hair, well oiled and neatly combed, his eyes were black as polished obsidian. His complexion, a talcum white, seemed not to match his other features. He was tall, over six feet, and he moved with the grace of a giraffe. All in all, Chandra presented a striking figure.

Still, Miles couldn't shake the feeling there was something peculiar about him, and he thought it singularly odd that NASA headquarters had so quickly found someone with the requisite security clearances. But eager as he was to get on with the experiments, he never bothered to question the appointment. After all, Chandra was only a technician. Albeit one with apparent good credentials.

According to Chandra's papers, he was most recently attached to Army research at Fort Detrick, Maryland, with USAMRIID, the armed forces premier biological warfare research center, which was now, by its own public relations propaganda, primarily devoted to cancer research, though Miles knew better. Their cover was partly blown when the news broke that the anthrax terrorist attack used a strain of the microbe called Ames, which, it turned out, had been developed at USAMRIID.

"We'll get the large rock out first," Miles told Chandra. "Sterilize it. Then put it through the MRI."

"Then the gas assays?"

"If you find cavities." As Miles watched the technician operate the robotic arms with the same easy professionalism as Lee, he felt a profound sense of relief. There would be no further delays. Progress would come quickly. Martian life, he was confident, would be confirmed within the samples, though not likely in the big black rock. That's why he wanted its analysis out of the way. So they could proceed to the mother load he knew lay in the other sample boxes.

*Beep! Beep! Beep!* Chandra's cell phone went wild, emitting an intermittent high-pitched screeching noise along with a series of undulating beeps and warbles.

"I see you've got one of those cursed things too," Miles snipped. But then it hit him. "Curious. The same thing happened twice yesterday. As soon as we opened that sample case. Hmmm."

"Look at this, Professor." Chandra handed him the cell phone.

Miles looked at the flashing display. "Same as yesterday. A constantly streaming alphanumeric string. What do you make of it?"

"It repeats."

"A coded message?" Miles knew if there were any electromagnetic emanations from the rock, the metal case would block it. "Put the lid back down."

Chandra closed the lid, the cell phone stopped, and its message screen went blank.

"By God," Miles rejoiced, "a signal *is* coming from that rock. Prepare it for scan immediately."

* * *

Miles felt a shiver of excitement. It was as if he were standing on the shore of eternity waiting for the mast of some ghostly ship of destiny to pierce the horizon. And, oh, how he longed to greet it. But, as always, there was the wait, the interminable wait. Seconds seemed like hours before the images began to emerge.

"Unbelievable!" Miles exclaimed through teeth clenching the remnants of a long extinguished cigar. "Just unbelievable!"

"In the beginning," Chandra said in a barely audible, almost reverent tone.

If he'd heard Chandra right, Miles thought the remark surpassingly peculiar. "What's that, Mister Chandra?"

"I said, 'It's just the beginning,' Professor."

*What a weirdo.* "Well, what do you see?"

"I see just what you see, Professor, a small, rectangular object, most certainly not naturally occurring."

* * *

Well past midnight, Miles ordered Chandra to use the diamond-blade circular saw for the last cut into the obsidian mantle, which accidentally grazed the box's face, causing the saw to whine and buck before stopping completely, its blade turned to a powdery pile of dust.

Miles ran his finger over the saw's blade, which was worn smooth. "I'll be damned. Harder than diamonds." He examined the box. Unbelievably, it was unscarred, not even the tiniest scratch. He glanced at Chandra, whose expression betrayed more horror than amazement.

"What's the matter, Mister Chandra?"

The man shook his head. "Nothing," he spouted in a razor-thin voice.

"Hmmm." With gloved hand, Miles freed the object from its obsidian carapace, quickly surveying it from every possible angle. "Just a little box of some sort."

"Magnificent!"

"I'd have said alabaster," Miles ventured, "before the saw. Can't be, though. It's way too light. Only half a pound, I'd guess." He continued to study the box, holding it out at arm's length, cursing himself silently for losing his glasses again. With the sleeve of his coat, he rubbed away the patina of dust from the face of the box. "What's this?" he joked. "A stop light?"

"An eye," Chandra said, pointing to the softly blinking red light.

"An eye, huh?" Miles held the box as far away as he could, but his arms just weren't long enough. "What do you make of these marks? Here, you take a look. Must've left my glasses back in the control room." He handed the object to Chandra. "Maybe some kind of hieroglyphics?"

Miles noticed Chandra didn't so much hold the box as caress it, his long, slender fingers gently stroking the smooth, white surface with its delicate inlays of precious stones and elaborate gold designs.

Miles needed a smoke. Impatiently, he drummed his finger on the table. "Well? Describe what you see."

"The principal design on the face is a modified ankh—its lower extremity being bifurcated. Of course the eye is the most conspicuous feature. The markings are certainly of a language, resembling, as you say, hieroglyphics—but not hieroglyphics. I can detect no seam. But we'll check it under magnification."

"If it *is* some kind of container?" Miles snatched the box away. "God! Are we stupid? We didn't try shaking it."

"What? No, Professor!"

"Guess you never celebrated Christmas," Miles said derisively, shaking the box like a child testing a gift. "Something's in there; I can feel it. Can we use the electron microscope?"

"If it will fit the chamber."

"Do it."

Chandra hesitated, his expression a mixture of shock and mystification.

"Well," Miles said impatiently. "Get on with it!"

For thirty long minutes Miles paced the hallway, his mind whirring, while Chandra set up the scanning electron beam microscope. A million questions had to be answered. What to do about storing the box securely? Whom to tell? And when? And another crucial question: Whom could he bring in for the language analysis? No, that one was easy. Roscha Venable, his old MIT roommate and one-time linguist at Columbia. Roscha had since moved back to town and now was special consultant to the National Security Agency on matters of cryptology. He was the only possible choice. *Roscha, you old fart—*

"I've got it!" Chandra's cry echoed through the lab like a commandment. "A seam!"

* * *

Miles looked at the clock on the wall. It was 4:15 A.M. For the first time he felt fatigue.

"Judging from the way it reacted to the diamond saw," Chandra said, "I doubt we could break it open without destroying whatever is inside."

"So, we'd better figure out how it's supposed to be opened. Got any ideas?"

"The workmanship is so extraordinary.... I doubt very much if it is a simple mechanical device. The seam itself is no more than a few angstroms across. And there is the question of the beacon, its power source and—"

"Yes, yes," Miles grumbled. "Evidently whatever's in there was valuable enough to warrant putting a homing device in the box. So you can bet it has a pretty sophisticated locking mechanism."

"If not something more."

"What?" Miles asked incredulously. "Booby trap? Possible, I suppose. But the question is..." He stared at the eye in the circlet atop the ankh. Its hypnotic soft red light winked rhythmically, in unison with the beacon's transmission. *At about the same rate as the human heart,* he thought, feeling the throbbing pain in his head.

"Could be pressure points, Professor. Or something keyed to the magnetic field around the living fingers—"

"Preposterous!" Miles snorted with contempt. "You're assuming that the intelligent life that made this box also had human anatomy, including fingers? That's a large leap, don't you think?"

"I suppose so," Chandra admitted. "How about sound, then?"

"A password?"

"Possibly."

For some reason, Miles saw images from the old *War of the Worlds* movie flash before his mind's eye, pictures of Gene Barry running in fright as the Martian monsters emerged from their spacecraft. "But it is also possible that our aliens communicated in ways other than sound, telepathically, perhaps."

"Certainly," Chandra said, curiously lifting an eyebrow, "they could have been more advanced than humans."

"Certainly very, very different anatomically, too," Miles asserted, now thinking of the aliens in the movie *Independence Day,* all buglike and grotesque. "No, we're looking at a problem of electromagnetics... some coded frequency pattern, probably in the same range as the beacon. If true, we may never open it. Hell, we can encrypt unbreakable codes even with our meager technology." He couldn't suppress a yawn. "I must be getting old." He thought how in his youth he could go without sleep for days, especially when in the thrall of some intriguing problem, such as this most certainly was. Reluctantly, he succumbed to the exigencies of fatigue. "Mr. Chandra, I think it's time to call it a night."

"I'd like to stay with it, Professor, if you have no objection."

"All right, then," Miles relented and started for his office, but he stopped suddenly, turning to his lab technician with a purposely-arched brow and his most intimidating scowl. "You *will* call me before you do anything with the box?"

Chandra nodded.

* * *

"Professor! Professor! Wake up!" Chandra shook Miles's chair. "I've done it. I've opened the box."

Despite Chandra's excited phrasing, his delivery was really quite calm. This made it all the more difficult for Miles to determine if he was awake or dreaming. Slowly his eyes began to focus. He looked at his watch: 6:40 A. M.. He'd been asleep only a short time.

"You say you opened the box? But how?" He looked at Chandra, who was putting the Bunsen burner under some water. "How, Chandra? Forget the damn tea—I want to know how?" For he'd really believed that there would be no nondestructive way to get inside the box.

"Serendipity, Professor. I was setting up the equipment to display the waveform so I could begin to analyze it. I had the recorder hooked up to it, along with a signal generator. In testing the set-up, I inadvertently recorded the homing signal's waveform inverted. When I rebroadcast it to the box, the eye stopped winking—and the box opened about a millimeter."

"Hmm. "Miles quickly twisted the explanation this way and that, testing the veracity of his technician. "Makes sense, I guess. Uh huh.... Whenever the box was closed, the homing beacon was on and the locking mechanism was engaged. Turn off the beacon remotely and the box— Did you look inside?"

Chandra stiffened. "No, Professor. I knew you would want to be present."

Relieved, Miles smiled and pushed the cigar box toward Chandra.

"No, thank you, Professor."

"I think I'll have that tea now, if you don't mind."

Miles leaned over and got a light off the Bunsen burner, letting the acrid smoke rise up the back of his throat and out through his nose. His body tingled with a sensation of imminent fulfillment. Such was the culmination of longing, not for the sexual, not for any mere animal appetite, not for anything so mundane, but for something uniquely human: the longing for revelation, for enlightenment, for understanding. He wanted to savor the mood, prolong it, for always the possibility of disappointment loomed: An empty box. No, he would wait a few more minutes, sip his tea and finish his smoke.

But after that fleeting thought he could resist the pull of curiosity no longer. He butted his cigar. "Let's go have a look."

* * *

The box sat like a bejeweled clam under a sterile hood just the other side of the wall from the animal cages in the containment area. As soon as Miles picked up the box the monkeys went berserk, rattling their cages, cringing, screaming and making an ungodly racket as they raced back and forth in their wire cells.

"Shut up!" he yelled and threw a Petri dish against the wall. He edged up the top of the little box about half an inch and nearly fell off his chair as an intense white light flooded out from the inside of the box. "This thing must have an incredible power source." Ever so slowly, he raised the top the rest of the way. Then he began to chuckle softly. "No alien life form here. It's just a book!"

"Not *just* a book," Chandra said, a subtle but unmistakable edge to his voice. "Obviously a book of some import, probably of religious significance—"

Miles shook his head in disgust. "Well, of course it is!" Lifting the diminutive book out of its cradle, he placed it on a black felt display cloth Chandra had somehow provided. "The cover material looks and feels like leather. Same design on the cover as the one on the box, a modified ankh with eye. Though this one's not winking." He gingerly opened the book, not knowing if the pages would simply collapse into a fine powder of long-deteriorated material.

"Good! The pages are intact," Chandra said excitedly.

With latex-gloved fingers, Miles gingerly leafed through the book, page by page. "Not surprisingly, the language is the same as that on the box. Pages feel like vellum." Soon he lost patience and using his thumb flipped quickly through the entire text. "Too bad, no pictures! That would have made things interesting, eh, Mr. Chandra?"

Something fell from between the pages.

"What's this?" Miles wondered, as he picked up a piece of fine, silklike white cloth with borders that repeated the ankh design. A brown stain ran nearly its entire length, which he estimated to be about ten inches long. "A bookmark, perhaps? What do you think? So far you haven't said much."

Chandra appeared dreamy-eyed as he beheld the book. "I think it's glorious!"

"What?"

"Perhaps a prayer cloth?"

Suddenly the lab's door-open warning sounded. Miles checked the monitor. Blalock was coming.

"What's he doing here so early?" Miles wondered out loud.

"What about the book?" Chandra asked.

For some reason, Chandra seemed as reluctant as he to reveal the find. "Vishnu," he said, feeling the familiarity of a first name was more appropriate for a prospective ally. "I think for the time being—"

"I'll hide it," Chandra whispered. "You stall him."

Miles met Blalock just outside his office by the control center.

"Miles," Blalock said with surprise. "You're here early."

"You, too," he said calmly. "Glad to see you're so dedicated."

Blalock half smirked. "I thought we'd get into that black rock today, and I didn't want to miss it."

"Yes. Well...because of Lee… I thought we'd better wait. Until the autopsy results, to be on the safe side."

"Oh?"

"Yes. Today I wanted you to attend a meeting at NASA headquarters on my behalf." He started moving toward the door as he spoke. "You'd better hurry; the meeting starts at nine thirty. You know what traffic's like this time of day. Just check with Larry Blumenthal when you get there."

As soon as Blalock was gone, he went back to his office and called Roscha.

## CHAPTER 5

Miles Lavisch sat outside the administrator's office at NASA headquarters in Washington, D.C., luxuriating in visions of himself accepting awards and accolades, for surely this would be the crowning glory of his already illustrious career. The world was always waiting to be astounded, and certainly he would not disappoint them. Indeed, not only had there been life on Mars but intelligent life. He'd made up his mind about one thing: Only he would be the messenger of that seminal news. He basked in a glorious reverie, imagining himself at the White House. It was a small, informal gathering. Champagne and caviar being served on White House sterling; violins and a piano playing softly in the eves; he was about to shake the President's hand...

"Only a moment more, Professor Lavisch," the secretary said, her gray-streaked brown hair tied up in a bun with a yellow pencil piercing it like a toothpick through chocolate pastry.

So what if Larry Blumenthal was his boss and NASA's chief administrator. To Miles, he was just another glorified paper shuffler and politico, and he didn't like to be kept waiting by anyone. Especially now, only twenty-four hours after discovering the book, for there was far too much to be done.

He fidgeted, sliding from side to side on the slick maroon leather sofa, shuffling through the usual array of out-of-date magazines. He saw the no smoking sign. *This will get some action.* He took out a long, walnut-brown Partagas and with his thumb, flicked a white-tipped kitchen match to life.

"*No! No! No!*" the secretary said, shaking her head and pointing to the sign on her desk, which she tapped woodpeckerlike with a gnarly finger.

Miles rolled his eyes and grunted but kept the match burning near the tip of the cigar. "I won't, if you'll tell him I'm tired of waiting."

"Patience, Professor. He has someone with him."

"Try him again, damnit!" Jumping to his feet, Miles poked the burning match in her face to hold her at bay as he maneuvered around her desk toward the oak double doors that led to Blumenthal's office.

"Professor Lavisch! I won't be threatened like this. As soon as Mr.Blumenthal—"

Before he could grab the polished brass handle, the doors swung open.

"Sorry to have kept you waiting, Miles." Larry Blumenthal smiled meekly. His face, accented with two hooded, puffy eyes, was drained of color. "Please come in."

"You know how much work we have, Larry. What's this all about?"

"I know, Miles, I know. This won't take long." He pointed to the man who sat at the small elliptical conference table in the corner.

Miles could see that the man, even though seated, was large, both tall and heftily built, but well proportioned. His blondish-white hair was neatly trimmed and combed. His florid face shown like a beacon, with spider-web veins crisscrossing his cheeks and the bridge of his nose, which separated two deep-set, searching eyes. A black double-breasted suit and a regimental-stripe tie, which vertically divided a luminescent white shirt, fit him like the crisp lines of a manikin. On his right hand was a Naval Academy graduation ring.

"Miles, "Blumenthal began, "I'd like you to meet Admiral Carl Snow. He's Director—"

"Of the CIA," Miles interrupted. He switched his unlit cigar to his other hand. "I haven't been living on the moon the last few years."

"I dare say, no one has," Blumenthal countered glumly, plopping down next to Snow.

Feeling somewhat flattered by the high-powered delegation, Miles extended his hand. "Pleasure to meet you, Director Snow."

But the admiral, without standing or offering his hand in return, just nodded and pointed to a chair...

* * *

Madras sat in his hotel room wondering why Pheras had not gotten back to him. He wondered if he'd mistakenly used his alias, Vishnu Chandra, when he'd left his message. He was so fatigued. He stared at his communicator, which lay on the coarse orange and beige blanket on the bed next to where he sat, and tried to will it to life. Nearly thirty-six hours had passed since the discovery of the Covenant, since his urgent call to his superior. He needed approval for his next move, and surely time was short before his cover was blown. He was not used to pretending he was someone he was not, and certainly not used to taking someone's life. Yes, it was necessary, he assured himself, but this assignment made him uncomfortable, and the guilt pressed in on him like a dull weight.

His communicator chirped to life. Lunging for it, he knocked it to the floor, then, in his eagerness, he kicked it under the bed just as he bent to pick it up. Vainly, he fished for it in darkness. It seemed to him as if some impudent force was toying with him, taunting him, egging on a growing frustration. Finally his fingers met the cool, black device, which he quickly squeezed, overly hard so as not to let it escape again, as if it were a menacing animal that had to be subdued.

"Pheras! Thank the Lord," he said breathlessly. "I was beginning to think—well, it doesn't matter. I've located the Covenant."

"Glorious! Even when the beacon's signal was confirmed I dared not hope..."

Merely the sound of Pheras's voice reassured him. His faith renewed, he spoke now with greater confidence, if not greater joy. "The last copy is now accounted for."

"Tell me about the man Lee. Your message said you'd had to cause his death."

"Yes. He had six months at best as it was. A fulminating cerebral aneurysm. He wasn't due for replacement, anyway."

"I see.... Then you have the Covenant?"

"Well, no. I wanted—"

"You must get it!"

He detected in Pheras's voice an unmistakable—and unprecedented—impatience, unbefitting his usually benign temperament.

"If they should manage to decipher it—"

"Impossible," he said confidently.

*"Impossible?"*

Madras could feel the rebuke. "For all practical purposes, yes! Given the short time frame."

"Just the same," Pheras continued, "if they did decipher it—however remote that possibility might be—our job would be all the more difficult. Get it now!"

"At all costs?"

"Be guided by your heart, Madras, but not blinded by it. You know what is at stake, as well as I. What about our candidate?"

"Her name is Molly Lavisch. She knows nothing yet. But indications are her father will draw her in."

"Good. But remember, if she is to be our Eve, she must face the coming challenges alone. What is the man's name?"

"Peter MacKenzie." He paused for a moment, uncertain if he should pursue his thought, for some things, he knew, would always be a mystery. Nevertheless, haltingly, the question coalesced, and then poured forth. "Her virginity. Is it really so important?"

"Emphatically, yes," Pheras replied. "If for no other reason than because it is of great importance to her. Remember, Madras, the weight of a challenge is set by the candidate who selects it. She chose this course some great while ago, though even she may not remember when or why."

"Knowing her history—and his—it will be very difficult for her."

"It's not the least of the hardships she'll confront," Pheras declared. "Beyond that, well, any individual outcome is never certain. Now, get our Covenant and hurry home. For time is short, and I need you here."

"I'll get it tonight," Madras said with renewed hope.

"Good."

"There's something—"

"I know," Pheras said. "The man named Lee. Let us hope no more killing will be necessary."

## CHAPTER 6

It was well past midnight when Miles pulled into his reserved parking space at Goddard. "What the hell is he doing here?" He was surprised to see Vishnu Chandra's ragtag Volkswagen Beetle. Racing through the double doors, he rudely flashed his badge to the guard without returning a gracious "Good evening" and hopped the elevator to the lab. He skipped the sterile gear and went straight to the control room. *Where is he?*

Not in the alcove lab, either. Nor the central containment area. Finally he went to the sterile hood, where earlier they had left the book. *Gone!* His knees weakened. Could Chandra have known that he'd planned to—? *Impossible.*

Frantically, he went from door to door, even the men's room—nothing. Maybe Chandra had taken the book, leaving his car as a diversion; perhaps he had an accomplice. But why? Money? Chandra didn't seem money motivated. But Miles couldn't be sure. Almost as an afterthought he opened the door to the cold room.

"What in God's name are you doing, Vishnu?"

"Professor! You nearly stopped my heart."

"You didn't answer my question."

"I was on my way—"

"The book—"

"Professor, you didn't think?" Chandra squirmed, exhaled a cloud of steam into the cold air. "I was on my way home from a late movie when it occurred to me that perhaps it would be better to keep the book in the cold room, just in case we inadvertently contaminated the pages. Some microbes might find the material appetizing—we still don't know what it's made of..."

Miles strained a stare. He could sense Chandra was up to something.

Finally Chandra's shoulders seemed to relax, as if his body could no longer contain the tension. He slumped into his chair. "Honestly, Miles, I thought you would welcome my initiative."

A thin fog developed as they talked. Cold began to seep into Miles's consciousness. Something wasn't quite kosher, yet he couldn't disagree with Chandra's reasoning. Besides, this might fit in nicely with his plans, because the cold room had no cameras. "Let's get out of here," he said in a deliberately conciliatory tone. "It's too cold." The little red eye winked as the door slammed shut.

"While I'm not unappreciative of your initiative, Mr. Chandra," Miles said, "in the future you will consult me before executing any such plans. Anyway, as I told you , Admiral Snow's men will be taking over the project in a few days. Until they do, it's best not to handle the box or the book unless I ask you to. Is that clear?"

"Of course, Professor."

"Good. Where's the remote control you made for the box?"

Chandra handed Miles the control, which he had jury-rigged from a circuit board that would produce the signal required to open the box. Like a standard TV remote-control unit, it worked with a point and click. "I think you'd better go home and get some sleep now. We've got a heavy day tomorrow. Come on, I'll walk you out."

"Please let me stay and help?" Chandra begged. "Surely there's something—"

"There's nothing that can't wait till morning." Miles stepped between Chandra and the corridor to the lab, trying to herd him toward the exit, but he continued oozing his way back to the cold room.

"It's such an exciting project," Chandra enthused. "It's been hard to sleep ever since—"

"Look," Miles said with a growing exasperation, "I just want to make a few notes, check the animals and get some papers ready for the CIA people. After that, *I'm* going home, too."

"But—"

"Good night, Mister Chandra!"

As soon as Chandra disappeared behind the elevator doors, Miles went to work. He pressed his thumbs against the latches on his ostrich-hide briefcase. Each latch sprang open with soft thud. Earlier that day, he'd carefully noted the dimensions of the Martian book, for he needed something approaching the same size and weight to double for it. Only one book in his personal library fit the requirements perfectly: an old copy of the *King James Bible.* Pocketbook size. His grandmother had given it to him for Bible school. Why he'd kept it even he couldn't guess.

He pointed the small, black remote control device at the Martian box and pressed the button. The red eye ceased its winking; the box silently opened. He had color copied the Martian book's cover, which he now glued to the cover of the Bible. "I'll be damned!" he congratulated himself, "that's not half bad. Long as no one looks too closely."

An errant shiver surprised him. He looked at the thermometer: one degree above freezing, Centigrade. His breath formed a light dew on the briefcase. Another involuntary shiver rippled up the small of his back, causing his Latex-gloved hands to tremble as he reached carefully inside the box and removed the alien book, delicately placing it on the black velvet cloth Chandra had used, enfolding it several times before putting it in his briefcase. He quickly replaced it with the Bible surrogate.

He looked at his watch: 1:30 A.M. He snapped the briefcase closed, exited the cold room and headed down the hallway, congratulating himself on how easy it had been to handle Chandra. He felt the better part of a cat burglar and a conman. It felt natural, it felt good. "If that brass-button sonofabitch thinks he's taking my project, he's—"

Suddenly, looming in front of him, was Blalock. Miles's heart pounded so hard that the Crosse pens in his breast pocket clicked together with the beat.

"Well, Professor," Blalock said sneeringly, "we keep meeting at odd times. Why do you suppose that is?"

"What are you doing here, Paul?"

"I was about to ask you the same—"

"You work for me," Miles said, noticing that Blalock's eyes fixated on the briefcase. "I'll ask the questions." The chill of the cold room quickly faded. Sweat began to bead on his forehead. A dull pain ticked at his breastbone.

"When are we getting into that black rock?" Blalock asked. "Or have you already?" He reached for the briefcase. Just then footsteps thundered down the hall behind them.

"Professor! Paul!" Chandra called. "I guess government scientists *are* the most dedicated."

"Chandra? I thought—" Miles quickly used the diversion to step away from Blalock.

"Actually," Chandra said, smiling oddly at Blalock, who looked slightly confused, "I was just leaving myself. Walk you out, Professor?"

Back at his car, Miles was relieved to see Blalock had followed them outside. At least he wouldn't be rummaging through the lab. And if Roscha wouldn't help him with the book, at least he'd have until tomorrow to get it back into its precious little box before Blalock could find out.

# CHAPTER 7

Miles had not spoken to Roscha Venable for several years, but their relationship had been forged in the fury of youthful exuberance and shared indiscretions, and had endured despite the corrosive effects of time and inattention. So Roscha did not hesitate to meet him on short notice.

On the way, Miles sifted through memories nearly a half-century old: memories of Roscha and him at MIT, in and out of trouble for pranks both lurid and vexing; memories of Roscha's unstudied brilliance; memories of Roscha's insatiable appetite for women, which on more that one occasion had nearly ended his career, a career that Miles had followed closely and not without a considerable amount of envy.

Roscha had taken his undergraduate degree in mathematics but had become interested in its application to linguistics and, by extension, to archaeology. So he had gone on to get his Ph.D. in ancient languages at Columbia and had remained there, eventually to become a fully tenured professor before leaving to do consulting for the National Security Agency in cryptology.

When Miles had told Roscha the meeting would involve very confidential discussions, Roscha had suggested his apartment in Bethesda, near Rock Creek Park. Miles was about to ring the doorbell, when the door swung open, startling both him and the young woman of about twenty-five who brushed by him with a smirk and a swish.

Behind her, a man in a silk smoking jacket appeared in the doorway. Not the dark-haired, bright-eyed, vigorous young man of Miles's memory—but what did he expect after so long a time? Oh, the hawkish features and swarthy complexion were still there, but Roscha was thinner now and slightly bent. His former dark hair, now completely white, billowed like a thunderhead above his thick eyebrows, which sheltered his blue-green eyes—and the formidable presence behind them.

"Hello, old friend," Roscha said, extending his hand. "It's been a long time."

Miles grasped his friend's hand while he turned to watch the young woman as she walked to the elevator, making last minute adjustments to her attire. "I see some things haven't changed," he said, smiling. "Fiancée?"

"Miles, *Miles,*" Roscha said, ruefully shaking his head, "you flatter me. No, I may be vain, but I'm not foolish. She comes with all the options—but I pay! Well, don't just stand there, come in."

Roscha's apartment had the same look as the apartment they had shared for a short time after their graduation from MIT. A typical bachelor pad, it was an unkempt assemblage of mix-and-match furniture, scattered articles of clothing, magazines, books, dishes with half-eaten food, overflowing ashtrays, and reams of computer printer paper. But there were also articles of genuine antiquity and great beauty. Paintings by Hieronymus Bosch and Salvador Dali—originals, not reproductions—hung side by side with rare Japanese silk-screens and erotic works from the Indian Kama Sutra. Egyptian and Greek sculpture stood on pedestals scattered about the room. Bookshelves bulged with rare, ancient works, intermixed with modern academic texts, many of which were authored or coauthored by Roscha himself.

"I see you haven't lost your penchant for collecting," Miles said, relieved that some things, it seemed, had never changed. "Nor your exotic tastes."

"Oh, yes," Roscha said. "I still like my knick-knacks. Afraid I can't offer you much in the way of food. How about some coffee?"

"Got any tea?"

"Sorry. Cigarette?"

"No, thanks. Prefer these," Miles said, counter offering one of his hand-wrapped Cubans.

Roscha shook his head, lit his cigarette, and inhaled deeply. "I must say I'm intrigued."

"Oh?" *That's good,* Miles thought.

"Yes." Roscha held his cigarette like a European, between his thumb and index finger. "Mostly by why you urgently needed to see me now, after all these years."

"Oh, I've kept close tabs on you, Roscha. You're a bit of a legend—"

"Don't be servile, Miles. It's unbecoming. Besides, you've no need to kiss *my* ass."

"Sorry," Miles said awkwardly. "I guess having to deal with politicians has infected even me."

Roscha leaned close to him. "Now, you said something about secrecy."

Slowly unwrapping his cigar, Miles carefully considered his reply. He bit the tip off his cigar, putting the bitter brown pulp politely down in the ashtray. "Are you aware of what *I've* been up to lately?"

"I do read the papers. You don't exactly have a low-profile job."

Miles dipped his head slightly in the service of false modesty. "As far as the secrecy... I've told no one about you or this visit because what I'd like to discuss with you may put you in jeopardy—as far as violating your security clearance, at the very least—possibly worse. So if you would like me to leave now without further discussion, I would certainly understand." Miles knew a concise and forthright approach was called for. Anything else would likely scare Roscha off. Besides, he knew his old friend shared his addictive curiosity, so phrasing the offer as he did was calculated to whet Roscha's appetite.

Roscha's expression turned sour as he sat for a silent, millennial moment before howling in laughter. He slapped Miles on the knee. "Of course I want to know. But you knew that, or you wouldn't have come here. Besides, if I don't like it, I'll just deny everything. Plausible deniability, right? Like any good politician."

"Okay, then," Miles paused, spun his cigar between his lips. "What is the most fantastic discovery you could imagine reading about in tomorrow's newspaper?"

"Come, now, would you have me play a game of twenty questions?"

"I'm quite serious, Roscha. Open your mind. Visualize the headlines!"

"Hmmm. You've discovered how to make cars run on water." Roscha gave a puzzled shrug and flopped backwards in his chair, shaking his head.

"*Think!* Not something petty or provincial. What would that headline read?" Miles wasn't just playing twenty questions with Roscha; he wanted Roscha's involvement in process even before he tried to set the hook. Too soon and Roscha might not be emotionally ripe to the concept.

"Miles, if you're trying to tell me that you've discovered life on Mars. Well, is that really so shocking. I mean everyone was betting—"

Miles shook his head, kept prodding, using his hands to try and drag out the required response, as if they were playing charades. "Come with me a bit farther, come on..."

"No! Intelligent life?"

"Yes! Roscha. *That* is the headline you'd read. Except you never will, because the forces of this government will not allow it."

"What makes you think this?"

"You know Admiral Carl Snow?"

"Not personally, but I do work for NSA, and we're on a tight leash from the CIA. It would be hard not to know something."

"He's dangerous. And not just to me. To America."

"From what little I've heard, I'd have to agree. He *is* ruthless. Back in the eighties his sub rammed a Russian sub and sank it. Then he refused to pick up the Russian survivors. This was in the Barents Sea, mind you. You can guess how long they lasted in that water."

"I don't remember hearing about that."

"It was hushed up. The President wanted him canned, but the Joint Chiefs and a few Rickover groupies talked him out of it, said he was one his best sub commanders and didn't want to make him a sacrificial lamb. At least that's the story. But the Cuban caper was the best."

"Cuba?"

"Yeah. After Al Zawahiri, bin Laden's top lieutenant, threatened us if we harmed the enemy combatants held in Quantanamo Bay, Snow had the prisoners fed a diet rich in pork, anything pork: bacon, ham, sausage, fried rind, kidney, you name it. And he made them wear pork-skin gloves everywhere, all the time. Really pissed 'em off. Made Zawahiri so mad, he started making mistakes. That's how we got him. Still, Snow's a bastard, no doubt about it. Certainly not a man you want to cross swords with."

"I'm afraid I already have."

"What happened?"

"He ordered me to keep the discovery quiet. Said some of his people would be taking over the project. That it's a question of national security."

"The easiest way out of this one, my friend, *is* to make it public. Get the evidence out in the bright light of public scrutiny. Then Snow wouldn't have any reason to seek recourse. Of course you'd never work for the government again. And who knows? They might even try to get you for treason. Use something under the Patriot Act."

Though Miles could tell Roscha was intrigued, he detected a growing caution, if not outright fear. He began to worry Roscha would accept his earlier offer and terminate the conversation. A growing tightness in his chest returned, though he'd tried so hard lately to ignore it. He started to perspire.

"What exactly *is* your evidence, anyway?" Roscha finally asked.

Miles relaxed a bit, for he knew once Roscha saw the book, he would be in. "I thought you'd never ask." He took out the book in its black velvet cloth. Slowly, almost lovingly, he disrobed it, taking care not to touch the book with his bare fingers, which would contaminate it with human oils. He tossed Roscha a pair of Latex gloves. "Here. These are for your own protection as much as the book's. We're not completely sure about the possibility of an unknown microbe."

"This came from Mars on the *Areopagus?*"

"Yes."

"Fantastic!" Roscha slowly turned the pages. His eyes glowed with the delight of discovery.

*Hook set.*

"Miles, it's fabulous!"

Relieved, Miles said, "Do you think you can decipher the text?"

"Possibly. I certainly have all the computer power I need." He pointed to the computer in the corner. "It's hooked directly into everything at NSA on a secure line. But there's no telling how long it would take. Is this the complete discovery?"

"We found a piece of cloth with a stain—maybe blood. It was folded inside the book like a bookmark. I plan on having Molly test for DNA."

"Does Molly know?"

"No. And the less she knows the better."

"I dare say, the safer she'll be. Won't the book be missed?

"It's secure for now," Miles said. But then he thought of Blalock. "The CIA isn't due by for a couple of days."

"Hmmm. Fascinating, fascinating," Roscha continued. "I'll just bet Admiral Snow would want this kept secret. Especially—" His seemed to catch himself. Then, rubbing his chin pensively, he said, "The astronauts who died in the fire."

"So? What are you thinking?"

Roscha lit another cigarette off the first. "There's a rumor circulating. Just a rumor, mind you." He gave Miles what seemed a cautionary glance. "Some are saying the fire was no accident."

"They were murdered?" Miles felt his heart skip several beats and he felt faint.

"Murdered because they saw something extraordinary, something extraterrestrial. Something the government—meaning some renegade like Snow—didn't want made public."

"So the paper was right."

"What paper?

"The *Post.* A couple of days ago they had a story saying Snow would testify at the inquest about the astronauts. It mentioned UFO groups making that claim. Which I thought was just nutty."

"Maybe," Roscha said. Slowly, he plucked an errant piece of tobacco from his lips. "But maybe not so nutty. HAM radio operators—so the story goes—picked up some of the transmissions between Houston and the *Discovery II.* They did mention UFO's."

"More rumors, huh?" Miles shook his head, as much to keep himself from falling out of his chair as anything.

"All unconfirmed, I'm afraid. But a possible connection."

The additional information made the soreness in his chest worse. He started to feel nauseous. "Then maybe this is more dangerous than I ever imagined and—"

"Rest assured, my friend." Roscha put his hand on Miles's shoulder. "It is!"

"Shall I take the book back, then?" His face began to grow hot. His heart raced painfully, and he was about to ask where the bathroom was.

"Don't be silly," Roscha said with his curious smile.

Miles then noticed his cigar had gone out. He settled back in his chair and sighed more loudly than he wanted to. Maybe things would work out. He began to feel better.

"What are your immediate plans?" Roscha asked.

"I'm going to announce it publicly in a day or so. I hope that you will be an eventual witness. If you can decipher some of the text, all the better."

"And what about Molly?" Roscha asked, his eyebrows arched with concern. "When are you going to tell her?"

"Perhaps I won't have to tell her. But if anything should happen to me, I'd like you to fill her in. Promise me that, my old friend."

* * *

"Hello, Paul." Bandar Bliss extended his chubby hand.

"Ambassador," Paul Blalock said and pretended not to see the proffered hand, quickly flopping down at Admiral Snow's large glass conference table. He didn't like Arabs, especially not this one.

Seemingly unfazed, Bliss removed his *kaffiyeh* and rearranged his raven black, braided pigtail. Otherwise bald, what hair remained grew from a small crescent patch low on the back of his skull and stretched over his corpulent frame almost to the extremity of his spine.

"Bandar," Admiral Snow said, entering through a side door. "Thank you for coming by." He handed Bliss a manila envelope.

The ambassador opened the flap and smiled. "Once again you've renewed my faith in the American spirit of generosity."

Snow lit a cigar without offering one to the ambassador. "Sorry you couldn't stay a while."

"Me too," Bliss replied, as he gazed at the cigar. "But my mother's in town, it's her birthday, and I promised to show her around before I take her back to Riyadh. She wants to visit 'The Devil's Den,' as she calls it."

"And what place would that be?" Blalock asked.

"The White House," Bliss replied.

Blalock and Snow glanced at each other.

"Well, give her my regards," Snow said. Then he patted Bliss on the back and started toward the door. "Now if you'll excuse us, Mr. Ambassador, but I'm afraid I'm late for an important—"

Bliss waved his hand and shook his head. "Not a problem," he chuckled, as he folded the manila envelope and stowed it in breast pocket. "Isn't that how you Americans put it? Your language is so quaint."

"Good a way as any," Blalock sneered. *God he looks silly. A* kaffiyeh, *a pigtail and a three-piece suit.*

Before crossing the threshold Bliss turned to him. A glint of fluorescent light shone strangely in his dark eyes. "Always a pleasure, Paul."

Blalock returned Bliss's dark gaze and could have sworn he saw slits for pupils. "Always."

Snow quickly guided Bliss toward the door, which he closed smartly behind him.

"Check the silverware," Blalock said, shaking himself like a wet dog. "Why do I always want a shower after seein' him."

"Now, now, Paul," Snow said sarcastically, placing a Scotch in Blalock's hand. "Neat, isn't it?"

"Right. Thanks."

Snow puffed erratically on his cigar. "He was very useful to us in the Gulf War. And we'd never have clipped the balls off that cockroach bin Laden without his help. We still need him."

"Maybe so, but I don't trust him."

"Neither do I!"

"Still can't believe that prick takes money. How many billions is he worth?"

Snow shrugged. "How many billions are there? Hell, his family owns better than half of all the oil under Saudi sand."

"Where'd a Saudi get a name like Bliss anyway?" Blalock wondered.

"It's his mother's maiden name. She's half Scottish. He uses Bliss in the Western world as a convenience. After the World Trade Centers, he sure as hell doesn't want anyone to know he's related to ol' Osama. And like most Muslims, he despises us. Of course that doesn't stop him from using us. Doesn't stop us from doing the same to him."

"Think he had his snake with him?"

"Who knows? He could have a foot fetish and I'd let him lick my feet—or better yet, I'd make you lick his. When we need him, we need him. He's still the highest placed source we have in the Middle East. But forget him. I'm more worried about our nutty professor. What's going on at the lab?"

"Nothing yet," Blalock said, more as a hope than a certainty. "The book's still in the lab. He hasn't even told me about it yet, so I guess he took your warning seriously."

"I doubt it." Snow slowly twisted his Naval Academy ring. "The guy's a weasel. I can smell 'em every time."

"Anything else on the UFO?" Blalock still couldn't believe there was one.

Snow shook his head. "We know they're out *there*," he said, pointing upward. "We've got to find out where they are *here*. This book may just tell us."

"Jack Beamis know about this?"

"Why?" Snow frowned at him. "You think he should?"

"Well, he is your deputy director."

Snow threw down a shot of vodka. "The fewer people the better."

"What about Blumenthal?" Blalock hoped he wouldn't need to take out someone like Blumenthal. Still, he'd do what had to be done. Because with every fiber of his Special Forces soul he believed that whatever the admiral ordered was necessary given the threat.

Snow barked a laugh. "He's one of us."

"Imagine that, I had no idea." Relief splashed over him like a cold shower.

"That's the idea with secrets, Paul."

"What's our next objective?"

"For now, just keep an eye on the book and Lavisch. I don't want to kill him if we don't have to. He's too high profile. Hard enough trying to contain this astronaut deal."

"I'm all over it," Blalock answered with enthusiasm. Then he thought, Blumenthal might be a hard one to swallow, but he would take great pleasure in icing that idiotic professor.

# CHAPTER 8

Molly watched AJ come out of Johns Hopkins Hospital and move fluidly and nonchalantly toward her car. She marveled that even now AJ projected an air of carefree irresponsibility. How that was possible, she could not imagine, considering that AJ had just discussed a bone-marrow transplant with her sister Katie's oncologist.

The many differences between them were understandable, if for no other reason than because Allison Jamison was privileged. AJ, Katie, and their two brothers had wanted for nothing. Christmas and birthdays were lavish affairs, given over to stupefying displays of material indulgence. In fact, AJ had told her, the two most important events of her life had occurred on birthdays. She had been given her first horse when she turned eight, and since that day, horses had taken up much of her time and all of her money. On her sixteenth birthday, she lost her virginity, and to this day viewed men the way she did her horses—big, dumb animals capable only of passing pleasure. The Lavischs' money went to doctor bills to keep Molly's cancer-ravaged mother alive and then, when all hope of recovery was gone, making her as comfortable as possible until the end.

Nevertheless, Molly did so very much envy AJ's flashy appeal with men. As far back as kindergarten AJ had taken an interest in every boy—or man—Molly had fancied. And she'd always come out on the short end of these battles. But then AJ, like most of their generation, easily used an enticement that she, herself, was not disposed to employ. Sex.

At first, Molly had thought it was her resentment of her father that made her keep the boys at arms length. Oh, she'd had plenty of chances, for, as her mother had often told her, the ever-rising tide of male libido, if given the chance, would wet every reed in the marsh. But later she'd noticed that the casual conveyance of this once vaunted "favor" by her friends—including AJ—had produced little in the way of lasting happiness, and had, among many, been the occasion of prolonged grief, not only for the participants but for the innocent issue, which too often came as an afterthought to but one poorly chosen moment of passion.

By now, her virginity had become a comfort, a treasured covenant unto herself, which she would confer upon the man she chose to be the father of her children. Old-fashioned? Yes. And it had been a promise kept at no small cost, but one which, until now, hadn't seemed too high. Until Peter MacKenzie. So far, AJ hadn't mentioned Peter. Perhaps she wasn't interested. Maybe this time things would be different. She sighed.

"It doesn't look good," AJ said as she slid into the car, immediately pulling the rearview mirror around to apply some lipstick.

Molly noticed some new crow's-feet had sprouted at the corners of AJ's blue eyes. "You know I'll do anything I can to help."

AJ smiled warmly and put her lipstick away. Then, almost dreamily, she said, "You know, she's the only decent one among us."

Molly's heart warmed at AJ's uncharacteristically reflective remark. "I'm meeting Dad and Uncle Malcolm for dinner. Why don't you join us?"

"Thanks. I'd like that."

* * *

Molly pulled into a parking lot around the corner from Tiovanni's restaurant, in East Baltimore. Not far from the docks, it had always seemed to her an odd place for so fine a restaurant, her father's favorite.

But now the prospect of seeing him coupled with the grim surroundings caused panic to rise in her as lurid memories of her youth flashed back. She was thirteen, blossoming into womanhood. He'd come home late, found her sleeping in a hot room without covers or clothes. The dank memory caused her stomach to knot. Down the dingy, shadowy street she saw the restaurant awning just as she felt a sharp elbow to her ribs.

"Just look right through them," AJ advised. "And walk fast."

Molly looked up to see a group of shaved-headed people in white robes who marched along the sidewalk in front of the Aquarian Genomic Research Center, a private bioengineering company made famous for its attempts, so far unsuccessful, to clone famous human leaders like Lincoln, Jefferson and Gandhi. No one believed the rumors that they were trying to clone the prophet Mohammed, but intelligence reports had suggested their involvement with militant Islamic extremists looking for help with the use of chemical and biological weapons.

The protesters marched two abreast, carrying signs. "Stop Human Genetic Experiments." "No Cloning." "Don't Play God." One that said "Ban Gene-Altered Foods!" had a picture of a deformed human fetus, all in bloody disarray, inside a circle with a line drawn through it. Zombilike, they marched by. One young zealot held out an old coffee can for money. "Please help," he asked in a small but sincere voice.

"Help us stop this blasphemy!" Another said, "Help our children dying of cancer because their mothers ate genetically altered food."

"Or from pollution," his female companion added in hostile tone, glaring at the cigarette hanging from AJ's fingers.

"Get a job," AJ snarled.

Molly put a ten-dollar bill into the can.

"You're such a sap," AJ said, rolling her eyes.

"What about Katie? And the jury's still out on genetically altered food."

"It's too late for Katie. And if it tastes good, I'll eat it."

Inside the restaurant, the maître d' led them through a dining room of rabbit-warren alcoves. Irregular white plaster arched columns designed to simulate rough-hewn rock were less than charming but afforded privacy. Past an archway framed by beautiful maidenhair ferns, alone in a dark corner, she spotted him: A large cigar in one hand, a martini in the other.

*At least he hasn't lit it yet.*

"Molly," he said delightedly. "And AJ, nice to see you too."

"Uncle Malcolm!" Molly said, kissing his cheek. "I can't believe I still get you and Dad mixed up!"

"It's the bowties," AJ declared. "One of them has to switch."

Molly pointed at the cigar. "You don't smoke."

"No. It's your father's. I was just trying to fathom his fascination for them. Our tastes in most things are so similar."

"Well, brother," said Miles as he plopped down with a huff, "you look like a thorn between two roses. Have a drink with me, girls?"

"You know I don't drink," Molly said, feeling her face begin to warm.

"I know you ought to," Miles said.

"Yes, please," AJ responded brightly. "Martini's fine, but hold the olives." She ran her fingers through her blond hair, and then shook her head to fluff it out, as a horse shakes its mane. "Molly quite drinking after our senior-year trip to Ocean City, when she—"

"Enough, already!" Molly could see her reflection in a baroque mirror that hung on a pillar across from the table. Her freckles had disappeared in a sea of red.

Malcolm laughed. "Why no olives, AJ?" He popped one into his mouth and stuffed another inside a small piece of flatbread.

"Don't like the green ones. What's that you've got?"

"Lebanese pita. This little pocket—" he outlined the bread's small rim with his finger "—is a symbolic ear."

Miles took the long, tawny cigar from Malcolm and waved it like a baton, as he took out a cheap BIC lighter.

"What's the matter?" AJ asked. "Couldn't find any of your signature kitchen matches?"

"They're getting harder to find," Miles said. He flicked the lighter to flame.

"Oh, Dad, you're not—?"

"Leave him alone, Molly," AJ snipped, then turned back to Malcolm. "Whose ear?"

"The Egyptian gods, my dear," Malcolm responded. "Osiris married his sister, Isis. Together they ruled the underworld."

"Fascinating, Professor," AJ said, cradling her chin in her palm and leaning toward the man. "Especially if incest turns you on."

The remark fell on Molly like ice water and caused an uncontrollable shiver. She looked at AJ, then Malcolm.

"Want my jacket?" Malcolm offered.

"It is chilly in here," Molly admitted. "Thanks." She edged her chair farther away from her father, who beat the side of his martini glass with the big cigar and seemed unaffected by the remark.

"As I was saying," Malcolm continued, "in ancient Egypt this bread was sacred. It was called Pharaoh's bread, and the priests placed it in tombs with the mummified Pharaohs to nourish them on their way to the underworld. The ears were symbolic of a wish that the gods would hear—and answer—their prayers."

"But does it taste good?" AJ asked, rocking her head jauntily.

Malcolm tore off a little ear of bread. "Try it."

Rather than taking it from him, she leaned even closer and opened her mouth. The tip of her pink tongue darted out and flicked the morsel from his hand.

Molly closed her eyes. *My God AJ!* She knew that with AJ, flirting was as reflexive as breathing. Sometimes she wished she could acquire that native response. She watched her father drain his martini. With a devilish glance, he flicked his lighter on and off, teasing the tip of his cigar with the flame, as if trying to provoke her. Again she felt her face and neck warming, so quickly she turned back to her uncle, who was stuffing another olive into an ear of bread. "Why are you plugging its ears?" she asked, trying to distract herself. "Don't you want your prayers answered?"

"Prayers? Miles snorted. "Supplications to nonexistent phantoms. Did prayer give us TVs? Airplanes? Cell phones? No. If you want to count on something, count on man's intellect. Given time, science will answer all man's prayers." He gestured with his empty glass at the waiter.

"And what about women, Miles?" AJ said, wagging a finger at him and munching bread.

"Some would say that *science* has been more of a hindrance than a benefit to man's spiritual progress," Malcolm pointed out in a good-natured tone. "Our intellect may have brought us far, but the human heart? Well, I'm afraid, it's still stuck in the stone age."

"My dear brother," Miles replied, waving his still unlit cigar, "if it weren't for the gloomy prospect of our mortality, I fear there'd be no need for that kind of heart, much less a God."

"Then I'd be out of a job," Malcolm grinned.

Molly watched the end of the swaying cigar as if it were a cobra's head. She decided to change the subject before the brothers got into another serious argument, or before she did. "I'm surprised you didn't mentioned the astronauts the other day at the lab."

"Terrible news, wasn't it?" Malcolm exclaimed as he peeled back the edge of another piece of pita. "What does it mean for your project, Miles?"

"Nothing," Miles said flatly.

Molly noticed he'd let the flame of the lighter bring an orange glow to the end of his cigar. "I met a man at your lab the day Kim Lee died," she said, tingling at recalling Peter MacKenzie's touch. "He said he knew the astronaut who commanded the *Areopagus* mission. He thinks they were all murdered. In fact he was there to see if you knew anything about it, Dad."

Miles sniffed disgustedly. "I can tell you this: The contamination story NASA gave was rubbish. We got the rocks right away. There *was* no wait. Hell, as long as the seals on the cases weren't broken, they were safe. And they weren't broken. If NASA had suspected contamination, it would have kept the rocks."

"You knew some of the crew, didn't you?" Molly asked.

Miles nodded. "Two of them."

AJ looked at Molly. "I think the whole thing is scary. Did you tell your father about the Gypsy's warning?"

"A Gypsy!" Miles guffawed. "Now you've really gone off the deep end."

Molly telegraphed AJ an angry glance. "We were at a carnival. It was just for fun."

"What's the message?" Malcolm asked.

"Oh, I can't remember," she lied, trying not to pout. *She can be such a bitch. She knew my father would do this.* She focused on the tip of her father's cigar, which glowed brighter.

"Well, *I* can," AJ announced. "I was spooked. She said, in effect, the world is about to end and that Molly was going to—"

"She said," Molly interrupted in self-defense, "'beware bellchapel' or something like that. She had a thick accent."

"No," AJ corrected. "She dropped the phony accent at the end. She said, 'Tell your father Bell and Carla said beware.'"

Miles blanched. His cigar fell from his hand onto the floor. He quickly bent to retrieve it, brushing the sparks into the antique Persian carpet with his shoe.

"I met a Bill Quincy and a Carla Pascal at your lecture, didn't I?" Malcolm asked.

"Good grief, Dad!" *Your passing will not be easy.* She repeated the Gypsy's warning silently. Her stomach quaked. "Do you know what that means?"

"Do you?" AJ repeated.

Miles shook his head. "Malcolm's right. They were Mission Specialists, part of the crew that went up to get the *Areopagus.* They were to ensure the integrity of the samples. Escort them to the lab. She must have read about them—and me—in the newspapers. I *am* a famous fellow, you know."

"But she doesn't know you're Molly's father," AJ said.

"Nice people, as I remember," Malcolm said absently, gazing into his glass of ginger ale.

Miles stared coldly at her. "Can you really be that gullible, Molly? You're supposed to be a scientist." He shifted his glare to Malcolm.

Molly felt Malcolm take her hand and squeeze it gently.

"Miles," Malcolm started quietly. "That's a bit harsh, don't you think? Oh, I don't know about this Gypsy—she's probably just a good actor. But sometimes I think we mock prophecy at our own risk. All great religious tradition tells of a Judgment Day. Or some watershed event for humankind. So do virtually all primitive cultures. Most point to this very time as the end. Even modern science, physics—"

"For Christ's sake, Malcolm!" Miles's face darkened under rising eyebrows. "If I didn't know better, I'd think your brain was switched at birth. What're you going to tell me next? That you're moving to a survivalist commune in the mountains? Or that you're going to shave your head and take up a sign like those Krishna types outside?"

"Prophecies," Molly said, burning with resentment, "don't just come from religious kooks. What about H. G. Wells? Or Jules Verne? And what about that white buffalo born on a ranch in Montana not that long ago? It fulfilled a prophecy of the Sioux. They say the coming of the Great White Buffalo signals the end of the age—"

"And the demise of the white man," Malcolm added.

"Maybe it's just an albino," she continued, taking on strength as she forced herself to look at him, "but it's the first."

"Or Star Trek, for that matter," Malcolm added. "Science fiction writers have foretold a great deal. Are they all just good guessers, guessing from an infinity of possibilities? Or are they modern-day prophets who hear the whisperings of revealed knowledge?"

"Really, brother, you *do* shame me."

"Shame *you?*" Malcolm huffed. "Do I need a crowbar and a welding torch to crack open that closed mind of yours? This is *my* area of expertise. And I can tell you that many familiar ancient prophecies are being reappraised in light of new scientific evidence. Yes! By scientists, no less. Why even the great physicist Freeman Dyson said recently that "'Religion has a much more important role in human destiny than science.'"

"Horseshit!" Miles pounded the table with the flat of his hand. "Or should I say buffalo shit," he mumbled under his breath. "A stupid albino, for Christ's sake. What'll you say when the next one comes. And there will be more. What then?"

"But you'd have to agree," Malcolm said, "the timing is mighty suspicious. Do you know of Nachmanides?"

"Nostradamus?" Miles scoffed.

"Open just a crack, brother! *Not Nostradamus.* But an altogether different thirteenth-century philosopher and mystic. Tell me if you recognize what he said. I'm paraphrasing some, but he said when God created the world it was *an entity so thin it had no substance to it. Just a dot of space.* And that *time didn't 'grab hold' until matter filled the universe.* Sound familiar."

"The Big Bang?" Miles sniffed. "Just another coincidence."

"Really?" Malcolm's gray-brown eyebrows mirrored his brother's. "Why, man's very existence is still a profound enigma. No one can yet explain the sudden emergence of so complicated a being as we. And not all that long ago."

"What now, little brother? You'd dispute evolution?"

"No! Evolution is fact."

"Well, then!" Miles said.

"But random mutation," Malcolm continued calmly, "doesn't account for modern man's sudden appearance only a hundred thousand or so years ago. Look, Miles, all I'm saying is that there is more to this universe than our feeble powers of imagination can discern, and we ought to be more humble about our inadequacies. That's all."

"Anybody seen a menu around here?" AJ asked wearily. "I'm hungry. How about you, Miles?"

"Blessed are the peacemakers," Malcolm conceded, "for they shall soon eat." Then he laughed.

"Funny, Malcolm!" AJ clapped.

Molly picked up two menus, tossed one to her friend and began to scan the other. "I don't suppose they have hotdogs here?"

"Oh, God!" AJ gasped. "Hotdogs again. Don't you know they're not good for you, *Doctor* Lavisch?"

"Yeah, well, as you're fond of saying, 'Nobody's perfect.'" She glared at her father. *How can identical twins be so much the same yet so different?* "By the way, Dad, what became of that beautiful black rock I saw? Find anything interesting?"

"That's another boil on my ass," Miles fumed. "Bastards want to take the project away from me now." He flicked the lighter's flint wheel. "Well, it'll be over my dead body. But I don't want to talk about. However, my good daughter, I do need a favor?"

Molly hoped it wouldn't be another offer to come work with him. Then she looked at his cigar. "Will you do me one?"

Miles held the flame steady. The cigar's tip glowed bright orange. A small streamer of bluish smoke dribbled into the air. He glanced over at her. "I'll be sending you something I want analyzed for possible DNA. Can you do it?"

She exhaled a loud sigh. “Of course I will. What is it?”

“I don’t want to bias your analysis,” he said sarcastically and puffed a huge cloud of acrid smoke in her face, “but it looks like blood.”

# CHAPTER 9

Molly stared blankly at her computer screen. Her thoughts drifted. She was part of the NIH group that first helped to map the complete set of human genes. Though Celera Genomics, a private company in Rockville, Maryland, run by a former NIH colleague, had clearly beaten her team to the punch with a "rough-draft" version of the sequence, they soldiered on, for determining the genome's sequence was the easy part. Determining each gene's exact function, posed a much more difficult—and more important—undertaking. Much remained to be done. But in the last five days she'd made no headway. Ever since meeting Peter MacKenzie.

Her attraction to him was an unfamiliar admixture of the gravitational pull of sexual longing and the curiosity surrounding the unknown. And the feelings frightened her. She forced herself to focus on the computer. Letters designating the DNA building blocks—the bases that formed pairs bonded together as the steps in the spiral staircase of this ancient and life-ordering molecule—flashed by: *a, a, g, a, t, c.*

"Four simple chemicals," she chanted in nursery rhyme fashion, "made you and me and the birds and the bees. Adenine, Guanine, and Thymine, too, and don't forget Cytosine, or a ghost'll get you." She leaned back in her chair and stretched. "Only about two-and-a-half billion more to go. Then what?"

She knew the eventual payoff for her efforts, and the efforts of thousands of others around the world, was the emerging science of genetic medicine. At least that was the stated purpose, but she knew the real power—and danger—in her work lay in eugenics, the ultimate tool for improving humankind. And she knew that day was fast approaching.

It was a day her father, much more than she, longed for: the creation of an entirely new species of human. He had danced around his lab like a schoolboy at a pep rally when the news of the sheep "Dolly," the first cloned mammal, had been announced. His alchemistical fervor was shared by many, though not all, in the scientific community. For others, like Jeremy Rifkin, the developments signaled man had reached a foreboding crossroads.

"Man making man," she murmured, knowing it was now possible. "What will we create with that power?" Yet she had to admit, her father was right about one thing: Mankind could no longer count on natural evolution to improve the species. If improvements to man's unyielding—and very flawed nature—were to be made, those changes would come only by dint of human intervention.

She sighed and clicked the mouse pointer to print. While the printer buzzed away in the background, she fiddled with her locket. She opened it, looked longingly at her mother's faded image. How she'd loved her. And in the locket's other golden half, her father. How much she'd once loved *him*, how hard she tried now to suppress her seething resentment, to find some scrap of forgiveness. A tear meandered down the edge of her nose.

He'd told her she'd never be a doctor. He'd said she was too cold, too timid, too heartless. She still wondered if he'd been right.

She was first given patients in her fourth year of medical school, and by the end of her internship she knew that maintaining an emotional distance would be impossible. Pediatrics had been the worst. How could any sensitive, caring person remain professionally detached from the crack babies, babies with AIDS, or those suffering from Fetal Alcohol Syndrome? To her, the desperation and the degradation of humanity was at once pitiable and reprehensible, for in the end most of the misery was the result of sad personal choices. It was the day-to-day dealing with those sad choices that had almost killed her.

First she developed an ulcer, then colitis, and finally a debilitating depression. Reluctantly, she'd gone into research, which is what her father had planned for her all along. He had never let her forget the failure.

*Yes,* she thought, *it* is *possible to care too much.* Was that what the Gypsy had meant? Or had she, as she knew her father thought, just been a coward? She snapped the locket shut with a sharp *click.*

Her lab assistant, Brenda Cruise, entered the room, juggling a stack of Petri dishes and a sheaf of manila folders, several of which fell to the floor in a shower of paper and clattering plastic. "Oh poop!" she cursed, bending to pick up the litter of saucer-shaped dishes and lids. "Package, Dear. Came by courier. I put it in your office."

"Thanks, Brenda. I'll be right back."

In her office, she looked at the small, plainly wrapped little box with her father's return address that sat on her desk, and then, because of her fatigue, thought about leaving it for tomorrow. She wondered why he'd been so vague about the source of the sample. So she guessed it had something to do with the Martian project. Was this his sneaky way of getting her involved?

Nevertheless, she'd promised him a quick turn-around, and so, reluctantly, she snipped the binding string and removed the brown paper with its grocery-store label. Apparently he'd wrapped it himself, which she thought altogether odd, given his nearly religious avoidance of anything that smacked of domesticity.

She would have Brenda do the analysis of the suspected blood. If all went well, she would know at least what species the blood came from in just a few days. She flipped off the top, tilted the box—a shoebox from the shoes she'd given him for Christmas—and shook out a silken ribbon.

"What?" she gasped uncontrollably. Her eyes riveted on the border's design. "The Gypsy's pendant." Suddenly the image of Kim Lee's face as he lay dying in her arms exploded in her mind; his terrified expression frightened her to the point of nausea. Then, as if in ugly counterpoint, the Gypsy's warning jolted her like an electric shock.

She picked up the phone and dialed.

"Uncle Malcolm!" She exhaled his name with relief, not even aware she'd been holding her breath.

"Molly, dear," the buoyant voice said. "Is everything all right?"

"Thank goodness I caught you."

"Why? What's wrong?"

"I'm worried about Dad. And I don't know what to do about it."

"What's happened?"

She told him about Lee, about her father's suspicions concerning Chandra and Blalock, about her concerns regarding the Gypsy's warning.

"And I didn't mention it the other night, but the Gypsy also said I was going to die."

"That is strange." Then he chortled. "You don't get many repeat customers that way in the fortune-telling business."

"Malcolm! It's not funny anymore."

"Now, now, Molly. I hate to agree with your father on this, but I do think you're taking this a bit too much to heart."

"I thought so, too. Until I got the sample Dad wanted me to analyze. Remember at dinner?"

"What was it?" her uncle asked.

"A cloth ribbon with a stain and a design—the same design the Gypsy had on her medallion."

"You're sure?"

"You know I collect antique jewelry—like Mom. And I've never seen anything like it. I even checked my books."

"And you think the cloth came from the Martian samples?" Malcolm asked incredulously.

"I don't know, but where else?"

"He couldn't tell you, even if you asked. Security," Malcolm said, then paused. "And it was the same design as the Gypsy's?"

"I'm positive."

"Hmmm." There was a long cleft of silence. "It's could be a prayer cloth. Or some such. Trouble is, I've never heard of anything quite like that design either—if I'm visualizing right. I'd like to see it. Can you fax me a sketch in the morning?"

"Of course.... Uncle Malcolm?"

"Yes?"

"It's just that I feel so stupid about it all."

Malcolm laughed tenderly. "My dear, you don't have a stupid bone in your body. Always listen to your intuition. Always. I don't know about the prophecy or what this cloth means, but I wouldn't totally discount it, either. Not in light of recent events."

"What do you mean?" It wasn't the kind of comment she was expecting to hear, even from him, a man who had debated, some thought very successfully, the great Joseph Campbell. Unlike Campbell, for whom all was mere mythology, Malcolm believed some prophecies revealed hidden, but still knowable human potentials.

"Unexplainable happenings around the world. All with spiritual meaning for some cultural tradition or other. Each day seems to bring something new and more bizarre."

She sighed heavily. "You're not making me feel any better."

"I don't want to alarm you, Molly. Let me put it into context. As we were discussing the other night, virtually all the world's religious traditions believe in a day of reckoning or an Age of Aquarius or a Judgment Day or some existence-altering event. Most surround the return of some savior or magical being that will usher in the new era. There's the Kachina of the Hopi Indians. And one for the aborigines, the Zulus, and the Mayans—"

"You mean like the white buffalo thing I mentioned the other night. God, I don't even know why I recalled that."

"That too," he agreed. "It goes on. Because we're a predominantly Christian culture, most people think only of the return of Christ, but parallels exist everywhere. A lot of people attribute it to a Jungian collective memory of a pre-existence in which a plan for the universe was known to all."

"Jungian?"

"Carl Jung, the psychiatrist and philosopher—"

"Oh, yes. I vaguely remember from psychiatric rotation in med school."

"Fascinating man. Dismissed by many as a mere mystic. If you remembered the buffalo thing, you probably heard about the Cistine Chapel, didn't you?"

"Vandalism, wasn't it?"

"No, not vandalism. Thirty years after Michelangelo finished his famous ceiling, he reluctantly accepted a commission to paint the rear wall as well. It turned out to be the largest fresco ever painted. It was meant to depict the Last Judgment. Michelangelo put his own portrait among the damned. Well, last week his self-portrait disappeared. Gone. Left a hole in the painting as if it were never there."

"But how?" she asked, fearing that all her education was somehow failing her in her hour of need.

"No one knows," he continued. "It's been played down because frankly no one *can* explain it. But it's gone—clean as a whistle. There's nothing left in the spot but fresh, dry plaster showing no sign of ever having been painted. Ever. But the plaster is old, not new. It dates from exactly the right period."

"Oh my God!"

"There's more. Just yesterday, the stone at Mecca disappeared."

She felt a shiver and drew her Afghan up over her legs. "The one the Archangel Gabriel was supposed to have given Mohammed?"

"Uh-huh."

"Who would want to—?"

"No one knows how. Or who."

"There'll be a war over that," she stammered.

"If Islam has been looking for the ultimate excuse for a *Jihad* against the West, they've got it now. Our war on terrorism will probably evolve into something more awful, I'm afraid."

"Malcolm, will you speak to Dad? Find out what he's up to? Or at least make sure he's being careful? I don't know what else to do."

"Of course, dear. But it sounds as if you're the one who needs to take care. You will, won't you?"

"I'll try."

He seemed to recover some of his cheerfulness. "But remember this: keep your eye on the Eastern Gate of Old Jerusalem; it's been sealed with stone for centuries. Judaic tradition has it that if it is ever again opened, it means that Judgment Day is near."

# CHAPTER 10

Peter MacKenzie raised his glass. "To you, Molly."

"And you," she squeaked. Her heart pounded so hard, it nearly shook the drink from her hand. Their glasses tinkled in toast. She took a big gulp of wine. She'd promised herself just one drink, remembering AJ's comment about Ocean City. A welcome splash of warmth radiated through her body. She didn't care if Peter's only interest was in her father at the moment, for she intended to change all that. She glanced self-consciously across the room, where an older man in a black tuxedo, gray, oil-slicked hair tied back in a short ponytail, played piano.

"Nice place, Peter. Come here often?" She cringed even as she said it and averted her eyes.

"A little fancy for me, but I thought you might like it."

Her face burned. Was her unease so obvious?

He shook his head grimly. "Molly, I won't bite. Promise. Now I know why you and AJ ran off at the airshow before we had a chance to talk."

"Oh, no, it wasn't what you think—"

"What's the matter, then?" He leaned back in his chair with a puckish grin. "Afraid I might want to sleep with you tonight?"

She spat out a thin reed of the wine she'd just sipped. "N-No," she stuttered, quickly mopping up the wine. *Get hold of yourself!* "Maybe I'm afraid *I* might—ah-ah, sleep with me. I-I-I mean sleep with you—I-I mean. *Sheeessh.*" She took a deep breath and stared at the ceiling. "What did AJ tell you?"

"Nothing, really." He laughed wickedly. "But I am flattered you'd considered me a candidate. And I agree with you. It's best to get sex out of the way first thing. Gets a relationship off on the right foot, don't you think?"

"I appreciate the honesty." *Did he say, Relationship*? For her the word was electric, so charged with meaning that it hung in the air like a cloud. She took a quick sip of her ice water, keeping the glass to her lips as she blew in air, trying to cool her blush with the backwash.

He plucked the cherry out of his Manhattan, never taking his eyes off her, took a sip, and tossed the cherry aside. She twirled her locket, slowly at first, but under his gaze she unconsciously spun it faster, wildly, until he reached over, stuck his finger in the arch of the whirling locket, which wound around his finger and came to an abrupt stop. "Sorry. It was making me dizzy."

Her face ablaze, she couldn't look at him; she looked out the window instead. The sun, though already behind the taller buildings, bathed the bustling city streets in a comforting orange glow. She felt his eyes on her. Mercifully, the waiter arrived.

"I didn't see hotdogs on the menu," she stammered. "Don't you have a children's menu?" The waiter apologized but said no.

*"Hotdogs?"*

"They're my comfort food. Reminds me of the baseball games my Uncle Malcolm used to take me to."

"Guess we have something in common."

"Hotdogs?"

"No—more of a Cracker Jacks fan, myself—I meant baseball. I've got a great collection of trading cards. Actually have an Honus Wagner. Ever hear of him?"

She shook her head, looked down at her hands, which she had tightly clasped together, fighting the urge to touch her locket. Finally, exasperated with herself, she said, "Can we start over?"

"Suits me."

She extended her hand. "Pleased to see you again, Peter MacKenzie. How've you been?"

They shook hands. They laughed. They declined another invitation by the waiter to order dinner and instead got another drink. They talked animatedly for half an hour or so about this and that—mostly Molly's research, her cat, the events at the air show and baseball. She purposely avoided discussing her father or the astronauts. She wanted some mystery to remain; that way, maybe he'd ask to see her again.

"Well, Peter, all I've done is talk about me. What about you? Your weekend flying job can't be all that you do?" She dipped her head quizzically. "Unless you're independently wealthy?

"You don't strike me as the gold-digging type."

"Just curious."

He hesitated, rubbing the scar on his chin. "That *is* what I do. Before that, I was a fighter pilot. A naval aviator." He paused, gave a thumbs-up and saluted. "Did that for about ten years. Until I lost an airplane."

"They're kind of hard to misplace, aren't they?"

"I like a good sense of humor. No, I meant I had to eject

"I guess you're lucky to be here."

"Yeah..." He seemed to drift away for a moment. "Hell, I was a whole inch shorter for a year after. I was in the hospital for a month with several fractured vertebrae. Anyway, my back never completely healed, so I got taken off flight status. I'd had enough of it anyway, I guess." He drained his Manhattan. "Hey," he said, eyes twinkling, "you know the first thing I asked the doctors when they fished me out of the drink?"

"What?"

"I asked if I'd ever be able to play piano again."

"Not if you'd be able to fly again?" She thought it an odd joke, unworthy of him.

He glanced at the piano. "Tell me the truth, did you really play baseball?"

"Sure did," she said proudly. "Little League. Pony League. I even played in high school one year. My Uncle Malcolm was my biggest booster. But then I got serious about being a doctor, so I concentrated on the studies. There's just no future for women in baseball."

He nodded. "The biggest regret of my life is I didn't get to play when I was a little kid. If you don't play early, it's tough to catch up—"

"Oh, *I* know," she laughed, trying too hard to be funny. "You played *piano* instead, right?"

Without a word, he got up from the table and went across to the piano where he whispered something to the old man, who vacated his seat. Then Peter took his place. He looked at her with arched eyebrow and started to play. And he played beautifully. And what he played was utterly magical to their moment, a song from one of her favorite old black-and-white movies, *Casablanca*, with Humphrey Bogart and Ingrid Bergman. He began to sing the words, his rendering sincere if not accomplished:

"You must remember this, a kiss is just a kiss, a sigh is just a sigh.... The fundamental things apply, as time goes by...."

She clapped as hard as she could. "Bravo! Bravo!"

Back at the table, beaming a broad grin, he said, "Aren't you sorry you doubted me?"

"I never will again, Bogie."

"Hey, I like that. Me Bogie, you Ingrid. Beats me Tarzan, you Jane, huh?" He looked at his watch. "Well, sad to say, but just like in the movie, one of us has got to go. Only this time, I'm afraid it's Bogie who goes and Ingrid who's left watching the plane depart."

"Sorry we didn't get to talk much about my father's project, but I can tell you this. He agrees that NASA's public statements about the fire are untrue."

"I know they lied. I just can't figure why."

"My father's giving a lecture at the Air and Space Museum tomorrow at eight. Maybe you could come. I can introduce you then."

"Okay. Must be big news from the *Areopagus* samples?"

"I don't know. He just asked me to be there. I promised I would be."

Outside streetlights had just begun to flicker on, as the sun, already set, slowly rescinded its bounty of summer light. The evening air was warm, the sidewalks busy with city life. As she put the key in the lock, she looked at him expectantly.

He reached over to her, slipping his hand deftly around her waist. "I know what we agreed about sex, and I mean to keep my word, but—" He pulled her to him and kissed her softly, discreetly on her mouth, not lingering long nor pressing with deep passion. Her lips stung deliciously, and she wanted more, but it was over before it had begun. She almost wished...

"That was sweet," she whispered, trembling so much that she dropped her purse, which emptied its contents onto the sidewalk, including the sketch of the Gypsy's ankh she'd earlier faxed to her uncle.

"What's this?" he said, picking up the sketch.

"An odd piece of jewelry. I'd never seen anything like it before the Gypsy at your air show."

"Lilah Blackwell?"

"Who?"

"She's the Gypsy. I know her. I never saw that on her, though." He fished out his key ring. On it was Apollyon's gold pendant.

At first she felt oddly relieved, for how strange could the image be if they were selling them for trinkets? "Please tell me you got that out of a box of Cracker Jacks."

"Tooth Fairy would be more like it. I got it off a guy who said he was an angel." His head dropped, as if he'd been hit. "It was the last time I saw Bo."

She felt the blood go out of her face and shivered. She thought about her father's bloodstained cloth, but decided not to say anything.

## CHAPTER 11

Peter yawned, pulled on his khaki pants both legs at once and bounded off the bed. Quickly buckling his belt and zipping his fly, he headed for the window. On the way he pulled on a gray Navy sweatshirt, checked the time on the Rolex he'd gotten for a song in the Philippines on his second cruise, then threw open the window and took in a draft of fresh country air, sweet with the smell of new-cut hay. He had come straight to AJ's from his date with Molly the previous evening. And after last night, he was hungry as well as sleepy, though the hollow feeling he had went beyond the need for food. He picked up a Cracker Jack box off the vanity, shook it and peered down inside. *Empty.*

He'd avoided going home since news of Bo's death, afraid that Beth would be there waiting. She'd left a dozen messages on his machine. He wondered how long he could put off talking to her. For how could he explain to her what Bo had meant to him? Talking to a woman in the way that would require was a chore he didn't feel up to. For the bond between him and Bo, an ageless link between soldiers of every era, was more certain than blood. Yet their allegiance went deeper still. Had it not been for Bo, he would never have won his wings, would never have fulfilled the vaunted image he'd set for himself the day he'd learned his father was gone.

Which was why his own act of betrayal rumbled around his gut like a red-hot piece of iron. He'd wanted to square things with Bo. He'd tried last Christmas Eve, failed. But then blind circumstance—and the *Areopagus* mission—had kept them apart. He certainly couldn't have done it over the phone. He was coward enough already.

*Then it was too late.* Death steals so many unspoken truths.

So Bo's murder needed more than avenging. His death needed meaning. Before all was said and done, he promised himself, it would, and he would be the creator of that meaning, if necessary by his own ultimate sacrifice.

He sighed as if something huge had sat on his chest, pushing the wind out of him. No. He could put off seeing Beth no longer. *Tomorrow,* he said to himself. *I'll see her tomorrow.*

With that behind him, he would continue pumping his contacts in the Intelligence community for information, which had so far yielded little. Peculiarly, the usual underground grapevine had abruptly withered. Everyone seemed to be holding back, reluctant to discuss anything remotely linked to the *Discovery's* crew or the *Areopagus.* Even old mutual friends of his and Bo's, people at the Defense Intelligence Agency, the CIA and the Center for Naval Analysis, revealed nothing but the expected niceties conveyed when a fellow warrior has fallen.

More bizarre was the stonewall he'd faced among his own associates at his home-base at NIMA, National Imagery and Mapping Agency in the Pentagon, from which he'd taken a leave of absence because of Bo. They even began to grill him on why he wanted to know, said they'd pass on his request to Langley, which is not exactly what he'd intended. The last thing he needed now was a high profile. Something was being hushed up. Something big.

That left Molly Lavisch—and her father. She would be easy. Especially after last evening.

Just then he saw the rim of the sun peer over the bluff just beyond the barns. Its yellow rays splashed onto the pasture, creating a vast golden pool of light. It reminded him of the sun on the water the day he and Roy Corbett had crashed his F-14. But he quickly squelched that thought and turned to look over his shoulder to the ravaged bed where AJ lay sleeping, her slender legs askew, half on, half off the bed. He watched a wisp of her blond hair moving slightly in the gentle breeze of her breath, revealing one of many tattoos. Why in God's name did women think tattoos could improve on their naturally interesting feminine curves? For some reason, Molly came to mind. *I'll bet she doesn't have any tattoos.* He tossed the empty Cracker Jack box next to AJ's head.

"Sun's up," he said loudly. "Better feed your horses."

"They can wait," AJ told him groggily. "Come back to bed. Last night was even better than the first time." She laughed like a drunken barmaid, flopped back onto her pillow, her blond hair fanned out around her face like the rays of the sun.

He sat back down on the bed, kissed her deeply and gently squeezed her breast, rubbing her hard nipple with his thumb as he did. He felt her unzipping his fly, but he took her hand and stood up, looking around for his jacket.

"You're such a tease," she said and picked up her compact with its little mirror and began to examine her face. "God! These crows' feet are gaining on me."

"You've got nothing to worry about." He scrutinized her carefully, assaying the burning blue eyes, the hair bright and blond as sun on a sandy beach, the lips pink, soft and swollen. Suddenly, she was every woman he'd ever known, a vapid cutout that he could, if he wished, shuffle like a deck of cards, to be played one at a time, over and over, in a game of solitaire. It was a fleeting but painful feeling.

"Why do you have to go?" she pouted. "You don't have be anywhere today." She threw the covers off, spread her legs. Caressing herself, she licked her lips, taunting him.

He managed a tired half-grin, thinking she looked like Lilacs from Christmas Eve with Bo. "All night is all there is, sweetheart. Don't you ever get enough?"

"Not of anything I like. And I like you."

He took out his wallet and started sifting through his trove of business cards, notes, old receipts, match flaps from some of his favorite bars, looking for Molly's card. "Where's your phone? I've got to get in touch with Molly."

"What do want to talk to *her* for?"

"Jealous?" he said without looking at her.

*"Of her?"* she sneered. "You've got to be kidding. She's handicapped, poor darling, and I don't just mean her limp."

"What do you mean, then?"

"She just doesn't know how to get what she wants, is all."

"For example?"

"She wants you."

"Oh?"

"Oh, *puleeease.* Your not going to say you don't know. False modesty's unbecoming. Especially in a hunk like you." She smiled, batted her eyes playfully.

"My best friend died because of something to do with the *Areopagus* mission. Her father has a big part in that; he may know something. That's all I'm interested in at the moment—" He winked. "Besides you, sweetheart."

She sat up and started to dress. "Sure that's all?"

"I'm sure. And I don't want you involved. Not yet anyway. I'm supposed to meet her old man tonight at one of his lectures."

"And what about the rest of the day?"

"I've got some business to take care of." *Old Cap*, he said to himself. The thought conjured comforting memories. "I'll call you this afternoon."

She reached for her panties. "What *do* you do, anyway? Not just fly airplanes I hope."

"You and Molly been comparing notes?"

"What?"

"Never mind. Yeah. Just that."

But he couldn't help watching her put one luscious leg, then another into her lacy panties with the open crotch, the nipples of her small but firm breasts still slightly swollen. He decided to stay a while longer.

When they were through, he pulled on his khakis again, both legs at once. She lit a Marlboro with her dainty gold horse head lighter.

"This time I've *really* got to get going," he said, kissing her one last time and patting her on the buttocks. "We'll get together after old man Lavisch's lecture. Might be pretty late. I'll call you later."

"Come to think of it, don't bother. I won't be here." She rolled out of bed and began to dress.

"Yeah? Where're you going?"

"My sister Katie's funeral."

## CHAPTER 12

*You don't look too good, Cap*, Peter MacKenzie thought as he sat by Captain Bob Donaldson's hospital bed. He'd known Cap most of his life, first as a friend of his dad, later as his new father after his own dad failed to return from Vietnam. Cap was always there and always good for a story, usually about his exploits as a World War II P-51D Mustang fighter pilot. God, how he loved the old man. But now he wondered how much longer Cap could hang on. Would it be a stroke, presaged by his worsening dementia, or his longstanding emphysema that would take him? Either way, he thought each sad visit to the hospital would be his last.

"Would you believe me if I told you I met the Babe?" The old man choked.

"Ruth? Sure, Cap." It was a story he'd heard perhaps a dozen times—and only in the last week. It was the increasing fragility of Cap's memory that disturbed him most.

Cap nodded, the nasal cannula bobbing up and down in affirmation. "Yep. In 'thirty-six, when I was just twelve. For all his faults, he was wonderful to kids. Always gave a hawker twenty dollars to take care of all his young fans. I know, I *was* one."

"A softy, huh?"

"Yep. Met Ted Williams, too. In a bar in London during the war. You know he was fighter pilot, don't ya?"

"I remember you'd told me that, Cap."

"No man will ever hit like he did again. Not just Texas Leaguers, either. He was a sorcerer. A magician. He could make a frozen rope outta smoke. Time after time."

He'd heard this one, too, and he laughed. "You mean he could hit a hard line drive—or a homer—from a fastball? You're datin' yourself with references like that, Cap."

Cap coughed away the accumulating phlegm. "Still got the baseball cards I gave ya 'cause your mom made you play piano instead of baseball?"

"You bet."

"Even the Honus Wagner? That one's the best, the one that came in the Sweet Caporal cigarettes?"

"Sure, Cap. Worth over half a million, I'm told. Though I'd never part with it."

"Pittsburgh Pirates," Cap said dreamily, his eyes watery with memories. "Those were the days... Yep. My father smoked those Sweet C's. And seeing where I ended up, I really admire old Honus for not wanting his name associated with tobacco products. They did it without his permission and he made 'em stop before they'd made maybe fifty or so. He was thinking of kids like me."

"Yeah," he said and sighed. "A true sportsman. Trouble is, there isn't much sportsmanship left in sports these days. The old warrior ethic is gone. Sports heroes used to be like knights of the roundtable. People with courage *and* class. Most players today are just overpaid thugs—and not just in baseball."

"Sad, isn't it? Especially for the kids."

"Oh, there's a Cal Ripken Jr, here and there. Not many, though. No Williamses or Wagners or Babes." Cap nodded agreement.

"Yep," Cap said with wise, aged eyes. Then he shook. He made guttural sounds, which rumbled through his speech. "Son, all I can tell you is, some of life's most valuable lessons are its most painful." He did his best to sit up higher in his bed, but made no progress, so Peter heaved his frail body up, cranked his bed more erect, and put another pillow under his head.

"You mentioned a 'warrior ethic.' But, Pete, courage isn't always so easy to define. Oh, I agree with you about the weakness of the human spirit, but war ain't exactly what you think—"

"Oh, I was in a war, Cap. A couple of 'em, remember? Didn't get into any dogfights like you. But then I didn't get shot down, either." He lifted an eyebrow and cast a joshing glance at the captain, who paused and wiped the drool from the corner of his mouth with the edge of his pillowcase. Peter noticed it was bloody.

"I'm dying, Pete—"

"Come on, Cap. Surrender isn't in your vocabulary."

"Yep. I always loved you like my own son. And before I go there's somethin' I want to tell you." He looked away for a moment, coughed up more bloody phlegm. " No.... Somethin' I *have* to tell you. Something I've never told *anyone* before. Ever." He stretched out his hand.

"Sure Cap," he said, taking the old man's bony hand, with its silvery skin, thin as tissue, and its large, ropey veins that stood out like little blue mountain ridges across its back.

Cap started almost in a whisper. "It was Christmas Eve nineteen forty-four—may God have mercy on our souls. In the prison camp. We were all outside by the fire pit, where we had to eat what little food they gave us. Otto—Otto Kessler, he was camp commandant and a colonel in the Waffen SS—always made us eat outside, even on the coldest days. Some of us died because it was too hard to stay warm enough to eat—you'd shiver so hard you couldn't get food to your mouth even if you had it. Anyways, they'd bring a large, black, cast-iron kettle out twice a day and hang it from a metal tripod over the fire pit. There was never much in it, though, nothin' but the same slop they gave to a bunch of hogs they kept for butchering behind the electrified fence next to our barracks. Yep, we saw 'em do it—throw some to hogs, then the rest in the big black kettle. Just leavin's from the enlisted men's mess, mostly rinds, bones and gristle, and occasionally a half a potato. And you know what our treat was?"

"What?"

"Otto always made sure they put a whole animal head in, usually a sheep or a pig—once it was a dog, a stray they ran over with a truck. Odd, 'cause the Germans loved their dogs, generally speakin.' Some men would fight over the bits of flesh from the heads, even fight over the eyes, some of 'em. Everything got ate, even the hair. Can you blame us? Only this for over two hundred men?

"Anyways. They made us chop our own wood every day. Always just enough to heat the pot, never enough to get us all warmed up, even by taking turns around it. Two guards would come with an axe and dump a few pieces of wood. Then they'd assign someone to chop. Always took several of us 'cause we were all so weak. Cold that year, too.

"On this particular day, a fight broke out. Over what, I don't remember. My best friend, Bernie, and a guy whose name I can't recall. This guy was trying to hit Bernie with the axe. He was a new prisoner, not weakened by the privations we'd been suffering under. He had strength all over Bernie, so we tried to stop it.

"Well, I was trying to break up the fight when who shows up but Otto, with his jackboots all spit polished. Had his silver-tipped baton and Princess with him, his all white German shepherd. I'll never forget that damned dog. She was meaner'n Otto. 'Cause he fed her human remains. We'd seen it. Sometimes he'd let her attack one of the men just for laughs, and if anyone tried to help the poor bastard, he was shot.

"Well, Otto singled out me and Bernie and the other guy and asked who started the fight. No one spoke. So Otto handed Bernie the axe and commanded him to chop my head off! My head! for crying out loud. Two guards held my head down on a tree stump. I was so weak I didn't even struggle. At that moment I *wanted* to die. I pleaded with Bernie, 'Please kill me and let this misery be over.' But Bernie—God bless his immortal soul—wouldn't do it. So Otto motioned to the guards to let me go and take Bernie. Then Otto grabbed the axe and before we knew it, he'd cut off Bernie's head. Oh, God," he whimpered like an inconsolable child. "Jesus, Mary and Joseph...God bless him.

"Yep. But I was actually happy for him—'cause I knew his pain was over."

"Jesus," Peter said softly. His uncle had been in that war, too. A prisoner of the Japanese. He'd always wondered why his uncle had never wanted to talk about it. Now he understood.

"But that wasn't the worst." He started to hack again.

"Can I get you anything?" His face had started to turn that God-awful purple color again. He wondered how on earth the story could get any worse.

"Nope. I'll be fine.... That bastard—Otto—that bastard put Bernie's head into the big black kettle! And so help me God, Pete, I didn't eat anything of Bernie. I didn't. The others did. Fought over pieces of him just like he was a pig or a goat or a dog."

The old man's pillowcase was soaked with tears. He paused, coughed some more, ever turning a darker shade of reddish blue, then went on: "I've never told anyone this before. Nope. No one. It's horrible, but you gotta believe me. I didn't eat his flesh. Bernie's head was in there for days. 'Till every bit of him was consumed, brains and all. But I didn't eat. Do you know how much *real* hunger hurts?"

He felt a sympathetic pang, shook his head. He didn't want to know for real.

"What I learned, son...what I want you to know...is we always have a choice. Do you understand me?"

Before he could answer, Cap began to cough and heave violently, clutching his chest, his face contorted and dark. Peter rang for the nurse and then ran to the door. He yelled as loudly as he could for a doctor. Seconds later a brigade of nurses stormed into the room, accompanied by the duty Resident. Working furiously on the old man, they were about to pull the curtains when Cap stopped convulsing and grabbed the curtain to hold it open.

"Pete!" he called.

"What is it, Cap?" He looked directly into his eyes, those azure blue eyes with the peculiar little yellow flecks in the iris just around the pupil, unlike any eyes he'd ever seen, not anything like the eyes of an old man should look, but clear, bright and full of life. Eyes he would never forget.

The dying man smiled. "Don't worry about me, son," he said in an eerily normal voice. "I'll be seein' you again sooner than you think...."

The doctor closed the curtain. Peter took a walk. His stomach churned. Not so much for the old man's pain but for his own.

When he returned, the nurse was putting new sheets on the old man's bed, whisking out the wrinkles with her chubby little fingers.

"Where's the old-timer?"

A tear trickled over the mound of her cheek. "I am sorry," she said.

He wondered who would hear his confession now, who would hear his story. Or did it even matter?

# CHAPTER 13

"It's gone," Blalock said in a strained voice. Even as he forced out the words he could feel the heat from the response he knew those words would elicit. He leaned back in the polished yellow oak chair, pushing off from the small glass table in Admiral Snow's private anteroom.

*"What?"* Admiral Snow shrieked. "You freakin' idiot! How? *How, Paul?"* The admiral's florid face seemed to swell.

Automatically, Blalock drew his head in. He knew first hand Snow's habit of summary judgments and equally summary punishments. "Apparently the lab tech took the case and the book—"

Snow kicked a chair across the room, shattering the glass front of a cabinet.

Blalock flinched.

"Christ almighty!" Snow bellowed. "What the hell good was it having a camera in there? And who is this, this—" He shuffled through the briefing paper Blalock had given him.

"Vishnu Chandra," Blalock said in soft, fuzzy tones, hoping to dampen his boss's fulminations by setting a likely example. "But I thought your buddy Larry Blumenthal sent him when Lee died. Besides, who'd of thought some lab technician—"

"Obviously not you, Inspector Clousseau."

"We haven't been able to find a thing on him," Blalock complained.

"No birth certificate. No social security number. No wants or warrants. It's as if the guy never existed."

"And this bilge rat, Lavisch. Damn that sneaky little sonofabitch. After I ordered him—" Snow dropped down into a chair across the table and shook his head with jerking msssssotions, before slamming the table top with the palm of his hand, cracking it with a sharp screech.

Jumping to his feet again, he paced like a caged animal. "He told you and Haverhills about the book?"

Blalock looked at his watch. "No more than an hour ago."

"And says he's going public tonight at the Air and Space Museum?"

"That's what he said. When he told the people at the museum he had an important announcement regarding the *Areopagus* project, they bounced the scheduled speaker." He began to feel better, thinking the worst of the storm had passed.

"So he hasn't told anyone else yet?" Snow asked in a slightly more subdued tone.

"No," Blalock said firmly. "He wouldn't have had any reason to before now. I've got someone watching his every move."

"Somehow that's not much comfort," Snow snorted. He poured a double shot of Jack Daniels and bolted it, then kicked the leg of the table, knocking Blalock's briefcase to the floor.

"All he has are pictures, right?"

"And a big reputation," Blalock said, feeling a bit braver. "Some people might believe him." He watched Snow in the wall mirror as he paced back and forth behind him, alternately twisting his Naval Academy ring and cracking his knuckles.

"Yeah, he's trouble all right," Snow muttered. "I knew I'd end up having to kill that sonofabitch." He spit the words like fifty-caliber bullets. "Haverhills, too."

Blalock felt better now. He rocked back in his chair confidently,

"That will be no problem."

Suddenly he found himself staring at the ceiling. The back of his head stung. Little white stars floated in the edges of his vision. Admiral Snow looked down on him, seemingly from a mile high, his face huge and red, his eyes bulging and swollenss.

"Get on it, then!"

"Yes, sir!"

"And Paul?"

"Sir?"

"No more mistakes."

# CHAPTER 14

"Stop here!" Molly cried. *What's she doing out of the hospital?*

Peter abruptly pulled the Ford Explorer to the curb, nearly taking out a parking meter and causing several pedestrians to jump in fright. "Hey! Where're you going?"

The door flew open. Molly leapt out and started down the sidewalk at a fast walk, dodging people only by virtue of her peripheral vision, for she focused solely on the young women who seemed determined to widen the distance between them.

"Katie! It's Molly Lavisch!" *Why isn't she stopping?* "Katie!"

"Boy!" Peter said, panting as he caught up with her at the corner of 9th Street and Independence Avenue. "That bad leg sure doesn't slow you down much."

Molly felt her face screw up into a scowl, but not from his remark, which she hadn't even noted. She stamped her foot, more in frustration than in anger.

"There I go again, Doc," Peter said in a silly voice. "Ya see I got this bad case of foot-in-mouth disease...."

"I know that woman. Why didn't she stop?" She looked at him, unable to ascertain why he looked as puzzled as she felt. "I know she heard me, and I know she saw me."

"It's getting pretty dark. Sure it was who you thought it was?"

"Positive! It was Katie Jamison, AJ's younger sister. But it can't be. She's supposed to be in the hospital."

"Then it's *definitely* not her."

"What do you mean?"

"Because Katie Jamison is dead."

Molly suddenly felt faint and leaned into Peter's chest. He felt so good. She imagined herself to be Ingrid Bergman's character, in Bogart's arms, waiting for her fateful departure in the final scene of *Casablanca*. She pushed away from him. *God, I've got to stop fantasizing.* "That's horrible. Poor Katie. But how—? When did—?"

"A few days ago," Peter said. "I was sure AJ would've told you. Some kind of rampant infection because of the radiation. Staff something. Antibiotics didn't touch it."

*"Staphylococcus.* But how do *you* know all this?"

"AJ told me. The funeral was today."

*"What?"* She had that sinking feeling again, for more reasons than one. "I can't believe she didn't tell me. We were just at the hospital. Wait! *She told you?"* Even before he answered, she knew AJ had won again.

"You might as well know," Peter said with the look of a man who's just discovered he has no clothes. "We've been out a few times—"

"You *what?"*

"*She* called me."

"Tell me, Peter, why did you want to go out with me if you're dating AJ? Never mind, I already know—my father"

Peter glanced away and shrugged.

"But I thought after last night—"

"Look, she was your friend. I thought she might help me get to know you."

"And my father?" She stomped away, bypassing his Explorer, refusing to look at him. But he kept talking to the side of her face.

"The museum's close," Peter said. "We can walk. Molly. Stop, would you!

"M-M-Maybe this date was just a b-bad idea."

"AJ said you stuttered when you got really upset."

"O-O-Oh, m-my God!" She kept walking away as fast as her limping gate would carry her. Her vision blurred slightly from tears, but anger quickly dried them. She stopped so fast he bumped into her. "What else did she tell you?"

"Come on, Molly," he begged. "I'm sorry. Look, I didn't sleep with her, if that's what you're thinking."

"Oh, sure," she said with all the ill will she could muster. "And just what else did she tell you? Did she tell you about Ocean City our senior year. Or did she go all the way back to our childhood? Did she tell you I snore when I sleep? Did she tell you about—?

"About Glen."

But Molly was thinking of her father, not her former fiancé. "Oh, *AJ!"* she yelled. The warm evening air, which had moments before felt so invitingly romantic, now brought little crystals of sweat to the space above her upper lip. She walked faster, trying to move some air over her scorching face.

"What did you expect?" Peter pleaded. "He's a lawyer. Hell, Molly, all men are not alike."

She hoped the look she gave him hurt as much as the pain in her heart.

"Well, all right, mostly alike."

"Is that supposed to be funny?" Molly kept walking, more slowly now, just sauntering toward the museum, but her mind raced far ahead. She thought about Glen—and his wife. Is this how she'd felt on hearing of his philandering? She was glad she hadn't slept with him. And so what if Peter MacKenzie wasn't her Bogart; she never had to see him again, though her heart shuddered at the prospect. Then again, what if he were telling the truth? Wasn't she convicting him without a trial? Without proof? Didn't she owe him that much?

"I apologize, Peter." She felt calmer now, in possession of her dignity again, or what was left of it.

"No, me, Molly. Honest."

She even managed a tiny laugh. "It's okay, Peter. Really. What you do is none of my business. As for last night...well...I guess I made too much of it."

"No, you didn't. I—"

She raised her hand to stop him. "That's my fault, not yours." Then she said almost cheerily, "Let's hurry up or we'll be late for my father's lecture."

* * *

Peter looked at the name on the entrance: Lockheed Martin IMAX Theater. It annoyed him greatly that for thirty pieces of silver, the Smithsonian Air and Space Museum had sold out to commercial interests and changed the name that had honored aviation Great, Samuel P. Langley. He scanned the forum, which was already crowded, finally locating two isle seats midway up the steep mountain of seat rows on the right side of the auditorium, giving them an acute angle, at quite some distance, to the lectern.

His main concern was to get to Miles Lavisch. He'd already heard talk that Bo and the others had been sacrificed because of something they had seen, possibly a UFO. Though he thought that a stretch, he wondered if the *Areopagus* had discovered something alien and if that in some way might be connected to the satellite reconnaissance photos he'd seen over the last couple of years.

Despite what people imagined, images of suspicious objects were not always flying. In fact, they usually were not. Those quirky pictures of *Unidentified Metallic-Looking Objects, or UMLO*s as they were known in the intelligence community, were a constant source of speculation. Most of the pictures had been from desert areas such as the Sahara and the Kalahari, and in recent years a bunch from *Ham Hai,* the Gobi Desert, in China. Paleontologists working a dinosaur dig there had made startling reports. And there were others, many others. Of course, most of the intelligence community pooh-poohed the possible extraterrestrial connection, laying it off to heat-induced mirages, or other optical artifacts, especially for the desert ones—even spy satellites had their limitations. But something was behind those pictures and the hundreds of other reports of sightings made by reliable witnesses around the world since 1947.

Plus, he'd heard Admiral Snow might be engineering this whole caper. As a former Navy man himself, and despite his myriad other shortcomings, he was, at bottom, a staunch patriot. He had to believe old Admiral Snow had good reason to do whatever had to be done. But if that meant that Bo was somehow a traitor, well…he just couldn't, *wouldn't* buy it.

"Hey," he said, gently nudging Molly, "I think I know that old guy over there." He pointed to a slender little man with a shock of pure white hair rising above dark, hawk like features.

"You know him?" Molly asked incredulously.

"Old college professor of mine at Columbia. Roscha Venable, if that's him."

"It is Roscha. He's a good friend of my father's." She lifted her red eyebrows. "Why didn't you use him for an introduction?"

"Yeah, that's him all right," Peter said, ignoring her inflammatory question. "Tough old bird. Had a nasty reputation for bedding his female students."

"Roscha?" Molly lurched in her seat and looked stunned. "I can't believe it.... Or maybe I can. He's looked at me rather oddly ever since I was teenager. When Dad's finished, we'll go over and say hello."

Peter winked at her, slipped her hand into his. Its daintiness impressed him. But she didn't squeeze back. Worried that he might have blown his chances, he suggested they all go out for a drink after the presentation, but she ignored him. Abruptly, the hum of the crowd diminished as the lights lowered.

"There's my father," she whispered.

Miles Lavisch stepped up to the microphone. He set his briefcase down by the lectern and pulled a sheaf of papers from his breast pocket. He put on his reading glasses, which hung from a chain around his neck.

She leaned close to him: "Well, he finally got a chain for his glasses—he's always losing them. Watch, next he'll light a cigar." She shook her head. "He always starts that way."

"No smoking allowed. Too much danger to the old aircraft."

"That's why he'll do it."

From what AJ had told him, Miles Lavisch was a brilliant, if pigheaded, scientist who would win no prizes as a human being. He'd been worse than a lousy father. According to Molly's childhood confession to AJ, he'd sexually molested her, which reminded him of Bo's critical remarks about the Professor last Christmas Eve.

One thing he could certainly believe: the pigheadedness. For he'd also detected a good case of it in the Professor's only daughter, who sat beside him now with the expectant gaze of an innocent child. He cocked his head slightly. The light caught her face in a different venue, this one wise and womanly, or perhaps sly and crafty. Which was she? He rubbed the scar on his chin, which itched furiously.

On stage, Miles shuffled his papers, then paused, looking over the crowd intently. In the audience, feet tapped, bottoms fidgeted; a low murmur became a buzz. The time for the presentation to begin was far past, with no explanation. What was the old fellow up to?

Peter whispered, "Think he's looking for you?"

She shrugged. "Doubt it. At least he's not smoking."

Miles stepped back behind the lectern. He took a handkerchief out of his pocket and cleaned his glasses. He looked at his papers and the console, then at side of the stage, as if looking for someone, and then at the giant screen behind him.

"Your father sure knows how to work a crowd."

Then, almost casually, Miles reached over and pushed a button on the lectern console. Behind him, the five-story screen burst to light, illuminated with a picture of an object.

To Peter, the image seemed more appropriate to a lecture on archaeology or antique collecting, rather than space science. White, baroquely decorated, with a curious eye on its cover, it resembled a jewelry box more than anything else. He thought at first someone had goofed up the slides. But he knew better when Miles looked at the picture without comment.

Miles paused again, looking out into the crowd, squinting. He looked impatiently over to the curtained margins of the stage, moving his head side to side, as if scanning. Presently, he turned back to the lectern. "Thank you for your patience, ladies and gentlemen. I have been asked to read an announcement: 'In his introduction, our host, Mr. Stephens, made a gross understatement when he said you are a privileged group. For tonight you are much more. You are explorers on the shores of a brave new world, participants in a grand—even universal—adventure. For what you see behind me, ladies and gentlemen is nothing more nor less than—'"

*Bang!*

The screen behind Miles Lavisch went red with two nearly simultaneous thunderclaps that shook the electrified atmosphere. His head whipped back sharply then forward as he collapsed in a shivering heap in the center of a growing crimson puddle.

*"Nooo!"* Molly wailed as she lunged for the stage, climbing over rows of seats, frantically trying to pick her way between the struggling human tide that pushed and shoved and fought its way along the choked isles, making for the exits.

Peter tore after her, momentarily becoming separated by a human wave that carried him sideways, as it swept toward the exits. Catching up, he reached for her, but quickly lost her again. Finally, he managed to grab her arm, but a huge man, arms flailing, fingers clawing, eyes bulging with fear, came between them.

*Bang! Bang!*

Two more shots cracked the panicked air, this time from the opposite side of the auditorium, up in the far corner from where they'd sat.

Peter's eyes registered another flash before the sound crashed his ears.

*Bang!*

Molly went down, pinned under the huge man with bulging eyes.

*She's hit!* As soon as Peter thought it, he was looking up into the recessed lights several stories high. Still holding her arm, he'd gone down with her, and they were both partially buried under the rubble of many human bodies. He felt something wet and slippery, like oil. He knew instantly—*Blood!* Turning his head to the side, he saw the pinkish gray of brains! A bullet had entered the back of the fat man's head and exploded out the front of his face, most of which hung by a flap of skin to the side with his nose and part of his lips still attached. Guttural, choking sounds, emanated from his heaving body, which gushed a final horrid gasp that frothed with bubbly bright blood.

The smell of brains, blood and bodily fluids flushed Peter's nostrils. Vomit rose in his throat. More shots punctured the wild din of screaming, shoving human flesh. *Christ!* he screamed to himself. *We'll be crushed to death before they can shoot us!* The realization hit him like a bullet. *Molly's a target!*

He struggled to pull himself and Molly from underneath the ghoulish carcass, his hands and shoes slipping in the dead man's blood and urine. He fell again. Someone's shoe pinched his neck, pinning him back down. Then with a final desperate tug, he rose, freeing himself and Molly, who rolled over and looked at him with the most terrified eyes he'd ever seen. At least she was alive.

"This way, Molly!" He dragged her toward the red exit sign. But they were knocked down again by the stampeding crowd. A dozen sharp heels dug painfully into his flesh; an elbow nearly knocked him silly. Rising, he pulled her to her feet and started again for the exit. But she resisted with a surprising power.

"M-M-My F-father!"

"Come on!" Peter yanked her by her blood-soaked hair out the exit. But still she fought with a mulish determination, trying desperately to get back to the stage. He slapped her hard. Again, harder. "Goddamnit, Molly! They're trying to kill you too!"

*"D-D-D-Dad-d-d!"* She yanked away, but he held firm.

"It's too late!" She broke free. Again he tackled her, pulled her to feet. *"Listen!"*

"Let me go, Peter!"

"Don't you understand? He's gone."

"N-N-N—"

He knocked her cold with his closed fist.

# CHAPTER 15

Molly Lavisch opened her aching eyes to see a vaguely familiar woman floating just inches above her. For an instant the image spun. She felt queasy. The woman stared back at her with wide, frightened eyes, her red hair fanned out around her face like an aura.

A sudden awareness that she was looking at herself in a ceiling mirror caused her to bolt upright, which precipitated an excruciating pain in her head. Her jaw hurt too. But with recognition came no reassurance, for she lay in a strange bed, dressed only in a man's shirt, without a clue how she had gotten here. Wherever *here* was.

Warily, she looked about the room. A man's room, to be sure: a brown leather jacket with squadron patches, a hunting rifle on a deer antler rack. She saw pictures of him and the airplanes he had flown; pictures of him in his navy uniform, starched white and crisp; pictures of him as a young boy, one with him holding a shotgun alongside a motley looking black dog holding a dead duck in his mouth; pictures of him and what must have been his family, one with his father, also in a navy uniform, holding him as a toddler with an airplane model almost bigger than he was. Pictures of Peter MacKenzie.

Then her eyes fell upon the chair by the window where her bloodstained clothes lay. She began to sob.

"I heard you crying," Peter said, placing a cup of steaming coffee on the nightstand beside her." He handed her an eight-hundred-mg Motrin tablet. "You'll need this after that Mickey Finn I gave you."

Painfully, she sat up. "So that's why my head feels like its about to explode." She massaged her jaw.

"Sorry I had to hit you," he said sheepishly. "But you were hysterical. Though I can't say I blame you."

"My Dad," she cried, collapsing back into bed. He was dead. Really dead. He'd seemed so indestructible, so permanent. Yet, perversely, another part of her rejoiced. "I've got to see him, make arrangements."

"Are you nuts?" he laughed. "You're not going anywhere."

She looked at her wrist; her watch was gone. Panicked, she slapped her hand to her throat. *My locket!* Thank God it was there. "What time is it?"

"Almost eleven."

"I've got to get home." She tried to get out of bed, but her head spun viciously. She'd felt quite lame.

"You remind me of me." Catching her legs, he swung them back up on the bed. "It's my turn to play doctor. You get some rest. It'll take all day to get that Finn out of your head. We can make plans later."

"I've got to call Uncle Malcolm. I've got to get home. Periwinkle, he—"

"Periwinkle?"

"My cat, remember?" She guessed by now he'd forgotten all about their Casablanca night.

"Well you can't go home," he said firmly. "It's not safe. Don't you know someone just tried to kill you?"

"Me? I don't believe—"

"Come on! You can't be that naive. And I know you're not stupid." He arched a smooth, black eyebrow and put the coffee up to her lips. "The bullet that blew that guy's brains all over us was meant for you."

"It was a mistake. It had to be."

Peter snorted, "Yeah, like Nicole marrying O. J. You're a target. And they'll take another crack at you. You can count on it. The question you should be asking is, Who would have reason to kill you and your father?"

"Dad, D-Dad..." She rubbed her eyes, not wanting to start crying again. Regaining her composure, she took a sip of coffee. It was boiling hot and bitter, almost like molten metal. It burned in her stomach just as the image of the Gypsy now burned in her mind. *But how could the Gypsy have known?* No. She would not, could not believe in some carnival fortuneteller's prophecy. That meant the Gypsy must have had something to do with her father's death. But how? Maybe Peter was right and the bullet that killed the fat man *was* meant for her. The Gypsy's warning now looked more like a threat than a prophecy.

"No idea?" Peter said, topping off her coffee cup She shook her head violently. He smiled at her. She recalled their first date, how dreamy it was, how utterly fantastic. *Yes, fantasy.* She said the word to herself and looked at him. My, how she wanted him; the pull was gravitational.

"Not that I like being hit by men, but thank you for last night."

Peter playfully put his fist up to her jaw. "I said I was sorry. And did you expect me to leave you there?"

"Plenty of people would have."

"Well, my name's not 'plenty.'"

She strained a tiny laugh, but his businesslike answer was not what she'd wished, not the warm nurturing response of a lover—or even a friend. His expression changed to something quizzical, almost clownish. She'd been a fool to let herself feel the things she'd felt only yesterday.

"Speaking of last night." Peter put down the coffee pot and puffed the pillows under her head. "It sounded like your father was about to make a big announcement. Really big. Any idea what that might have been?

"No. Except—"

"Except, what?"

"Oh, nothing—it's crazy." She gathered every scrap of her depleted energy, sat more erect, her face itchy with tears.

He sat on the bed beside her. "Nothing's crazier than what happened last night."

"My father had given me a swatch of silken cloth. It had a stain he thought was blood, and he wanted me to analyze it. The strange thing is, he wouldn't tell me where it came from. But I'm sure it had something to do with the Martian stuff he was analyzing."

"*All* of this has something to do with the Mars project. What do you think it was?"

"I don't know, but it had a design just like the trinket on your key chain."

* * *

Peter made another pot of coffee. Out his window, he watched the ceaseless ballet of departing and arriving flights at National Airport. As usual, huge flocks of sea gulls milled about the approach end of runway 18, menacing approaching aircraft. Every few minutes they would scatter, as air cannons used to frighten them away randomly fired. But the effort was largely futile, as the sea gulls quickly learned to accept the noise, a temporary inconvenience to their incessant search for food in the small neck of water between the airport property and Gravelly Point Park.

The chaotic performance mirrored his own confusion. He thought about going to the police. But what could they do? Molly was not the victim. And while he was sure she was a target, how could he prove it? Even if he could, he knew how poor "police protection" could be, and he'd probably lose access to her. But then there was this question: Had she told him everything she knew? He didn't believe she had. She had to know something more, a reason why someone would want to kill her and her father. The *Areopagus*, Bo Randall and the *Discovery II* crew—and now Miles Lavisch—shared some deadly linkage. His greatest fear was not that Admiral Snow had tried to erase them but that he might have had a valid reason to do so. In any event, with Professor Lavisch gone, she was his only lead.

He took another sip of coffee. One thing was certain, as long as she was with him, he was a target too.

* * *

At Peter's urging, Molly used the payphone on the corner outside Peter's apartment. She called her lab first.

"Molly! Oh, Molly!" Brenda Cruise gasped. "It was all over the news. I...I... Is there anything I can do?"

"Yes, there is," she replied, struggling to avoid a break down. But her voice shook uncontrollably and she began to sob. "C-C-Could you take care of P-Periwinkle, a-a-at least for the next c-c-couple of d-days."

"Where are you?"

"I-I'm staying with a friend." She too a deep breath, held it, then exhaled while holding the receiver away from her mouth.

"Cause several people were here already this morning looking—"

"Who?"

"A tall Indian-looking guy. Black hair. Eyes like Frosty the Snowman. Wait, I've got it written down—Vishnu Chandra. I told him I hadn't heard from you and didn't know when you'd be back. Same for the other two—"

*"Other* two?"

"Said they were from the police. Looked more like the Men-in-Black. Never took their sunglasses off. Couldn't honestly say who they were because they didn't show any ID, and I was too nervous to ask."

"If anyone else comes or calls, just tell them I'll be gone a few days, okay?"

"Sure, love. Anything else? I'm just so shocked about your father."

"Hasn't Uncle Malcolm called?"

"No."

*That's odd.* "Have you finished Dad's DNA analysis?"

"Not yet. I got sidetracked, but it'll be done in a day or three."

"Put it at the top of your list, okay?"

"You got it. Anything else?"

"No. And Brenda…" She thought of telling her to be careful. But about what?

"Yes, Molly?"

"Thanks. I'll call you in a few days."

Next she tried Malcolm's office, and then his home. He was not at either place, so she left him a message on his machine. She checked her phone-mail messages. It took her ten minutes to get through the first sixteen, mostly messages having to do with her father's murder: condolences, a couple of overzealous funeral homes offering their services, Brenda again. But no messages from the police. Nothing from Malcolm there either. The last message was from Roscha Venable.

"Molly," he said in a strained, reedy voice, "I hope this message reaches you before it's too late. Listen carefully! Your life—and mine—are in great danger. Do not go to the police or go home. Or anywhere else you would normally go. They're after you. Soon, probably me, too. We must talk. But not in person. Go to the Big Red Ride. Remember, Molly? When you were a little girl. The Big Red Ride. There is a pay phone there. At the stone tower. Remember, Molly, it's the last chance I'll have to help you. The Big Red Ride tonight at ten...."

* * *

When Molly came back to Peter's apartment, she found him watching the news. He clicked off the TV.

"Nothing on the tube," he said. "What'd you find out?"

"Roscha called," she said, unsure if she should be telling him. "He wants to meet me."

"He knows something then. Where'd he say to meet?"

She sank into a crushed-felt chair and put her head in her hands and vigorously rubbed her face until it burned. She was sure now; she didn't want Peter involved any further. "I've got to go back to my apartment. I look silly wearing your clothes."

"Look, Molly, you've held up well so far. Don't do something stupid now."

She shook her head, looked down at her locket. "Roscha said the same thing. About not going home." Picking up her bloodstained clothes, which he'd put in a blue wire wash basket, she gasped loudly, and then quickly threw them down, as if they'd concealed a snake. "I'll be the first to admit, I'm not thinking clearly. But I know it's not fair to involve you in this."

"Some bastard damned near shot my head off. I *am* involved! Tell me your size—"

"My size?" She saw he had a pad and pencil at the ready.

"I'll get you something more feminine to wear. It may not be high fashion—"

"No Peter—"

"Yes, Molly, it's the only way." He took his jacket off the rack, flopping one arm into it as he spoke. "I'm not going to get killed for something somebody only thinks we know—or have." He looked at her, with his other arm only half in its sleeve.

She saw his stare turn cold.

"Unless you've been lying to me?"

She stared at her locket, not wanting to look at him, afraid he'd see right into her heart and expose her plans. "You think I've got something to do with this, don't you? You think I did something.... Or my father." She launched out of the chair, threw up her hands, and shook her head, pacing quickly for the door.

"Settle down, Molly," he said in a much calmer tone. "That's not doing us any good." He moved beside her and put his hand behind her neck, pulling her to him. "Look, I'm sorry about your father. Last night would've knocked the wind out of anyone. But we've got to work together if—"

"What?"

Peter looked out the window. "If we're going to survive.... Now where and when are you supposed to talk with Venable?"

"Tomorrow night," she lied, "at ten o'clock...at a pay phone in the old Glen Echo amusement park. I think."

"What do you mean, you think? You're not sure?"

"Pretty sure," she told him. "He told me to meet him at the Big Red Ride. When I was only five or six Dad and Roscha used to go to a spot near there to fish. On the way, they'd always take me to the park so I could ride the big carousel—"

"Yeah, I know about that. My mother took me there too. What's that got to do with a red ride?"

"Roscha would tell me wild stories about the big roller coaster they had before my time."

"That's been gone since the early sixties." He gathered up her old clothes, putting them in a laundry basket.

"Roscha used to tell me that so many people got killed on it, they called it the Big Red Ride of death. I don't know if that was because of the supposed blood from all those dead people or because the cars were red. According to him, one day the whole line of red cars jumped the tracks just after the crest of the second big hill, killing twelve people. Guess he was sure I'd remember."

"Guess he was right."

"He says we're in danger. Roscha and me."

"Evidently he knows why. And he's going to tell us tomorrow."

* * *

Peter sat with his legs propped up on his ottoman. He'd been watching Molly's reaction to everything very closely. So far, he could detect nothing but genuine emotion and concern for her father and her uncle's unknown whereabouts and, well, everyone and everything, including her damned cat. Now this.

The evening news reported nothing new on Molly's father, but it was reported that Dr. Melvin Haverhills had been found dead in his car at a rest stop on the Baltimore-Washington Parkway not far from Goddard. He'd been killed execution-style, with two bullets in the back of his head. Dr. Paul Blalock was missing, as was Vishnu Chandra.

"Oh, my God!" Molly gasped, putting her hand over her mouth. Then she muttered, "They killed Doctor Haverhills too."

"Who was he?"

"My father's colleague on the Mars project. So were the other two. I'd met Blalock, but not Vishnu Chandra. I know Dad hated Blalock, and he was suspicious of Chandra, though I don't really know why."

"Just missing? Not dead. Hmmm…I mean if they weren't so particular about hiding Haver-what's-his-name, why would it be different with the others? Maybe they're involved in some way for the other side, whoever *they* are."

"Could be," Molly said. "Brenda did say Vishnu Chandra was at the lab this morning, looking for me."

Peter sat down beside her and put a glass of brandy in her hand. Without thinking, he began to gently stroke the waves of her baby-fine red hair. "Any idea why he'd be looking for you?"

Abruptly, she stood up. "There was no message from AJ when I called. Have *you* heard from her?"

Her query caught him off guard. He feared she was losing control, and her petty jealousy was beginning to annoy him. "There was a message from her on my machine, but I haven't called her back. Maybe she's trying to locate you."

Molly gave him a peculiar, almost sly look. "And Uncle Malcolm's never called me back."

"Look," he said, trying to soothe her, "I don't think we should be calling anyone else just yet. Our friends have certainly set up surveillance on you. For all I know, they've already figured me in this—though I don't see how. Not yet, anyway. Give me some time to figure out where we're going with this before you do anything. Okay?"

"Okay, Peter, anything you say."

* * *

Glen Echo sat on a ridge overlooking the Potomac River. The most popular amusement park in the greater Washington area up until the 1960s, it once boasted a large roller coaster, a giant swimming pool, ballroom, bumper cars, shooting gallery, and numerous other rides and games. Now, aside from a baroque carousel, which still operated part-time, it enjoyed a new life as a center for artists and writers and as a playground for busloads of children on day trips.

When Molly pulled into the large parking lot by Minihaha Creek, across a rocky ravine from the old amusement area, it was deserted. She shut off the engine, checked the time on her Camry's digital clock, whose glaring 9:42 p.m. shone in Toyota blue-green, and surveyed the area. From where she sat, she could see the dim aura of the street lights along Clara Barton Parkway, beyond which lay the river, a couple of hundred yards away, enshrouded in deep darkness. She'd ducked out while Peter was gone to get her dinner. She told herself one last time that she'd done the right thing by not involving him. Now her terrible guilt for having lied to him vied with her crushing fear that she couldn't handle this alone. She got out of the car.

Crossing the wooden bridge that spanned the black ravine, she entered the shadowy area of the poorly lit amusement compound. After more than twenty years, her memory of the park was blurry. Trying to avoid what little light there was, she crept along the narrow, winding footpath. Except for the distant roar of the river as it crashed over the rocks at Great Falls four or five miles up river and an occasional car passing up the hill on MacArthur Boulevard, the park was still. Dead leaves from the late-summer drought crackled disconcertingly beneath her feet. She stopped. Thinking she heard a car enter the parking lot she had just left, she crouched low and waited, silently shivering from the surprisingly chill night air that circulated through Peter's oversize shirt and baggy trousers. But, no, the car drove on; the noise faded. She heard another. Each time, her muscles tensed and her stomach knotted.

Then she heard the stones popping from beneath the tires of a car that rolled stealthily into the parking lot close to hers, lights and engine off. Just some kids necking, she told herself, but the thought did not keep the hairs on the back of her neck from bristling. Another car made the same cautious entry but stopped perhaps a hundred yards away before coming all the way into the parking lot.

Quietly she made her way along the path.

*Clang!*

She'd inadvertently kicked a Coke can. *Wonderful!* She ran the rest of the way along the row of buildings closest to the road and headed towards a light in a larger complex of buildings. There, in his second floor office, under a fairly bright florescent light, sat a man with epaulets and a Smokey-The-Bear hat, his back to her. A sign on the building said PARK POLICE. *Thank God!* A big Seth clock on the wall said 9:59.

She saw the dark outlines of a phone about twenty yards away, near what she remembered was the refreshment stand. *But Roscha said a stone tower.* She decided to wait for the phone to ring in the shadows of a giant hydrangea bush, whose fading blooms now expelled a sour bouquet.

Only seconds later a phone jangled, but not the phone she had been watching. The ring came from somewhere behind her, back in the shadows by the police station. She couldn't avoid the light as she crossed the short distance to the building. Finally she saw it. The tower, a rough-hewn stone building, three-stories high, stood in darkness right next to the police building. She jerked the receiver from its cradle.

"R-Roscha?" she whispered.

"Are you sure you weren't followed?"

With the sound of Roscha's voice came the image of her father. "I-I-I d-don't think so."

"Get hold of yourself, Molly," he scolded. "You didn't drive *your* car, did you?"

"Yes," she sobbed. "Wait." She made herself take a huge breath, as if she were going to swim the length of a pool underwater. She held it for several seconds, and then blew the warm, moist air as hard as she could down the front of her shirt. "Okay, I'm back with you."

"Listen carefully. The people who want us will stop at nothing. You must assume you were followed. I'll be quick, and then you must go. Leave your car. Get a bus, walk if you have to. Understand?"

"Okay. Okay." She squinted into the darkness, but her tears caused the light to ripple and scatter in little flares, obscuring her vision. "Oh, Roscha, what happened? Why Dad?"

"Just listen! Your father gave you something to test in your lab."

"Yes, yes, the cloth. It had a strange design."

"That's it."

"And a stain." She took another quick breath. "He wanted it analyzed for DNA. It's still at my lab. Why, Roscha?"

"The *Areopagus* brought back more than life on Mars. It brought back proof of intelligent life, alien artifacts—"

"What?"

*"Listen!* Were you at his presentation?"

"Yes." She felt herself start to sob again, but choked it back down deep inside her. "I saw you there."

"Then you saw the slide on the screen. That little jewel box case had a book in it. A book from Mars. That's why your father called me. He brought the book to my apartment. I was to keep it only a day, make copies and give it back. But—"

"Then you still have it?"

"Yes."

"Does anyone else know you have the book?"

"Only you. And they'll think of you first when they look for the book. I promised your father I'd tell you if something happened. To be honest, I wouldn't have if I wasn't sure they'd be contacting me eventually anyway. But I won't wait around for them."

"Who *are* they, Roscha? Why do they want to kill us?"

"The CIA's behind it, though I'm not sure why. And they'll be after you. If you can, leave the country."

"But what are we going to do?"

"I advised your father the best thing would be to decipher the book and get it out in public. That's what I intend to do."

"You don't know what it says, then?"

"Not yet. I'm going to need help with that. But it will take time. I can't even guess how long. That's why you have to stay in hiding. Until you hear it on the news."

"I don't know how to hide from my cat, much less government agents." Now more that ever, she knew she'd made at least a tactical mistake in not letting Peter help her. *The Gypsy was right. I'm going to die!* "W-W-What's does the cloth have to do with this?"

"Your father said it came out of the book."

"But why was Dad murdered? What do they—"

Two shadows caught her attention. Appearing against the refreshment building, they moved slowly, in and out of the shadows, toward her.

"Roscha, someone's coming!" She picked up a handful of pebbles and threw them at the window where the police officer sat, hitting squarely behind his head with a loud crack.

No response.

"There's no time," Roscha warned. "Leave now! Stay in hiding until you hear from me or until this is made public. That's your only chance. Goodbye and good luck!"

*Click!*

"Roscha! Wait! Rosch—"

A hand closed over her mouth, muffling her scream, while an arm grabbed her around the waist and pulled her away from the phone just as a chunk of rock exploded off the stone tower where her head had been. With a muted *pop, pop* more bullets zinged by only inches away, lifting her hair in its breeze.

"It's me, Molly," the voice whispered, as he pulled her further into the darkness.

*Peter!*

"Come on. This way."

"But the policeman—"

"He's dead!"

*Pop! Pop! Pop!*

The pinging and twanging of ricocheting bullets trailed them as they ran into the shadows, along the row of arcade buildings, past the popcorn stand, the theater and the old shooting gallery.

"I saw at least two of 'em. Over there. Remember the old bumper car pavilion?"

She nodded.

"We've got to make it to that. Then if we can make it to the river, we'll have a chance. You'll have to be fast. How's that leg? Can you do it?"

She swallowed hard, nodded as he tugged her forward. A volley of bullets thudded into the earth at their feet, following their short sprint across the open, lighted area.

"That'll screw up their nightvision!" he gasped, jerking her to a stop. He pointed at two more men ahead, running to cut them off. He pulled her behind him, dashing for the old Spanish Ballroom, beyond which, through thick bramble, lay a steep but shallow drop-off to the Clara Barton Parkway, and beyond that the old C&O Canal and the Potomac river.

Tendrils of viny undergrowth and clawlike briars tripped them again and again, slowing them dreadfully, as sounds of their pursuers crashed through the brush behind them. Finally reaching the embankment, they slid down to the roadway in a hail of rocks and rubble, falling on each other in a lump at the side of the highway. Across the road lay darkness and safety. They scrambled to their feet.

"Stop!" a deep voice behind them ordered. "Hold it right there or you just sucked your last lousy breath."

A man dressed entirely in black with a ski mask clung precariously to an overhanging limb with one hand while he trained his weapon on them with the other. He had a clear shot.

A car approached, slowed, then sped away.

"All right," Peter said, raising his arms and prodding her to do the same, "we're not moving. Don't shoot."

"Down here!" the man shouted."

Little clumps of dirt and gravel broke loose under the masked man's feet, creating a mini-landslide, but he managed to hold his aim. All of sudden bright headlights illuminated the pavement before them, and the roar of a truck drowned out whatever the man said next.

Impelled by some unseen force, Molly lunged in front of the oncoming truck, dragging Peter, caught completely off guard, helplessly behind her. The truck's brakes locked, screeching like a wounded animal and streaming a trail of acrid smoke from the vaporized rubber and asbestos brake linings, which was followed by a squishy thudding and scraping sound, then a thump, then silence.

Stopping on the other side of the road, she couldn't keep from looking back with a twinge of guilt as the driver fell in his panic to get out of the truck's cab, then made his way to the man's crumpled body.

"Oh, Shit!" the driver screamed hysterically. His twitching head with eyes big as moons glared at them. *"Holy Jesus!* Where'd you people come from? I never saw him. I swear!"

*Pop! Pop! Pop!* Sparks sprayed up from the center of the roadway like small volcanic eruptions. This time she didn't have to pull Peter. He pulled her, tripping and stumbling, into the darkness toward the sound of the rumbling water. Her leg slowed them, but he dragged her as if she were a rag doll. His strength amazed her.

*Pop! Pop! Pop! Pop!*

Molly could see the bright flashes, which now came from at least three different locations. To live past the next few seconds would, she was sure, take something of a miracle.

"You've got to go faster, Molly."

"I can't!" Her leg hurt, her arm too. They fell down behind a small concrete maintenance bunker, perhaps fifty yards from the river. Several bullets slammed into the concrete blocks inches above them, spewing a shower of sparks and small, rocky shrapnel.

"With their nightvision equipment, I'm surprised we made it this far; we'll never make it back to the car."

Peter's head twisted back and forth. His labored breathing came in sharp, bellows like gushes, reminding her of AJ's horses after she'd run them too hard. He choked out the words, "Can you swim?"

She hesitated, desperately wondering what he had in mind, then nodded.

Peter reached up, momentarily exposing himself to the gunfire, and tipped over a large metal garbage barrel.

*Pop! Pop!... Pop! Pop! Pop!* More sparklers from near misses. "Sonofabitch!" Peter jerked down behind the barrel, grabbing his arm.

Terrified, Molly tried to look at the wound, but he wrenched his arm away. "I'm okay. Get in, feet first."

Now she saw what he'd had in mind. "No! I can't. If it's between being shot and drowning, I'd rather be shot."

"It'll float!" he argued. "I'll be right behind you. Once we get in the river they'll never get us. We'll live!"

She shook her head, as much from revulsion at the idea of the insides of the barrel as from fear, but the words "we'll live" reverberated in her mind.

"Get in!" Peter screamed. Just then a bullet from a different angle ricocheted off the top side of the barrel. "They're repositioning. Soon they'll have a clear shot. Do I have to beg you?"

In an oddly heartening way, she thought he sounded like an exasperated spouse. *Dagwood.*

"See you later..." And he started to get into the barrel.

*Maybe not Dagwood!* "Wait!" She pulled on his bloodied arm.

"Ouch!"

"Oh, God, Peter! I'm sorry."

"I know, I know, damnit. Get in!"

"If I drown—" She screwed up her face at the smell of the rotting food and refuse, looked over at him. He shook his head, and then he braced his back against the blocks, put his feet on the barrel and kicked. She rolled over slowly at first, hearing the soft shushing of the grass against the outside of the barrel as she fell bruisingly from one side of the barrel to the other. Quickly the barrel picked up speed, bumping and bouncing down the grassy incline. She felt as if she were in the inside of a washing machine on spin cycle. Abruptly, there was silence, a falling sensation and a loud splash, followed by the shock of the cold Potomac water. She involuntarily squeaked a reaction, and then gurgled as she submerged into the liquid blackness.

Upside down in the barrel, under water and running out of air, she kicked her legs, but it didn't help. Unbidden visions of her father's ravaged body emerged, blending with feelings of her own imminent death. She saw the Gypsy and the ankh, heard the Gypsy's words.

*I won't die!* she thought defiantly, kicking even harder. Then she felt something on her ankle. Her first breath of air was like a rebirth, cool, sweet and life giving. There was Peter with his finger over his lips. Up above, their assailants walked back and forth along the bank, their guns clacking at their sides.

"They're dead. They gotta be," one of them said.

"How do you know, smartass?"

"Nobody could survive what they—"

"You don't know shit from Shinola. You wanna tell the boss you got 'em, you go right ahead. I'm sayin' I ain't so sure."

Then she heard another voice, this one strangely familiar.

"Shut up, you two! Let's get outta here."

# CHAPTER 16

Peter sat on the dock at his mother's home and looked out across the West River. He could hear the luffing of sails, prim and white, as the boats otherwise silently plied the dark green waters. There were also the sounds of engines, the gasoline-powered crab boat, which lazily worked its mile-long trot line, and the masculine diesel of the cabin cruisers flying high on the water in headlong pursuit of nothing in particular save the conceited proclamation of its owner that he'd found the good life.

He'd grown up here, only forty miles east of Washington, D.C., where as a boy he'd swum the brackish waters; fished for rock and bluefish, spot and perch; hunted canvasbacks and bluebills and geese; crabbed for Chesapeake Blues. And this was where he had run two nights before with Molly after coming ashore a half mile downstream from Glen Echo park and walking the towpath along the C&O canal the rest of the way to Georgetown and a late-night cab ride.

He'd told his mother a tall tale of a wild party, of running the car into a ditch, and of deciding on the spur of the moment to visit home. She surely didn't believe the story, for she was accustomed to his lies; but she'd accepted his explanation without question or complaint, fair exchange for the pleasure of an infrequent visit from her son, or so he supposed.

He figured they'd be safe here for at least a day or so more, until the CIA realized no bodies had turned up down river. Besides, no one knew he was involved yet, so they wouldn't look here.

What Molly had told him confirmed his suspicions about Bo Randall and the other astronauts: their deaths had been no accident. What he didn't understand was why was the CIA was willing to kill to suppress the discovery of extraterrestrial life? Could they have had a good reason?

If what she'd said was true, and he by no means fully trusted her, the book was her only possible bargaining chip. He thought again about handing her over to the FBI as he'd planned, but to do so now might be a fatal error—for both of them. No. He'd wait a while longer on that.

Roscha had left few clues, only saying he would need help to decipher the book. So Peter had spent the previous day on the WEB. He'd searched the computer databases for any title authored or co-authored by Roscha Venable over the last thirty years. A real loner, Roscha had worked with only two others, both of whom were associated with Ben Gurion University in Israel: an expatriate Lebanese national named Brandon Hadid and a Palestinian named Youssef Sharabi.

The river air was cool. He rubbed his arms, but pain reminded him of the bullet fragment still lodged just under his skin. It started to ooze. "Better let Molly fix this after all," he said absently, dabbing with his handkerchief at the blood trickling down his bicep while he thought through his plan.

First he'd visit his friend Clancy Turnbow, see if Clancy would front him some cash—no credit cards from here on out. He'd also taken the Honus Wagner baseball trading card from his collection, which he'd kept in a fireproof safe behind a false wall in his childhood bedroom. Lord how he'd hate parting with it. He hoped it wouldn't come to that, but if ever he ran out of cash, the card would be almost as good as gold. He patted his wallet.

A platoon of waves from a passing cabin cruiser caused the line on his Boston Whaler to stretch and groan as it jerked the dock with each successive wave that caused the boat to rise and fall.

*We'll see Clancy. Then head for the Middle East.*

* * *

"Smells great," Molly said.

"Good morning, dear," Peter's mother said. Margaret MacKenzie, who at sixty-two could easily have passed for fifty, stood at the stove, pouring pancake batter onto a griddle already crackling with a brace of eggs and crisping bacon.

"Where's Peter?" Molly asked, not a little afraid he'd left her.

"Out on the dock." Margaret handed her a steaming cup of coffee.

"Thank you, Mrs. MacKenzie. You've been so kind—I mean dropping in the way we did."

"Ohhh, nonsense," she said, smiling. "And please don't make me beg you to call me Margaret. Mrs. MacKenzie sounds sooo old."

Molly watched Peter sitting with his legs swinging over the end of the dock. All he needed, she thought, was a straw hat and a bamboo pole and he could have been Huckleberry Finn. She watched silently, unwilling to break the spell, to spoil the pristine moment. Out beyond him she saw Chesapeake Bay Bridge slicing across to Kent Island, on the Eastern Shore. The world seemed utterly at peace, like the tranquil bay itself this day. What, she wondered, would the waiting world think when it discovered for the first time that human consciousness was not, perhaps, the crown jewel in God's creation?

Her own non-reaction to the news of extraterrestrial life had surprised her. Maybe because of the things Uncle Malcolm had said. Or maybe this *was* the rebirth of the world. She laughed a silent, nervous little laugh, aware that the no matter how much she tried to mitigate its meaning for herself or to belie its source, she kept thinking about the little dark eyed woman and her prophecy. "Well, she was wrong about me," she murmured. "I didn't die last night. I'm alive."

"What's that, dear?" Margaret said.

"Oh," she startled. Feeling her face warm, Molly hoped she hadn't said something she shouldn't have. "I was thinking how Peter looks like Huckleberry Finn, sitting on the dock like that."

"Like him, don't you?"

Now her cheeks burned. She averted her eyes, and sipped her coffee. She liked Margaret, who reminded her of her own dimly remembered mother, who seemed always to know the basis of her emotions. "He's been very nice" was all she could say.

"I wish that boy *would* get married. It'd do him good to settle down. It's my fault."

"Oh?"

"When Peter was just five or six, his father was gone a lot—away at sea. He was a Navy man too. I was young and unhappy. And I made mistakes—several. With other men. Peter—"

"Margaret," Molly interjected, not really eager to hear the sad details. "You don't need to tell me—"

Margaret waved her frying spatula as if to brook no interruption. "Peter knew, and he hated me for it. He idolized his father. What he doesn't know—and I'd never tell him—is that his father was a drunk. He was suspected of being drunk when he finally killed himself flying in Vietnam. But because he also saved someone else in the process, instead of a court-martial he got a Navy Cross."

Molly glanced outside at Peter again, seeing him with new eyes. "I just lost my father." Inwardly, she began to tremble.

"Oh, dear," Margaret comforted. "I *am* sorry." She gently rubbed Molly's back, making grand, warm circles with her knowing hand.

"Peter blamed me," Margaret continued with an obvious bitterness. "He thought I was the only reason his father volunteered for a second tour. But the truth is, he didn't plan to come back."

Molly watched the woman deftly flip a half-dozen eggs, one by one, and then neatly arrange some bacon on a draining rack.

Suddenly, Margaret MacKenzie put down her spatula, turned away, and started whimpering. "There's no idol like a dead idol. Even though Peter loved music—he plays the piano, you know—he took up airplanes, which I don't believe he ever really liked or had much of an aptitude for. He nearly flunked flight school—if it weren't for his friend Bo." She wiped the tears from her cheek with the hand that still held the spatula. "But don't tell *him* I said that. No, his Navy career was just a monument to his Dad, and, I suppose, a way of constantly reminding me."

*There're all kinds of betrayals*, she thought.

The toast jumped out of the toaster. "Because of me... " Pausing, she picked up the plate of eggs and bacon, then, as if recalling a distant tableau, she stared sadly at Molly and said, "Well, because of me, I don't think he really likes women."

* * *

After breakfast Peter took Molly for a tour of the waterfront in the Boston Whaler. He showed her the fabulous estates; the large riverside marinas lined with million-dollar yachts and sleek sailboats; and the smaller creek marinas, crammed with boats for oystering, crabbing, fishing and clamming.

The bay was white with fluttering sails and foam and spray from colliding wakes. All of which helped create the cachet of the Chesapeake Bay, whose tourist slogan was "The Land of Pleasant Living." But the great shellfish bay—that's what the Indian word Chesapeake meant—was dying, the victim of over development, over fishing, overuse by a burgeoning human population with flush toilets, weedless lawns and a greedy appetite for crabs, clams, and oysters.

He'd witnessed firsthand the moribund progression throughout his years with sadness and alarm, as first the great swarms of canvasback and redhead ducks dwindled to small vestigial flocks, gone largely because wild celery and other of their favorite aquatic grasses had all but vanished due to pollution. Later, the hardhead, rock and spot fish had all but disappeared, before stringent restrictions had managed to bring some relief. Then it was the oyster's turn, fished nearly into oblivion with rapacious patent tongs, which scrapped the bottom clean, taking everything, including favorable rough-ridged bottom habitat. Now, even the hardy blue crab was succumbing to unrestrained appetites and degraded aquatic habitat.

At last they reached Clancey Turnbow's, Peter's fortunate friend who had an airstrip right on the edge of the bay. Of course, he had the obligatory boat as well, two of them, one sail, one powered, though his house was nothing special, a drafty three-story clapboard, with tiny, cold rooms and bowed hardwood floors.

By contrast, Clancy's aircraft hangar was first-rate. Big enough for four light planes, it usually housed his two planes—a beautiful red S-2B Pitts Special aerobatic plane and a Beech Bonanza—and a couple belonging to visitors.

But planes were just a hobby for Clancey, who in real life was a bum, albeit a very rich one.

Clancey's father had run one of the biggest junkyards on the East Coast. Nobody realized how much money there was in junk until Clancey's mother and father were killed, ironically, in a car accident. Clancey got everything, but ended up selling the junkyard to pay estate taxes, netting three million dollars. He hadn't done anything since but play with airplanes, often with Peter. And drink, mostly when he was not flying—sometimes when he was.

This day, however, they did not fly. Clancey had custody of his kids for the day and was dutifully distracted. But he did have time to advance Peter a loan of ten thousand dollars, for which Peter gave him a note, promising to make good in about a month.

After profuse thank-yous, they returned to his Mother's early in the afternoon.

* * *

Shortly after returning from Clancey's, Peter relaxed with a beer as he watched Molly dive off the dock into the cool river water. Moments later he watched her climb the three steps to the lower platform of the dock. She wiped the water from her eyes, slicked back her red hair, which clung like a flame to her pale white back, and held her face to the sun. He saw her nipples neatly outlined against his mother's old one-piece swimsuit. *Dripping wet suits her.*

With that thought, AJ came to mind, and he mentally relived the last time they'd made love, the last time he'd tasted her, felt her. Oddly for him, he felt the need to call her. Somehow, he felt he owed her an explanation as to why he'd be gone—for a very long time—and he didn't want her raising any unnecessary questions. Besides, since AJ didn't know what he was up to anyway, the risk was, he calculated, modest, if any. So he picked up the phone and dialed.

"Peter!" AJ gushed. "Where have you been? I've called a thousand times."

"Figured you had. Been kinda busy. Listen, I'm going to be out of town for a few weeks. And I—"

*"A few weeks?* Oh, Peter, I'll go crazy."

"Me, too. But I got a chance to ferry a plane to Africa. And like you said, it's what I do."

"Can't I see you before you go?"

"There just isn't time, sweetheart. I've got a million details to take care of before I go."

"You're not with Molly, are you?"

"Come on, honey, you know better than that."

"No, I don't."

"Look, this Africa trip came up suddenly. Molly and me never got together. Why would you even ask?"

"Because the CIA is looking for her. They were here."

"At your farm?"

"Uh-huh. They claim she and her father hatched some plot to sell the Martian soil, or some such. They said Miles was killed. And I haven't been able to locate her."

"That's pretty bizarre."

"Not really. Miles was a prick with a capital 'P.' Believe me, there'll be no Papal eulogy."

"Hmmm. There goes my chance to talk to him."

"Where are you, anyway? I'll come to you—"

"No, no. There isn't time. I just dropped by my mom's to say goodbye. She had something I needed to pick up, but I'll be leaving before light in the morning. I'll miss you, sweetheart."

"Peter," Molly called, entering the room wrapped in a towel and holding her wet bathing suit. "Where should I—? Oh, sorry, didn't see you were on the phone."

Peter quickly covered the receiver and pointed to a rack in the corner.

"Who was *that?*" AJ probed. "Sounds too young to be your mother."

"Oh, my sister just dropped by. Listen, sweetheart, got to go. I'll call you in a day or so."

# CHAPTER 17

It was 8:49 P.M. when Jack Beamis arrived at Admiral Carl Snow's house in McLean, Virginia. As deputy director of the CIA he was second in command. He was supposed to know everything Carl Snow knew, and that was what troubled him.

First there was Snow's inquest testimony a couple of days ago regarding the *Aurora* project, a long-rumored new spy plane, which Jack knew didn't exist. Oh, they had a new spy plane, all right. But it was a much different aircraft, far more advanced, far stealthier, created at Snow's personal direction. Capable of sub-orbital flight, it was designed to counter unspecified sub-space threats. The rumored *Aurora* was a decoy, and the deception had proved remarkably successful. Even *Jane's* had published pictures of it refueling behind a KC-135 tanker, in the company of a gaggle of F-15 Eagles. Yet Snow had said it did exist. Lying to senators went beyond Snow's usual sleight-of-hand. But worse, he had testified that the Agency had no involvement in or knowledge of the NASA people's deaths—Doctors Lavisch and Haverhills.

Now this.

Earlier that afternoon he'd mistakenly opened a package of correspondence intended for Snow. Among the contents was a copy of a one-page report marked, *ULTRA-EYES ONLY, MAJESTIC TWELVE,* whose contents both puzzled and frightened him:

**To**: The Director

**From**: Field Operations Agent MQ-2-PB

**Distribution**: M-12

**RE**: Operation White Blanket/Surveillance Report

**Subject**: Dr. Miles Lavisch.

**Disposition**: No longer actionable.

**Subject**: Dr. Molly Lavisch

**Disposition**: Contact broken at 8:12 P.M. E.D.T. Whereabouts unknown.

**Subject**: Mr. Vishnu Chandra.

**Disposition**: Unable to verify personal historical data. Efforts to establish contact thus far unsuccessful. Whereabouts unknown. Intentions unknown. Country of affiliation unknown.

**Subject**: Alien artifacts.

**Disposition**: Missing.

PB

He returned the memo to its manila folder. He had known Carl Snow for half his career and for all but the last few of those years, Snow had had his full respect and loyalty, but lately he never quite knew what to expect. His mood swings had become more pronounced, his schemes increasingly risky, bordering at times on the edge of irrationality. More than once Snow's policies had nearly caused international crises. Like the mining of harbors in North Korea. That was his idea, though few others knew that. Eventually it provided the necessary pretext for a war to remove nuclear weapons from the peninsula. It had worked, but not before several nuclear exchanges led to the destruction of Seoul and a half-million casualties.

*That was been only the beginning.*

But this was different, more personal, more erratic: If the Agency had been involved in the murder of a civilian, the President would have to be notified. And who or what was MAJESTIC TWELVE? Not the putative secret group that was the butt of a longstanding joke in Intelligence circles? The one everyone knew of? The one everyone knew was the first great cover-up of nothing? Like the so-called Roswell UFO mystery?

"Well, I don't know what the old cod is up to," he said to himself, switching off the car's ignition. "But I owe him the chance to explain."

A prim-looking young Latino women dressed in the traditional black and white maid's uniform seated him in the study. While he waited, he nervously scanned the well-appointed room, which had the look and feel of a big-city library, with its floor-to-ceiling bookshelves that he estimated must have contained at least a thousand titles. A ladder on wheels provided access to top shelves. The subject matter did not surprise him either, perfectly reflecting the Snow's Napoleonic bent. There was a large section on the subject of warfare—land, sea and air. Another large section contained volumes on seafaring and naval activities, and a fair number of titles encompassing the full spectrum of political and historical thought.

On Snow's working desk, stacked three or four high, were books whose titles he could not quite make out in the dim light, but he could see the letters UFO.

*He really must be off his nut.*

"Evening, Jack."

He jumped up as if caught in some sordid act, but quickly sank back into his seat.

"You must be rigged for silent running, Carl." He was never sure whether to address him as Admiral or Carl or Mr. Director. Snow would accept only the mode of address congruent with his present state of mind, and that was difficult to predict.

"We submariners will never get the salt water out of our bilges, eh, Jack?" Snow, wearing slippers and a tattered U.S. Naval Academy terrycloth bathrobe, lit a Chesterfield cigarette, spitting out some errant strands of tobacco. He opened his desk drawer and pulled out a bottle of Stolichnaya vodka and two glasses. "Nightcap?"

"Make it a double." Just what he'd need to get through this.

"This damned stuff's the only good thing the Rusky's ever made. Submarines—no good. Airplanes—naw. Women—ehhh... mostly too fat. Ice?"

"Neat. Thanks." He took the whole shot in one gulp.

"Atta boy, Jack."

The admiral pulled Jack's hand with the empty glass down to the table and poured him another. He quickly dispatched that one too. "Now," the admiral said, slipping into the chair across from him, "what brings you here at this hour, Jack. Couldn't be *good* news."

He slid the manila folder across the table, avoiding Snow's eyes. "What's this about, Carl?"

Admiral Snow opened the folder, looked at it, and after a long pause, tossed it back. He then poured himself another vodka and said evenly, "What do you want to know?"

"For starters, what is Majestic Twelve? Not the silly UFO group we've all laughed up our sleeves about for half a century?"

Snow didn't answer. He sipped dreamily on his drink and appeared to be weighing his options.

"And the civilians—Doctors Lavisch and Haverhills, the others? Why kill them?"

The admiral's eyes calmly rotated to his, as if they were targeting him. Snow put his feet up on the arm of his chair. He felt the threat just as acutely as if the man had put a gun to his head.

"What would you say if I told you that there was an alien presence on Earth? At this very moment?"

"Little green men?" He laughed reflexively.

"If you like."

"I'd say you've been drinking your own bilge water. Or too much of this Russian vodka." He put his glass down.

"It's true, Jack. And we've known it since Roswell, in nineteen forty-seven."

"Not that Majestic Twelve crap again. A UFO crash in New Mexico?" He shook his head and laughed, trying not to sound nervous. "The Air Force put that to bed in ninety-five. It was only a weather balloon. But you know that, Carl."

Ignoring him, Snow rolled on. "Alien bodies were recovered and stored at Wright Patterson."

"I heard that part, too. Lunacy!"

"I know it's become almost a cliché, but it's true," Snow said matter-of-factly. "All true. The remains are still at Wright Pat. Not

Area 51, not the way in that idiotic movie—what was it? *Independence Day*? No, just where the early UFO *nuts* said they were." He laughed like a braying farm animal. "Hilarious, isn't? I mean the irony of it?"

"You can't be serious?" Grabbing the vodka bottle from the admiral, he said, "You've been watching too many old X-File episodes, Carl."

"Dead serious, Jack." Snow got up and went over to his desk, unlocking a small safe. He threw a pile of black and white photos on the table. "And then there are these."

"What am I looking at? Autopsies of accident victims?"

"Yeah, you could say that. Look at the close-ups of the area behind the ears."

"Looks like an odd shaped scar, similar to an ankh."

"Exactly right." Snow put his foot back on his chair.

"So?"

"So. We found the same scar on all three."

He took a sip of the clear, prickly liquid and, based on what he was hearing, thought he might need another. "I still don't get it."

"Remains of three *humans.* At least we think they were human. All were found alongside the little gray men in the Roswell crash."

"No! And you think... What?"

"We don't really know what they were or why they were there. We couldn't detect any abnormalities other than the scar."

"You think they were aliens, too?"

Admiral Snow shrugged. "They were in the company of aliens. If it looks like a duck..."

He decided against another drink; better to keep his wits about him.

"But how could all this be true, with no one's knowing all these years?"

"No one knew about the Manhattan Project, 'til Hiroshima. No one knew about the B-two or the F-one- seventeen...'til we wanted them to. Hell, have you forgotten about the things *we* should have known about but didn't: the North Korean nukes? The Iranian nukes? Thank god the Israelis took care of that problem for us. No, when proper precautions are taken, secrets can be kept. But then no one should know that better than you, Jack."

"That's just it. I *should* know."

"Not about this one." The admiral swirled his vodka, looked at him with almost feral eyes. "Only M-twelve, only a handful has known, for over fifty years."

"But why keep a secret like that? The whole world should know about—"

"National security." Snow chuckled. "I know, it's such a cliché, but it started that way. Look, the Cold War was just getting under way. We knew the Russians would have the bomb before long. And just two years later in forty-nine, they did. Soon after, they had the H-bomb, too.

"They were behind us only in delivery capability. We knew that wouldn't last long, either. The Roswell craft represented a phenomenal leap in technology. If anyone owned it, it had to be us. And no one wanted to panic the public. Oh, I know, I know, that sounds corny today, but remember what Orson Welles started on the radio back in thirty-eight?"

"But why keep it secret? Why now? That wouldn't happen today."

"Maybe, maybe not. Even after the 'X-files' as you said, and all the movies like 'Independence Day' and the others, people would still panic if they truly thought... Well, if they_*knew* the truth."

He felt himself shaking his head.

"But you know how lies are," Snow resumed, "once you start one, it takes on a life of its own, gathers its own momentum. Hell, it's how you and me make a living. Would you like to be the one that admitted the government's been lying all these years? Every chairman of the joint chiefs for fifty years has been a member of M-twelve. You think they all want their careers ruined, their good names."

"What about the President? He know?"

Admiral Snow shook his head. "None of 'em have ever known. Only military. *Sheeet!* You think people distrust our institutions now? Besides, it would also be an admission of our inability to protect the nation. And after nine-eleven? Hell this is orders-of-magnitude different. The public would demand every head in the military."

"I'm sorry, Carl, but you haven't convinced me of the need for all this. Just what kind of threat does all this represent? It's been well over a half century; nothing's happened yet."

"We think these aliens pose a long term threat, and we haven't been able to do anything about it. And until we figure out what they are up to, it's best kept a secret. Hell, what they're planning could take generations to complete. We just don't know."

"What about Doctor Lavisch, then?"

"He discovered a book in the material the *Areopagus* brought back from Mars—"

"A *book?*"

"A book in an alien language. And he—against my direct orders—was determined to announce it to the world, before we had a chance to see if it could be deciphered. We don't want *them* to know we know. He had to be stopped."

Beamis squirmed in his seat, unable to contain his growing discomfort.

"Jack, hear me out. We don't know that it doesn't contain the battle plan to conquer the Earth."

"And you think it's related to the Roswell thing?"

"We can't be sure, but a partial manuscript—in English—was recovered with the bodies at Roswell. It was too badly charred to get much information from it. But what we could get suggested some kind of infiltration was under way even then. There was mention of a 'Reconciliation Project.' We really don't know what that means. But are you willing to take the chance that the *Areopagus* book and the Roswell document are unrelated? That it's all just a benign coincidence?"

"But a civilian, Admiral? Wasn't there some other way?"

"Anything less would have been irresponsible."

He paused, studied Snow's face, trying to sort out all this crazy information. "And you really believe we're threatened?"

"I do. And not just this country. But I can't tell you anymore unless..."

"Unless?"

"Unless I introduce you to the others. Then we can give you a full briefing. What do you say, Jack?"

"What about the President, Carl? I still say he should be notified. Will you brief him, too?"

Admiral Snow sighed. His head bobbed almost imperceptibly as he stared off through an open window into the coal dark atmosphere of the night. "What if I say I can't guarantee that?"

"I guess I'll have to trust your judgment for now."

"But I suppose you're right," Snow said with unusual calmness. "Times have changed. The President should be in on it. I'll recommend that to the others." He dropped his foot to the floor. "Can I count on you?"

"Never let it be said I didn't love my country first."

"Good." Admiral Snow stood up. "In a way, I'm glad you've found out. We could really use your help—especially now. We'll meet tomorrow. My office, if that's all right with you. Say about nine-thirty?"

"Nine-thirty."

He smiled, gathered his material, and wiped his sweaty palm on his pants before shaking Snow's hand.

Outside in the crisp night air he wondered if he would be able to reach the President tonight.

* * *

Admiral Snow watched Jack Beamis's taillights disappear down his long driveway and wondered whether the growing volume of leaks was going to finally sink him and Majestic Twelve. *I'm sorry, Jack. You were a good sailor.*

A call came in on the secure line on his desk. It was Paul Blalock.

"Admiral. Good news." His voice was celebratory. "We think we've found Lavisch's daughter."

"You know what to do about that, but I've got something else even more pressing."

"What's that?"

"Beamis knows."

"Not Beamis," the man gulped.

"It'll have to be tonight."

# CHAPTER 18

A bone-rattling vibration shook the rafters of Peter MacKenzie's childhood home and ripped him out of a deep sleep. An eerie white light drenched his room, flickering to the rhythm of the pulsation. As if from the bottom of a well, he heard Molly and his mother screaming for him.

*Helicopter!*

He jumped from bed straight into his pants and shoes, pulling on a shirt as he made his way to the back of the house, where he found Molly and his mother peering out the window at a large dark sedan midway down the gravel driveway, which presently disgorged what seemed a small army of black-suited men carrying weapons.

"Mom, get down to the boat with Molly and get ready to go."

"But son, what's—?"

*"Now!"* He found his old Remington 12-gauge shotgun in the hall closet and chambered three deer-slugs, heavy chunks of lead sufficient to take off a man's head, or take out his spine.

Still hovering just above the house, the helicopter's searchlight swept the perimeter of the property. Its light shimmered off the silver poplar leaves, rippled over the shrubs, the lawn furniture and faux Greek statuary, creating demonic dancing shadows, among which he saw two men dressed in cat-burglar black, edging their way toward the house. One of the men carried a satchel.

"Come on in, you bastards!" Peter raised his gun, ready for the men to crash the back door, but instead he heard the helicopter's noise abruptly recede. Instinctively, his feet began to move, way before any conscious awareness of the threat—*bomb!* He never even felt his feet hitting the floor as he raced for the back door. But just as his hand hit the latch, the searing fireball of the satchel charge turned the house into a cloud of wood, brick and glass shrapnel, its shockwave hurling him halfway to the dock. He landed face down with a loud, hard *whumpf.* Stunned, he rolled over to what he thought was up and saw flickering splashes of light, but they weren't the nighttime stars. He tasted dirt, smelled lilacs and new-cut grass. Faintly at first, but growing quickly in volume, he heard a woman screaming.

"I-I-I...I'll g-get him."

The ominous whine of the chopper grew louder. Out of the corner of his eye he saw Molly climb out of the boat. Clawing at the night air, he struggled to his feet, rocking unsteadily before collapsing. He forced himself up again but staggered back toward the house, thinking he'd forgotten something important. *What?* His Honus! He fell back on his rump; his wallet crushed against his butt. *Got it!*

"Not-not t-t-that way!" Molly screamed, as the searchlight swept an arc between them.

A searing pain shrieked in his head. Dimly, he caught a glimpse of Molly hiding behind a lilac bush, just feet away, but he couldn't make his legs get him there. Suddenly, she was at his side, lifting him by his belt. He stumbled backward, collapsing into a heap, pulling her down. Why wouldn't his legs work? Luckily, the choking smoke from the burning house, pushed toward them by the chopper's downwash, now also screened them from view.

*"P-P-Pe-eter!* You-you've g-got to—"

"I know," he responded groggily.

"Peter, get down here this instant!" Margaret MacKenzie shouted to him, as if he were an obstreperous nine-year-old.

He couldn't get off all fours, so, with Molly pushing him, he crawled toward the darkness and his mother's voice. Suddenly he was spinning, rolling over and over until—*Boom!* He hit something hard and wet.

"Son! Are you okay?"

A faint odor of fish mixed with gasoline. Where was he? He rolled over and felt a sharp sticking pain. *The boat! I'm in the boat.* As if in slow motion, he watched Molly lift the mooring rope free of the creosoted wood piling, which flickered like a totem in the firelight, just as a bullet tore a big chunk off inches from her hand.

"M-M-Margaret, c-c-can you s-start the boat?"

*"No!"*

"Oh, God! P-Peter, *Peter h-h-help us!"*

The chopper's searchlight found them just as another explosion wracked the carcass of the fiercely burning house. Pushed back by the concussion, the helicopter seemed to struggle for a moment to get its bearings, then veered off into darkness again.

*Good ol' gas water heater.*

Unmoored, the boat drifted away from the dock into the darkness beyond the orange glow of the blazing house. Peter drew in a deep breath of cool night air, along with some brackish water, which caused a fit of coughing, which helped brighten his consciousness, just as the searchlight again penetrated the smoke, completing his resurrection. Hauling himself up to the control wheel, his hand twisted the key and seventy-five horses of Mercury outboard engine surged to life with a wail of sound and water. With the throttle jammed full forward, the Boston Whaler lurched into the blackness, nearly flinging them all overboard.

"We've got to make Clancey's," Peter yelled. "Or we're dead." He hugged the shoreline, trying to stay in the shadows of the trees near the water's edge, for the full moon, racing in and out of clouds, sporadically exposed them as a bright, white target for the helicopter maintaining station behind them. At least, he thought, the bright moon made their night-vision equipment unusable; they'd have to stick with their searchlight.

"Goddamned moon!" he shouted, as cloud-shrouded moon broke through again, forcing him to dip in closer to shore than he knew was safe. *If we hit a sandbar...*

Bullets raked the water and the boat. He zigged and zagged and did donuts, changing speeds abruptly. He tried every evasive maneuver imaginable, but the bullets always crept back to the mark. The boat was fast taking on water from the hits.

"Molly, you've got to bail or we'll never make it! Never mind, there's Clancey's. Hold on tight." Without slowing, he bypassed the dock and rammed headlong into the marsh reeds and cattails, running the boat well up onto shore. More shots streaked through the boat as they scrambled out and ran for the tall stand of trees that bordered Clancey's grass runway. Momentarily, the searchlight lost them, but the harpylike copter circled back and with a predator's uncanny sense soon found them.

"N-now w-w-what?" Molly stammered.

Margaret collapsed in the reeds, clutching her chest, seeming to struggle for air. Her hair wet and stringy, Peter thought she looked vulnerable in a way he'd never experienced. "Peter," his mother gasped, "I can't go on. You'll have to leave me here. I don't know what you've gotten yourself into, but I can't help you. Good luck and God bless—both of you."

"I can't leave you." He tried to pick her up, but she pushed him away.

"Go!"

Several bullets tore through the side of the boat where they crouched.

*"Now, son!"*

"Clancey'll take care of you," he told her. "Tell him to take you to Tangier Island. I don't think they'll bother you once we're gone, but—"

"Just go!"

With that he kissed her, grabbed Molly's hand and dashed for the hangar. He saw Clancey's lights go on and hoped he would not shoot them before the copter did. Then he glimpsed Clancey in the glow of the helicopter's searchlight, racing a storm of bullets as he ran to meet them at the hangar's entrance.

"Shit! That friggin' copter's tearing my place up. What the hell's goin' on, Pete? You sellin' drugs or somethin'?"

"No," he said tersely as he punched the red button that started the giant bi-fold hangar door on its way up. He could see the helicopter sweep around in a wide arch, repositioning for a better shot.

"What then?"

"They're trying to kill us! No time to explain. Mom's down in the reeds. Take care of her, will you? Clancey, I need your Pitts!"

"Get the hell out of here, boy, before they blow my hangar!"

Clancey took Peter's hand and squeezed it, but he didn't feel it. Suddenly it occurred to him that he'd have to fly the damned plane. At night. His arm, his control-stick arm, uselessly numb, he stood frozen in the pale moonlight, paralyzed by the flashback. It was night. He sat in F-14 on the catapult. He joked with Roy Corbett, as he always did before launch. Suddenly, he was drowning—he'd never been able to fly at night since.

Closing in for the kill, the copter maneuvered into position in front of the hangar and began to descend.

"What's wrong, son?" Clancey shouted. "You hit or somethin'?"

"I don't, I can't—"

"Damn, I forgot! He crashed at night in the Navy. Hasn't flown at night since!"

Molly grabbed the keys from Peter's hand and started to climb in.

"No!" Clancey howled. He grabbed her foot before she stepped on the wing. "This thing's fabric. Tear it, and you won't fly it anywheres! Even with him flying, you'll probably kill yourselves. Gimme the keys and get in front. Step here. I'll strap you in. Quick!"

A hail of bullets dug furrows up to hangar entrance, a few ricocheted off the interior of the hangar causing little lightening bug effects inside. Peter beat his arm against the door jam. "Clancey! I can't!"

The copter continued its slow descent close to the hangar opening, sealing off their only escape route.

"It's now or never, boy!"

Willing himself into the cramped, dark cockpit, Peter managed to flip the master switch and start the fuel pump. Using both hands, he pushed the mixture in to get a fuel prime. Finally he remembered the keys.

Clancey reached in and inserted them, then started to push the skullcap with its David Clark headsets onto Peter's head, but he pushed them away. "No time!" Without the headsets, he would not be able to talk to Molly, nor she to him, but it wouldn't matter.

"Thanks, Clancey. I—"

"You're welcome. Now get the hell out of here, will ya?" He gave a quick thumbs up, then turned the key for Peter. The 260-hp Lycoming engine exploded to life with wind and noise. As the copter began to settle in front of the hangar, almost low enough now for its lights—and its guns—to see under the upper edge of the hangar door, Peter pulled the canopy down and locked it with numb fingers, letting his hand fall to the throttle, jamming it forward with a blast of power that created a dusty smoke screen and sent the little red Pitts charging out of the hangar like a bull out of a rodeo chute, just missing the descending helicopter, which flashed by in his peripheral vision. A bullet struck the cowling, causing a flare of sparks. The engine sputtered and popped but quickly came back to life.

He knew that tall stands of oak, sycamore and chestnut flanked both sides of the narrow runway and the Pitts had no landing light. He'd have to taxi by feel. All he could see was a slightly lighter strip between two black walls—until the searchlight splashed his face, momentarily blinding him. But he couldn't stop and went for what he thought was the center of the runway before gunning the engine at full throttle and pushing the stick full forward to pick up the tail and allow him to see out in front. Suddenly a wall of trees loomed before him. He yanked the throttle back and jammed left rudder; the plane rocked dangerously then spun around into the copter's searchlight, which unwittingly gave him just enough light to get going again. Quickly correcting his path with rapid jabs of the rudder, he opened the throttle full, roaring down the strip, racing a stunning moon as it broke through a cloudbank.

*Thank God for that moon!*

Massive tree trunks flashed by, just inches off the wingtips, as the Pitts, veering left and right, accelerated quickly to flying speed and broke ground.

Already they were on him. "Goddamned moon!" he yelled. He pulled hard to the right, jumping just above the tree line, then dipped to a few feet above the water, again using the shoreline to help hide his movements. He jerked his head around. "Shit!"

They were right there, only a few hundred yards behind. Their Bell Jet Ranger shouldn't have been able to pace a healthy Pitts, and he was going flat out. Something was wrong. Then he felt it, a subtle vibration that quickly grew in intensity. The manifold pressure dropped, just as the deep navy blue sky, pinpricked with starlight, brightened again.

A bullet ricocheted off one of the flying wires. He knew a failed flying wire would upset the structural integrity of the wings, making high-G-load maneuvers dangerous and those were the only moves that would save them.

*That chopper pilot's good.* He pointed the Pitts upward, asking every farthing of its performance, twisting and jinking violently, just as he and Roy had done in their F-14 Tomcat in the Persian Gulf dodging SAMs, the surface-to-air missiles that seemed to rise like angry mosquitoes from every angle of the desert floor. He moved the controls by instinct, by a craftsman's faith, for he still had no feeling.

*Twang.* Another bullet hit a flying wire. Now he dove to the surface of the bay again, close enough to see whitecaps.

"That's it," he said with abject contempt, racking the plane into a five-G turn toward the north and the Chesapeake Bay Bridge. He strained against the acceleration, which mimicked gravity at five times normal, pulling the blood from his head and pushing him hard into his seat, wanting to make him loose consciousness. He knew Molly would've blacked out, at least for a few merciful moments, but it might also cause a wing to separate.

From just a few feet over the water, the Pitts shot up to two thousand feet, never following a straight line for more than a second or two. He looked back out of a steep turn. *Lost him!*

But instantly the searchlight illuminated the cockpit. He pushed the nose over steeply, aiming for the center span of the bridge. Tracers blurred by like fireflies in his peripheral vision.

With a loud *twang* and a shower of sparks, a bullet severed a flying wire on his left wing, rocking the plane violently as the airflow over the wing radically changed. Gritting his teeth, he pushed the stick forward, nosing over harder at more than three negative G's. The forces reversed, now trying to fling them out of the plane. Only tight straps held them in. He prayed Clancey had strapped Molly in tight enough, too, as the Pitts fell like a meteor toward the dark, placid bay waters.

*"Oh, shit!"* he screamed. Almost misjudging the pullout, the plane skimmed only inches above the water, which at this speed may as well have been concrete.

Then he saw it. Between the span of the two center towers, a large ship sat at anchor catty-corner across the space. *Too late!* He pitched the nose up slightly and aimed for the small bright spot between the freighter's deck and the bottom of the bridge's twin spans.

*Thank God for that moon!* Skimming the deck, the Pitts barely cleared the space between two cranes that rose like dead trees from the deck stacked two-stories high with containerized cargo.

A firm pullback on the stick sent the Pitts racing skyward in a large arching loop. He tensed his legs and stomach muscles, while exhaling against his closed mouth and nose, trying desperately to stay conscious, straining against the 6-G pull. For a second or two everything went black, no moon, no clouds, no stars. As the Pitts shot upward, gaining several hundred feet of altitude before going inverted, he regained his sight. Just in time to see the aviation red warning lights on the bridge's towers flash by beneath them. He rolled the Pitts upright, completing a perfect Immelmann turn, heading 180 degrees back to the other side of the bridge, back toward Annapolis. Quickly, he dipped a wing to look below.

For the hot-dog copter pilot, fixated on the image of the Pitts, it was too late to stop, turn around, climb away, or find a way through. The moonlit bay beneath the bridge erupted into an orange-red fireball of jet-A fuel and burning metal, Plexiglas and human flesh. The Pitts's wings rocked violently with the shock wave.

Up front in the moonlight, he saw a shock of red hair fluttering violently in the slipstream. A wave of relief gushed over him. She was still with him.

# CHAPTER 19

Peter had mooched a free ride on a friend's half-empty Learjet charter flight to Montreal only hours after he'd had landed the bent and broken Pitts in pre-dawn darkness at Frederick Municipal Airport. From Montreal, they would strike out for Tel Aviv in search of Youssef Sharabi, who, Peter had learned, was no longer at Ben Gurion University. Brandon Hadid, Roscha's other former collaborator, was no longer a possibility, as he'd been killed on a dig in the Negev only six months earlier. With Sharabi, he hoped, they would find Roscha, the book, and possibly the reason behind what was, by all appearances, a rogue action by his own government.

He detected a slight power reduction, and the nose of the jet lowered slightly, beginning its descent. He estimated they'd be on the ground in Montreal in fifteen minutes, where they'd meet a man who promised to provide the necessary papers for their international travel.

Joseph, not his real name—Peter would never know that—would meet them, or have them met, which was not completely clear. A wealthy Israeli of uncertain political or moral affiliation, Joseph had made millions in illegal arms trade, selling to the Arabs, the Afghanis, the Sudanese and any other Third World country with disposable cash and a gnawing dispute with its neighbors—or its own people.

Once, Peter had tipped him off to a customs inspector who had exposed Joseph's contraband shipment of Stinger missiles on its way to the Hezbollah in Libya. Peter was really helping *his* government by having the missiles intercepted. Only by strange providence did that also help Joseph, in whose mind this fortunate confluence of events had created a debt owed to Peter. Because of this, Peter had had to make but one call, and Joseph pledged the documents would be waiting for them in Montreal, no questions asked. But he still had one troubling thought: How reliable could someone like Joseph be?

The co-pilot, an attractive young woman doubling as a flight attendant, entered the cabin with a tray of coffee and nuts. "Care for anything, Miss?"

Peter gently nudged Molly, who appeared lost in thought.

"What?" Molly looked at him with glassy eyes, as if he were a complete stranger.

"Would you care for some coffee, Miss?" the attendant offered politely with a quizzical look on her pretty face. "I'm sorry, no one gave me your name."

"Molly, ah...Bumstead. And no, thank you."

"Bumstead?" Peter laughed. He noticed tracks of dried tears leading from her bloodshot eyes. "Thinking about your father?"

"Uh-huh. And Uncle Malcolm...and your mother and Clancey and…." She ran her slender fingers through her hair until reaching the top of her head and locked them, as if trying to keep her head from falling off her shoulders. "How did they find us?"

"AJ," he said bitterly and instantly felt the heat from her glaring green eyes.

"Fine way to talk about your lover."

"Remember the phone call when you came in from swimming yesterday?"

*"That was AJ?"* She unbuckled her seatbelt and wrenched around in the cramped seat to face him.

He hadn't seen her this mad since the night he'd told her about AJ the first time, the night her father was killed. "She must've recognized your voice."

"Why didn't you let me speak to her?"

He ignored her silly question. Slowly shaking her head, she stared at him with an expression he thought fell somewhere between accusation and disappointment. In retaliation he cocked his head, purposely arched his eyebrow and stared her down.

"Men *are* all alike," she said nastily. "Their loyalty extends about as far as the end of their— " Her face erupted in red. "I mean—why would she do such a thing?"

"Money, probably," he said, his mind still filling in the blank she'd left, which begged some very interesting questions that would have to wait. "I know she was strapped; the banks were after her big time. She told me the CIA came to the farm."

"Well I can't believe it," she said archly. "I won't! I-I mean—I-I do—about you. But s-s-sh-she wouldn't—"

Surprisingly, he felt ashamed. "And you think it's easy for me to believe?" he asked insincerely. "No, Molly, I thought it through a million times. It couldn't have been any other way." In truth, AJ's betrayal didn't much surprise him. He pretended not to notice when Molly took a deep breath and held it.

"Despite what you say, she's still my best friend."

He looked out the window and almost solemnly he said to himself, *No she isn't,* and he realized, perhaps for the first time since the Smithsonian debacle, that this was a much more dangerous situation than he'd thought. The plane's flaps began to screw down. He felt a slight pressure in his seat from the enhanced lift they provided. He wished they could lift his spirits as well.

* * *

Going through customs in Montreal had proven a nerve-fraying experience. Peter and Molly had been pulled into a side room and forced to disrobe while their duffle bags were thoroughly searched. Then, just as abruptly as they had been taken aside, they were released. Nothing had changed except for a new bulge in Peter's jacket pocket.

Joseph had come through for them; the documents were all there. Their flight to Tel Aviv on El Al 401 would depart in thirty minutes.

A short way down the concourse Peter spotted a prototypical airport lounge, all plastic and chrome, with gaudy orange faux-leather chairs and the obligatory TV, tuned to the obligatory sporting event *du jour,* this time a soccer game. Typically crowded, wall-to-wall faces with dour expressions betrayed the same inner anxiety. He knew the syndrome well: people never got over the their natural apprehension about the admittedly unnatural act of climbing into an oversized beer can and hurtling through the stratosphere at nearly the speed of sound. People wanted speed, wanted unencumbered freedom. But that came with a price: the possibility of catastrophe. And since September 11, 2001, radical Islam had focused that possibility to a fine point indeed. Thanks to people like his ironic savior, Joseph, the world was awash in variants of the shoulder-launched Stinger missiles, especially the Russian SA-18 Igla. Islamic terrorists had made good use of them, bringing down several airliners before counter measures were installed and even these were not foolproof. That explained why, in consideration of the quantity of alcohol consumed, airport bars were such quiet places. People were contemplating disaster. Which was precisely why he needed a drink.

Picking their way through the garment bags and briefcases, skis and golf clubs, dodging waitresses balancing trays with fresh drinks heading away from the bar and others with empty glasses on the way back, they made the bar just as two weary-looking travelers got up to leave.

"That was lucky," Molly said.

"I don't believe in luck," Peter countered gruffly.

She ordered a Coke. He got a beer.

Thinking of her response to the flight attendant, he asked. "Where'd you come up with a goofy name like Bumstead, anyway?"

"Oh," she giggled, "it's because I'm a big 'Blondie' fan. You know, the comic strip. I've loved it ever since I was a kid."

"I always liked those old movies. But I'm afraid I identified more with Mister Dithers. Dagwood never made a good decision in his life, except maybe to marry Blondie. Guess that's why you like her, huh? Because she pulls all Dagwood's strings, makes him look like a...well, a *Bum*-stead."

"You can be funny." She methodically curled the paper straw cover into a roll.

"Well isn't that about the only thing a feminist would like about Blondie, being as she was such a good mother and family woman?"

"Oh, I get it," she said. "You think feminists are all anti-motherhood? Well, they're not. And if believing that women should have the same opportunities as men makes me a feminist, I guess I am. But it might surprise you to know that I like Blondie precisely *because* she's a good—and smart—mother. A career mother."

He watched her rolled up a straw like party kazoo. "You know what really pissed me off? That movie *Fargo*. Did you see it?"

"Uh-huh, with the female cop someplace up north."

"North Dakota."

"What about it?"

"Here she was a nine-months pregnant police*man* who tracked down these contract killers. For the sake of her *career*—and her outsized ego—she puts her unborn baby in the line of fire. Now, come on, that was totally unnecessary. And you know what the worst part was? You never heard anyone criticize that. Instead it seemed everyone—especially the feminists—applauded her as such a great role model. What the hell is this world coming to?"

"When I said women should be able to do anything, I didn't mean I thought they should view motherhood as a part-time job. It *is* a career, probably the most important one there is."

"Not probably, it is. These days, most Americans think kids are pets. That's about how much attention parents give 'em. Hell, daycare is no better or worse that puttin' your kid in a kennel. The last thing the world needs is another woman firefighter. Or lawyer. Or cop. Or you name it. But we could sure do with some better mothers."

"You're fond of children then?" She inclined her head toward him and gave him that goofy nest-building smile he'd seen so many times before.

"Kids make me nervous."

"Why? To use one of your favorite expressions, 'They don't bite.'"

"Not if you don't let 'em." He wagged his hand back and forth in a feigned slapping motion.

She shook her head and said resolutely, "Well, I could *never* harm a child. Never. I know that much." She paused reflectively. "Anyway, I love Blondie. She's intelligent, resourceful, wise and wonderfully good humored. And while Dagwood may not be the sharpest knife in the drawer, I'd take him. He's loving, kind and thoughtful, if somewhat accident prone."

"Just call me Mister Dithers—" Someone caught his eye. Roy? Roy Corbett? He nearly fell off his stool.

"What's wrong?" Molly said, trying to steady him. "You act like you just saw a ghost."

But Peter couldn't answer. Propelled by shock, he started making his way through the crowded bar toward the young man wearing a Lufthansa first officer's uniform seated at the far side of the bar. The man blinked at Peter for a second, then looked away, quickly throwing a ten-dollar bill on the bar. With one last furtive glance, the man disappeared into a gang of newcomers before Peter could reach him, but reappeared some distance down the concourse. Peter ran after him, stopping only when the man exited through doors marked Flight Duty Personnel Only.

Returning to his stool, Peter signaled the bartender for another beer. "I must be losin' it."

"You look awful. Who was that?"

"A dead man," he said flatly.

"You mean that pilot who just left in a hurry?"

"Yeah, him. Couldn't be, though. I saw him die."

"Then it's simple. It couldn't have been...whoever." Molly shoved the beer the bartender just set down into Peter's hand. "Here, drink some beer."

"If it wasn't Roy, it was his twin. And I know he didn't have one."

"What was Roy to you?" She massaged the wet paper ball between her fingers, then pushed the end of her straw over it.

"Roy Corbett, my RIO—radar intercept officer. He flew with me in the F-fourteen. Remember the problem I had at Clancey's? Remember me telling you about my accident on the aircraft carrier?"

"Yes."

"Roy was with me that day."

He told Molly how he had taken a cold catapult shot off the USS *NIMITZ* on his last Mediterranean cruise. A night mission, his F-fourteen, along with Roy Corbett, had dribbled off the flight deck like a toy off a kitchen table and plunged over sixty feet to the water, then sank well beneath the surface before Peter managed to reach the ejection handle. Fortunately, the reliable, rocket powered Martin-Baker seat had carried them out of the water and high enough for their chutes to deploy. In the warm but stormy sea waters twenty-five-foot waves took him and Roy up and down like yoyos. Peter had managed to separate from his parachute harness before the wet chute could pull him under, and light a flare.

Roy was not so lucky. Stunned and in shock, he panicked, flailing about as he struggled to stay afloat. He screamed for Peter, who quickly swam to his aid, but Roy nearly pulled him under before he could push away and save himself. The vision of Roy Corbett's terrified face, flickering in the flare's light, as he slipped beneath the dark green waves for the last time would haunt him forever.

"Roy didn't make it," he whispered, then hung his head and closed his eyes hard.

Molly put her hand softly on his shoulder. "Doesn't sound as if it was your fault."

"How would you know?" he snapped. He caught a glimpse of himself in the mirror behind the bar; the face glared accusingly back at him, and he had to look away. "If I just hadn't waited so long to pull the damned handle. But I was—"

"Afraid?"

"What the hell do you know about being afraid?"

"Nothing, Peter, nothing at all." She said it in a crusty voice, as she hammered the straw's tip on the counter top. "I was just trying to help you. To be your friend."

"Patronizing me isn't being my friend."

"Maybe I don't know a lot of things you know, Peter. But I do know this: People don't come back from the dead. If you'll recall, I'm a doctor. When you quit feeling sorry for yourself, meet me in the boarding area."

"Like Katie Jamison?" he blurted into his beer, loudly enough so he was sure she'd hear. "Have you forgotten AJ's sister?" When he looked up to watch her go, a wet spitball struck him dead between the eyes. Molly lowered the straw and, without smiling, spun around and headed down the concourse.

* * *

"Look who's still with us." Peter pointed to the last row of seats in the rear of the Boeing 747. It was Mr. Madras, the lanky East Indian who had sat quietly in the rear of the Learjet staring at his laptop all the way to Montreal, and who now, catching them staring, smiled faintly, then returned to his reading. While Peter thought it an odd coincidence, no alarms went off, for there just wasn't any way, he figured, that their presence on that flight could have been known.

Buckling up, just as a muted bump signaled the closing of the last cargo door, he felt a tingling in his right arm, an unpleasant reminder of their predicament. Seconds later the giant craft lurched backwards from the gate. Molly sat with her head stuck in the emergency procedures material as the flight attendant made her presentation; she hadn't said a word since they boarded.

He'd managed to pick up a copy of the *Washington Post,* which he quickly scanned, looking for some mention of the events at his mother's house the previous night or anything about Molly's father.

"Mad at me?" he ventured cautiously, without taking his eyes off the paper.

No reply.

"Well here's something that might interest you." Folding the pages in half, he placed the newspaper's 'Metro' section on her lap and tapped his finger on a headline.

"My God! All it mentions is a fire without injuries in a *vacant house.*" She read aloud: "Says, '...The owner, Mrs. John MacKenzie, could not immediately be reached. The cause of the early morning blaze is suspected to be a faulty gas water heater.'"

"Whatever we're into, it's huge," he told her. "Even the CIA would have a hard time justifying an action like this."

"Your mother—?"

"She's all right. I got a call off to Clancey on Tangiers Island. They made it fine. I told him to stay there until he heard from me again. Or until he reads about us in the papers." He dug down into his flight bag.

"Give me the comic section," she ordered brusquely.

"Want some?" He tipped his bag, which overflowed with boxes of Cracker Jacks.

"You're such a little boy."

"Let's call it a peace offering," he said, popping a piece of caramel-coated popcorn into his mouth and pushing the bag closer to her. "Take one."

She looked away. "No thank you."

"That's what I like about you; you're *sooo* polite." He handed her the rest of the newspaper with something wrapped inside. "Here, maybe you'd prefer this."

Finally, she looked at him, her face quizzical but noncommittal. "A book?" *Blondie Trivia, the Funny's First Family.* "Blondie!" Then, hesitating, "Thanks, Peter." She said it in a hushed voice, as if trying to cling to her anger. She looked at the Cracker Jacks. "Maybe I will have some after all."

He shook the box of candied popcorn and peanuts side-to-side and peered inside.

"What are you doing?"

"Looking for my prize." He fished around until he'd found it, excitedly tearing away its thin paper covering. But as soon as he had the toy, he jammed it back into the box, quickly crushing it and putting it on the tray for the flight attendant to trash.

"Wait a minute. I can't let you do that."

"What do you mean?"

"Well what was it?"

"Something stupid."

She grabbed the box and upended it on the tray. Out fell a tiny plastic pistol.

# CHAPTER 20

Madras laid the metal briefcase down on the bed in his Tel Aviv hotel room. With delicate, reverent movements, he thumbed in the required sequence of numbers on the combination lock, and pushing gently, opened the briefcase. He lifted out the beautiful Martian bookcase, placing it on a purple velvet display cloth, its glowing red eye winking in unison with its silent beacon.

Alongside it he set a small candelabra with three white candles. Using complimentary hotel matches, he lit them, along with a thin stick of incense, which he then placed in an ornately inscribed gold dish. He poured a small portion of red wine from a flask into a matching chalice. Unbuttoning his shirt, he reached behind his neck and undid the clasp of a necklace, from which hung a single ornament—a gold modified ankh. Carefully, he positioned the ankh with its forked tail onto the bookcase's corresponding figure, where they perfectly overlapped. The eye ceased its winking.

He removed his shoes and sat down, crossing his legs in the lotus position, took a sip of wine. Bowing his head, he closed his eyes and made the sign of the cross on his breast as he said a silent prayer.

But his urgently bleating communicator sabotaged his meditations.

"Hello, Madras," the willowy female voice said. "Lilah Blackwell. You summoned me?"

"Yes. I spoke with Pheras earlier today, and he wants me to expedite the return of the Covenant. Within the bounds of our mission, of course. I thought it would be easy, but—"

"How can I help you?"

"I'm following our Eve—Molly Lavisch—and the companion who will test her, but—" He hesitated, not knowing if he should be asking someone of Lilah's stature for help in such an assignment, or if she would do what he thought was necessary.

"Molly Lavisch does not have the book," she said emphatically.

How he hated to have his mind read. "But she must know who does?"

"Yes. She knows. I can't tell you any more than that. But if you wish I can come and help in any other way that I can, within the bounds of the law."

Madras knew she meant God's laws, not man's. "I know that Pheras doesn't like you to use your powers in this way. But I thought under the circumstances, because of the Covenant—"

"Of course, we would like to. But you understand why we can't?"

But of course he didn't in this case, or at least he was uncertain. "I guess I have much to learn."

"Learn this," she commanded. "The abolition of the will to choose is an impossibility. Worlds upon worlds could pass away, saving not one. What would last would be Consciousness and Free Will."

"Forgive me. It was a foolish thought. I do have much to learn."

"We all do," she said, softening her tone. "Life *is* learning. What I mean to convey to you now is this, If people think their future is fixed, they fail to exercise their own power to change that future. They deny their own free will often enough themselves without our interference.

"And you must remember, Madras, I can see only outcomes based on the present moment's configuration, not a preordained future."

In a moment of selfish pique, he risked an affront. "But what about Molly Lavisch? You told her of her coming death."

"We all die, Madras. I told her little more than that. Besides, Pheras has special plans for her, given her role in the present configuration."

"What will Pheras do if I don't—can't—recover the Covenant?"

"Madras, Madras," she said with the patient timbre of a mother, "you must simply do the best that you can."

"I would feel better if you were here."

"Very well."

"Tomorrow?"

"I'll meet you at your hotel for dinner."

* * *

Youssef Sharabi had just lain down on his cot with his pocket tape recorder and was about to make some notes on the morning's accomplishments when a dark-skinned little boy wearing the vagabond garb of a Bedouin threw back the flap of his tent and burst in.

"Great One! Great One!" the boy shouted. "Someone coming! Look! Come quick!"

Sharabi looked out the tent to the northeast in the direction of Baghdad, where the boy, frantically hopping up and down, pointed. Judging from the plume of dust that rose into the pale blue desert sky, they were, indeed, going to have company.

"Kopi," Sharabi said calmly as he pulled the boy by the neck to his side. "I want you to do me a favor." He turned the boy around and held him by his shoulders while he looked him in the eye, for he wanted to convey a precise meaning. "Go down to the river and bring back some refreshments for our guests. Don't rush. Look in on the men while you're there and report back. Can you do that for me?"

"Yes, Great One."

Sharabi watched the boy charge down the sandy slope and shook his head. Again he looked to the approaching vehicle. *Who could this be?* Unexpected visitors at his remote dig were rare and worrisome. If trouble it was, at least Kopi might be spared. A month before, Kurdish rebels had passed through, stealing everything they could carry off, including the fuel reserves, forcing him to spend the rest of the year's budget to resupply. But worst of all, it had taken him a month to recruit new laborers to replace the half of his workforce the Kurds had scared away, putting his project hopelessly behind schedule.

Picking the binoculars off the hook on the tent post, he scanned the smoky column of dust rapidly snaking its way toward him. "Not the Kurds. But who?" He searched in front of and behind the white Land Rover for evidence of other vehicles, but saw none.

"Here is drinks, Great One," Kopi said, panting heavily, as he threw down a goatskin water bag and a twelve-pack of Coors beer, for which Sharabi had acquired a fondness back at Columbia University.

"That was fast."

"Kopi run whole way. Quick, quick."

"Good boy!" he said with all the genuine pride of a father. "Now take it into the tent for me." So much for my ruse to get Kopi out of harm's way, he thought. He scanned the excavations about a hundred yards down the hill, making sure that the workers were still doing just that: working. Progress of late had been slow, due, he thought, to his new foreman, Moab, whose harsh treatment of the men had begun to sap morale and already had led to more than one defection. "Good, good," he said, seeing the requisite movement around the fluted columns of a long-buried city, uncovered just two weeks before.

He could hear the Land Rover clearly now, as it strained in its lowest gear to make the top of the bluff where his tents stood firmly against the sky, defying the strong desert winds and providing a commanding view of the river a quarter-mile below, where the motor boats were moored.

"Should Kopi get gun, Great One?" the boy asked excitedly.

"Guns are not the good things you seem to think they are, little one. You above all should know that." He continued to scan the visitors with his binoculars as he spoke, unable to suppress a big smile. "No, Kopi, we won't be needing the gun. Get the beer." He laughed playfully and slapped himself on the thigh. "Get the beer, Kopi! I'd recognize that white hair anywhere."

The Land Rover bucked and shuddered to a stop in a choking cloud of dust immediately in front of them. Wasting no time, the Iraqi driver hopped out and without so much as a smile, a bow or a hoot began to untie the ropes holding down a large footlocker strapped to the top.

Roscha, beaming, gave Sharabi a big bear hug. "Youssef, my old friend. How are you?"

"I'm...I'm surprised is what I am, Roscha. *Surprised!*"

"No doubt."

Tugging on Roscha's shirtsleeve, the Iraqi driver pecked the palm of his hand with his index finger.

"Oh, yes, yes—money," Roscha chuckled, reaching for his wallet. He hesitated before handing the man his money. "I hate to put you on the spot like this, Youssef, but I think this good fellow wants to be on his way, and, well—" he looked around forlornly— "it seems you've got the only accommodations in town. Can you put me up for a few days?"

"I'd be offended if you didn't stay," Sharabi told him. "Kopi... Kopi, where's that beer?" Hearing the sounds a pop-top popping, he threw open the tent. "Kopi! You little beggar!" But before he could grab him, the boy dropped the remains of his beer and scurried down the hill toward the dig.

"Camp rats are getting bigger all the time," Roscha quipped.

They sat down in the shade under the tent near Sharabi's work table, on which lay hundreds of artifacts, all nicely cleaned and tagged with little yellow data cards.

"How long will you be staying?" Sharabi asked, still unable to fathom the circumstances that would prompt Roscha's sudden appearance.

"Until you're sick of me, I'm afraid." Roscha removed his sunglasses and lit a cigarette. He slipped his silver and gold lighter inside the cellophane outer wrapper of his Marlboros, placing them on the table beside him. He wiped the sweat from his brow with his forearm. "I had considerable difficulty in finding you, Youssef."

"That's good!"

Roscha took a sip of beer. "Mind if I ask what you are into here? No one wanted to tell me anything about where you were or what you were up to."

"The museum is simply following my instructions," Sharabi said cautiously.

"Here I thought you were still at Beersheba. Now I find you're with the Rockefeller Museum in Jerusalem. What happened? I thought you liked Ben Gurion."

"Ben Gurion didn't share my vision for this project." Unable to contain himself, he leaned forward, grabbing Roscha by the shoulders and, with the fervor of an evangelist, said, "Roscha, it's so exciting. You won't believe what we've found here. I can't believe it myself. It's a find, Roscha! A *find!*" Then, seeing Roscha's glazed look, he grew wary, his body tensing. He straightened in his chair.

"You don't think—" Roscha chuckled. He reached over and patted Sharabi on the knee. "Relax, old friend. I'm not here in any official capacity."

"In that case, have another beer."

Roscha flicked the butt of his cigarette away and reached for another. "Hey!" He grabbed for the sash on Kopi's burnoose, but the boy got clean away.

"Kopi! *Kopi!*" Sharabi barked. "Bring back those cigarettes! Right now! Or I'll...I'll circumcise you. *Kopi!*"

"Cheeky little fellow," Roscha said with a smirk. "He yours?"

"No, he's not *mine,*" he said, though the thought of it did not displease him. "But I guess I've assumed responsibility for him. He's the reason I'm here."

"Oh? How so?"

"Because of what he just did to you, actually. The little thief stole my camera in the market in Baghdad. Just ran up, bold as brass, and snatched it. When I caught him, he tried to barter for the camera with this." He reached into his pocket and produced a potshard with tiny wedge-shaped markings.

"Cuneiform," Roscha said with seeming indifference. "Certainly not uncommon in these parts."

"Not at all. Except where he found it. Here. Where no evidence for human habitation had ever been found."

"Still...I don't see the what's so unusual. I mean...I can see how it's a new site, perhaps another city on the order of Uruk or Kish—and that's great. But—"

"Think about it, Roscha. Think where you are right now. Only thirty-five or forty miles northwest of Ur, the oldest known city in the world. About twenty miles southwest of Babylon. Twenty or so from Uruk to the southeast. But don't forget, Uruk and Babylon are on the *other* side of the Euphrates from Ur. Everyone has always wondered why there were no other habitations like Ur on the west side of the river." He stamped his feet in the dusty earth. "Here."

Roscha shrugged.

"The boy stole it from the Marsh Arabs who took him in. Just south of here. Of course, when they threatened to cut off his hand, he ran away, ending up in Baghdad. Ordinarily I'd have turned this over to some graduate assistants and gone on to something else. But the location. That's what got my attention, the *location.* The boy swore the shard had come from here. I don't know why I believed him. So I came." He paused to finish his beer, crumpling the can between his palms and tossing it with a clink into the trashcan. "But what kept me here is what we found below the first layer." He took another beer and handed one to his friend.

"Go on," Roscha prodded.

"We found another layer."

"Come on, old friend. That's not at all unusual either. You know—"

He waved his arms excitedly, dismissing what he thought Roscha was thinking. "But here, as they say, is the kicker. The lower level was a *more advanced* habitation than the top, not more primitive."

"That is the opposite of what you'd expect."

"What's more, there's at least one other level, much deeper. We just began uncovering it three days ago." He put his hand on Roscha's shoulder. "And, are you ready for this? The geologic stratum it's in is at least fifty thousand years old! *Fifty thousand!* Perhaps much, much older."

"It can't be!"

"I assure you, we've double-checked every measurement. It's true, all right."

"Let's see, that would make it about ten times older than Ur, which goes back, what? Three to four thousand B.C.?"

"We think about thirty-five hundred B.C. And the Sumerians who built it were still fairly primitive at that stage. Well, I don't need to tell you."

"Yes, " Roscha agreed, "that is Interesting. And you're sure about the strata? It couldn't be a geologic anomaly?"

Sharabi shook his head emphatically, pleased that Roscha had at last seen the significance of the find.

"Impressive, Youssef. Now wait 'til you see what I've—"

Just then Kopi marched brazenly between them. Sharabi grabbed him and tried to turn him upside down in an effort to shake out whatever contraband might be hiding in the labyrinthine folds of his clothing. With that, Kopi gave out a high-pitched shriek, putting his hands between his legs in an apparent effort to keep his clothes from riding up and betraying his privacy. Feet fluttering like bird wings, he begged Sharabi to let him down.

"All right, then!" Sharabi relented and plopped the boy down, dislodging an empty beer can and Roscha's Marlboros. The degree of Kopi's indignity took him by surprise. "Let that be a lesson for you, then." He tossed the cigarettes to Roscha.

Backing away, Kopi scowled like a cornered convict, until Roscha handed him a cigarette. "Next time, ask."

After a few puffs, the boy broke into a fit of coughing and barely managed a "Thank you, Great One," before sauntering off, puffing and hacking as he went.

"Like it or not, you've made a friend," Sharabi laughed.

"He's a funny one. And he's cultivated a pile of bad habits for such a short life."

"Yes. Very modest about his body. Won't bath. So I throw him in the river when he gets too ripe."

"Where are his parents, anyway?"

"Killed in the second Persian Gulf war. In Baghdad. Two of the 'collateral casualties,' so called. Father was Sudanese, mother Syrian. Hence the dark skin but otherwise Caucasian features.

"I told him he could stay with me and help me on the dig as an 'advisor.' Thinks he's a big shot now. I'm fond of him, though. He keeps me company."

A low, murmuring sound drifted up from the valley below, a chanting sound that rose and fell with the undulating breeze.

"Afternoon prayers?" Roscha asked.

"All the workers are Muslim. Only way you can get them to work is allow them their five prayers a day."

"Which reminds me," Roscha said, "what's a good Christian boy like you doing here? How'd you get permission? Iraq's a very unfriendly place again, since the Americans left. It took half my net worth in bribes plus calling in some very old debts just to get in the country."

"I'm Palestinian, remember? We've always backed Iraq."

"Ahhh... A meager show of gratitude is better than none at all, I suppose."

"More importantly, Roscha, what are *you* doing here? I haven't heard a word from you in, what? Six? Eight years? Suddenly you show up on my doorstep, as it were, from half-a-world away. What could have motivated an action so drastic as that, I'm wondering?"

"It's simple, Youssef. I need your help. Desperately."

"Desperation's a strong word." He offered Roscha another beer.

"If anything it's a gross understatement."

"All right, then. Just what's this all about?"

"I'm eager to tell you. But first, can't an old friend get anything to eat around here? I've been a long time on a dusty road."

"Kopi!"

* * *

Roscha had fallen asleep halfway through a meal of cold mutton stew and pita bread, and still he slept.

"Why does he sleep, Great One?"

"He's exhausted from a long, and perhaps hazardous, trip. He'll be all right. Come on, let's go down and check on Moab. I want to see what's happened on the third level."

The site was unusual, a revelation caused by a fortuitous natural event. The largest flood in millennia had carried the Euphrates far from its banks, raging for a devastating period of several weeks. Many lives were lost as hundreds of towns and villages were washed away; the debris and bloated bodies churned to the surface for weeks afterward, finally ending up in the Persian Gulf, hundreds of miles downstream. As a consequence, a meander had developed in the river about a mile from its normal course, forming a hook-shaped gouge in the bluff face, the result being the present site, exposed vertically—and conveniently—from the top of the bluff nearly down to the level of the rogue river, whose edge now lay some quarter of a mile away, its course permanently altered. Although the edges of the two top city sites were fairly well exposed, a third distinctive pallet lay much deeper in the alluvial mud.

Sharabi, as is the right of any discoverer, had taken the liberty of naming the site Ur-el-Sharabi, after himself and the top level's similarity in all respects to the ancient Ur. Logically, they had begun the excavation at the top level, removing layer by layer, moving both inward toward the heart of the bluff and downward, carefully shoring the fragile walls of the excavation as they went, recording everything with still photos and videotape.

They had found the usual pottery shards and fragments of clay tablets with cuneiform writing, which Sharabi, expert at reading the long-since-deciphered cuneiform, had read as grain manifests and tax levies. They had found other unremarkable bits and pieces of stoneware—except for one beautiful alabaster vase with human and animal figures—along with small bits of badly oxidized copper, which no doubt had arisen from copper implements expected to be associated with the relative age of the top layer, which is to say something on the order of three to five thousand years.

But it was the second layer, already partially uncovered, and the third—and possibly deeper layers—that fired his imagination. Luckily, the part of the city revealed by the flood on the second level appeared to be a temple, judging from the elaborate ceramic tiles in cobalt blue and gold that lined an apparent entranceway, or processional, at the top of some highly polished stone stair steps. He knew well that in ancient times, temples were the repository of a culture's grandest achievements: its writing, its history, and, perhaps most importantly, its view of the eternal. So this was where the bulk of Moab's men now worked, slowly, carefully digging away the soils of the ages, penetrating ever deeper into a mystery: Why were these structures, these finely crafted ceramic tiles, on a caliber with the much later, magnificently beautiful work in Babylon, here at a geologic stratigraphic level of between ten and possibly as much as twenty thousand years?

“Great One!” Kopi ran onto the narrow plank that connected the platform on which Sharabi stood to the foyer of the temple. The planks swayed and bowed as he ran. Laughing gleefully, he seemed to relish his recklessness.

“Be careful, Kopi!” Sharabi yelled. “Watch your footing!”

“Look what Kopi found,” he said, beaming proudly, as he held out a gold Egyptian ankh in perfect condition.

“Where did you find this?”

“There. By the large rock.”

*“Kooopi*, are you telling me the truth? Let me have it.”

The boy drew back. “No. Belong Kopi.”

“We’ll check with Moab. If it belongs to no one here, you may keep it.”

Sharabi didn’t have to look for Moab; he heard his lash. It wouldn’t be long, he thought, before he and Moab would need to have a serious talk, for he couldn’t tolerate the delays losing more workers would mean.

“Moab, would you come down here, please?”

The tall, dusky man with the scared face all pinched out at the nose so that he resembled a weasel, stuck his riding crop into his sash belt alongside his revolver and descended the ladder.

“Yes, Sharabi?”

“This ankh.” He handed the piece to Moab. “One of your workers must have lost it.”

“There is only one Egyptian, Habib Amar. I will ask him.”

“Better ask them all, just in case,” he said, knowing that Moab would more than likely just keep it rather than keep asking. “How’s the temple coming? Will the hallway be cleared by tomorrow?”

“This afternoon, if you wish,” Moab answered flatly, placing his hand menacingly on his revolver.

“No more of that, Moab,” he said as sternly as he could. “Understand?”

Moab said nothing, turned quickly and climbed back up the ladder, shouting curses at the workers to pick up the pace.

"Excellent!" Sharabi said to himself, relieved he'd confronted Moab without some major blowup. Yet deep down he knew that wasn't the end of it. "Well, Kopi, shall we go see if our guest has revived?"

* * *

Roscha opened his eyes, saw the tan canvas of the tent and was crestfallen. Truly, it had been but a dream, a pleasant one to be sure, one devoid of the feeling that now settled over him: the feeling that he was no more than a hunted animal.

Even with Sharabi's help, he doubted his ability to decipher the book. Without a decipherment, the book could have come from anywhere. True, the materials of its manufacture might tell the tale, but the book could be easily hidden or destroyed. No. Only the text itself could establish its extraterrestrial origin in some as yet unknown way.

But he knew deciphering the text would be next to impossible without some kind of key. Examples illustrating the dilemma abounded: the inscriptions in square soap stones found in the Indus Valley, known for centuries yet resisting every attempt at decipherment; or the better-known example of Egyptian hieroglyphics, which had to await not only the genius of Champollion but the Rosetta stone.

*Genius* and *the Rosetta stone.* "I'm bright," Roscha said to himself, "but I'm no genius."

"Well, Kopi," Sharabi said, entering the tent where Roscha lay, "I see our guest has awakened. Be a good boy and go to the river for some more American beer. Check that the boats are properly moored while you're there. And Kopi, don't drink the beer!"

"Yes, Great One...." The boy hesitated, turning to Roscha.

"What's on your mind?"

"Kopi have cigarette, Great One?"

"Sure," Roscha shrugged and looked at Sharabi. "Here, keep the pack. Beats having him steal them."

"Have you rested well, Roscha?"

"I have, old friend." He sat up and sighed heavily, stretching out his sore arms and rubbing them briskly.

"It's the desert air," Sharabi said. "Makes your bones expand and contract like an old house."

"Well, old brittle bones anyway. No, I'm afraid there's more to it than that."

"Do you feel up to finishing our conversation, then?"

"We must, Youssef. I'm afraid time is short—for me at least." He lit a cigarette and pulled on his boots. He began by telling Sharabi of his meeting with Miles Lavisch, the book, Miles's murder and the attempt on Molly's life. He told him how he had escaped, disguised as a Capuchin monk, with a phony passport and visa he had used for years to visit Cuba and the live sex shows in Havana. How he had used an old acquaintance at the British embassy in Israel, who had put him in touch with the proper corrupt officials in Jordan and Iraq, who then arranged more phony papers and transportation.

Finally, Roscha opened his large trunk and removed a briefcase, from which he withdrew the Martian book wrapped in the purple felt cloth. Handing Sharabi some cotton gloves, he'd started to unwrap the book when Moab stuck his head in the tent.

"Sorry to disturb you, Sharabi, but I thought you would want to know." He handed Sharabi the ankh. "No one among the workers would claim this."

"You're sure?"

"Yes. And there is this." He handed Sharabi a cotton bag. "One of the men working in the temple area on the second level just found it."

Sharabi reached in the bag and held up a finely worked, richly inscribed gold chalice. "Fabulous! Good work, Moab. Tell your man he'll get a bonus, as will you." He put the chalice back in the bag and set it down. He put on gloves and picked up the remarkable little book.

Roshca watched him examine it. Sharabi carefully opened it, turning to the first pages of text. When he did, he gasped.

"Never seen anything like it, have you?" Roscha said, not at all surprised by Sharabi's reaction.

"Five minutes ago I would have said no."

"What?"

Sharabi reached into the bag and handed Roscha the chalice. "Look."

Roscha walked out into the bright sunlight, where he examined the characters on the vessel under magnification. Though not a language identical to the Martian in the book, it was nonetheless very similar. Some characters, even some words—though very few—were exactly the same. Most, perhaps fifty or sixty percent, lacked any commonality. *We have a chance!* he thought.

Kopi arrived with the beer, along with a look of deep concern. "Great One, why was Moab standing outside your tent so long?"

"What do you mean, little beggar?"

"He stood against Great One's tent whole time Kopi walk back from river."

# CHAPTER 21

Roscha Venable stood, with Youssef Sharabi, on a makeshift scaffold on the second level of the excavation at Ur-el-Sharabi, watching impatiently as Moab coaxed his workers with taunts and curses and occasional lashes of his riding crop. One last stone blocked the entrance to a suspected royal tomb. For the first time since Miles was killed and his own life became threatened, Roscha felt he had a chance, however slight, to save himself.

"This must be how Carter felt when his feeble light first pierced the darkness of Tutankhamen's tomb," Sharabi said in a reverent tone.

"Speaking of Egyptians," Roscha said, steadying himself on the shaky scaffolding, "What about the ankh Kopi found? I mean the link between the Egyptian and the Mesopotamian cultures isn't hard to swallow, but the depth at which it was found is astonishing."

"And the similarity to the symbol on your book!" Sharabi added.

"Ready!" Moab bellowed.

The thick rope well tensioned, all eyes turned to Moab, awaiting the final order to exert themselves to the utmost in an effort to dislodge the massive stone. Moab paced rapidly up and down the length of the rope, eyeing every man. Then, slapping the huge slab with his riding crop, he yelled, "Heave! Heave!"

The thrumming ropes stretched to the limit, but the stone moved only a couple of inches.

"Heave!"

The men grunted fiercely, their feet sometimes breaking traction, sliding, and causing showers of small rocks to cascade down the steep bluff. Grudgingly, the stone moved another few inches.

"Heave, you laggards!" Moab cursed, as he walked up and down the line, haphazardly whipping the men with his crop. "Put your backs into it!"

The men grunted and groaned, their sweat-muddied faces contorted with the effort as ropes creaked and twanged and fibers snapped. One let go of the rope with a painful scream, but Moab lashed him, kicked him aside and picked up the end of the rope himself.

"Heave like the stone is on Allah's own neck!" Moab shouted.

The great stone twisted, making a loud crunching sound, then cracked in two, falling to the side. The entranceway was clear.

Roscha covered his mouth with a damp handkerchief. "If this dust would just settle."

"I can see well enough," Sharabi said. "Let's go."

Sharabi went first, Roshca following close behind. Shining his light into the thickly soiled darkness, through a long-closed portal to the dim past, Roscha couldn't believe what his eyes beheld. With a background of cobalt blue ceramic, as beautiful as any in Babylon, embossed white alabaster figures, accentuated with gold and precious stones, lined the walls, telling vivid stories of the life of the day, much like the walls of Egyptian tombs, though with much superior craftsmanship and artistry.

"Look, Roscha!" Sharabi directed the light at his feet. A huge sun made from an intricate pattern of tiny colored tiles formed the floor of the room. Emanating from the central sun were twelve rays. Each ray contained the same script found on the chalice, along with a human figure. The pointed tip of each ray touched an outer circle, which circumscribed the entire sun-and-ray figure. Several feet farther out, yet another circle encompassed everything. It was also divided into twelve sectors by lines drawn from the tips of the twelve rays. Within each sector was a constellation of stars.

"Are you thinking what I'm thinking?" Roscha asked rhetorically, knowing what his friend would answer.

"The Zodiac!" Sharabi gasped excitedly. "The Babylonians were supposed to have invented astrology. This changes everything."

"Maybe the Babylonians discovered it the same way we are now," Roscha thought out loud. "Look at this, Youssef." He pointed to a pictorial comprised of several human figures surrounding what looked like a very large domed shaped figure, which initially he thought was a burial mound topped with a bright red stone.

Sharabi wiped away the ancient patina with his handkerchief. The mound had legs! Three short supporting legs. Coming out of the center of the mound was what looked like stairs, on which were a number of human figures carrying various unidentifiable objects.

"Spacecraft?" Sharabi gasped.

"Could just as easily be something else," Roscha argued, but he didn't believe it. "Some monolithic temple...or...or who knows what...."

"Sure looks like a flying saucer, though, doesn't it?" Sharabi shined his flashlight in his own face. He was smiling broadly.

"I'd have to admit, the Martian book suggests a compelling link."

The alabaster figures continued all the way down the wall, a ceramic scroll whose entire length told glorious, if mysterious, stories of a past people's lives. Several pictures showed mastodons and other upper Neolithic animals, now extinct, but the renderings were much more naturalistic and sophisticated than those at *Lescaux* in France from about the same dating.

Descending a staircase, they encountered water.

"Moab!" Sharabi called. "Get some men with buckets. We need to clear the water from the bottom of the stairwell. Bring some lanterns, too."

"Don't you have a generator?"

"We do, just no gas to run it. Cursed Kurds! Have to save what's left for the boats and the truck. We'll use it if we have to."

They set up a half-dozen kerosene lanterns around the perimeter of the gallery, in whose flickering soft yellow light the figures on the storied wall danced eerily, as if a magic potion had resurrected the ageless dead, who again went about the daily burden of their lives. A dozen workers formed a bucket brigade. Soon water began to gush from the tomb.

* * *

"Sharabi! Sharabi!" Moab yelled. "Quickly!"

Instead of the water flooding the entire tomb, it only filled the stairwell at the entranceway, leaving the tomb itself completely sealed off by a wall of what appeared to be clay, probably glazed over brick or stone, which formed a doorway. Workmen scrubbed away a thick layer of mud with coarse rags and sponges to reveal an astonishing work of art.

Roscha's heart skipped a beat when he saw it. "Same characters here as the inscription on the chalice."

"Yes," Sharabi said. "We'll no doubt find it throughout, unless I miss my guess."

"Must be the royal pair themselves," Roscha guessed, scanning the beautiful full-length color portrait of a king and a queen, resplendently arrayed in what appeared to be funereal attire. For the fresco also contained images that suggested a trip to the afterworld, the means of conveyance being something that looked very much like the saucer-shaped object they had seen in the main gallery.

"A double tomb?" Sharabi's eyes shown large in the flickering light. "Could we be so lucky?"

"It does appear the journey was booked double occupancy. You'll want pictures before we deconstruct the fresco, won't you?" Roscha didn't want to step on Sharabi's archaeological aspirations; he wanted Sharabi to be the one to okay the tomb's opening. Oh, he could not have cared less at this point about the scientific niceties of preserving data, and if necessary, he was more than willing to forge on alone, secretly if circumstances demanded.

"Kopi!" Sharabi shouted, his voice echoing in staccato reverberations that produced trickles of loose earth. "We'll let the men clean all this mud first."

"I am here, Great One." Kopi slid down the bluff face from the top, causing a small landslide and sending a good deal of dirt on top of the workers below, finally landing in a heap in front of Sharabi and Roscha.

"Go and get my camera," Sharabi said. "The one with the flash attached. And, Kopi—"

"Yes, Great One?"

"Bring a gas can, too. We're going to need the generator." He looked at Roscha and shrugged. "Hurry, now.... After the pictures, we'll try to cut out the perimeter. Just in case it is a door we can open without ruining the fresco. You agree?"

"Whatever you say, old friend. It's your dig." He only wanted to hurry.

All afternoon they worked with crowbar, hammer and stone chisels, but to no avail. The door, if such it was, would not budge.

Roscha was about to suggest they try the diamond-bladed saw and worry about reconstructing the fresco later, when all the workers dropped their implements and began to congregate on the steps of the main gallery.

"Prayer time." Sharabi said. "Let's break—"

"Wait a minute." Roscha grabbed his arm. Something had caught his eye. "Let me have your flashlight."

"What do you see?"

"Look at the queen's scepter," he said, pointing to a bright spot showing through the mud. "The yellow of the gold shaft is lighter—much lighter—on the last third or so. See?"

"Why yes," Sharabi acknowledged. "It's been painted over."

"And look here...around the loop of the ankh, where the scepter points. There's a slight depression. Like—"

"A key hole?" Sharabi asked.

"It's certainly in the right position—"

"Doors with hinges and locks hadn't been invented twenty or thirty thousand years ago."

"Even I knew that," Roscha said peevishly. A shiver rippled through him as the enormity of the discovery struck him.

Sharabi took a stone chisel and a hammer from his leather tool bag. "Hold the light, will you?"

Luckily, pictures had been taken, because the clay crumbled into a million tiny pieces. Reconstructing the fresco now would be difficult, if not impossible.

Sharabi stopped for a moment, appearing to be unsure. Roscha feared he wouldn't want to go on.

"Oh, hell," Sharabi finally said. "What's the difference now." And he went back to his chiseling.

The material used on the repair was clearly different from the remainder of the fresco, leaving open the possibility of preserving the rest. After just two more strikes, the last portion of the inscribed area fell away, revealing a horizontal slit in the stone about three inches high and six inches long. Sharabi picked up a steel tamping bar. "Now, if this is what I think it is..."

With surprisingly little effort, the sliding stone lock disengaged. They both pushed on the huge stone door, but it opened silently with little force. They again looked at each other, this time with the look of two boys standing on the precipice at the edge of a quarry swimming hole, wondering who will jump first.

But Roscha knew the etiquette. "After you, Youssef." Sharabi nodded, then entered the tomb slowly. Roscha followed with the same reverent deliberation.

Sharabi moved his flashlight quickly, panning the entire tomb in a matter of seconds. *"Empty!"*

Roscha's heart sank. "That explains the door."

"It must have been robbed millennia ago. Look here!" Sharabi walked along the beam of light, which now fell on the sarcophagus in the middle of the chamber; its beautifully sculpted cover lay propped up against the side. "Nothing! Not a single blessed bone!"

"Let me see that flashlight." Roscha knelt down by the sarcophagus cover, running his hands over the rough gouges and grooves where gold had been chiseled from the death masks, his fingers dipping into the eye pits, where once precious stones surely had lain. Moving down to the breastplate of the king, he stopped. "Maybe not a complete disappointment, old friend," he said, his heart racing. "Look at this."

The inscription carved in alabaster on the breastplate was short: only twelve lines, ending with a single word of four characters.

"Same language as the chalice."

But there was more. Roscha found the same discourse repeated below in the language from the Martian book. "You said you didn't believe we could be this lucky? Well, we just won the Powerball."

Outside, the excited voices of the workers, who had started to trickle back after their prayer, rose to a din. "Moab! Moab!"

"Let's close it up for now," Sharabi said. "I don't want anyone else in here yet."

Crossing the threshold of the door, they encountered Moab. "The tomb, Sharabi. I want to see it." His tone verged on a demand.

"I've sealed it for now," Sharabi told him. "We'll need time to consider the proper disposition of the tomb's—"

"But I helped to discover…. I have a right to—"

"No!" Sharabi said forcefully. "You have only the right to leave if you don't follow my instructions. Besides, there is nothing to see."

"The tomb was robbed," Roscha confirmed. "Probably many times over the centuries."

Glaring at Sharabi, Moab placed his hand on his gun, wheeled around and retreated up the stairs.

"He's one to worry about," Roscha said.

"I know. But for now we need him."

"Anyone you can trust to watch him."

"Only you, me and Kopi."

* * *

Roscha was tired. His bones ached. His muscles were sore. He was not used to so much physical labor. But, he thought, it all made the beer, cooled by the deep waters of the Euphrates, taste all the better. "What do you make of all this, Youssef?" he said, picking up the Martian book and waving it in the direction of the tomb. "The Martian book, the tomb, the ankh...."

"I think we are in the midst of another Copernican revolution."

"Meaning?"

"Think about it. What must Copernicus have felt like when he first realized with certainty that the Earth was no longer the center of his universe?"

He slowly mulled the antiquarian proposition. "I'm not sure I follow you."

"It just proves, once again, that our perceptions rule our behaviors, no?"

Roscha groaned as he lifted his stiff legs onto the cot. He propped himself up with his sleeping bag. A scarab beetle raced out from underneath and crawled up the tent post beside his head. "Depends on your point of view, I suppose."

"Exactly," Sharabi said. "Until Copernicus, people lived their lives in the certainty of the Church's edicts on such issues—for them the Earth *was* the center of the universe." Sharabi popped a date into his mouth, chewing quickly as he spoke. "Not that that kind of conceit is the province of religion only—"

"Oh, it's the best part of it. Just look at the Muslims and the Jews—"

"And the Christians." Sharabi took a swig of beer. "Oh, yes. Make no mistake. A Holy War there will be."

"What's Copernicus got to do with this?"

"In his day, the guiding faith was religion. No more. Not in the Western world. Science is today's religion, science and technology. We scientists are just as guilty as the high priests of the past." He pointed his beer-filled hand at the tomb. "Like our friends in that tomb. And the result is the same." He guzzled the remainder of his beer, crushed the can between his palms, and then flopped down in his canvas chair, slapping his hands on his knees. "We've forgotten that science is a method of finding truth—it's *not* truth itself. Not even the only road to truth."

Roscha was not at all sure that he agreed with his friend. He knew Miles Lavisch wouldn't. *Poor bastard. I just don't want to be next.* He watched the beetle hitching its way up the post to about his eye level. "Truth is a large subject, old friend—"

"And our powers to know it so weak."

"Oh, truth isn't always so hard to find. It's just that it is easier to believe blindly in something than to get to know its truth. That takes too much work for most people."

"Truth lies all about us like sparkling gems," Sharabi declared, "but we roam the world in dark glasses. And when we do notice a faint glint of it, we pick it up and, as often as not, discard it, unable to accept what it is because what it implies about us is too unpleasant."

"Yeah, same thing I guess." Roscha nervously flicked open the top of his lighter, then closed it. He pondered his next move. He wondered how Sharabi would react when he told him he was leaving, or if he should tell him at all. "People don't like the truth when it conflicts with their own self-image and their own prejudices." He held his cigarette against the tent pole, letting the smoke drift up around the beetle.

"You've got it right," Sharabi agreed. "But make no mistake, our view of ourselves—of humanity—will never be the same when word of all this gets out!"

"You're right about that. And just as in Copernicus's time, someone always wants to suppress new knowledge—for whatever reason. If it's not the Church, it's the government. If it's not our enemies, it's our friends."

"Or ourselves."

Roscha ran his fingers through his bushy white hair, brushing out the accumulated sand of the day. He continued to flick his lighter on and off, thinking of Carl Snow and the CIA's considerable resources, wondering how soon they'd find him. When he thought of his predicament, he wished Miles's had never shown up on his doorstep. But nevertheless, wasn't this what he'd gone into science for in the first place? The sheer joy of discovery? He blew smoke rings at the helpless beetle, which seemed to be paralyzed by the fumes. "What about the ankh Kopi found?"

"Probably an archetype," Sharabi posited. "An example of parallel invention."

"Maybe."

"But I've been thinking about the Martian connection. Did you know that the ancient Arabic name for Cairo, Egypt, was Mars?"

"I didn't!"

"But I'm afraid all we can say for sure about the ankh, and all this, for that matter, is that there was some communication between beings on Mars and Earth, some many eons ago."

"Over thirty thousand years ago. Maybe more." He thought Sharabi looked tired.

"Unless we can somehow decipher the book…" Sharabi threw his hands up.

"We may never know." And that was what scared him.

Sharabi sipped his beer and leaned back in his creaky canvas chair. "I thought we had a chance today at the tomb—with that sarcophagus."

"Me too." Roscha took another drag off his smoke and inhaled deeply. He blew it at the beetle, which seemed to vibrate oddly, then drop to the ground on its back, its legs running on thin air momentarily, before regaining the upright. "Thought we had our Rosetta stone."

"Yes, too bad. Two strange languages pose twice the problem. But you know, it was interesting. The inscription, I mean. It's like Catholic liturgies. In English, then repeated in Latin. Exact same form."

Roscha butted his cigarette on the back of the hapless beetle as it tried to crawl beneath his cot. He felt his expression fall somber. Then, intending not a hint of humor, he said: "Well, it may as well be Martian."

* * *

Sharabi's bare arms were pimpled with goose bumps. The rose colored pre-dawn sky was cloudless. For a second, Roscha's parting words the previous night caught in his mind. He shivered. We'll concentrate on the lowest level we can reach today, he thought, as he dumped a streaming ribbon of sand from his boot, like the sand from an hourglass.

Below, the day's first prayers rose to Allah. Sharabi, as was his habit, took the binoculars and scanned the work area. As the prayers ended, the men began to congregate near the tents on the top of the bluff, instead of dispersing to their various work areas as usual. That's odd, he thought. Moab always gave the men their orders for the day's work the previous evening, so that work could begin without delay early the following morning. And there was Kopi, kicking up a cloud of dust as he ran up the hill toward him. What was he up to so early in the morning?

"Great One!" the boy said, panting. "Moab is gone!"

"Gone where?"

"He took one of the boats!"

# CHAPTER 22

Peter lay on a lumpy bed in a cheap Tel Aviv hotel where he and Molly had checked in as Mr. and Mrs. Amadeev, a name the mysterious Joseph had selected for their phony documents. The room had the stale, moldy smell so familiar to bargain-basement travelers, but at least the linens were clean, and it had a radio, if not a TV.

He listened to an English-language station that played top-forty hits by Hooty and the Blowfish, 'NSync and other groups he'd never heard of and liked even less; he wished they'd play some Country. Patsy Cline. Conway Twitty. Or Faith Hill. Hell, he'd even welcome the Beatles at this point. Yet the familiarity of the pop form, all-American as it was, brought only small relief from the vexing homesickness he felt. Perhaps because, unlike at any other time—even when he'd been to war—he didn't believe he'd see home again.

He took out his wallet and removed a frayed and yellowed piece of paper bound with plastic. It was the last letter he'd received from his father, postmarked Saigon, Vietnam. He read it whenever he felt the grip of lonely isolation. Yet today it failed to cheer him. He wondered if his father, had he lived, would have been something like Cap. But then he was gone now too.

He flipped out his Honus Wagner card, kissed it and thought that if he had any security at all in this world, this was it, in both form and substance.

"What's our next move?" Molly asked from the bathroom, where she'd gone to wash up.

"After today... I'm just about out of cards to play. Who'd of thought an archaeologist's whereabouts would be top-secret stuff? Well, we know he's moved to the Rockefeller Museum. So I guess we'll go to Jerusalem tomorrow."

"It is strange," she called from behind the door. "What could be so hush-hush in the field of archaeology, anyway?"

"I don't know. We'll find out in the morning."

Molly walked out of the bathroom, as usual fully buttoned up in the cotton pajamas she had picked up in London. But he could not help noticing the firm curve of her breasts and the way her nipples rose, causing the blue print fabric to crinkle slightly as it pulled away. Her hips were womanly wide and inviting. Her freshly washed face glowed pink from rubbing with the coarse linen washcloths, giving her an even more blushing, youthful appeal. Her hair, fluffed full with a towel into disarray, flared about her head in uneven curls, like red flames, framing her face in an oval aura of heated light.

"You know," he said with serene confidence, "we've been together for nearly a week. Eating together. Even sleeping together—well, in the same room, anyway. And you know what?"

"What's that?" She stood before the small oval mirror with its spider-web of cracks, striking an almost domestic pose. She began to brush her hair, seeming only half interested in what he'd said.

"We haven't even kissed since our first date. I must be losing my touch."

She turned to look at him, but quickly turned back and continued brushing. "I'm sure I wouldn't know. Besides, we haven't exactly been on holiday."

"No, but we're not talking rocket science, either. Insert tab 'A' into slot 'B.'" He noticed the first flourishes of a blush brighten her upper chest and neck, and the idea of what thoughts must have engendered that reaction delighted him.

She brushed faster.

He caught her eyes in the mirror. She stopped brushing. He moved closer, holding her with his eyes, never risking so much as a blink. Slowly, he put his arm around her waist, turning her, then pulled her close. He felt not a whisker of protest. "Now," he said, feeling the familiar rush of easy conquest. “About losing my touch. You’re not going to spoil my reputation are you?”

“Shouldn’t that be my line?” she said without retreating.

He felt the warmth of her body, even before they touched, smelled the faintest hint of the perfumed soap she’d used. Lilacs. His favorite.

They embraced as all lovers do, with passion, trepidation, and hope. His hands moved from her soft, still-damp red tresses to her shoulders, on down her back, his fingers exploring the tiny valley of her spine, then up onto the soft mounds of her buttocks. He felt her nipples harden under her pajamas as he pressed them into his chest. He experienced her lips as none before, like a returning innocence, a renewal. The sensation shocked him. He reached for her buttons.

She pushed him away.” No,” she said softly.

“But I want you,” he whispered, nuzzling her neck. He felt her hot breath on his shoulder.

“Peter,” she sighed, sitting him down on one bed while she sat across from him on the other, “it pleases me that you find me attractive enough to—”

“Enough?” he sniffed. “Molly, you don’t know just how attractive you are.”

She hesitated a moment, looked down at her toes, her blush now seemed in full flower.

He moved over beside her, but she quickly exchanged places with him, moving to the other bed.

“Please listen, Peter.” She drew herself up, as if about to make a some momentous pronouncement. “Considering what we’ve been through together already—practically a lifetime’s worth of shared experience...” She laughed, throwing her head back and stretching her hands out, pressed together as if in prayer. “I really do feel like Mrs. Amadeev. But—” She wrinkled up her face.

“Let’s skip the small talk—”

“No. We have to talk.”

He started to move toward her but, seeing her body stiffen, thought better of it and sat back down. “We’ve got the CIA, the FBI and God knows who else after us. They all want to kill us. We may be dead tomorrow. All we've got is each other, Molly. And I want you. Now!"

"It would be nice if you *needed* me, as well." She cocked her head to the side, pausing uncertainly.

Funny, the women he'd known of late hadn't much cared about that.

"You'd think at nearly thirty I'd, I'd," she stammered, "be good at this by now."

"Good at what?"

She squirmed.

"Trust me," he countered. "You've got all the right equipment, and you're not going to tell me you don't know how to use it?"

Sensing he'd made some progress, he moved beside her, but she stood up.

"What I mean is, there's no denying our animal nature. Believe me, I'm just as turned on as you."

"That's good to hear...." He couldn't quite see the connection.

At first she looked rather hurt, but then she knotted up her hands and punched the bed. "But...But... I am not an animal. Not just an animal, anyway."

"What are you, a zoologist?" he laughed.

"You mean AJ didn't tell you? She told you everything else."

"What are you babbling about?"

She started to cry. "I-I can't, Peter. My-my-my b-body is sacred to me. It-it's a treasure I'll give as a gift to the man I m-marry, the man who'll father my-my-my children."

He felt like a fool when he realized it. "You mean you're a-a-a—now you got me doin' it—you're a *virgin?*"

She nodded.

"I didn't know there were any of you left." He threw back he head and chuckled.

"It's not funny."

"Yes it is. And AJ was right about one thing: You don't know anything about men."

She wiped her tears with her pajama sleeve. "And you're no Einstein with women, either. What makes you think I want to hear about AJ at a time like this?"

"You brought her up, not me." Oddly, the comment stung him. He flopped back on the bed, shaking his head in disbelief. "She was wrong about something else, though?"

"Oh?"

"You're not just a crippled plain Jane."

She started to sob, collapsing onto the bed. "No. AJ's right. I *am* a plain Jane. I don't know anything about men. M-m-maybe I'm j-just jealous of her."

He watched the blades on the wobbly ceiling fan beat the warm, musty air. He wanted to laugh out loud again, but he couldn't bring himself to do it. He watched her pull herself together, her puffy red face full of dignity, and he thought how pretty she really was. He saw her take one of her big breaths and hold it. He was beginning to sense her signals. She looked at him like a stricken puppy.

"If you'd just let me explain my feelings—"

"Not necessary," he said with an edge he immediately recognized as childish pique. Suddenly he felt shallow and clumsy. "But you know what? I think it's the other way around."

"W-What do you mean?"

"I honestly got the feeling AJ was jealous of you."

# CHAPTER 23

Paul Blalock sat next to Carl Snow in the admiral's limousine as it streaked through the Whitehouse gates and headed down Pennsylvania Avenue. They had just left the President, who had wanted to express personally his condolences at the loss of Jack Beamis and wanted to be kept apprised of any progress on the investigation into his death. *My God!* he thought, squirming uncomfortably on the black leather seats. *Who's next? The president himself?*

Blalock slipped off his wire-rimmed glasses and brushed back his close-cropped reddish blond hair, damp with sweat. Out of the corner of his eye, he stealthily tried to assess the inscrutable admiral's mood. Events had skidded too far out of bounds, beyond his control and, perhaps worse, the admiral's. He was just a passenger now, swept along by some hidden logic. Killing civilians was one thing, but doing the deputy director had not set well with him. What was even more immediately troubling was the admiral's silence. Since losing track of Molly Lavisch a few days ago, Blalock had been expecting the unpredictable man to explode, but Snow had asked for no updates, given no orders. His silent non-reaction was ominous. With Snow, nothing could be taken for granted, and Blalock worried that the admiral now found him expendable as well. *Especially if I can't locate the book.* Unfortunately, he had no leads. He looked sideways at Snow and just wished the man would just say something—anything.

But the admiral, as if in a trance, stared out the window, maintaining the shield of his thoughts, rolling a cigarette end over end, back forth between the fingers of his left hand like a baton.

Suddenly, the limo phone warbled to life.

"Snow, here." After a moment's listening, he put his hand over the receiver and with a raised eyebrow said, "Someone who says he knows something about Miles Lavisch's death wants to talk to me."

"May I suggest you take the call, sir?" Blalock advised lamely.

"Put him through."

The admiral's ruddy complexion blanched. His scalp pulled back as his eyes widened. A disparaging stare formulated itself and came to rest on Blalock. It was the look that always made his rectal sphincters pucker.

"Admiral?" Bewildered, Blalock had never before seen even a subtle failure of the admiral's composure.

"Well, well, Professor Lavisch. I'm glad the rumors of your violent death were so wildly exaggerated.... Of course we could use your help, Miles." There was a pause. "My office in an hour? Very well, then, the Castle steps at the Smithsonian in thirty minutes." He hung up.

*"Miles Lavisch?"* Blalock gagged. "But how?"

"That's what you damned right better be finding out, Clousseau."

Blalock hunkered down in place, grinding his clenched fists hard into the leather seat. "Does he have the book?"

"No. But he says he knows who does."

* * *

Miles Lavisch was exhausted. He'd been sleeping in his car for nearly a week. He was dirty, hungry and scared as he approached Admiral Snow and Paul Blalock, who sat on a bench across the street from the Smithsonian's red stone Castle building on the mall between the Washington Monument and the U. S. Capitol.

To Miles's surprise, he'd walked past them unnoticed in his street-person garb: dirty, grease-stained overalls, brown herring-bone tweed jacket with frayed green elbow patches, ragged buff fedora, and a crudely fashioned fake beard. He carefully surveyed the crowd, swollen with hundreds of school children and the ever-present tourists, for possible Snow confederates. Satisfied he could make a safe retreat in the crowd if needs be, with heart pounding, he sat down between Snow and Blalock without looking at either.

"Greetings, Miles," Snow said with obvious false cordiality.

"Looks like you could use a shave, Miles." Blalock observed snidely.

"I want to live," Miles pleaded. "That's all I want."

"And we want the Martian book," Snow said matter-of-factly. "That's all we want."

"Why bargain with him?" Blalock sneered. "Because of him, several innocent people have died, including, apparently, his own brother."

"I'm supposed to believe that's my fault?" Miles hung his head and carved grooves in the sandy earth with the edge of his shoe and wondered if he'd made a mistake. His chest stung with every labored breath. "I never dreamed it would come to this. I thought you'd arrest me before I said anything about the book, not start shooting—"

"Oh, bullshit." Snow spit a streamer of nasal phlegm as he draped his arm across Miles's shoulders, where he nervously rapped his Naval Academy ring on the wooden bench next to Miles's ear.

Blalock laughed. "Our Punctilious Professor would have us believe he didn't think we'd shoot."

"No, Miles," Snow declared. "You're a calculating sonofabitch. You knew, all right."

The truth was, Miles really felt no remorse at Malcolm's demise, having long resented the presence on the earth of someone with his body but of such a flabby intellectual disposition and such squishy moral sentiments. "I want to make a deal, Admiral Snow. I can help you get the book. And, yes, you could say I've been properly chastised. If I live to be a hundred, I'll never mention alien artifacts—"

"Now he's a psychic," Blalock snapped. "Predicting the future."

Out of the corner of his eye, Miles noticed Snow flick Blalock's neck.

"You, my fat friend," Snow said slowly, "are in no position to make deals."

Now Miles's head swam disconcertingly. He'd been off his medications and he knew his blood sugar had to be off the charts. He felt helpless and confused. Maybe they already had the book. What then? His heart thrummed in his ears. "Really? You think my daughter has the book, don't you?"

Snow stopped tapping his Academy ring on the bench rail. "Go on, professor. "

"No, I won't say any more. Not until I have some assurances."

Admiral Snow took out a Cuban Partagas cigar, pinched off its tip and handed it to him. Then, lighting it, he said in the casual tone of a schoolboy, "There's no longer a need to harm you, Miles. But I will insist that Paul stay with you. Just until we can recover the book."

"I have your solemn word, then? On my safety?" Admiral Snow nodded. "All right, then…Roscha Venable has the book. And I think I know where he might be."

# CHAPTER 24

Bandar Bliss luxuriated in the warmth of a hashish fog. Lying half buried in a pile of brocaded silk pillows, each painstakingly hand-embroidered with designs featuring men and women in various forms of sexual congress, he surveyed the opulent surroundings of his Baghdad home, his favorite of five princely estates scattered about the Middle East, and was for the moment content. Sucking an idle draft from his hookah, he drifted into dreamy semi-consciousness. Until the annoyingly incessant *bing-bong* of the door chime cut through his drug-induced reverie. It was late, past ten o'clock. Why hadn't his manservant Omar gotten the door? *Useless tripe.* With his fleshy elbow, he jabbed Tatia, a raven-haired sixteen-year-old Pakistani girl whose parents had her sold into bondage for less than one hundred Saudi riyals.

"Get up, woman. Go see who's at the door."

Quickly complying, she returned but a moment later. "It's a man named Moab," she said numbly. "He says you'll want to see him."

"Did he say why?" He hit his hookah once more, feeling the warm, moist smoke drench his lungs. His mood, however, was no longer elevated.

"He says you know him," the slightly built girl added. "Says he sold you some statues last year...someplace in the Negev. He says there's an American in the desert who's found something he knows you'll want to buy. Something big." She stood motionless, glassy-eyed. She covered a sleepy yawn with her petite hand. "What must I tell him, Master?"

"Send him away." He threw a pillow at her, making her jump like a frightened rabbit as she disappeared behind the diaphanous doorway curtain.

Just then Bliss's cell phone rang, somewhere deep among the folds of his silk robe, but he was unable to locate it. Like the doorbell, its ring was coarse and irritating. Frustrated, he ripped the sash free and tore out the lining, finally reaching the pocket-sized phone and flipping the cover. "Admiral Snow?"

"Mister Ambassador," Snow began. "Sorry to bother you at this late hour."

"No, no," Bliss assured him, surprised at Snow's unusually reverential tone, which he took to mean that Snow wanted something badly—and quickly. "It's always a pleasure to hear from you, Admiral. And please, call me Bandar."

"It seems once again we find ourselves in need of your special talents."

"Of course of course. I'm at your service as always. How can I help?"

"We're trying to locate a couple of Americans in your neck of the woods.

"How do you say—neck?"

"In your area, Bandar. A Mister Roscha Venable and woman named Molly Lavisch. We think he might be with a Palestinian named Youssef Sharabi. The woman is looking for him. So they might be together."

"I know of a Sharabi, an archaeologist—"

"That's the one. I'm faxing you a picture of Venable and the woman now. If you help us... Well, you know the drill."

"Please, please, Admiral, allow your humble servant to serve." He was already thinking how much he could hold the old bastard hostage for. It wasn't a question of money, as he knew everyone thought. Oh, one could never have too much money; such was true. But it was revenge that was now of paramount interest. Snow was a powerful American, whose arrogance tested his own, and now he needed him, Bandar. He laughed silently. Did Snow think that he hadn't noticed every slight, every nuanced jab from him and his lackey Blalock? "If I may ask, sir, what do you want with them?"

"We think he may be trying to sell classified documents."

"And if I find him?"

"Just call me. We'll handle it from there."

"Very well. You will be hearing from me." He flipped the phone closed. *Moab? Where have I heard? Ah, yes... That dig rat.* "Tatia! Don't keep or guest waiting. Bring him in. Quickly!"

* * *

Roscha sat frowning on the cot in Sharabi's tent as he watched Sharabi dart in and out of the tent with his binoculars. "What are you going to do about Moab?"

"What can I do? For now, I've got the men back to work on the third level. But I'm afraid we can expect trouble—sooner rather than later."

"What kind of trouble?"

"No doubt Moab thinks the tomb is loaded with priceless antiquities. He's gone to Bliss or someone like him."

"Antiquities dealers?"

"Thieves!" Sharabi said. "Oh, some, like Bliss, fancy themselves something more, high-class collectors of rare antiquities or even amateur archaeologists. Moab will offer his services to one of them. Either that, or he'll come back with a band of his own thugs and steal whatever he can. In any case, there will be trouble. I know it."

"What can I do?" Roscha asked the question aware of his sounding less than enthusiastic. In truth, he'd decided to leave. He already had just about as much trouble as he could stand, and besides, the empty tomb probably meant he'd have to come up with Plan B, for the CIA couldn't be that far behind.

Sharabi took a Colt 45 automatic pistol out of a footlocker and handed it to Roscha. He took the cool, heavy metal pistol. He didn't know one end of a gun from the other. Now he knew he'd better leave sooner, rather than later. "You're serious?"

"I'll not let them destroy everything I've worked for. If it means a fight, a fight they'll get. If you want to leave, I'll understand."

"Who is this Bliss, anyway?"

"His hobby is being Saudi ambassador to the U. S. But he's better known in these parts as a snake. A sadistic, monumentally greedy snake. Story goes he was an identical twin, but he killed his brother in the womb. Others claim he's one of Saddam Hussein's large flock. Oh, I don't know how true that is, but still..." Sharabi fidgeted nervously. Suddenly he jumped up, stuck his head past the tent flap, and looked right and left, like a crook on a lookout.

"You've got to get a hold of yourself. Maybe you should contact the authorities—"

But Sharabi ignored him, plopping down in his canvas chair, shaking his head. "So they say, besides money, Bliss loves only two things—his mother and *snakes.*"

Roscha laughed. "Just a cute 'n' cuddly mamma's boy, eh?"

On his feet again, Sharabi didn't respond and continued to pace. Roscha motioned him to sit down, which, haltingly, he did, before jumping up again. "And I'm serious about the snakes. He imports the venomous ones from all over the world—vipers, cobras, mambas, you name it. Rumor has it he killed Brandon Hadid by putting a cobra in his tent."

"I didn't know Brandy was dead."

"Murdered!" Sharabi resumed his jack-in-the-box act. Grabbing the binoculars, he walked outside, babbling as he went.

Now less frightened than he was annoyed, Roscha fairly shouted: "Would you please sit still a moment? What do you mean, murdered?"

"By Bliss. Just last year. Of course nobody could prove the snake belonged to Bliss. How could they? But Brandon was sleeping at the time—and his tent had a canvas floor, no holes. It couldn't have gotten in on its own. And Bliss is known to have ended up with many of the most valuable finds from Brandon's dig. Which is illegal. Which is why he's *persona non grata* in Israel, even in an official capacity."

Roscha stretched and stood up. He was tired, not eager for a fight with anyone. He tossed the gun aside and followed Sharabi outside the tent. He thought about telling Sharabi now that he'd be leaving, but thought better of it. Suddenly Kopi came running between them wielding an oddly shaped object as if it were a sword. He slashed the air in great flourishes, pretending to vanquish some imaginary foe. By odd chance, some significant factor of shape or texture or coloration registered in Roscha's mind. He glanced at Sharabi. "What does he have?"

"A stick?"

"Kopi! Come here!"

But the boy continued his imaginary warfare, laughing and shouting a curious mixture of Arabic and English curses as he made mock charges at both men.

"Cigarettes?" Sharabi said with a shrug.

Roscha took out a fresh pack of Marlboros and dangled the bait. The young warrior stopped. "What do you have there, Kopi? Can I see it?"

"A mighty sword, Great One. *My* sword."

"Where did you find it?"

"Down there." He pointed to the excavation area. Cautiously, he walked up and reached for the cigarettes, but Roscha withdrew them.

"Tell you what, Kopi," Roscha said, "I'll give you another whole pack of cigarettes just for letting Youssef and me look at *your* knife. It is *his* knife, isn't it, Youssef? Finders, keepers—it's still the law of the land, even here, isn't it?"

Kopi stepped forward and reached for the cigarettes, but held the object behind him

Roscha pulled them back. "First the knife!"

Finally the boy handed the knife to Roscha. "I'll be damned!" His heart nearly took leave of his chest, for it was clear this was indeed an important find. "Take a look, old friend. You're better at cuneiform than I."

"Ha!" Sharabi smiled hugely. "Kopi just may have found our Rosetta stone."

* * *

Sharabi watched the rising tail of dust behind the approaching vehicle and wondered how much help Roscha would be when the chips were down. "I knew it! Bliss. Has to be, it's a limo. Better put that knife away, Roscha."

"What are you going to tell him?"

"Nothing."

"Why not just show him the tomb? There really isn't anything to steal."

"He'd never believe we hadn't hidden the nonexistent treasure."

The sun dipped low in the desert sky, growing redder with each degree of descent; its still-strong rays painted the sides of Bandar Bliss's white-on-white Mercedes limousine a soft pink. Above, to the east, the nearly full, ascendant moon began its trek across the heavens of the encroaching night, as the overloaded limo, bouncing on its worn out shocks, heaved to a stop beside Sharabi's truck. Out stepped the driver, who smartly opened the passenger door with a swift, smooth motion, then bowed until his head nearly scraped the ground. On the other side of the car there emerged two muscular men whose very appearance implied threat, but who were not visibly armed. Bliss rolled out, adjusting his kaffiyeh, the sash of which was supported by an embroidered silk rope studded with little golden cobra heads. He put his hand into the pocket of his white British regimental jacket as if to retrieve something but withdrew it empty, patting the pocket gently. Behind him Moab cowered like a mangy lapdog.

"Good evening, Mister Sharabi," Bliss began, extending his hand. "I believe you already know my associate, Mister Moab Abdul—"

"I know the snake." Sharabi caught himself. "Oh, forgive me! I forgot. You *like* snakes."

"I'm gratified you know who I am."

"Only by reputation, which I'm sorry to say, isn't flattering."

"As for Mister Abdul," Bliss continued, "he's a man of ambition, if not exquisite breeding."

Sharabi sneered and spit on the ground near Moab. "An ambitious thief! He stole one of my boats—and God knows what else. And he's cost me at least two day's work."

Bliss shrugged. "As I was saying, Mister Abdul lacked employment. I had a position." He looked over his shoulder into the limousine. "Come, my darling. Don't be shy." With that, his young concubine slid across the expansive white leather seat and planted her shoeless feet on the sandy ground.

"What are you doing here?" Sharabi demanded abruptly.

"Moab tells me you have some articles that may be of interest to me." Bliss seemed to survey the compound as he spoke. "These archaeological projects are always under funded, emmm?" He paused as if to gauge the effect of his words. "Perhaps a sizable donation in support of your efforts here might interest you?"

Sharabi thought how transparent the man was, how lacking in finesse. He stared at Bliss and his entourage, assessing the odds if the confrontation deteriorated beyond its dismal beginnings. He glanced at Roscha, who stood silently beside him with arms defiantly crossed, and felt slightly better.

"So you see, Mister Sharabi, I'm here on business. If you show me what you've found, I might be able to help you."

Sharabi stiffened. "We have nothing to sell."

"Moab tells a different story. He says there's a tomb and—"

"We have nothing to sell! He's right about the tomb, but it was cleaned out long ago."

"And a very interesting book," Bliss said, stepping closer to Sharabi, his posture looser, friendlier. "Come now, where's that fabled Palestinian hospitality? Have you nothing to offer weary travelers? If not food, perhaps a cool drink, while we talk a bit more, eh? But allow me." With the clap of his hands, Bliss summoned the driver, who quickly produced an ice chest, and then stood at attention, awaiting further instructions.

"What do you say, Mister Sharabi? May we sit awhile in your tent?"

"All right," Sharabi relented, "but *Mister* Abdul and the others stay outside."

Inside the tent, Sharabi positioned the requisite number of canvas chairs in such a way that he could keep an eye on the entrance and be within reach of his 45. Bliss, after several futile attempts to fit his wide bottom into the narrow chair, finally sat on the ground. Sharabi knew the polite thing would be to join his discomfited guest on the floor, but he and Roscha retained their seats. He took no small delight in the scowl that came instantly to Bliss's face as he nodded to his dutiful young slave, who quickly took to his side on the floor.

"Bandar Bliss," the Arab said with a smile, extending his hand to Roscha. "I'm sure it was just an oversight that Mister Sharabi didn't introduce us."

"Roscha...Roscha Venable."

"And what brings you here, Mister Venable?"

"Just a visit to an old friend," he said with a weak grin.

"I see. Well..." Bliss glanced at Sharabi. "May I call you Youssef?"

"Mister Sharabi will do nicely."

Unfazed, Bliss removed his kaffiyeh, allowing his braided pigtail to fall down his back to the ground. "Well, *Mister Sharabi.* Since my reputation precedes me, you must be aware of my interest in antiquities. You also must know that I deal fairly with men who deal fairly with—"

Sharabi grunted, his distaste for the man growing by the second.

"I can even be generous. *Very* generous." Bliss gently massaged a slight bulge in his right-hand pocket. "Oh, I know, I know. You've no doubt heard some frightful stories about me."

"Brandon Hadid was a good friend of mine," Sharabi declared accusingly.

"And mine." Roscha added.

"But as you can appreciate, any man of considerable reputation is always the object of some—shall we say—bad press." His belly rippled with a slight chuckle. "The envious grumbling of lesser fish, my friend. That's all it is. And we all know what happens to lesser fish."

"And what's that?" Sharabi turned away the proffered snifter of brandy.

"Why," Bliss smiled, "they get eaten." He laughed louder this time and removed his hand from his pocket holding a small, mottled greenish-brown snake, its tongue darting furiously in and out as it writhed between the Arab's fingers.

"That's an asp!" Sharabi cried, almost falling out of his chair.

"Relax," Bliss said calmly. "You're quite right, it is an asp. And he would be exceedingly deadly if he still had his fangs." At that moment the snake bit down on Bandar's little finger. "There! You see.... Little devil. He bites, all right. You might say we have a love-hate relationship. He loves the warmth of my generosity, but hates to be handled." He laughed in a peculiar tittering way, somewhere between condescension and contempt. "Reminds you of women, doesn't it?"

"Being cold-blooded, it's more likely the warmth of your body he finds appealing," Roscha offered. "And speaking of women, can't a successful man like you afford shoes for his best girl?"

"Why? She would only need shoes if she had somewhere to go. Isn't that right, Tatia?" The girl dropped her eyes and said nothing.

Sharabi decided to take a more civil tack, thinking only to get rid of Bliss for now, so he could make more permanent plans. "Perhaps I misjudged you, Mister Bliss; you seem to be a reasonable man. Surely you understand anything I find is the property of Iraq, first, then the university, where it can be negotiated. So you see, even if I had something, which I assure you I do not, I couldn't sell it to you. Now it's been a long day. The sudden departure of *your* man, Moab, has left things in a bit of a muddle. We're very tired."

Bliss's expression changed suddenly. He stared piercingly at Sharabi. "Very well, *Mister Sharabi,* I'll be blunt. I understand you have a book from the planet Mars, odd as that may sound. I want it! And I am willing to pay handsomely for it. More money, I'm sure, than you would see in several lifetimes of your work—"

Sharabi stood up and threw back the tent flap. "I think you'd better be going."

Outside, the bright light of the newly risen moon mixed with the afterglow of the just-set sun, painting the desert a soft but eerie bluish orange. Bliss threw back his arms and inhaled a draft of cool desert air, then, with obvious pleasure, exhaled loudly. "Nothing quite so bracing as desert air in the evening. Promotes good health, don't you think?"

Sharabi ignored the attempted pleasantry.

"Consider my offer, Youssef." Bliss said, handing him a business card. Then he climbed aboard the limo. The darkly tinted window whirred down. "Don't be a little fish."

# CHAPTER 25

Molly and Peter climbed into a cab outside their hotel near the Church of the Holy Sepulcher, where, according to the Gospels, Jesus of Nazareth was laid to rest some two thousand years before. She looked up at a bright morning sun that seemed to paint a halo around Peter's tired looking face. To her, he looked more handsome than ever. Then thoughts of the previous night dimmed her spirits. She wondered if she'd done the right thing in rejecting his advances. She couldn't explain to herself anymore why her virginity mattered so much, but it did. *I guess AJ won again.*

"Rockefeller Museum," Peter told the cabby, who jabbed the accelerator. The cab jolted forward, sending several pedestrians leaping for the curb, as they careened onto Ha-Zanhanim, heading for Herod's Gate and East Jerusalem. The cab slowed as they passed the Arab marketplace. She rolled down the window. While the cab inched along at a walking pace, she marveled at the scene, which—without the cars—could easily have been from the time of Christ.

Sights, sounds and smells blended into a single sensation, forming a timeless expression of human life in the living: young boys with their brown donkeys, heavily laden with pita bread or olive wood, plowed through the crowds like ships through a turbulent sea; beautiful Palestinian women, dressed in lavishly embroidered, brightly colored dresses, boxes of figs on their heads, swayed as they walked down crowded streets, darting in and out of narrow alleyways; human voices speaking in various tongues commingled with the clanging of cookware, the clatter of feet and hooves, and music; the aroma of baking pita, numberless herbs and spices, human musk—even roses—tested her senses.

Now in the Muslim Quarter, the long black coats and hats of the Orthodox Jews disappeared, echoing the ages-old conflict between these pious, feuding peoples. Like most of the world, she'd followed with great hope the repeated attempts at peacemaking over the years, but little ever seemed to change. Then the World Trade Center cataclysm. And the Road Map became just another dead end. Now it seemed the radical Muslims had gotten their way: the world in a spasm of *Jihad*. Once again Gaza and Jericho were under Israeli control, and once again an atmosphere of violence and sudden death descended on the ancient city.

Was it this place, Jerusalem, this disputed home to three of the world's great religions with its war-zone atmosphere, that caused her to wax so melancholy today? Or was it a growing affection for Peter, which she hopelessly resisted with every doubt? Even as she thought it, she edged closer to him, close enough that her knee touched his thigh. This alone, this slight touch, was thrilling.

"This is the Eastern Gate," the driver said. "The Rockefeller is just up ahead."

The thought of what Malcolm had said about the prophecy of the Eastern Gate began to form in her mind just as the cab clipped the curb, momentarily bouncing up on two wheels. It slammed back down with a jarring screech as the driver jammed on the brakes, throwing them violently up against the front seat.

"What the hell're you doin'?" Peter barked.

*"Intifada!"* the driver gasped, pointing frantically up ahead. Then he shoved the car in reverse, tires squealing.

*Boom!*

A truck riding their bumper rammed them, blocking their way. "Go left! Left!" Peter shouted. But the driver froze, throwing up his hands, as people ran everywhere in front of the cab.

Perhaps a hundred yards ahead, Molly saw a large crowd of rock-throwing, club-wielding demonstrators. They had stopped a bus with a pile of burning tires that sent columns of sooty black smoke boiling into the cloudless blue sky. Surrounding the bus, they beat a ragged staccato against its sides with sticks, pipes and baseball bats. Even at this distance she could hear the horrified screams of the passengers as they covered their frightened faces against the shattering glass. Then a group of five or six attackers approached the bus in line abreast formation and began rocking it up and down. It looked as if they were trying to turn it over onto the black lump of fire and create an awful funeral pyre.

Suddenly, from overhead a whistling barrage of teargas canisters arced into the fray, exploding just feet in front of them. Frantic, the cab driver jerked his head right and left, searching for an escape route. But there was none.

She looked at Peter. "What now?"

"Sit tight," he told her, looking out the rear window. "Here comes the cavalry."

"The what?"

"Police... maybe military."

The milling crowd grew closer and she more nervous. Stones brought up sparks from the pavement near the cab. Several clinked off its fender. She winced. *Bang!* Gunshots cracked. She jumped. The smoky air parted enough for her to see two of the rioters near the bus fall, sending the others scurrying to take up cover behind it. Her chest tightened, her lungs shrieked with pain as the teargas flooded them.

Suddenly a spray of shattered glass stung her face. A bullet had smashed the windshield.

"Come on!" Peter yelled.

Three cab doors flew open at once. The bloody-faced driver went left, but was struck down immediately by a rock or a bullet. She started after him, but Peter grabbed her by her belt and pulled her across the seat and out his side toward an alley, which was already jammed with people trying to escape.

"This way!" Peter commanded, jerking his head toward an alley.

But she broke away, running back to the driver. She felt his neck. "He's dead!" She looked for Peter, but he was several yards away, near the wall of the old Eastern Gate, beckoning to her with waving arms, shouting for her to get down.

Before she could wonder why, she saw him. Bursting from the main body of the mob like a madman, a young protester carrying an AK-47 charged toward them, firing.

An Israeli policeman rushed to her side. "Get behind me!" Kneeling, he took quick aim at the advancing boy. But before he could fire, Molly heard a sharp *wappp!* And the policeman fell backwards onto her, bleeding from a shoulder wound. His pistol, still smoking, lay next to him. Firing incessantly, the crazed boy came closer and so did his bullets. *"Learn what intifada means! Jews die! Jews die!"*

*BOOM!*

A huge explosion knocked her to the ground. Shrapnel stung her arms, face and neck and the brightness of the day instantly faded to darkness. Dazed, she struggled to see Peter through the smoke and dust. Seconds passed like hours before she could finally see. There, where the fabled Eastern Gate had been, was a gaping hole in the old city's wall. But no Peter.

*"P-Peter!"* She got to her feet. There he was, writhing under a pile of rubble between her and the Palestinian boy, who was knocked down by the blast, but now, retrieving his gun, was back on his feet. For some reason, the boy focused on Peter. He marched with deadly determination toward him, his gun rising as he took aim. She watched the scene unfold in cinematic slow motion, every detail magnified with vivid crispness. She could see Peter move his head, see him following the barrel of the gun. A step or two more and she knew the boy would fire. Peter's hand went up in futile defense against the metal-jacketed bullet that would surely end his life with smashing bone and flesh.

*"N-Nooo! P-P-Peterrr!"* The sharp report of a shot deafened her as the boy flung his rifle into the air and crumpled into a lifeless lump. As if through someone else's eyes, using someone else's brain, she stared at her hand and dropped the policeman's smoking revolver.

Peter rose shakily to his feet. Numbly, Molly ran through a haze of smoke, dust and teargas for the boy, who now lay drenched in blood, crying out for his mother. Molly barely noticed or even cared when bullets tore through her pants leg, just missing her flesh. She fell to the boy's side just as Peter wrapped both arms around her waist and pulled.

"L-Let-let, let me go!" she screamed, struggling to break free. "I-I-I m-must help—"

"Leave him!"

Kicking free, and without really knowing why, she slapped Peter's face. "H-Help me!"

"He's dead, Molly!"

"H-He's j-j-just a child!"

"Not any more," he said and pulled her toward the alley.

"I-I'm g-going back—"

"No you're not!"

The sting of his slap shocked her. She slumped to the pavement. Limply, her head spun, lolling on her shoulders. She felt faint, thought she'd vomit. She breathed in short puffs. Finally she managed to hold one big breath, exhaling in loud, choking coughs. "Malcolm..." She took another big breath. " Uncle Malcolm was right..."

# CHAPTER 26

As the last glimmer of Bandar Bliss's limo lights had faded into the desert darkness, Sharabi and Roscha brought out the knife and the Martian book.

Roscha realized that Kopi's discovery was a godsend. A magnificent ceremonial knife about eighteen inches long, its handle, comprising about a third of its length, was of finely engraved ivory, with several dozen human and animal figures depicting scenes of hunting, war, ritual sacrifice, and various celestial bodies—including the crescent moon, which was juxtaposed with the domed object with legs seen in the tomb.

All of this was, indeed, very beautiful and interesting in its own right—a find of immense archaeological consequence. But it would have been of little value to him without the text.

A narrow rectangular space running vertically down the center of the handle was divided into three equal sections. The bottom and middle sections had the same twelve-line inscription found on the sarcophagus in the tomb, the bottom in Martian, the middle in what was now clearly an intermediate language. But the top section was in a modified cuneiform, which contained the usual wedge-shaped characters but also a goodly admixture of pictographs. The other side of the knife had a different and somewhat longer inscription, also in the three languages. While a direct reading of the text was not possible because of the lack of complete correspondence between any two languages so differently conceived—not to mention the dearth of total words—perhaps two hundred and fifty, counting both sides of the knife—because of the cuneiform, at least a partial decoding was now within reach.

Before he knew it, hours had passed unnoticed, as together they struggled to tease out the meaning of the text. Piece by piece, layer by layer, gradually, the soul of a mystery began to unfold like the petals of a rose.

"You know," Sharabi said, "there's a knife in Paris—in the Louvre—that's almost identical to this, except for having no inscriptions. Fourth millennium B.C. Egyptian, I believe."

Roscha knew the piece. "Jebel el-Arak."

"That's it! Beautiful. Has the same neatly worked flint blade as this. Same craftsmanship."

Roscha handed Sharabi the knife. He felt that with Sharabi's expertise in cuneiform, he might know enough by morning so that he could leave. But then there was the nagging question of the pictographs. "You were right, looks like some kind of simple prayer."

"Or perhaps poetry," Sharabi offered. "Hmmm...the details are so small and fine. Hard to imagine whoever did this didn't have a magnifying glass. Has to be liturgical, though. It has a cadence, like the inscription on the sarcophagus. But this other side seems to be something about a journey, a trip or something, and a war—or some other calamity."

"Those look like the royal names," Roscha ventured, pointing to the knife's lower extremity. "Can't be sure, though. It's not straightforward cuneiform. It has—"

"Yes! I know," Sharabi said. "Pictographs. Unusual. Not quite like anything I've ever seen. But some of the words are familiar. It won't be easy, but we can do it. I'm certain of that."

"Isn't that Mars, Youssef? Look in the upper right-hand corner at the astronomical formation."

"Resembles celestial depictions found in much later astronomies. Remember the zodiac?"

"It's definitely Mars," Roscha said excitedly. "Good God! There it is in text, too, just to the right of the astronomical symbol—"

"It has to be it," Sharabi agreed, his eyes wide. "The pictograph stands for Mars!"

"Looks like the top part of the ankh."

"It does, doesn't it. And here it is in the prayer—"

Roscha laughed, delighted. He just couldn't believe their good fortune. "And the modified ankh is everywhere in the text. Just like in the Martian book."

"But I still don't get its meaning. Do you?"

Roscha shook his head. "My eyes are blurring." He removed his glasses and rubbed the bridge of his nose. For the first time, he noticed his head hurt.

"Perhaps we should get some rest," Sharabi suggested, "and take it up again tomorrow morning."

"You go ahead, old friend." Roscha was too close to stop now; he was sure he could complete the work without help in a few more days. He put his glasses back on, never for a second taking his eyes off the knife and the Martian book.

* * *

Sharabi arose at daybreak. He silently approached Roscha's tent, but hearing the profound snoring that emanated from within, decided not to disturb him. "Better get the men started working first," he muttered.

Two hours later, satisfied that Habib Amar, Moab's replacement, understood his instructions regarding the day's work plan, which was to begin digging on the third level, bypassing further excavation around the royal tomb for the time being, he started back up the bluff. He had gone no more than a hundred yards when Habib Amar began shouting for him to come back.

*"A worker has fallen!"*

* * *

The man Roscha Venable saw enter the tent bore little resemblance to the man he had last seen only the night before. Sharabi's arms were scraped raw and bloody. His face was pale and drawn, his hair matted with congealed sweat, dirt and blood, his clothes tattered and torn.

"What the hell happened to you?" Roscha asked, handing Sharabi a beer. "You look like you mud wrestled a banshee and lost." He pushed a chair under Sharabi, who immediately collapsed into it. "Sorry I didn't join you today, Youssef. But I've been absorbed by the text. It's—"

"We lost one of the workers today," Sharabi muttered, shaking his head wearily. "A cave-in." Then Sharabi told him of the day's efforts to save his worker Hosne, who had fallen through the floor of the tomb into a chamber in the third, and deepest, level.

"I'm sure you did everything you could," Roscha said with outward sympathy, though to him the death of a mere laborer was inconsequential as measured against the import of his current endeavor. "You're damned lucky to be alive yourself."

Sharabi knocked two dirt-encrusted artifacts gently together. "Just before the cave-in, he managed to get these out to us." Some small measure of debris fell away after a couple of taps, revealing a hint of shiny metal. "I should be using a dental pick on these, but…." With greater force he hit them together again. Two large pieces of dirt separated from the smaller of the two objects, freeing a silvery object, which fell to the floor.

"Well, I'll be damned!" Roscha felt as if he knew what it was but couldn't bring himself to articulate it. He handed it to Sharabi.

"Cherubic figure on the handle. Very high quality. Looks like a silver baby spoon. Can't be silver, though—"

"Yeah," Roscha agreed. "No tarnish." He bent down and picked up the other piece, with yellow flecks showing through a patina of dirt. "No mistaking this. It's gold." He easily rubbed away the remaining encrustation. "It's our Martian ankh. Exactly like the one on the book.... What's that you have?"

Sharabi had pulled yet a third piece from his trousers and tossed it to him.

About the size of a large man's hand, it was comprised of a double cylinder, a smaller diameter one on top of a larger diameter one of slightly greater length. There was a small circular structure on the top of the cylinder near what must have been a handle, because it fit quite nicely into his hand. At the other end was a tiny bead of solid silver metal. A piece had been broken off between the lower cylinder and the presumed handle. Roscha hefted the object, gently tossing it up and down, assessing its weight and character. "Wonder what this could be?" He gave the object back to Sharabi.

"I don't know," Sharabi said, a troubled look on his face. "But when you just now pointed it at me, I got the distinct impression it was a gun."

* * *

When Sharabi found Kopi in Baghdad, he had been a street urchin, living by his wits—which meant he was a thief. Like the others of his ilk who worked the streets near the marketplace by day, he slept on the hard, cold streets at night. It was a habit hard to break. So, since living with Sharabi, Kopi had slept out under the stars, just a short way behind Sharabi's tent; and just as on the streets of Baghdad, he slept lightly.

Perhaps it was the muted clatter of firearms or the rustling of clothing; perhaps it was the intonation, only whispered, of some familiar voice that stirred Kopi to consciousness. A flashlight moved like a shooting star around Sharabi's tent. He heard more talking, this time louder. Yes! he thought so. It was Moab in Sharabi's tent.

Kopi moved closer. Another voice. He stuck his head under the edge of the canvas tent and could see that Moab and the two men who had stood with him by the limo on the previous night held guns on Sharabi. Guns fascinated Kopi, but they frightened him too. He had seen firsthand what they could do. And now he was terrified for Sharabi, but what was he to do?

"Where is the book?" Moab asked.

"There is no book," Sharabi replied defiantly. "And what right do you have to come bursting in here—?"

Moab slapped him. "Shut up!"

Kopi's heart struggled against his fear. If only he could get to Sharabi's gun in the duffle bag near his cot. He reached under the tent, but he was too far. Suddenly Moab motioned to his two men, and they moved nearer to him. He withdrew his hand, shaking, certain he'd been discovered. Instead, he saw through a tear in the tent the two men grab Sharabi. One stuffed a rag into his mouth.

"You're not such a big bossman now, eh?" Moab mocked and drew his knife. "Hold him. For each lie, I take one finger." He positioned the knife on the second joint of Sharabi's right index finger and pushed slowly through the flesh. Blood spurted out with each beat of Sharabi's heart.

Sharabi's muffled scream made Kopi wet himself. He wanted to scream, too, wanted to run to Great One, but fear checked him. He crept around the tent's edge, closer to the duffle bag holding the gun.

Moab put the severed finger in his pocket. "These will make nice trophies. The book, Sharabi?" He removed the rag from bleeding man's mouth. Sharabi spat at him. Moab nodded to his henchmen. Again Sharabi struggled uselessly against the burly men. The rag went back in his mouth. Another horrible scream, another finger into Moab's pocket.

This time Kopi reached the bag. Nothing there! Then he saw it. Sharabi's gun hung holstered out of reach alongside the binoculars on the tent pole. He was helpless. *Great One Roscha.* He eased the tent flap down and began to crawl on his elbows. Just passing the corner of the tent, the nearly full moon broke out of a cloud bank, brightly illuminating two more men with rifles. He froze, but only for a second, for the moon again did its disappearing act. He was free to make his way back to Roscha's tent. "Great One," he whispered, shaking Roscha's cot. "Great One," he whispered louder, rocking the cot more violently.

"What?" Roscha mumbled groggily. "Kopi?... What are you doing?" He grabbed his cigarette lighter, but the boy snatched it.

"No! Great One! Men with guns! Come quick!" Kopi did his best to make his voice urgent and commanding and was relieved when Roscha immediately complied, rolling off his cot. But he started in the direction of Sharabi's tent. Kopi clutched his shirt and pulled him back.

"No, Great One! Many men. Must go! Now!" Several rapid flashes and the loud report of rifle and pistol fire sealed the argument. Roscha grabbed his footlocker and pointed to the end. "I've got to take this. Get on the other end!"

"My knife?" He was not leaving without it.

"It's in the trunk!"

Kopi wasn't sure he believe him and tried to open the trunk.

Roscha pushed him back. "I swear. Now come on." He started to pull the footlocker toward the Land Cruiser.

"No!" Kopi whispered urgently, jerking his head toward the river. "Desert no good. The boat."

Then Moab shouted, "Get the American!"

"Go start the boat!" Roscha yelled. "I'll get the trunk."

Shots chased them down the bluff, falling far and wide, thanks to the transient moonlight, which was now extinguished by another column of thick clouds. He looked back, relieved that Great One was close behind. He was glad, too, that Great One Sharabi had made him learn to start the boat's motor, which burst to life just as Roscha untied the mooring lines and pulled the footlocker into the boat. As they sped up the river, the night sky brightened, not from the moon but from the glow of the flames consuming Sharabi's tents. His Great One of Great One's was gone forever. He began to cry. Now, he thought, he must cling to Roscha for survival.

* * *

Roscha was glad he'd kept Kopi close at hand; he'd been helpful not only because of his facility with the local language but also because of his vast knowledge of the seamy haunts of Baghdad's back-street, black-market cadre. Once in Baghdad, with Kopi's assistance, Roscha had arranged for them to catch a ride to Jordan on a converted tanker truck whose insides had been cleaned and partitioned to carry contraband instead of gasoline or oil.

From Jordan they had hitched a ride on a fishing trawler for the short trip across the Dead Sea to the West Bank city of Mar Saba, then on to Jerusalem, where Roscha reported the attack on Youssef Sharabi's compound and his murder to the people at the Rockefeller Museum. Though he now owed Sharabi a debt that would remain unpaid—with his old friend's help, he'd made much progress in deciphering the text of the Martian book—he could not allow himself to dwell on the past, for that new knowledge now impelled him with great urgency toward an uncertain destiny in a faraway land. Eager to stay on the move, they'd quickly left Jerusalem for the port city of Haifa, on the Bay of Acre. It was nearly noon when their bus stopped near the shipping terminal at the harbor. Roscha and the driver lifted his trunk off the top of the bus, but when Kopi tried to help, Roscha motioned him away. "Kopi, come here." He pulled off his belt, unzipped the inner liner and took out five one-hundred-dollar bills. "Take this."

"Thank you, Great One. But Kopi wish you keep for me. So Kopi won't lose when we—"

"That's just it, Kopi," he said unemotionally, "*we* aren't going anywhere. You are staying here—"

"But Great One!" Kopi grabbed Roscha's sleeve. "How can you go without Kopi? Who carry Great One's trunk? Who to warn you of danger? Who—"

"I'm going very far away, Kopi. It's dangerous."

"Kopi love danger—"

"You're just a kid. You should be in school. And you should be in a family. Not living in the streets like some sewer rat, whether it's here or in Baghdad. I wasn't cut out to be a father—*and I won't be one.* Understand?"

"Kopi not need school. You Kopi's family now...now that Great One Sharabi dead."

"Look!" Roscha said, trying not to be too hard on the boy; after all, he probably wouldn't have made it this far without Kopi, helping carry his unwieldy trunk across three countries and hundreds of miles and all. He spotted a police officer on the corner across the street. "See that policeman over there? Go to him. He'll help get you situated, once you tell them your circumstances. You speak English pretty well, so you'll have no problem getting placed in a school—and with a family."

"No school!"

"You're not coming with me, Kopi. That's final!" He picked up the end of his trunk. "Go back to Baghdad, for all I care. There's enough money there for that, too. But I don't recommend it. There's a better life here, if you want it." With that he walked away, dragging his trunk along the dock on the waterfront, where large freighters of many nationalities were berthed side by side for a mile or more along the pier. He'd gone only about a hundred feet when Kopi ran up and stopped him.

"Great One not leave Kopi with no cigarettes."

"Here." He threw him the pack. "Keep it." Dragging his trunk down the street, he turned every few feet to see if Kopi was still there, which he was, leaning up against a lamp post puffing and coughing. He was still there when Roscha entered the Overseas Convoy Shipping Company.

# CHAPTER 27

After the attack and explosion at the Eastern Gate, Peter had decided to walk the rest of the way to the Rockefeller Museum to allow them both time to dissipate an overload of adrenaline. He moved through the dense, scorching Jerusalem air as if stalking through tall grass, his legs like lifeless weights. Despite the heat, Molly shook so hard her teeth chattered. He reached out to put his arm around her, to hold her, but she pulled away, walking with soldierlike determination, her face blanched white as the stone houses that rose from the earth like the half exposed bones of some long buried skeleton.

He looked out over the Judean desert. The air had a surreal clarity; the sun shone with overbearing intensity. He could see all the way to the Dead Sea. *So she killed for me. And a kid, no less.* The thought provoked a peculiar emotion, an admixture of surprise, gratitude, pride and affection. "Are you going to be all right?"

She kept walking with her slightly off-balance gait, like a car with a flat spot on its wheel, but her words remained locked up behind a silent scowl.

"Well excuse me, Molly. But I, for one, am damned glad to be alive. It's a condition I've become fond of over the years, and I intend to stay that way—a*live.* And I'll tell you something else. You want to waste your days pining away over every stray cat, lost dog or punk kid who went wrong, be my guest. But don't ask me to do it with you. And don't try to sell me a bag of guilt about it, 'cause I won't buy it."

"Stop it!"

"No you stop it!" He grabbed her arm, but she wrenched it away. "I'm sorry for what happened back there, Molly. I'd change it if I could, but I can't. And you know what, it's not my fault. None of this." He stuck out his hand and quickly spun around and was thinking not just of their predicament but also of the world's. "Our chances are better together. But maybe you'd like to go it alone? Or we—"

"We? Our?" She huffed the words. "Those words require a mutual understanding *we* don't have." She stopped abruptly on the steps of the museum and glared at him. "Do you know what happened back there? Do you? *Really?* Can you possibly understand what that meant to me?"

"Yeah," he said with calm confidence and without a trace of conceit, "I know it means you love me."

"I-I-I h-*hate* you!" She slammed her fisted hands down to her sides. She inhaled so hard, he thought her breasts would burst from her shirt. "I don't even know who you are," she gasped through clenched teeth. "But from what I've seen so far..."—Another deep inhalation— "... you're vain and arrogant and cocksure of everyone and everything. Well, lucky you! We should all be so fortunate. The trouble is, Peter, when all you care about is yourself, you don't care about much at all."

"Thanks for the compliment," he said with determined sarcasm. "So you think I'm a selfish jerk. Well, okay. But you know what? I'm all you've got right now. For better or for worse. Like you said, we're as good as married in this thing, *Mrs. Amadeev.* So you'd better pull out of this death spiral you're in before we both crash and burn."

Molly's face, so red her hair melded into it in a single fiery mass, trembled as she struggled to speak. "A-And you hate children!" She collapsed onto the museum steps and began to cry.

"Does that mean you were shooting at *me?* Instead of the kid? Guess I *am* lucky. Lucky you're a lousy shot. Now pull yourself together. We're late for our appointment."

* * *

The news that they had missed Roscha by only a day was bad enough. What was worse, the curator at the museum informed them that Roscha had said he was leaving the country, but didn't say where he planned to go. Exhausted and depressed, they'd languished in their hotel room, each brooding wordlessly, until late afternoon when Peter, in a last-ditch effort, decided to call all the hotels in the phone book.

If Roscha was still in country, he had to be staying somewhere. Even if he was now traveling under an assumed name, someone must have seen him.

He'd tried them all. All except the King David Hotel. As he dialed, he felt as if this was his final, fateful catapult shot all over again, and he prayed the outcome would prove more favorable. His call got transferred, multiple times, ricocheting between Housekeeping, the Front Desk, the Concierge and Reservations until finally, by felicitous chance, he ended up with the bartender.

"Yes, there have been several Americans here in the last couple of days. I remember him. In his sixties. Hawkish features, yes. Great mound of white hair. He's traveling with an Englishman. Big guy with a red handlebar moustache." The bartender thought he'd had heard the men say they would be leaving the country tomorrow.

* * *

Sitting anxiously in the bar of the King David Hotel, Molly's anger at Peter was tempered by her excitement over the prospect of finding Roscha. For the first time in her life, perhaps, she felt she needed a drink. Eagerly pointing to a tray with fruit-and-umbrella drinks being carried to an adjacent table, she told the waiter, "I'll have one of those."

Peter glanced at her, the scar on his chin bent up slightly in a half grin. "My, my, but you are full of surprises." He reached for her hand, but she jerked it away.

"It's dark in here," she said coolly, idly snapping her locket opened and closed. "I hope we don't miss him."

"Listen, Molly" Peter said bleakly. "What's bothering you is that kid back there."

She ignored him. "Wonder if you can get a hot dog here?" Letting go of her locket, she crossed her arms over her breasts like a shield.

"You didn't kill him."

"What?" She rolled her eyes and purposely avoided any hint of a smile.

"What I couldn't figure out," he continued, "was how the kid could have been hit so hard."

"I shot him! That's how. Bullets hit hard."

"Now wait a minute. I know you *think* you did. At first I did too."

"So?" She suspected this was just another "AJ story."

"When I looked up, I saw you drop the gun. But, at the time—because of shock and all, I guess—it never even occurred to me that you couldn't possibly have hit the kid. Because you don't know anything about guns. Hell, you probably wouldn't have got it to fire if the cop hadn't used it first."

"You can't grow up with TV and not know about guns." She shook her head in disgust.

"Do you know what a safety is?"

"No…but…" She started to think, to hope. *But how?*

"That's exactly what I mean. Over and over again, I reconstructed the scene from memory, and there he was, every time."

"There who was?" Her heartbeat tugged pleadingly at her breastbone.

"The guy who shot the little *bast*—the boy. A soldier who was standing right behind you. Didn't you see him?"

"I don't remember seeing anyone." Hope began to fade.

"Because he was behind you. On the other side of the cab. His gun barrel was smoking, and he held his aim right on the kid. I swear."

"But how can you be sure it wasn't my bullet. Even I could've made a lucky shot." Hope reemerged. One scintilla heaped upon another, for the last thing she wanted to believe was that she had, in fact, killed a young boy, however misguided he may have been.

"Luck? First of all, it's a jinx to say you're lucky even when you believe it. No. Because the boy was hit too hard. Didn't you see how his rifle flew up in the air. Hell, he was knocked off his feet by the impact. Small caliber, low velocity bullets—pistol bullets—won't do that."

"But he was just a kid." Luminous hope was now piled high, sufficient to instigate the beginnings of a tiny smile. "Are you sure?"

"I can't prove it." He scratched his scar. "You're just going to have to trust me."

Trust him? Once again her smile faded. How long ago was it? Only days since she'd sworn she'd never doubt him again. *My Bogy?*

"Of course," he shrugged, "if you insist on believing the worst…."

"I believe you, Peter."

"Molly?"

"Yes?"

"Let's make a pact," he proposed, just as the drinks arrived. "No more fighting between you and me. Let's save it for the bad guys. Okay?"

"Let's drink to it," she said cheerily. But a more somber thought dampened her mood. "Why do you suppose a brush with death makes one so much more keen to live?"

"It's called war euphoria. 'Nothing in life is so exhilarating as to be shot at—and missed.' I think it was Churchill who said it. I experienced it in combat. You learned it today."

"For the third time," she mumbled.

"What's that?"

"Just that you were right yesterday." She took a big sip.

"Oh?"

"About living. We're not dead yet. And now more than ever, I want to live, Peter, just as much as you. To my last breath. To the end."

"Boy, after the other night—"

She touched his hand, blushing, for she instantly sensed what he was referring to. "You think I'm a prude. Is that it?"

"Well, you are about the only adult virgin—"

"*Shhh!* Don't be a jerk." She started fondling her locket again.

Peter laughed what seemed a good-natured laugh, without the derisive edge she'd so often heard from him. "Don't forget our pact," he said, wagging his finger. "We both need to be looking for Venable—or his friend."

"Actually, I'm glad you brought up last night, because you never let me explain why I feel the way I do about—well, you know."

"Oh, yeah—*Hee Hee*—I know."

"Stop it!" This time she laughed at herself. "It's what you were saying the other day about mothers, but maybe you didn't realize it."

"Oh?" He tossed aside a maraschino cherry with its stem neatly tied in a bow.

"Do you recall the song that started 'I believe the children are our future. Teach them well...' and it goes on?"

"I suppose so."

"Well, I think it's true. When I was a little girl, my father built a birdhouse and hung it from a rafter on our front porch. Before long, a pair of house wrens set up housekeeping. "They were so cute and interesting. I watched them all that summer. Together they built the nest, but when she'd laid the eggs, it was entirely up to him to bring her food while she warmed the eggs with her body.

"What an incredible bond of faith!"

"And he worked so hard. If he'd failed for whatever reason to bring her food, she'd have been forced to leave her eggs, and her babies would've died. It took both of them working together. Without that bond of trust, that fidelity of purpose, the species wouldn't survive. Those birds know that instinctively. They don't even have a choice about it.

"But we do. That's why I don't believe in casual sex. It 's cheapened our whole regard for what human life means. It's led us to devalue children. No one's trying to deny anyone pleasure. It's not about pleasure. It's about love and or uniqueness and a regard for our future. Our future as something more than just animals. I don't take that responsibility lightly. If that makes me weird in your eyes or anyone else's, so be it."

While she spoke, Peter made more bowties out of cherry stems. In metronomic accompaniment to her story, she absently snapped her locket opened and closed.

"That's a nice sentiment," Peter said, "but what if you don't want kids?"

"But I *do*."

"But I can't help wondering if part of your *conviction* doesn't have roots elsewhere."

"Oh?" She felt the temperature rise in her cheeks again. "And just what are you implying?"

"That a part of you doesn't like—or trust—men. Maybe because of your old man—"

"Stop! Please!" *Before you mention AJ.*

"Let's just say I'm having a hard time mourning your father's passing."

Her head swam, and she felt faint. She didn't know whether to slap him, kick him or shake his hand goodbye. Somehow she composed herself, suddenly incredibly aware of how much she'd already stuttered around him. Determined to carry on at all costs, she got up to leave not certain if she'd come back. She took a deep breath. "Good grief, must be the alcohol," she said evenly. "But I've got to go...literally. Where's the bathroom?"

Passing through the dining area, a man alone at a table attracted her attention. *It couldn't be.* She moved a little closer, peering through a small forest of hanging plants. *Blalock! He must be on the run, too.* Jubilant at seeing him still alive, she started across the room, but a woman stepped in front of her, blocking her way.

"Pardon me, Madame," the dark-eyed woman said, "but may I find you a table?"

"No, thank you. I see someone I know and—"

"Perhaps a table over there," the woman insisted, almost shoving her.

Molly tried to advance, keeping her eyes on the man, but with every step, the woman stood in her way. Annoyed, she finally looked at the woman more closely and nearly fainted. "Lilah Blackwell?"

"Who? I'm sorry, Madame, but you have me confused with someone else. Let me help you."

*Let me help you.* Now Molly knew it was Lilah. She remembered the way the Gypsy had said it in just that same cadence, with just that same tone. Oddly, Lilah now directed her attention back to Blalock's table, where two men had joined him.

One man's coat pulled back as he sat down, enough so that she could see a gun. *CIA?* Hidden from view, she heard Blalock say, "Go get him. He's been in the head long enough." One of the men got up and left, while Blalock and the other man stayed.

"Lilah, Peter is—" She looked around but the woman had vanished.

Forgetting her urgent need to pee, Molly rushed in panic back to their table. *Peter's gone!* Had he been picked up too? Or, as she most feared, had he finally become fed up with her and just left? Her heart raced. Her vision started to narrow. She walked quickly, trying desperately not to run and call further attention to herself, heading for the exit...but where?

# CHAPTER 28

Her mind numb, her hand shaking, Molly finally managed to get the key in the door of her hotel room. *Please be here.*

The room was empty, Peter's flight bag gone.

Her emotions alternated between anger, thinking he'd deserted her, and unalloyed loss, if truly he'd been captured. But then there was also the emotion of relief, because now, perhaps, she would never have to know for sure what his true feelings for her were. She hated that cowardly feeling and dismissed it.

*Now what? Uncle Malcolm?* She went for the phone. Just as her hand touched the cool plastic, it jangled. She jumped back as if she'd touched a snake. *Peter?* It rang again. But what if it weren't him? What if it were the police? CIA? Another ring. She stared at the black instrument, which may as well have been a gun in a game of Russian roulette. It rang once more. Soon it would stop, opting her out of this unwanted game with its unattractive choices. *No. It might be Peter.* She snatched the phone mid-ring. "H-h-hello."

"Front desk, Mrs. Amadeev. We have a message for you."

* * *

The message had been to meet Peter at the Grand Hotel bar, where Molly found him seated at a booth well hidden in a dark corner. "And you said *I* was full of surprises," she said as she sat down beside him in the booth. Nudging closer, she determined in that instant of blessed reunion to do whatever it took to keep him.

"Sorry for leaving you," he apologized. "But it couldn't be helped."

"When I didn't see your bag at the hotel, I thought...."

"I told housekeeping to take the whole mess, such as it is, for cleaning."

"I propose a new pact: No more surprises."

"How about no more pacts. That way, neither of us will be disappointed."

She quickly scanned the crowded bar. "I don't see Roscha."

"It's not Venable I found—

"But—"

"It's your father."

*"What?"* She felt as if he'd doused her with ice water. "My father's dead. Why would you—?"

*"Shsss."* He put his finger up to her lips.

Now she knew he was deadly serious.

"I know, know," he whispered. "I'm seeing dead people again. But I would never have said it if I wasn't certain."

"Certain?"

"As I can be. I only saw him once."

"But it can't—"

"Listen. It gets better. He was with our mustache man. Big guy. Red, waxed 'stache, just like the bartender said. I tried to catch them in a cab, but we lost them in traffic. Finally found their cab here. Trouble is, I checked at the front desk. Your father's not staying here. Not under Lavisch anyway. But the Bellboy said he'd seen the man with the mustache, just not today."

"We've had this discussion before," she reminded him, thinking of their airport encounter. "Dead people don't come back to life.

"It was *him*," Peter said emphatically.

"There's a simpler explanation. Uncle Malcolm."

"Your father has a twin?"

"Identical, except my father has a port wine birthmark on his scalp. Remember Gorbachev's? You can just make it out through his thinning hair. And he smokes cigars. Uncle Malcolm hates smoking as much as I do."

Peter twisted up the corner of his mouth and slowly shook his head. "Then it *was* your father. He had a big ol' cigar. I saw that much."

"Then it probably wasn't Malcolm, either. Just—"

"A look-a-like?"

She nodded. "Like your Roy Corbett." Then she told him what had happened back at the King David Hotel, about seeing Lilah.

He scratched at the scar on his chin. "This is getting spooky. Especially after what your uncle said about the Eastern Gate."

"And all these dead people?" Her head swam, overloaded with uncertainties. "It's crazy."

"As for Lilah," he said, his voice rising slightly, "it makes sense she's mixed up in this. She's probably CIA. Blalock? That only makes sense too. He'd do the same thing we are. Must've been picked up, though. Which means they're onto us. And there's something else..." Suddenly, a voice on the television over the bar was talking about Youssef Sharabi's body being brought back to his hometown of Nablus for burial. "Hmmm…no mention of Roscha Venable. We've got to get out of here tomorrow. Guess I'll have to hock my Honus Wagner after all."

"Pardon my intrusion," said the man in the booth just behind them, who had arrived unnoticed. "But I couldn't help overhearing. Did you say you're looking for a man named Venable?" He draped his arm across the top of the booth, as he flicked open the top of his lighter and thumbed the flint wheel. With a starburst of sparks, the lighter flared to life, for the first time illuminating his face, with its magnificent red, highly waxed, handlebar mustache. Puffing away, he applied the flame to a large dark pipe, which stubbornly refused to make smoke. Lean and hard, face well lined, tanned and leathered from obvious close acquaintance with the elements, he appeared to be in his mid-fifties, with steady blue eyes and blond hair, except for a tinge of gray at the temples. He wore the hallmark khaki safari jacket, replete with high-caliber bullet loops, which were empty but stretched from prior use.

"You know Roscha Venable?" Peter asked.

"Depends...." The man motioned to the empty seat across from them. "May I?"

"Please," Molly said, her voice elevated with hope.

"Name's Reginald Bell, but Reggie'll do nicely." He extended his big, calloused hand to Peter, then Molly. He sat down, taking a tobacco pouch out of his pocket. "Mind if I smoke?"

"Not at all," Peter said. "I'm Peter. This is Molly."

Bell tapped his pipe on the table, emptying its spent contents, which he then swept off the edge into his cupped hand, before transferring the remains to the ashtray. He then refilled the bowl of the briarwood pipe with tobacco, tamping it neatly into place and, with a flip of his well-worn Zippo, its brassy interior showing through the chrome-nickel finish, he lit it, puffing a steady column of steel-blue smoke into the already smoky barroom air.

Molly found the sweet, if somewhat pungent, aroma of the marinated tobacco surprisingly pleasant, unlike her father's harsh cigar smoke that she'd come to detest.

"Where do you folks know Roscha Venable from?" Bell asked cagily.

"He's a friend of the family," Molly told him. "My Dad and him go back to their college days."

"What about you?" Bell said blandly, dipping his head toward Peter. "You know him too?" "He was a professor of mine in college. But I doubt he'd remember me."

Bell puffed impassively on his pipe for what seemed an eternity before saying, "Mind if I ask why you're looking for him?"

"He has something that belongs to my father and we—"

"The truth is," Peter interrupted, "Roscha kinda got our ass in a sling, and we need him to get us out. Beyond that, we can't say."

Bell chuckled and blew a perfect circlet of smoke, which he then blasted apart with the rest of the drag. "Nothing has quite the bite of an honest answer. Does he know you're looking for him?"

"He doesn't know," she said.

"Maybe he doesn't want to be found," Bell posed.

"I think he'd want to see us," Molly said confidently. "What I said about him and my father is true."

"We mean him no harm, if that's what you're getting at," Peter added.

Bell tapped his Zippo on the table and looked at them. Then, leaning back in his chair, he called to the bartender, "Another round here, if you please." A hint of a smile curled the corner of his mouth. "You two seem okay to me."

"Where is he?" Peter asked. "We'd like to see him now if we can,"

"That'd be a ticklish proposition." Bell paused, looked at his watch.

"Is he in town?" Molly sensed an impending disappointment.

"Offhand I'd say he's somewhere off the coast of Ethiopia, in the Red Sea."

"On a ship?" Molly said, incredulous. "Headed where?"

"Mombasa," Bell said. "From there, he'll have to make his way up to Nairobi by train. That's where I'm meeting him. Nairobi's my home office. And our jumping off point—if all the bloody supplies I ordered are ready. Can't depend on anything these days but surly help and blowflies."

Peter frowned. "Jumping off for where?"

"Venable's hired me to take him on a safari."

"A *safari?"* She glanced at Peter, who appeared more surprised than even she. "What on earth for?"

"Oh, not a hunting safari. And he really didn't need me to go where he wants to go. But for whatever reason, he said he liked the security of being with someone who knows how to handle a gun."

"Guns!" she said disgustedly, thinking of her father—and the boy. "I'm sick of guns."

"Anyhoo," Bell said, downing the rest of his brandy, "the price was nifty right. So there you are."

"Where are you taking him, exactly?" Peter asked.

"If he cares to, Mr. Venable will tell you. That's if you're coming with me tomorrow."

A surprise belch erupted from her. " 'scuse me.... We're coming. Jesss, jesss, tell 's when 'n' where." Ambushed by her drinks, she began to feel warm, confident and cheery, if somewhat out of control. But she decided to go with the feeling, for once, and see where it took her. Given their predicament, what did she have to lose?

"Looks like she's had a bit too much fun," Bell said to Peter.

*Is he talking about me?* She giggled to herself.

"Flight leaves at eight o'clock a.m.," Bell announced. "But we'll need to be there a couple hours early to make sure we can get you on and get your papers straight. Don't think they'll be a problem, though. This flight's never full. If you two can meet me here—in the lobby—say five o'clock, we'll head for Tel Aviv."

Still frowning, Peter rubbed his chin and said, "No offense, but what's a white hunter doing in Jerusalem?"

"None taken." Bell smiled, the tips of his mustache curled up like the horns of a Cape buffalo. "I'm through here a couple of times a year. Got a rich Saudi client who likes to shoot Arabian Orynx on a preserve in Oman, among other things. He doesn't need me either. Just likes to compete with me on the shooting. Bloody nasty bloke, too. But—"

"Let me guess," Peter said. "The price was nifty right."

Bell chuckled as he nodded.

"One more thing," Peter pressed. "Do you know a guy named Lavisch. Older fellow. Balding. Kinda fat. Smokes big cigars."

"No one I know," Bell said firmly. "Well, sleep tight, chaps. See you in the bright and early."

* * *

Peter laughed to himself as he walked with Molly, stabilizing her inebriated gait, glad that she'd decided to loosen up a bit. He'd never heard her talk so much about anything, especially herself. And, strangely, these little ingenuously offered pieces of her life intrigued him in a way utterly foreign to him.

She'd babbled on about her father and AJ and her childhood and Roscha and her job and Katie; about how she missed her cat, Periwinkle, her home, her lab, her routine; about how worried she was about her Uncle Malcolm, whom she had not been able to reach. She allowed as how she had forgotten all about Brenda Cruise and the Martian cloth, how she'd determined to call Brenda and Malcolm tomorrow before they left for Nairobi. She'd been in the bathroom for a long time when he called to her.

"You okay in there?" He listened for sounds of retching but heard none. Perhaps she wasn't as sick as he thought she should be, given what she'd had to drink.

"Yes.... Be right out."

She sounded as if she were sobering up. But when she fell up against the door jam shuffling out of the bathroom, he changed his mind. She wore only a large towel wrapped around her, tucked into her cleavage, breaking high across the tops of her thighs. Little glimpses between the folds told him she wore nothing underneath.

She navigated unsteadily, letting go of her hold on the door jam, then having to reach quickly for him as she crossed the short space of floor that separated them. She put her arms around him and gazed up at him with her big green eyes, smiling impishly.

"Peter, I've been thinking. 'Bout a lot of things, actually...the other night...what I said." Her head dropped to his chest, as if she'd fallen asleep, but, with apparent effort, she pulled her eyes back to his. He steadied her with his hand behind her head, thinking how pretty she was, even drunk.

"Been thinking.... You know, you saved my life today—again."

"You have it backwards, don't you? I remember you saving me?

"No-No, you! How many times now?" She put her index finger to her temple as if digging for the memory. "Four times already—God. " She dropped her eyes.

"I'd say the saving's been pretty much equal."

"You know what the Chinese say?"

"What's that?"

"If you save someone's life, they belong to you." She wobbled slightly.

"Then I guess we belong to each other."

"That's what I was thinking. We make a good team, huh?"

"Suppose we do."

"What I-I-I mean, though, is, t-thanks for not leaving me—again. When you weren't at the hotel... I thought you did, and it scared me. But... but not for the reason you think."

She started to fall backwards and he put his arm around her waist, supporting her. "You promised never to doubt me, remember?"

"You *are* my Bogie," she murmured. "And I'm your Ingrid—forever."

"Sure you don't mean Dagwood?"

She slapped her hand limply on his chest; her head thudded against him, nestling against his heart, lingering for a moment. "No," she whispered, holding up her thumb and index finger. "Maybe Dagwood, too. J-jess a little."

She nuzzled into his shirt; her hair smothered his face with her fragrance, intoxicating him. He pushed her back, trying to gauge her intention. "Molly—?"

She put her finger to his lips. "No, No, No, Peter. Pleease let me fin-finish. I know I'm no AJ—she's *sooo* pretty. But I'm not so bad, am I?"

He shook his head slowly and couldn't suppress a grin. "Molly," he said softly, kissing her on the neck, wanting her intensely, knowing she'd never believe he wanted her in just the way she might wish. "You don't have to—"

She frowned and slapped his chest again. She pushed away from him, teetering on her own just inches away, struggling to hold her head up as she untied the fold that held her towel between her breasts. The pure white towel fell in a heap around her feet.

"What you said at the museum is true. I *do* love you, Peter." Her head lolled side to side against his stolid heart. "Even though sometimes my head says I hate you, my heart says otherwise."

"Now ain't that just like a woman," he joked. "Always of two minds—and they never agree."

He took her in his arms, kissed her hungrily as they fell together onto the bed. She lay back. He took in the sight of her, pausing to savor her beauty. He kissed her, nuzzled her neck just behind her ear. And then he heard muted, snuffling sounds coming from her. *She's snoring.* Laughing silently, he rolled her over and was about to cover her when he saw it. There, on her right buttock, was a tattoo that said "Hell's Little Angel" in blue encircled with a single long-stem red rose. He patted it lightly, then pulled the blanket over her and retired to the other bed.

# CHAPTER 29

Ndobo, a coal-black Waliangulu from the Lake Naivasha area of the Masai Mara and Bell's headman and gunbearer, met Peter and Molly at Jomo Kenyatta International Airport. He loaded their meager belongings onto one of Bell's Land Rovers and, after dropping by Bell's headquarters, where preparations were already underway for the trip to Lake Victoria, in Uganda, saw to it that they were properly delivered to the New Stanley hotel.

Looking at their one piece of luggage the desk clerk gave Peter and Molly a curious stare, then handed Molly a key to room three-twelve. "And your key, sir, room three-thirteen, across the way. Just as you'd requested."

"Which way to the bar?" Peter asked.

"The Thorn Tree," the clerk replied brightly. "Just around the corner to your right. Hope you both enjoy your stay."

"Oh, one more thing," Peter said. "Can you tell us when Roscha Venable gets in?"

Quickly checking the bookings, she said, "This evening. Six o'clock train. Will he be staying with you, then, Mr. Amadeev?"

"No, we have other plans. But thanks."

"Other plans, *Mr. Amadeev?"* Molly whispered, more hurt than worried about Peter's unannounced change of plans. "Why separate rooms?"

"If you're up for it," he said wearily, "we've got time for a drink before the train gets in."

She followed him into the barroom, which was rapidly filling with hotel guests and locals cheerily ordering what must have been their customary post-five drinks. Here and there a smattering of good-natured banter erupted, spiced with an occasional hoot of laughter. On the wall above the bar, which was well stocked with an international blend of spirits stacked in four tiers like a terraced garden, there hung a gallery of game heads: A zebra, its white and black coat yellowed with age and neglect; a ferocious-looking lion with blackened mane appeared ready to pounce on the unsuspecting patron; and a fearsome Cape buffalo, all rumpled and baggy-skinned, with bottomless brown eyes and a hint of its pink tongue showing.

"American beer," Peter told the bartender. "Any kind you got."

"Club soda with a twist of lime, please."

Peter chuckled and turned up the corner of his mouth, making his scar crinkle peculiarly. "With all you drank, even sleeping all the way over on the plane didn't help much, huh?"

"No, it didn't. My head is screaming. My mouth feels like a dust rag. To be honest, I've never had that much to drink before. Well, maybe once—"

"Ocean City?" he sniggered. "Hell's Little Angel?"

*"You saw it?"* She felt the inexorable blush start to warm her breast and cheeks.

"You *had* to be drunk." He guzzled his beer, then tapped the empty glass on the bar for another.

"It was the first time I tried to be like AJ. It didn't work."

"And last night was the latest?"

"Peter, I'm...I'm sorry about last night. I behaved badly."

"Molly...don't..."

"Oh, I don't mean about what I said—"

"Molly..." He shook his head. "Listen to me. You have nothing to apologize for. *Nothing.* If anything, I should apologize to you."

"You apologize? For what?" She watched him quickly down his second beer. She noticed his shoulders lower as he seemed to relax a bit, even the tension lines in his face smoothed out.

"Plenty," he said. Then he looked up to the animal heads above the bar.

She angled her head upward, following his gaze. "Not wishing you were one of them, I hope."

"Actually, I was."

"Why on Earth would you?"

"Because it's over for them. They don't have to fear the predator anymore." His expression turned strangely sorrowful. "Take that zebra. When he was alive all he ever had to worry about was eating, chasing girl zebras and running from something trying to eat him.

"Just like us?"

"Just like us." He pushed his empty beer glass away. "Except he never had to worry about doing the right thing."

"Because he's just an animal."

* * *

Molly stood with Peter in an alcove at the train station from which they had a clear view of Ndobo, who held a large sign with Roscha Venable written in big red letters high above the heads of the swirling crowd, just as the dusty brown train lumbered in. She watched the cars, heavy-laden with a rich assortment of African humanity, disgorge their human cargo. She remembered the tourist guidebook from the hotel, which described a typical trainload: businessmen from as far away as Kampala; craftsmen from Gilgil and Limuru, their ebony carvings strung on ropes around their necks; farmers from Lake Naivasha bringing chickens in wicker cages, along with whatever produce they could haul in burlap sacks; schoolchildren back from a day trip to Nakuru; tourists, mostly British, German and American; mothers from the hinterlands carrying sick children to hospital in Nairobi; and legions of the idle unemployed, garnered from far and wide along the railway, seeking a new life in the big city. But the real-life travelogue that unfolded before her was even more amazing, and she only wished the circumstances could be different.

Finally she saw him "There he is!" She pointed to Roscha's huge white mane, which shone like a beacon amid a sea of brown heads. She thought he looked like a frightened animal.

Peter nodded. "I see him. Let's go."

"Wait, Peter." Perhaps for the first time she realized she really didn't know Roscha very well. Most of what she knew was second hand from listening to her father's stories, and except for the night at the museum, she had not even seen Roscha since she was a little girl. "Let me talk to him first. I don't want to spook him." She was about to call out his name when someone grabbed her purse. "Hey! Come back here!" She took off after the young boy with the Arab headgear, who, strangely, ran toward Roscha, disappearing behind a conga-line of Kenyan *askaris*, the local policemen, carrying confiscated elephant tusks, each pair of them toting a heavy post of ivory, one after the other.

"Roscha!" Molly shouted, ducking limbolike below one long ivory beam, before popping up in front of him. Swaying side to side, she tried to get a glimpse of the little thief, who clung desperately to Roscha's pant leg and avoided her eyes. "That boy stole my purse!"

Roscha's expression went from frightened-animal to that of a man who'd placed his foot on the first step of the gallows. "Molly! You're alive!" He reached behind him and grabbed the boy, relieving him of the purse as he roughly pulled him up in front of her.

"He's with you?" she asked, bemused.

"Hell no! Well...temporarily I guess. He belonged to a friend in Iraq. Then stowed away on my ship coming here. It's a long story. But what are you—?"

"We lost track of you in Israel. But we ran into Reggie Bell—oh, please don't be angry. You're our only hope."

"Our? Who's with you?"

"Peter MacKenzie." She waved to Peter, who waded through the swirling crowd toward them. "He was with me the night Dad—they're after him now, too."

"Trying to talk here is crazy," Roscha shouted. He turned to Bell's gunbearer. "What's your name?"

"Ndobo, Bwana. This way." He led them out of the station into the relative quiet of the cool Kenyan evening.

"Where are you staying?" Roscha asked.

"Reggie put us up at the New Stanley," Peter said, catching up with them and extending his hand. "Peter MacKenzie."

"So I hear. Your name sounds familiar. Do I know you?"

"You have one helluva memory, Professor Venable. I was in one of your classes at Columbia."

"Hmmm.... You must have been a lousy student."

"Why do you say that?"

"You can't be too smart. Getting yourself mixed up in this. What has Molly told you?"

"I know about the Martian book. What I don't know is why the CIA would want it hushed up. They certainly can't justify their killing people over it."

"You haven't mentioned any of that to Bell, have you?"

"Nothing specific—"

"What exactly does that mean? Never mind. How'd you find Bell, anyway?"

"Just a piece of luck," Molly said.

"I don't believe in luck," Roscha said.

* * *

It was well past midnight when Peter, Molly and Roscha returned to the New Stanley for a nightcap after having had dinner with Bell, during which it was mutually agreed that Peter and Molly would accompany Roscha to the northern rim of Lake Victoria.

As they sat down, something about the bartender instantly attracted Peter's attention. A handsome young man of about thirty-five, with thick bronze hair and crystalline blue eyes, he beamed a huge smile as he asked to take their order. Trying not to be obvious, Peter studied him carefully. Somehow, he was sure he knew this man. But from where?

While the bartender made their drinks, Roscha told them of his journey: of how he had left the country the very night Molly's father was killed and how he had called Molly at Glen Echo from half-way around the globe; of his experiences with Sharabi, Bandar Bliss, Moab and Kopi; of the tomb and the inscriptions on the sarcophagus; of his escape with Kopi; of the partial deciphering of the Martian text, made possible by Sharabi's knowledge of cuneiform and the knife Kopi had found; of how the text contained a map that indicated there was something at the falls on the north side of giant Lake Victoria, though what he could not yet say. Yet he was certain whatever *it* was had some great significance, as a major portion of the text was devoted to it. He told them he hoped he could finish the translation before they got there.

The youthful bartender returned with a tray of drinks. Peter stole another glance, marveling at the subtle happiness that brightened the man's every movement. And those knowing eyes: a purity of spoken blueness, with curious little golden flecks in the iris near the pupils. Where had he seen them before?

"Will there be anything else?" the bartender asked, setting the drinks before them with a graceful flourish and holding Peter's gaze unusually long. "I'm going to be closing up now."

Feeling slightly uncomfortable, Peter averted his eyes, and the bartender was called away to another table.

"Roscha," Molly said, wearily, "Maybe we should think about giving the book to the CIA. Sooner or later, they're going—"

"No!" Roscha barked. "We've got to know what the book says, and I've nearly completed the translation. Then we'll have bargaining power. Without it, we'll have nothing. Besides, I think I know why the CIA would kill to get this book. They—"

Two patrons waiting to pay their bill hovered close to their table, seeming to take note of Roscha's comments.

"Go on, Roscha," Peter urged, desperate for some clue. "Why?"

But Roscha pushed back from the table and stood up. "Bell said we'd push off at five, so I'll see you two in the morning."

Molly got up too.

"Where're you going?" Peter asked her.

"I'm going to look for my locket. It's been missing ever since the train station."

## CHAPTER 30

Progress was agonizingly slow, as the Land Rover whined in low gear, struggling snaillike over the rocky terrain. A fierce sun streamed in through the side window, scorching Peter's face. The stiff African atmosphere afforded not a sigh of a breeze. He looked at Bell, who clutched the wheel with a certain deft assurance as he adroitly dodged another large boulder. When Peter thought about it, he had to admit he admired, even envied, Bell, whose knowledge of the bush, animal behavior and firearms were encyclopedic. Bell's life was the kind of adventure Peter, himself, had always wished for. But why, he wondered had Bell lied when he'd asked about the man with the cigar? The man he'd thought was Miles Lavisch. He realized that the very things he admired about Bell would make him a formidable adversary.

Just then, the Rover's wheel dipped into a small crevasse, nearly throwing Peter out of the truck as it whip-lashed from side to side. Grabbing the roll bar, he shouted above the engine, "If that's your way of showing us you're worth your 'nifty price,' it's not necessary."

Bell laughed, gunning the engine, as he teased the clutch in and out, gingerly picking his way through the dense mopane scrub. The Land Rover backfired in complaint. An odd-looking cousin of those sometimes seen on the streets of American cities, this working Rover purposefully sported a two-inch pipe bush guard, which surrounded the body like a bulging muscle, and a massive roll bar, made of even larger pipe, that encircled the Rover vertically. A stainless steel screen covered the fenders and the radiator. Thick steel plates protected the vulnerable underbelly. More like a tank or an armored personnel carrier, this Rover was ready for any unforeseen encounter, whether with an angry rhino, a hidden rocky outcropping, or an unseen chasm.

"How much farther?" Peter asked.

"Couple of miles...maybe three."

Picking up speed as the land opened up, a wild, primal surge of adrenaline activated Peter's every sensory nerve. Colors were brighter, more distinct; sounds had sharper, crisper edges; his nostrils filled with a summer-baked smell of dried— "What the hell's that?"

Bell slammed on the brakes.

"Pew!" Molly gasped, waving her hands in front of her nose. Kopi made a ugly face.

"What in God's awful heaven is that smell?" Roscha piped.

"Putrefying flesh," Bell told them. "Don't know what from...." He leaned out the side and looked up into the hazy blue afternoon sky. "That's bloody odd, though."

"What?" Peter asked.

"No vultures." Bell shut down the engine.

"So?" Roscha said. "Can't we just keep moving? It's too damned hot to just sit."

"Vultures have a sixth sense about death," Bell explained. "It's almost as if they can hear an animal give up its life. And there's definitely something dead around here. Sorry, Roscha, it's part of my license. I have to report poaching if I find it. Won't take a minute. Ndobo!"

"Yes, *Baba,*" the tall black man answered, using the revered *Fanagalo* word for father. Without the need for elaboration, he took Bell's Winchester .375 H&H Magnum off the rack in the back of the Rover and met Bell outside.

Fascinated, Peter watched as Bell took the weapon, pulled the bolt-action up, back, then forward, chambering a cartridge a bit longer and about as fat as his middle finger. He then braced the butt of rifle on his thigh and held the trigger back while he lowered the bolt handle gently down into the locked position. Though he'd done a fair amount of shooting himself, both in the military and privately, Peter had never seen a rifle handled quite this way.

"Want to have a look?" Bell said in little more than a whisper.

Peter nodded instantly and jumped out. "Hey, what was that you just did with the rifle...the bit with the bolt?"

"Better than running around with a fully cocked gun whose safety may have slipped off. Quieter for stalking, too. All you have to do to re-cock is move the bolt handle up and back down again. Then shoot."

Peter winked at Bell. "Nifty." As they launched into the undergrowth, Peter decided to stay well behind the White Hunter. It would be all too easy for Bell to write his death off as a hunting accident.

* * *

Molly watched Roscha go out of sight over a ridge some twenty yards from the Rover, on his way to answer nature's call, while she and Kopi waited for Peter, Bell and Ndobo to return. Beyond the spot where his white hair disappeared, out across the plains below, she saw a giraffe cropping the sweet, tender leaves near the top of an acacia tree, while her two young played tag between her spindly legs. Strangely, Molly felt a bond with this giraffe; she even envied it. For it had fulfilled a yearning and a purpose she now knew so acutely. *Motherhood.* Did everything come down to this? Were we humans nothing more than animals after all? Hadn't Peter said just that in the bar in Nairobi? Near the horizon a herd of zebra kicked up a dusty cloud. She diverted her gaze fluidly from the African plain to the youngster seated beside her and smiled.

"Great Red One?"

"You may call me Molly," she said sweetly. "What's troubling you?"

"You pretty lady," he said.

"Why, thank you. Where did you learn to speak English?"

"How come you walk like?..." He rocked from side to side in his seat in an exaggerated imitation of her walking.

"Oh, my limp? I had polio—a sickness—when I was a little girl. It ruined my walk. Now, I've told you a secret about me. How about you? You didn't answer my question."

Suddenly, with a frightened expression, Kopi winced and grabbed his stomach.

"What's the matter?" She could see a small bright red stain near his upper thigh.

"Great Red One doctor?"

"Yes. Are you sick?"

Rubbing his stomach, the boy sniffled, “It hurts. Kopi scared.”

“Can I take a look?” She tried to pull up the hem of his burnoose, but he pulled away. “Kopi, if you want me to help you, you’ve got to let me look.”

“Will Kopi die?”

“Yes,” she said flatly, putting his clothing back in place. “But not from this. Why have you been masquerading as a boy?”

“Uncle wanted to cut me. Back in Sudan.” She pointed to the bloody area of her genitals. “Make me his wife.”

“Circumcision.” Molly shook her head, disgusted by the images recalled from a trip she’d taken to an American safe house for African refugees when she was a medical student. “Barbaric.... You poor thing. Well, you won’t have to go. I promise you that. And there’s nothing wrong with you. You’re just becoming a young woman. Here, let’s get you cleaned up.”

Suddenly Kopi grabbed her hand. “Molly not tell. Please!”

“You won’t be able to hide it much longer, I’m afraid, but all right, I promise. But you must promise me to stop acting like you think a boy should act.”

“Kopi promise.” Then she dug deep down inside the folds of her burnoose.

*“My locket!”* Molly opened it almost with a sense of desperation. With watery eyes, she stared at the frayed-edged pictures of her mother and father. *I almost lost you twice.*

“This for you too, Red One.” And Kopi handed her a Martian ankh.

* * *

Somewhere off to the left, Peter spotted Ndobo. Then he heard a soft buzzing. They continued through thick mopane and wait-a-bit thorns that painfully clawed at his legs and arms with their fishhook shaped spines. Each little insult he took as payback for Bo, for his own betrayal, his guilt, and he would gladly take more. He wondered if he’d done the right thing in telling Molly. The last thing he wanted was sympathy; he wanted somehow to pay.

Now Bell and Ndobo used only hand signs to communicate. Ndobo led at first, but as the noise grew louder, Bell assumed the point. Half-crouching, they proceeded silently through the undergrowth toward the frenzied buzzing.

As they approached a small clearing, Bell stood erect, in a relaxed slouch that said the stalk was over. "Well, I'll be hanged. Would you bloody look at that?"

Peter pushed forward past Ndobo, who was moving back as if he'd seen his own dead face. There in a small clearing was the biggest snake he'd ever seen, or part of it. Beautifully camouflaged in green, brown and tan reticulations, undergrowth hid over half its huge length.

"Is it dead?"

"No," Bell said. "Just indisposed. A Python. One of the biggest I've ever seen, though they can get over thirty feet. Appears he bit off more than he could chew, so to speak. Caught a little bushbuck, suffocated it the usual way by coiling and squeezing it. Then he swallowed it ass backwards up to its head."

"So it wasn't dead when he ate it?"

"Snakes don't eat carrion. No, he killed it all right. That's the rub. Got himself into a bit of a pickle, he did. As he was swallowing it, it must have dawned on him—if that's the right expression for a snake—that the antelope's horns couldn't go down. They would kill him. So he just lay there until the bluebottle flies laid their eggs, the eggs turned to larvae, and those millions of little maggot meat cleavers went to work, chopping their way through meat and cartilage. He's waitin' for the head to fall off, is what he's doing. Which it looks like it's about to do."

Peter gazed at the seething black log with revulsion, for if there was one of God's creatures he had an intense loathing for, it was snakes. "It's just a mass of flies. Sure he's alive?"

"Let's have a look then." Bell took the muzzle of his rifle and poked the snake in the ribs. Nothing happened. He poked harder. This time the snake pulled back into the tall grass at the edge of the clearing, antelope head and all, sending a veritable thundercloud of flies into the overheated air, fanning the stench even more. Bell's face contorted from the smell. "Ndobo!"

Peter looked at Ndobo, who stood well back, trembling slightly and clutching his talismanic pouch. "What's wrong with him, Reggie? He must've seen snakes before."

"Stroking his bones," Bell replied, an edge of concern in his voice. "His talisman. It's filled with various animal trimmings, bones, herbs, stones...all of which has been fully and well blessed by the local witch doctor.... What's wrong, Ndobo?"

"Bad *muti, Baba!"* he said before suddenly vanishing into the bush.

"What the heck was that all about?"

"Muti is magic. He means it's a bad omen."

"Witchcraft?" Peter said, incredulous. "I thought you were kidding about that stuff."

"Hardly, my friend. It permeates everything here, all the tribes, all the peoples in Africa. Something bad happens—anything—your goat dies, your kid gets sick, your wife has a baby feet first—it's because someone with a grudge put a hex against you."

"That could make you jumpy."

"I don't know why that snake spooked old Ndobo. But it's no joke to him." Bell started back through the bush at a normal walk. "You never hear about it back in the states, but a large bunch of the murders in Africa every year are ritual murders. They kill for body parts they use for magic. Mainly to put a hex or some enemy or other."

"You mean in the rural, tribal areas?" Peter pushed aside a branch of thorns, which broke, whipped back against his chest, stinging as its thorns penetrated his sweating skin. He reveled in the pain.

"Even in Johannesburg and Cape Town, my friend. You'd be surprised. What was it? Twenty…maybe thirty years back. A hired *Inyanga,* that's a witch doctor, was caught by British authorities trying to work some untoward magic on the crown prince and future ruler of Swaziland, who was a lad of only sixteen at the time. Turns out the former queen regent and the Minister of Home Affairs were in on it together. Hell, a goodly number of the leaders or former leaders of these African countries today are still cannibals—"

"Africa really is full of man-eaters."

"And not just the lions, Pete."

“Remind me not to offend Ndobo.”

“What I mean is ritualistic cannibals,” Bell continued as he pushed the brush aside with the barrel of his gun. “Which is to say eating human flesh for the purpose of magic. Idi Amin Dada was a cannibal; so was Emperor Bokassa the first of what used to be the Central African Empire. Of course I told you about the Mau Mau oaths. Lots of cannibalism in that. All based on magic—muti. And don’t think it’s just the country folk, either. Many of the university-educated city folk practice it too.”

“Wait ‘til Molly finds out who her competition is out here,” Peter joked.

But Bell didn’t laugh. “Oh, they’ll accept modern medicine—in addition to magic. They’ll see a Molly, but then go for a visit to the local Inyanga.”

Back at the Land Rover, Ndobo sat stiff and stone-faced at his station in the back of the Rover. Roscha, who now seemed oblivious to the entire event, sat quietly engrossed in the Martian text, every few seconds wiping the sweat from his eyes. They hopped in and Bell started the engine.

“What happened?” Molly asked. “Ndobo wouldn’t say a word.”

“Later,” Peter told her, looking at Ndobo with new eyes. Then it occurred to him, his chin wasn’t itching. He wondered if his infallible trouble-sniffer had finally failed him? No, he decided, there was no danger after all. Whatever scared Ndobo was just some stone-age notion of good and evil, ghosts and goblins, banshees and spirits. He looked at Molly and smiled, then realized she’d been sobbing. She handed him the newspaper he’d picked up for her just before leaving the New Stanley.

“What’s wrong? Blondie die or something?”

She folded the paper over so he could see the picture.

“I wish you’d stick to the comics.” He read the obituary, which detailed the all-too-brief life of a prominent Middleburg, Virginia, horse rancher, who had died of a broken neck in an apparent riding accident.

“Now I guess we’ll have to start looking for AJ to show up,” he said quietly thinking of Roy Corbett.

"There's something else," Molly said, handing him the ankh. "Kopi must have taken it off your key ring."

He quickly fished out his key ring, from which his Martian ankh still dangled brightly, reflecting the orange rays of dying African sun.

* * *

They'd been moving again for the better part of an hour when Peter noticed a subtle but distinct low rumble like far off thunder, even over the roar of the revving engine as it again strained in low gear, this time against rising terrain. "How close are we to the falls now?"

"You feel it, don't you?" Bell said. "No more that a mile, I'd say. Fabulous lake, the Vic, primary source of the Nile. Huge! Hundred and fifty miles across in spots. Surrounded by some of the most beautiful country in all God's creation."

Only moments later, with a *whoosh*, the Land Rover parted a particularly thick wall of thorny, matted scrub and burst into a sunny clearing with a house and several outbuildings.

"We have arrived," Bell announced.

A few seconds later, Wakambi, Bell's camp cook and overseer, arrived with the supply truck. Almost before the engine died, a swarm of perhaps fifteen or twenty children descended upon them like colorful, cheering locusts, loosed from a thatch-covered pavilion with desks and chairs and a blackboard about twenty yards away. Right behind them was a black man of slight build, with close-cropped hair. He wore blue jeans and a khaki safari shirt oddly supplemented with a bright white clerical collar.

"Father Easterbrook," Bell called, "I've got some people I'd like you to meet."

# CHAPTER 31

Molly stood with Peter on the edge of a promontory near the falls at Lake Victoria, only a short distance from Father Easterbrook's mission. The cool evening air combined with great clouds of mist created by water falling with a titanic force to the river below chilled her. She gazed out at the spectacular falls, the churning river and the beauty of the emerald lands beyond, and for the first time in her life felt whole. She slipped her arms around Peter. His warmth comforted her. She could feel his heart beating. His hands encircled hers in affirmation. The total strength of the roaring waterfall seemed to find focus in her feeling for him at that moment. And though surrounded by a storm of random motion, her heart kept a peaceful pace.

"Peter," she said softly, touching his ear with her lips. "I have something to tell you. And something to ask you." He turned to face her. The waning sunlight reflected off the mist, outlining his face with a golden aura. She thought he looked angelic. "Remember Lilah's prophecy?"

He rolled his eyes.

"Somehow she foretold the future."

He frowned. "Look, she probably did have something to do with your father's death. She's CIA. But telling the future? No way."

"But what about the ankh? That wouldn't be CIA."

"Don't talk silly."

"That's why I know she was right about me."

"What do you mean, about you?"

She backed away from him. "When someone like my Uncle Malcolm starts to believe, you have to wonder."

"You're not getting sick, are you?"

"No." She turned away from him for a moment, cast her eyes heavenward, watching the carefree clouds walk lazily by. "It's funny, but I've never felt better. And, Peter—"

"Look," he said, "here's what I've got in mind. Let's get out of here. Forget the book. Forget Roscha. Let's go to...to...I don't know. Tahiti or someplace tropical. Anywhere we can just live. You and me."

"Sounds wonderful. But..." She couldn't bear to look at him as she said it. "Lilah said I'd die soon."

"What? You can't—"

"And I believe her."

"That's insane! I thought you loved me, wanted to be with me?"

"More than life itself. But, Peter—"

"Then stop all this prophecy garbage. It's easy to predict the future if you're the one making it." He shook his head, picked up a rock and threw it into the mist. "Remember you said you'd always trust me? Remember, Ingrid? Well, trust this: I'll never let anyone hurt you again."

"Somebody said, 'Would I love you more if I loved truth less?'" She tossed her head wearily. "Call it intuition. Call it what you will but—"

"Voodoo? Molly, people can talk themselves right into a grave. Ask Reggie. It's all just witchcraft. He told me all about it."

"My *soul* knows it. I *am* going to die soon. I can't deny it. Or fight it."

"For the love of God, Molly!"

"Sweetheart, if you only believe in me—"

"Ya know, I never figured you for a coward. Nothing is fated. It... it would be like saying we have no free will." He turned away from her. "Every time I think I have you figured out…"

She touched his arm and spun him around, but he avoided her eyes. "Peter, please help me."

"Help you what? Kill yourself? To make this crazy prophecy a reality?"

Exasperated, she hung her head and struggled to find the right words. She knew it was going to be difficult, but not this difficult. She threw her arms around him again and held him. She heard the wind of his life—deep and rapid—rushing in and out of his chest, felt the pulsing of his heart against her cheek. She held him until his breathing slowed, his muscles relaxed, and his heart resumed a more subtle rhythm. "Don't you want to know what I wanted to ask?"

"I'm not sure I do."

"Oh?" She followed his gaze up into the yellowing sky of twilight. Now he looked like that little boy on the dock again, like Huckleberry Finn.

"When you killed—thought you'd killed—that Palestinian boy. Well you touched my heart in a way... I knew then..." He chuckled softly. "Then the other night you were so beautiful as you stood there naked. And when you told me you loved me... For once in my life, I felt it. Oh, I've heard the words before, but you made my heart hear them for the first time." He held her tight, squeezed her and rocked her. "Don't you understand what I'm saying? I love you. *By God, I love you,"* he shouted above the roar of the torrential waters. "That's something I'd never believed I could say to a woman. To anyone."

She kissed him with all her heart, her mind and her soul.

"Will you marry me, Molly?"

"Knowing I'm going to die soon?"

"If only for a moment."

"When?" Heart racing, her mind flooded with a million images of a dream fulfilled, even though she now believed it to be impossible.

"Tonight?" He reached in his breast pocket and retrieved a small, silver coated plastic ring with a clear plastic stone. "Here, I've been saving this for you."

"Cracker Jacks?" She laughed and kissed him again with a passion she only dimly knew she possessed. "My Bogie."

"Don't keep me waiting," he said jokingly. "Isn't that what Bogart would say?"

She nodded. "Of course it's yes. Let's ask Father Easterbrook."

He kissed her hard again. "I almost forgot," he said as they trudged along. "You had something you wanted to ask me?"

More gaily, more exuberantly than she ever thought possible, she laughed. It was a laugh she'd always wanted to be able to laugh, full of confidence and high spirit. Then she told him, "I wanted to ask you to marry me."

* * *

Molly was delighted that Father Easterbrook had agreed to preside over the nuptials. The ceremony would take place the next morning. She'd decided to make the formal announcement at the welcoming dinner, whose tantalizing aromas now beckoned. On her way to the dining room, she reflected on the dreamy moment, her heart an insufficient container of the joy she now felt. Yes, tomorrow would be the best day of her life, an affirmation of answered prayers and perennial hope, even if it meant today she'd have to endure a sizeable flock of butterflies that roiled her tummy as they gathered round the dinner table.

With Bell and Ndobo supplying the yellow-necked francolin, a delicious local game bird, and eland, a large antelope, Wakambi had crafted a feast of regal proportion. The large ebony-wood table fairly groaned under the weight of its bounty, which spread out conrucopialike before them.

She glanced about the large room, which doubled as a living room. Its walls were lined with bookshelves, with barely space for even one more thin volume. Sparsely furnished with an antique-Victorian flare, in pieces having originated in the British Colonial period, the living quarters nonetheless offered a floral-print, high-back sofa; a couple of well-worn armchairs; a hassock; two elephant-foot end tables with lamps; an ebony armoire to match the dinner table; and a china cabinet, also of ebony, and nearly devoid of crockery, in addition to the aforementioned dining table.

For the next hour, they sat and feasted and made small talk. Until finally Father Easterbrook pushed back from the head of the table, patting his swollen belly. "Whew! Reggie. What a treasure you have in Wakambi. Wish you'd visit more often."

"Are you ready?" Peter whispered to her.

Though nearly weightless with joy, she suddenly felt that funny feeling in her throat she got whenever she was about to stutter. "Would-would?"

Wonderfully, Peter seemed to grasp her difficulty without further elaboration and dipped his head in assent. He picked up a flagon of claret and walked slowly around the table, filling everyone's wineglass. Then, grinning broadly, he lifted his. "Sorry if I stumble over this, because I'm not much for public speaking. But I have an announcement." He winked at her. "Today—for the first and only time, I might add—I asked for a woman's hand in marriage. Something I never thought I'd do. And, yes, I mean Molly. Best of all, I'm happy to say, she… she..."

"Said yes!" she blurted, feeling instantly self-conscious.

Everyone laughed.

She jumped up and threw her arms around him. "Father Easterbrook will do the honors tomorrow morning. I hope you'll all come."

Peter kissed her cheek. "Thanks for the help; I needed it. And Reggie, I'd like you to be best man."

Bell stood up, hoisting his glass in toast. "To Molly and Peter. Bloody good show, Pete. From what I've seen, you've plucked a fine peach."

"We shouldn't forget Kopi," she said. "Kopi, would you be my ring bearer and hold my ring while we say our vows?"

"That's risky," Roscha smirked.

"Kopi's going to love it here," Father Easterbrook said, looking at the youngster. "We have a fine school—"

"No school!" Kopi screeched and stormed out the door.

"He'll come around," Bell said.

"By the way," Peter inquired between sips, "I've been wondering ever since we got here, why does someone with a Harvard Ph.D.—in cosmology, no less—give it up to be a priest in a place like this?"

Father Easterbrook sighed and straightened up in his chair. He put his hands together under his chin and paused for a moment. "Because I loved science too much. The way I should have been loving people. You see, the satisfaction of curiosity can be addicting—like so many things in life. And I was hooked."

"You're not suggesting curiosity is evil, are you?" Roscha said reproachfully.

"Not at all. The desire for knowledge is entirely natural. But one needs balance and I'd lost mine."

Molly thought of her father. If only he'd been able to reach the same understanding before he died.

"But oddly enough," Easterbrook continued, "it was a child's innocent game that made my decision easy. I'm sure you know the *Why?* game. Every three- or four-year-old knows it—they question everything at that age.

"Well, during one of these sessions with my niece, it struck me that if the game were carried to its logical conclusion, there would always be one last 'Why?'

"Think of it this way. Suppose I build a box that performs some function—a true X-Box, if you will. You can study it completely. Take as long as you like. Eventually, you will describe it at whatever level of detail you choose. Even down to the subatomic, or quantum, level, as we've done with our own world. But even if you succeed in describing it fully, in the end, you won't know *why* it exists. *That* is the last 'Why.'

"What you'll be left with is a description. But not, I'm afraid, an explanation. You'll be able to say what it looks like, how it functions, but not why. An explanation requires an answer to this last question. You see, unless I told you I made this box as a toy merely to please my child, you would never know this. Ultimately, our X-box is truly a metaphor for our own universe. And while science can give use very detailed descriptions, it cannot provide us with knowledge of *intention!* Only intention gives meaning. Intention reveals the heart of being. It is Free Will expressed."

"But science can't measure that," Molly said, following his story closely, searching for some shred of hope that the Gypsy was wrong after all.

"Exactly," Easterbrook agreed. "Take love. Can its existence be proved scientifically? Of course not! Yet would anyone deny its existence?"

Molly squeezed Peter's hand, gazed at his handsome profile and thought she at last knew the reality of that word.

"The same applies to the universe," Easterbrook continued. "Questions like, What happened before the Big Bang? Or, Why is the universe the way it is? Or, most importantly, Who are we? Why are we here? And why are we the way we are? Answers to these are unknowable by the exercise of intellect. This is the meaning of transcendence. And there is only one way to know the transcendent—"

"By direct access?" Roscha spoke the words like a challenge.

"Exactly, Roscha!" Easterbrook threw his hands up excitedly. "You must ask the creator himself."

Molly thought out loud: "Just as I cannot know your thoughts—your intentions—without your telling me."

"You're just trying to justify God," Roscha protested. "Or prove he exists."

Then, almost in a whisper, she heard him say, "But that's not necessary anymore."

"Anyhoo," Bell interjected, pushing his chair back and slapping his thighs. "It's near dark. I've got to make sure everything in camp is set. Ndobo will be back to take you to your tents."

"It's been most stimulating," Father Easterbrook said. "Thank you all. Would you join me in a brief prayer before you turn in?"

"Allow me, Father," Roscha countered soberly. "I'm going to read a prayer. A prayer from an inscription on a ceremonial knife recovered from an archaeological site in Iraq not two weeks ago by none other than our friend Kopi, wherever the little rat is." He looked around the room and under the table. "It's of an age that clearly predates Christianity or any other so-called modern religious tradition. Remember that! It's important.

"I finally deciphered it completely only this afternoon. In fact, Father, you unwittingly helped. You said the Lord's Prayer at lunch today. For some reason, it kept echoing in my mind all afternoon. I guess it was the rhythm of it—the cadence. But I still didn't make the connection until one of your school kids helped me see it by drawing a stick man in the dust. Anyway...here goes....

*Our Father, who art in heaven, Hallowed be thy name. Thy Kingdom come. Thy will be done...*"

He paused momentarily and looked around the room at every face, as if he were playing charades. A shadow of a smile creased the corners of his eyes. He recommenced,

*"...Thy Kingdom come...Thy will be done...On* Mars *as it is in heaven."*

"So you've deciphered the book." Peter said.

"The whole thing?" Molly's heart lightened at the prospect, for now, perhaps, she and Peter could return to America—and a normal life together. She turned to him. "Does this mean we can go home?"

"I don't think I bloody well get the joke. If that's what it is."

"It's no joke," Roscha assured him. "And it means, at the very least, that a prayer attributed to Jesus Christ predated him. Or what we know of him, here, on Earth. And that he—"

"Was a *Martian?"* Father Easterbrook shot back, his eyes bulging. "Preposterous!"

"Well, *on* Mars, anyway," Roscha clarified. "And well before he was here."

"What in bloody hell are you folks jabbering about?"

"What's the stick man got to do with it?" Peter asked.

Roscha shook his head disgustedly. "I'm embarrassed I didn't see it sooner, but from the beginning, the modified ankh stumped me. It appears throughout the text of the book, alone and in conjunction with the symbol for Mars."

"You have a Martian book?" Father Easterbrook asked with obvious disbelief.

Roscha nodded. "I couldn't figure out why because it just didn't quite fit in with the rest of the symbols. But today, watching some children drawing stick men in the dirt, it finally struck me. The symbol was a pictograph, like some of the others in the text."

"Pictograph...pictograph," Easterbrook muttered. "A picture, an actual picture of the thing represented."

"Correct."

Peter pulled the Martian ankh from around his neck and handed it to Father Easterbrook.

"You mean the ankh is a man?" Molly asked.

"Also correct," Roshca said confidently. "And in conjunction with the Mars pictograph, it means, essentially, Mars man, or *Martian.* Oh, before I forget, Molly, the stick man figure was all over the cloth your father asked you to analyze. Did you ever get the results from the brown stain on the cloth? The DNA analysis?"

She shook her head. *My God, I'd all but forgotten about Brenda and Uncle Malcolm.* But before she completed the thought, the electric atmosphere shattered as the door burst open.

"Perhaps I can help, Doctor Lavisch," said the man holding an Uzi automatic.

Father Easterbrook started to rise, "Who are you? What's this all about?"

The man pushed him back in his seat with the barrel of his Uzi.

"Paul Blalock!" Molly exclaimed.

"The man who worked for your father?" Peter put his arm around her and pulled her close.

"I told you I saw him in Jerusalem," she said.

"Just like the lady said," he laughed. "Paul Blalock, paleontologist extraordinaire. Right, Molly?"

"And CIA?" Roscha asked.

"Yeah." Blalock pointed to Bell. "So's he."

Peter frowned. "That true, Reggie?"

"Fraid so, chum."

"I knew finding you was a little too convenient," Peter muttered. Then he addressed Blalock. "Why did you kill Molly's father?"

Ignoring the question, Blalock turned to Bell, "Anyone else here?"

"Just children and the rest of my crew."

"Where's Bliss?"

"His mother was ill," Bell said with a shrug. "Said he wanted me to take care of this business for him."

"Good. Can't stand that fat sonofabitch, anyway."

"I'll be outside if you need me," Bell said and walked out.

"Why is the CIA here at my—?"

"First things first. Uh, Reverend, is it?"

"Father Easterbrook."

"Well, blessed Father, like I said, first things first."

"I'll ask you again," Peter demanded. "Why did you kill Molly's father? And why are you so damned afraid the world will find out about all this?"

Molly watched Blalock scan the room. He removed his wire rim glasses and brushed his hand over his head, making his close-cropped blond hair stand up in wet little spikes. Her father had been right about him all along.

"Well, all right," Blalock said, smirking like an adolescent thug. "Since we're all going to be one big happy family—for a few days anyway—I guess it couldn't hurt. Professor Lavisch was a traitor, pure and simple."

"He was no such thing!" Molly said with a lack of conviction that surprised her.

"Oh?" Blalock chided. "Perhaps you'd like to ask him yourself."

*"What?"* Her mind reeled. She clutched her locket. *Alive?* But how? She'd seen his shattered corpse with her own eyes. He was all too dead.

But as soon as the disheveled, ashen-faced man crossed the threshold, she felt pins and needles start pricking at her hands and feet, her sight dimmed and her mouth grew suddenly dry. *Malcolm?* Slowly and silently the man turned toward her, emerging from the growing shadows of evening. Her eyes focused instinctively on his hairline. The port-wine birthmark!

* * *

Filled with rage, Peter rushed to Molly's side and, with Father Easterbrook's help, carried her to the sofa. *This is it,* he thought. *The end game.*

"Well, well, old friend," Roscha said with mocking precision. "So you've thrown in with Snow?"

"Yes. And if you know what's good for you—"

"Oh, I can see how you'd want to make a deal, but setting up your brother?"

Miles looked away.

"You don't seem too happy to see your daughter, either," Peter told him, feeling vindicated as he noticed the port-wine birthmark. "She's been sick, thinking you were killed."

"As I was saying," Blalock continued, "against explicit orders from the highest levels, the good professor here tried to reveal information of the utmost sensitivity—"

"My father may be many things," Molly cried, leaping off the couch and running to his side. "But he's no traitor. He only wanted the world to know what it deserves to know." She hugged him. "Are you all right?"

Miles responded with a limp pat on her shoulder but said nothing.

"He's a renegade," Blalock snarled. "He plays only by his own rules. His ego's as big as an asteroid, and from what I can see, he doesn't care who he hits with it. He had to be taken out before he did real harm. Only we made a slight mistake."

"Is that true, Dad? About Uncle Malcolm. He's—"

"Yes!" Miles barked. "It was Malcolm you saw. And, yes, he's dead. And, yes, you will be too if you don't give up the book. That's the deal. Help them recover the book, we all live."

"Tsk, tsk, tsk," Blalock sneered. "Shame on you, Miles. See? That's just what I mean. He's lying again. He made no deal for you people. Only for his own fat ass."

"All right, Mister Blalock," Peter said cautiously. "You say there's a national security issue. How? What could it possibly hurt to reveal the book?"

"There's a lot you don't know, MacKenzie. And a lot I'm not at liberty to say. But there are reasons. And much more we need to know. Information possibly contained in that book. As someone in the Intelligence business—especially an ex-military officer—you should know better. And speaking of presumptions, how can you presume to say there is *no* security risk? Do you know what's in the book?"

"No," Peter answered quickly. "I haven't even seen it, neither has Molly."

Blalock looked at Roscha again. Putting his foot on the table, he tapped the muzzle of the Uzi on the tip of his boot. "What about that, Venable?"

Peter's own feelings of patriotism welled up, confusing him. Maybe Blalock was right; maybe Molly's old man was a traitor, another Julius Rosenberg or Aldrich Ames. *She wouldn't know.* As far as he was concerned, Miles was a scumbag, a child molester, just another brother of Cain. He didn't care if Miles was the "greatest scientist" or the greatest anything. And maybe Blalock did know what the book was about. For all Peter knew, Roscha was a traitor too. All he wanted now was to do the right thing—and live. *But not without Molly.* "Give him the book, Roscha."

"No!" Molly yelled. "Don't ask me how I know, but everything here is related. The book. The prophecy. The Eastern Gate in Jerusalem. Everything!"

Her reaction took Peter by surprise. "How, Molly? What if Blalock's telling the truth? We're supposed to be married tomorrow. Don't you want that?"

"Of course I do. But—"

"But what? Maybe this *is* a national security issue. And maybe your father *is* a traitor. Look what he did to Malcolm."

"Somehow I know."

"Intuition again?" Molly's obsession with Lilah and her prophecy was beginning to make him doubt his own convictions about what the truth really was.

"Call it what you want," Molly told him. "The book must be given back. But not to the CIA!"

"I don't have the book," Roscha calmly said.

The room fell quiet.

"Well, well..." Blalock paused as he strutted back and forth along the length of the table like a cock in a chicken coop, running his hand over his blond, crew cut head, glancing left and right at the assembled prisoners. "To answer Mister Venable's very apropos question of a few moments ago, the DNA from the stolen government property" —He looked directly at Molly— "Which we retrieved from your very efficient lab technician, Brenda Cruise, was from none other than *Homo sapiens sapiens."*

"Good God!" Roscha gulped. He planted his slowly shaking head in his hands. "*Human!* It's true, then. All of it."

"And what, exactly, does that mean?" Blalock demanded, putting the Uzi's barrel under Roscha's chin and lifting his head.

Roscha stiffened. "It sounds as if you know more than I do."

Blalock, whose rapid movements betrayed a growing impatience stared directly into Roscha's face. "Come now, Venable, I heard your little speech before we came in. Obviously you've deciphered a good deal of the book."

Miles joined the inquisition. "Why come *here*, Roscha, to the middle of Africa? Something in the book told you to."

Roscha sat silently for a moment, every eye on him. "I'll speak only to Admiral Snow."

"You may get your chance," Blalock said angrily. "But then again..." He whacked Roscha up side the head with his open hand, knocking him to the floor, where he lay motionless. "Maybe you won't. You see, Admiral Snow thinks I've botched this assignment so far. I need to redeem myself. So it would look very good for me if you gave me the book first. Otherwise the Admiral might have to settle for body bags. Get my meaning?"

# CHAPTER 32

Peter struggled to sleep as he lay on the knotty wood floor in the dining room, where only a few hours before they had all so happily celebrated his engagement to Molly, who now, above him on the sofa, slept soundly, her muted snore dainty and purr like. He wondered how she could sleep so peacefully after all she'd been through. *Reggie was right about one thing. She's a fine peach.*

Even without their current predicament, he doubted he could've slept. Outside, the sounds of the night were deafening. Insects mostly. But more unnerving were the high-pitched keening of jackals and the cries of bush babies that resided in the house-sized Baobab tree on the edge of the compound. Then he heard an earth-rumbling *uuurrrunghhh!* A lion. He wondered if it was the same one Reggie had pointed out earlier in the day a mile or more from the mission, the one he'd said would most likely keep its distance. But it sounded much closer now, all the more menacing because of the brooding darkness that lay just beyond the thin walls.

Blalock had promised that the new day would bring some unpleasant surprises if Roscha did not cooperate. Earlier, Peter had watched Blalock inventory his large briefcase. Among its ominous cargo were syringes, vials, and dental utensils, including a high-speed drill. Knowing interrogation techniques as he did, the outcome for Roscha was a foregone conclusion: He would talk, eventually, for the calculus of pain was inexorable. Then what? That question alone was an effective antidote to peaceful slumber.

Peter wondered how he and Molly could possibly escape now without Reggie's help. Alone, he was no match for the small cadre assembled against him. Even Kopi, who had rushed outside at dinner, had never returned, not that he could be of much help anyway. No. He'd have to bide his time, wait for the right moment and do some kind of Hail Mary.

Hours passed like eons, minutes like years, as he tossed like a feverish patient for whom time had become an amorphous, dilated dimension. But before he knew it, he'd drifted seamlessly into the twilight between sleep and waking. Suddenly, the vision of Roy Corbett's terrified face startled him, but he didn't awaken, as would usually be the case. Instead he felt trapped, a prisoner of his dream—if such it was.

"I should have saved myself, Peter," Corbett's ghostlike image, still dressed in his flight suit, said pitifully. "And so must you. So must we all." Then the apparition departed with a fiendish laugh.

Within the space of a dreamy heartbeat, Peter stood trembling at the gate of an old clapboard house on a precipice overlooking the ocean. The house, whose paint had long since weathered away from harsh onshore gales and neglect, appeared abandoned. Yet he knew someone or something awaited him within. Low, purple-gray clouds roiled in an unnatural way near the horizon, skittering and colliding in the dimming violet dusk. A flash of thunderless lightning coincided with the appearance of Lilah Blackwell, who waved invitingly to him from up ahead on the long walkway leading to the front door. She wore a bulky white sweatshirt, like a cheerleader's, with bright red letters that said GYPSY PRINCESS and a large ankh symbol that ran top to bottom, also in blood red. Suddenly, she pulled up the sweatshirt, exposing her breasts, with nipples the size of pink Oreo cookies, each a portrait, one a man, one a woman, like opposing pictures from a locket, though their identity was unclear. Above her left breast was the gold wings of the Naval Aviator, with its single upright anchor and shield.

She called to him, laughing in a silly, taunting way, and then said, "You're not dreaming, Peter," before running ahead, beckoning with waving arms for him to approach.

A gust of chill wind, salty and fishy with the smell of the ocean, pushed him off balance. He took a half-leaping step through the rusted wrought iron gateway. He blinked and Lilah was gone, quickly reappearing on the threshold of the door. Another gust pushed him, harder this time, like an invisible hand. Sensing a presence behind him, he turned and looked back. No one there.

"This is a dream," he heard himself mutter. "Isn't it?"

But this was no ordinary dream; he *knew* he was dreaming. A dream whose texture is at once so frighteningly bizarre and yet so vividly real that, on awakening, the dreamer may question the very nature of consciousness. A dream whose boundaries are defined by fear, an unfamiliar fear, not of mere physical death but of utter expungement of spiritual identity, of soul.

He took another step down the pathway, then another, and another, drawn helplessly onward to meet, he sensed, some secret destiny. He struggled against his will to retreat.

All at once he was inside the house, moving along a long, dark hallway at whose end was a door outlined by a light from within. His urge to run away was overpowering. Something or someone was behind the door at the end of this black tunnel. It—he—knew him, wanted him, and impelled him onward.

Whatever *it* was, he had to confront it. The presence he'd felt behind him was now at his side. Paralyzed, he could not turn to see who it was, yet he continued to move, as if floating, toward the door. Was the presence friend or foe? He could not tell. Closer now, only a few brief steps away. Behind the door he heard faint voices. What were they saying? Acid from his knotted stomach rose in his throat. Sweat drenched him like a soaking rain. The voices were louder now. They were calling for someone. They were calling for him...

*Peter!*

Molly's scream, along with the sharp crack of gunfire, wrenched him into consciousness. A body crashed through a wooden chair onto the floor in front of him. As Blalock's life oozed out, his exploded face twisted into a grotesque, fleshy smile. Peter instinctively pulled Molly off the couch to the floor behind him, shielding her from the shots that zinged through the open door, windows and walls.

For a moment, the shooting stopped. One of Blalock's men crouched low at the doorjamb, darting his head out and back, like the tongue of a snake, inspiring another short fusillade. Then Peter saw Blalock's gun. But before he could react, a phantomlike form flashed past him, scooped up the gun and disarmed Bell and the agent by the door.

*"Allah is Great! Allah is Good!"* the wild-eyed Arab yelled.

Moments later the front steps creaked and a dark blot of a figure, outlined against the growing pink light of dawn, swaggered across the threshold.

"Bliss!" Roscha blurted.

"You *know* him?" Peter asked.

Bliss laughed irreverently in the presence of the newly dead, as he turned Blalock's body over with the muzzle of his rifle. "Hello, Paul. What an unexpected pleasure! And you, Professor Venable, likewise, I'm sure."

"What the bloody hell are you doing, Bandar?" Bell demanded, unable to conceal his surprise.

"You keep fine company, Reggie," Peter sneered, wondering who else was not what he seemed.

Bell got to his feet. "These are Admiral Snow's men. You had to know they'd be here by now. You bloody told me to notify them!"

Bliss pointed his pistol at the center of Bell's chest. "It might be better for you to stay put for the time being. Moab, get this...this mess out of here." Then he pushed aside Father Easterbrook, who had begun to give last rites, kicked Blalock's corpse and pointed to the sole surviving CIA man. "Lock him in the storehouse with the others. Leave the holy man here."

Bell, in his usual unflappable way, took out his pipe and his tobacco pouch, along with his ivory elephant-foot tamper. "What bloody mischief are you up to, Bandar?" he inquired calmly. "You said Snow wanted them located and followed. Nothing more. And what's this nonsense about a book from Mars?"

Bliss drew up a wicker chair and with apparent difficulty, lowered himself down on its rickety frame, which popped and groaned under the load. "It's a mad, mad world, Reggie. Alliances shift. Plans change accordingly." He wiped away the accumulating sweat with the yellowing sash of his kaffiyeh and tried to lift one of his high-topped leather riding boots onto the edge of the table, just as Blalock had done only hours before, but couldn't manage it. "This African heat is insufferable."

"*He* wants the book, too?" Miles threw back his head, laughing. "And he's CIA? How ironic, in a Shakespearean sort of way."

"I've had just about enough," Father Easterbrook declared and moved toward the short-wave radio. "Whatever your business with these people, this is not the place for it. We have children here. Have you no regard for their safety? I must insist—"

*Bang! Bang!*

With vulgar detachment, Bliss squeezed off two shots, one at the radio, one at Easterbrook.

"Father!" Molly cried as Easterbrook fell backwards, collapsing at her feet.

"Leave him!" Bliss ordered. "He's only foot-shot. He'll live."

"I'm a doctor—"

"My, my..." Bliss's stomach jiggled with a snort. "Your spirit burns as brightly as your beautiful hair."

Peter watched Bliss struggle to heave himself up out of the chair and waddle over to Molly, his breaths coming in loud, husky volumes, like some rabid animal. As he approached, she recoiled, quickly crawling to the corner, where he followed, trapping her. With the barrel of his gun, he lifted a lock of her hair, then let it fall, strand by strand, across her face. When he bent over her, Peter knew he'd have to kill the man. From what he'd just seen, maybe Bell could be counted on to help, but it didn't matter. "Touch her again and I'll kill you."

Bliss turned the muzzle of his pistol and aimed squarely at Peter's head. "Bravely spoken." Bliss kept him within his scan as he stroked her hair again, this time with his hand, continuing down her shoulders.

"Stop it!" She pushed his hand away.

But he kept up, leaning in closer, slowly transgressing the rise of her breast.

Hoping the fat man couldn't react quickly enough to stop him, Peter leaped to his feet. But Bell grabbed his arm and held him back.

"Wait, Pete!"

*Whack!* Molly had slapped Bliss smartly across his round oily face.

Looking stunned, he stood motionless for an instant, then grunted, "You just stay put, pretty one—"

"I heard a shot," Moab Abdul shouted as he lunged through the doorway. "I ran all the way."

"No cause for alarm," Bliss assured him, returning to his chair. "Now, Roscha, there's no point prolonging this. Or need I remind you what happened to your friend Sharabi? Moab! Show them."

Moab reached into a small leather pouch that hung from his belt and retrieved a pair of human fingers, all gray and shriveled, their bones raggedly exposed, the heavy red-earth deposits of the third-level still packed under their nails.

"Don't tell him anything, Roscha," Peter said, suddenly deciding Blalock was right after all. "It's only a matter of—"

"Calm down, Pete," Bell urged, squeezing Peter's arm so hard he felt the nails dig in.

"I want the book," Bliss growled.

"Knowing him as I do," Bell said, "I'd recommend you give him what he wants."

"Yes!" Molly shouted. "Give it to him."

"A minute ago you said we shouldn't," Peter said, puzzled by her sudden change of heart.

Molly glanced at Blalock, then Easterbrook. "It's not worth anyone else getting hurt."

"Think of the children," Easterbrook added in short, choking gasps.

Peter looked at Roscha, who squirmed but avoided everyone's eyes.

"Let go of guns!" a small, brave voice yelled. Kopi struggled to stand erect under the weight of Bell's .375 H&H Magnum, which she held with fair precision on Moab's midsection. "Kopi shoot! Promise!" With some difficulty, she refocused the barrel on Bliss, then back to Moab in a labored sweeping motion, but neither man dropped his gun.

"Kopi, put the gun down.... Please," Molly begged.

"Leave the kid alone," Peter told her. He knew she was too big-hearted to deal with this situation, and this was combat. And in the quirky ways of war, Kopi just could be their savior.

"Bring the gun to me, son," Bell commanded.

"No! Here, Kopi." Peter challenged, sensing a Hail Mary. "You're doing just fine, kid."

"What do you think, Moab?" Bliss asked gruffly. "Will the little bastard shoot?"

"He knows how to use it," Bell warned. "I showed him myself. Come over here, son."

"Stupid boy," Moab said, setting his rifle against the wall and approaching Kopi without caution. "It's time this little camel turd—"

"Stop!" Kopi cried.

Moab hesitated, looked at Bliss.

"Kopi shoot. Promise." She raised the bolt handle up; then, without pulling the bolt back, she quite properly returned the bolt to its down and locked position.

"Good, good, kid," Peter coached in a whisper, remembering Bell's little trick.

"Look!" Moab jeered, reaching for the gun, "he doesn't even know how to—"

*Boom!*

The high-powered rifle's report reverberate like a bomb blast in Peter's ears as the copper-jacketed lead slug spun Moab violently around and slammed him against the wall, where he crumpled to the floor like a dishrag. Through the milky-blue smoke, Peter watched helplessly as Kopi, knocked off her feet by the recoil, struggled to move the bolt action for another shot. But instead of drawing the bolt up and back to eject the spent cartridge and pick another round off the magazine, she again just lifted the bolt up and put it back down. Bell and Peter lunged for the rifle simultaneously. He stretched out his hand, but Molly snatched his belt, and before he knew it, he was on his back, watching as a bullet from Bliss's gun tore the butt of the rifle from Bell's hand.

"Filthy wog," Bell cursed, gathering himself up and shaking his hand frantically. Blood splattered across the floor making little explosions of red, while Kopi re-shouldered the damaged rifle, aiming squarely at Bliss's gut.

"Kopi shoot again!"

But this time Bliss approached the child without the slightest hesitation. He grabbed the rifle barrel, put a booted foot on Kopi's chest, and kicked her back hard on her rump. Then, pointing his pistol between Kopi's terrified eyes, he pulled back the hammer and began to squeeze the trigger. "You little black dung beetle—"

"No!" Molly screamed, shielding the child with her body. "Don't touch him again!"

Bliss grunted. "Very well. You may have him...for now."

"Help me...help me, my prince," Moab pleaded as he writhed in a gathering pool of his own blood.

"Fool!" Bliss turned away and yelled, "Kufu! Bring the gunbearer."

Moments later Kufu, a short, bearded Egyptian, missing his left ear, entered with Ndobo.

"Baba," Ndobo called, "are you all right?"

Bell nodded. "Just a scratch."

Bliss, streaming sweat, looked at Bell as he spoke to Ndobo: "Mister Ndobo, I want you to take my man, Kufu, on a little safari. Bring me back—"

"What's this all about?" Bell demanded. "What do you need *him* for?"

Bliss ignored him and finished. "Bring me three serpents...two harmless, one venomous. Anything will do. A cobra. A mamba. An adder—whatever you can quickly put your hands on...so to speak." He growled a laugh. "Bring them back to me, each in a separate bag. Kufu will go with you to make sure there's no funny business." He motioned for Kufu to leave. But Ndobo did not budge, instead looking again at Bell.

"Better do as he says," Bell relented.

Bliss snorted. "Oh, good advice, Reggie. Good advice. Hurry along now, Kufu. This African heat is insufferable."

* * *

Father Easterbrook's small dining room was morguelike; its air, humid and fetid with the smell of cordite and warm blood, nauseated Peter. Outside, the afternoon was ablaze with a strong tropical sun.

Insects buzzed and chirped, harmonizing in a crude, metronomic rhythm with the ever-present low rumble of the waterfalls and the barks and howls of the monkeys. For the natural world, it was just another day of life, of eat or be eaten.

No one but Roscha knew where the book was or what it meant, and there was no point in pressing the issue now. Besides, Peter doubted Bliss would let them go even if Roscha did give up the book. No. Somehow he had to kill Bliss before.... He looked at Molly and couldn't finish the thought.

The incident with Kopi had renewed his hope that Reggie might now be an ally, if only temporarily. He glanced at Bliss. Could be anyone, he mused, the corner grocer, a barber, a shoe salesman, a loving husband and father, the savior of the world. Such was the banality of his face, which now seemed to brighten with the sounds of footsteps on the porch.

Kufu and Ndobo laid three identical gray burlap sacks on the floor in front of Bliss, and he got up to examine the contents. "Hmmm," he said with obvious pleasure upon opening the first sack. Opening the second, he hissed a chuckle. "Good, good, good." But with the third sack, Bliss's eyes got noticeably larger and a smile broke across his seeping face. "Excellent! Your companions will thank you, Ndobo, for making this an interesting contest."

Peter looked at Bell, who mouthed the question, "Contest?" then shrugged his handlebar mustache.

"Kufu," Bliss said pointing to Ndobo, "take him back to the storehouse. And hurry back. I want to get started."

* * *

As soon as Kufu reappeared, Peter felt his heart begin to race. He sensed they were running out of time. And before he could think, Bliss holstered his gun and placed a chair in the center of the room.

"We're going to play a little game," he announced. "A variation on Russian roulette—or perhaps 'Let's Make a Deal.' You know that old game show that asked what's behind door number one, two or three? It's was my mother's favorite. Of course I'll play...Who was it? Monty Hill, no?"

No one spoke.

"Well then," he continued, "I can see I have your attention. Here's how we'll play. One of you will sit here." He tapped on the chair with his pistol. "Then our contestant will choose bag number one, bag number two or number three. After that, he'll open it and without peeking—that's right, *nooo peeeeking*." His belly rippled with a laugh. "He—or she—" He glanced at Molly "will retrieve the serpent. If you refuse...." He looked at Kufu, who nodded and elevated the barrel of his gun in affirmation. "Choose well, my friends. You are playing for your life. Remember what I told Ndobo to get? Two choices are harmless. But one...ahhh, but one special one, she will, I promise you, yield an unpleasant surprise. She's a beauty, arrayed like royalty. But she has a nasty disposition. And the largest fangs of all her sisters."

Peter noticed Bell's mustache twitch when Bliss said "largest fangs."

"Of course," Bliss continued, casting his eyes upon Roscha, "the game can be avoided completely, if only our *old friend,* Professor Venable, will produce the book. If he does, Kufu and I will quickly depart. I have no reason to harm you. As I've already said, I have no liking for this climate." He wiped away a sheet of oily sweat with his kaffiyeh, which had taken on the appearance of a dirty dishrag. "Well, Roscha?"

"Roscha, please," Molly begged, holding Kopi close at her side, "give him the book. Father Easterbrook and"— She dipped her head at the groaning Moab. "He needs more medical care than I can give here. He'll die soon without a hospital."

"Come on, Roscha!" Miles joined in. "There's no point in keeping it now. Give it to him, for Christ's sake."

"I bloody well agree with Miles, Venable. It can't be worth dying for."

Zombielike and deranged, Roscha at last spoke. "Brandon Hadid," he said as if announcing a theatrical player. Then he looked at Peter with a wild expression and mumbled through barely parted lips, "Do you think there are things worse than death?"

*"What?"* Peter shouted. "Are you nuts? He won't kill *you*. He'd never find the book that way. But he'll kill us. And you know what, professor? *I'll* kill you if you don't give it to him."

"Good show, Pete," Bell chimed. "And you can count on me to second you. The jig's up, Venable. It's over. You—"

Roscha croaked, "There *are* worse things, Peter!" Then his head dropped back between his knees.

"So you are willing to let all your friends die, eh, Roscha?" Bliss growled. "Perhaps a round of the game will warm your heart—and loosen your tongue."

Peter saw Bliss look at Molly and jumped to his feet. "I'll go first."

But Bell stepped in front of him. "Not so bloody fast, Pete. Unless I've been fired, it's my job."

"Wouldn't want you to lose that fat government pension." Peter moved toward the chair, thinking he'd use the snake somehow to distract Kufu, get his gun and end this nightmare forever.

Bell pulled him back again, but Peter wrenched free. "Okay, you're fired!" Then he felt the barrel of Bliss's gun pinch his chest.

*"Ha! Ha!* This is more fun than I thought. You'll flip for it. That's right, isn't it? Flip for it? Another quaint American custom."

Bell quickly fished out a coin and flipped. "Call it, Pete."

"Heads."

The coin bounced on the floor and spun lazily on its rim for what seemed an eternity before settling down to its fated verdict. "Sorry, chum."

Peter wondered what Bell had up his sleeve, but for now, all he could do was watch. He pulled Molly close. "Some wedding day," he said, kissing her. "I'm sorry." She smiled a slightly sad wisp of a smile that seemed filled with forgiveness and, in equal measure, with resignation.

"Well, well, Reggie," Bliss sneered. "Aren't you the consummate professional? *Hee, hee*. I always said you were worth every *riyal.* Smart, too. As first player, the odds favor you." Affecting a far nastier tone he ordered, "Now choose!"

Bell took the chair as coolly as Peter thought he would and pointed to the bag on the far right. Kufu placed it gingerly on Bell's lap, then backed away slowly and took up his guard station by the door.

The hot, putrid air clung like thick syrup; each breath took its toll. Peter saw that Bell, brave as he was, could not control a slight tremor as he untied the cord binding the top of the canvas sack, for obviously he, more than anyone else, knew the possible dangers within. Only a pale pink rouge of color on the heights of his cheeks remained of what was normally his ruddy complexion. A drizzle of perspiration dampened his blond hair at the margins. He seemed to hesitate, glancing about the room, finally resting his gaze on Peter before quickly reaching into the bag.

"African egg eater!" Bliss rejoiced. "Ha! ha!..."

Bell flung the harmless snake out the door into the dusty yard, whose atmosphere now shimmered with heat in the blinding African sun. Quickly, the snake slithered back toward the porch in search of shade. Legs shaking, Bell resumed his place beside Peter.

"Well done, Reggie, well done," Bliss gloated. "Now, Roscha, will you reconsider, or should the game go on?"

"Roscha, I beg you," Molly pleaded. "Let him have the book."

"Don't beg," Peter snapped. "I'm next."

"Not so fast." Bliss leaned back in his chair, scanned the participants, taking a long time to speak. "I think not, Mr. Pete. Obviously Professor Venable has no emotional attachment to you. But...let's see. The boy—"

"N-Not K-Kopi. Not a ch-child!" Molly cried. "T-Take me." She stood up. But Kufu had already caught Kopi.

"Molly! Great One! Kopi hate snakes!"

As Kufu wrestled the struggling girl into the chair and began tying her in with a leather thong, Molly attacked like a leopard, jumping on his back, screaming, pounding and scratching furiously at his eyes.

"D-Dad, h-help me. P-Peter!"

*Bang!*

Everyone froze.

Bliss shoved Peter back with the butt of the still-smoking rifle, then, setting the rifle aside, he turned to Miles. "So this is your daughter?" He drew his pistol and held it to Miles's head. "She *is* your daughter, no?"

Miles quaked in his seat. His upper lip visibly quivered as he nodded uncertainly.

Bliss moved back, thumbing the hammer on the pistol. "I have a sister. And I can tell you my father would kill before he allowed her to be so shamefully humiliated. And he would kill himself before he'd let her know danger. *You,* Mister Miles. You will be our next contestant." "Peter! Help him."

"No, no," Miles blubbered. "No, no, not me. Please! Molly!" Bliss had to help Kufu drag him onto the chair. Kufu tied him in, leaving his hands free to explore the burlap sack, which Kufu quickly placed on his lap and retreated. Miles's normally radish-red face suddenly turned chalky. He mumbled incoherently. He vomited.

"Sit him up straight," Bliss ordered, motioning to Kufu..

Peter felt Molly fight for a deep breath. "T-Take me," she begged. "He's g-got a bad heart. You'll k-k-kill him." But he held her immobile until she exhausted herself.

"Get his hand in the bag!"

The Egyptian lackey dutifully complied, untying the sack and grasping the whimpering man's shaking arm. But before he could go further, Miles heaved a loud guttural sound and collapsed, tumbling onto the floor with a thud, still attached to the chair. Kufu quickly re-laced the bag.

*"D-D-Daad!"* Breaking free, she raced to her father's limp body, bawling miserably. "Ohhh...he-he's deaad..."

"The book, Roscha, where is it?" Bliss cuffed Roscha across the face with the barrel of his gun, but to no avail. Sobbing like a child, he rocked his head side to side, never uttering a word.

"Enough of this!" Bliss pushed the barrel of his pistol painfully into the space just below Peter's left eye and jerked his head in Molly's direction. "Put her in the chair."

"You sonofabitch!" Peter roared, trying to squirm away, but the pistol dug deeper into his eye socket until he wanted to scream. Then he heard the metallic *click* of the gun cocking. He fell back against the wall. Bliss pressed the gun ever more forcefully into the orbit of his eye. A dagger of pain lanced through his brain, blurring his vision.

“Choose!” Bliss snarled.

“There’re still two bags,” Bell told him. “She’ll make it.”

Becoming dizzy, his vision now double, Peter couldn’t decide whether to puke or pass out, when Roscha’s whimpering grew louder and he looked at Molly. “We’ll all be dead soon enough,” he said before again burying his head between his knees.

Kufu lifted Molly’s limp body onto the rickety chair, roughly snapping her head back by her ponytail as he lashed her down. Defiantly, she jerked her head forward, inviting the blade of. Kufu’s against her throat. A trickle of blood made its way down her slender neck.

“Kufu!” Bliss barked. “Would you ruin our game?”

Looking like a chastised mongrel, Kufu relaxed his knife, but before withdrawing, he cut off a sheath of Molly’s hair, which fluttered to the floor like a red ribbon.

With all his strength, Peter pushed against the gun in an effort to rise, but Bliss jammed it harder, squeezing his eye aside as the penetrating barrel created a blast of stars and pain. Through his remaining good eye, he watched as Molly’s delicate fingers untied the hemp cord on the earthen-colored sack. She held her head steady, without the slightest tremble. The string fell away. The bag yawned open. She closed her eyes and bit her lip. The sack wriggled as her hand plunged in.

*P-Peterrr!* Her hand yanked from the sack—along with the savagely flailing snake, its fangs still tenaciously embedded in her wrist. Her body went limp and she toppled to the floor.

Its skin a curious palette of tan, black and white, the snake hissed, writhing its pudgy body violently s it tried to slither away.

“Get it back!” Bliss yelled But too late. Kufu had quickly dispatched it with his broad knife. Even in death the headless serpent’s body continued to undulate menacingly.

Molly’s bloodcurdling wail, still reverberating inside Peter’s head, washed away his pain, and with all his being, he shoved past Bliss and flew to her side.

"Peter," she whispered softly, trying to rise. Her arm, already horribly swollen and beginning to turn purple, oozed from two puncture wounds with raised edges like little volcanoes about two inches apart.

"Just be still." He hopelessly wiped the edges of her wounds with his sleeve as she struggled to speak between little puffs of breath, which grew smaller even as their pace quickened. He kissed her, brushed the perspiration from her brow with his cheek, and stroked her radiant red tresses. For the first time since news of his father's death, he felt his eyes well with tears.

"We almost made it, didn't we?" she whispered.

"Molly... My Molly."

"No." She put her finger to his lips. A scant smile creased the corner of her mouth. "Your Ingrid, remember?" Her panting slowed. She struggled to get her good hand into her pants pocket.

"Here, let me." He took the little plastic wedding ring from the Cracker Jacks out of her pocket and placed it on her pinky, the only finger it fit. He looked into her green eyes, still liquid and bright. She smiled peacefully, holding tight to her locket, as if it were an anchor. With her other hand, she weakly squeezed his arm. "I told you Lilah was right." Her breathing seemed to falter, coming in uneven spasms. Then, without a hint of a stammer, she whispered, "I love you beyond forever and forever."

She fell limp and silent. He eased her head gently to the floor. But it was the end of his gentleness. Now his consciousness narrowed to a singular focus on Bliss's throat, at which he lunged with the fury of wounded animal. He saw his hands only inches from their target, when he fell into blackness.

# CHAPTER 33

Peter's first awareness was of a penetrating buzzing sound arising out of a black void, which, eerie though it was, nevertheless seemed familiar. Soon, the darkness gave way to an accumulating light, which melted the shadows, revealing a surreal, rosy landscape lined with red rivers flowing nowhere in particular.

Particle by particle, he gathered his consciousness, finally opening his eyes. The red rivers disappeared. He blinked hard against the hot afternoon sun streaming in upon his sodden face. He tried to roll over—*ouch!* Dried blood had firmly stuck his hair to the floor. Freeing it accentuated the already frightful pain in his head. Across the floor a mass of blow flies invaded Moab's eyes, mouth and nostrils, his bloated body already beginning to stink in the heat. Above the frenzy of flies, he heard whimpering.

And then he saw Molly. All physical pain vanished; he felt only an auguring heartsickness. She rested in the crook of Father Easterbrook's arm, still and pale. The priest, with eyes shuddered against tears that nonetheless seeped through, did his best to keep the aggressive flies off her face, which even now showed no horror, but rather an angelic peacefulness.

"Peter!" Easterbrook said, "Thank God. I thought you'd been killed too." He rocked Molly's corpse like a baby. "I'm sorry, Peter."

"Let me." Peter took her into his arms. He caressed her limp body, kissing her cool face. Still he loved the scent of her, loved the feel of her hair, her skin. "Molly, Molly," he murmured and thought just how empty Father Easterbrook's attempts at solace were. He looked at the man and said in an intentionally accusatory tone, "Why? That's your game, isn't it? Then tell me why!"

Easterbrook dropped his head, sobbing with renewed intensity.

"So this is the mercy your God shows his best. And she was the best. You know that." He looked at the hideous snake's partially coiled carcass in the middle of the floor; its head, flat and wide, lay nearby.

"A Gaboon viper," Easterbrook croaked, rubbing his leg above his swollen, blood-caked foot. "She died quickly, Peter. You can thank God for that."

"That's supposed to make me feel better?" Calmly, he picked up the severed lock of Molly's red hair and put it in his pocket. "Where'd they go?"

"To the promontory. They took Reggie and Roscha—and the boy."

He stood up and instantly grabbed his head, which spun violently. He nearly fainted, falling down on one knee. "Do you have a gun?"

"No.... Peter, don't kill him."

"Why? Because it wouldn't be just? There is no justice in this whole pus-filled boil we call the World." He began searching the room, looking for anything he could use as a weapon. "Don't you even have a knife? Anything?"

"What justice there is, we make."

"Frankly, Mike," he said, dropping the clerical honorific, "I think you're a fool. What's worse, I think I am too." He went into the kitchen, where he found a boning knife. "How long they been gone?"

"Only moments," Easterbrook blubbered. "Perhaps more. Oh, I don't know... But Peter, you mustn't sully her memory with vengeance. You'll be hurt more—"

"Save the sermon for the kids." Never looking back, he shoved the knife in his belt and left the pathetic man weeping with what remained of his dreams. Then he dizzily stumbled outside, where looking up into the searing African sun, he nearly fainted.

* * *

The roar of the falls resonated with the throbbing ache in Peter's head. He'd left the trail about twenty yards from the small clearing at the promontory, which now lay beyond a thick wall of mist-dampened underbrush. The pulsing pain seemed to make the jungle shimmer with an eerie metallic green hue, as he fought his way, vine by stubborn vine, closer to his target.

Then without warning, the world began to spin. He braced himself against a tree but couldn't hold on and fell helplessly to the ground, rolling to and fro uncontrollably, as the canopy above him swirled into a blue-green tableau of sky, trees and clouds. His vision grew dim and he thought he'd pass out. He heard voices just as vomit rose in his throat. Choking it back down, he took a deep breath and held it, recovering a bit. Then, using the low branches, he pulled himself erect and peered through the brush. There he saw Roscha trembling pitifully before Bliss, while next to him Kufu guarded Bell and Kopi.

"You're sure this is where you hid the book?" Bliss yelled.

Roscha nodded stiffly.

Bliss put the Glock .45 pistol against Roscha's temple and cocked it. "Well, where *exactly*?"

"Behind that flat rock," Roscha stammered, pointing to a patch of disturbed earth at the base of a large cleft boulder about ten feet away.

Peter could see the Martian ankh carved on one side of the boulder, near the top. On the other side was a more faded image of a dome-shaped figure he couldn't identify. He watched Kufu explore the crevice as far as he could reach, then turn and shake his head.

Bliss flung his arm toward the precipice. "You have exhausted my patience, Professor Venable." With Kufu's rifle hard to his chest, Roscha walked backwards in small dreadful steps to the ledge. Bliss had elevated his gun to aim roughly between Roscha's sunken blue eyes, when Bell took a step closer. Quickly, Bliss repositioned the muzzle on him. "I wouldn't, Reggie." The gun went back to Roscha. "Well? To live or to die—that seems to be the question of the day, doesn't it, Professor? Choose!"

"They must have taken it!" Roshca's body quaked, sending loose dirt cascading off the ledge near his feet.

"Who? Where?"

*"They!"* Roscha repeated, half turning to point to the center of the crashing white ocean of falling water. "There!"

Bell again edged toward Bliss, who snapped his pistol to the man's face. "That's two, Reggie. Three's the charm. I'd miss hunting with you again—but not that much. This no longer concerns you. If you're smart, you'll stay put and live to hunt another day. Now, then, Professor, I'm feeling generous today. I'll ask you one last time. Where is it?"

*"I'm telling you! They have it!"* he screamed, pointing again to the falls. "It belongs to them and they took it back."

Peter could see Bliss's pudgy finger begin to crush the trigger. He didn't care so much whether Roscha lived or died. No, he'd let the report from Bliss's shot be his signal to attack. So he repositioned himself, crouching like a sprinter and putting his foot against the base of a tree, and prepared to charge. Suddenly, Kopi broke away from Bell, pushed past Kufu, and ran to Roscha's side, wrapping her arms tightly around his shaking leg.

"Wait! Don't shoot!" Kopi's little voice barely rose above the rumble and fury of the falls. "Don't shoot! Kopi has book. Kopi has—"

"What?" Bliss's face softened slightly, his grip on the trigger seemed to ease. Again he motioned for Kufu to approach and investigate.

"Give it to me, boy," Kufu ordered.

With one arm still clinging to Roscha, Kopi reached into the folds of her over-sized cloak and made one swift stab with the ceremonial knife, whose jagged stone blade, judging from the volume of blood, deeply penetrated Kufu's abdomen. "*Allah!*" he cried, falling backwards as he raised his rifle to shoot. With a loud grunt, Bell dove for the gun—

*Bang!* The lead missile from Bliss's Glock sent Roscha flying off the ledge, along with Kopi still gripping his pants leg.

Seizing the chance, Peter rose quickly from his crouched position. Too quickly, for his vision shrank to a narrow tunnel, as if he'd just pulled too many Gs turning his F-14 in a dogfight. Slowly, he slid back down the trunk of the tree, puking and trying to do it silently. He rolled over on his back, momentarily paralyzed, but out of the corner of his eye, he could see Bliss turn his pistol on the two wrestling men, firing twice without hesitation or much aiming. A small red explosion erupted on the meaty portion of Bell's thigh where the first bullet dug in. The second round apparently hit Kufu in the heart. Now his lifeless body pinned Bell to the ground, briefly shielding him from a third killing shot.

Unhurriedly, Bliss waddled over to the intertwined men, grabbed the back of Kufu's shirt and lifted him up, at the same time fully extending his arm. It was a shot he couldn't now miss. "So much for the Brit's reputation for brains."

Peter's fierce kick sent the Glock flying over the precipice. Grabbing Bliss's ponytail, he yanked him violently backward, sending him to the soggy earth with a squishy thud. At last he had Bliss where he wanted him, flat on his back with him on top, riding him like a rodeo bull. Bliss convulsed desperately but his own bulk helped keep him down, as Peter buried his thumbs deep into the man's throat. With primal satisfaction, he watched Bliss's eyes bulge, dark, liquid, and frightened as he writhed beneath him. To see his pain only excited his frenzied grip; he bore down harder, with every fiber of his strength, wanting to be done with this filthy job even as much as he was sure it had to be done. But above the howl of the raging falls, which seemed an affirmation of his own fury, a small, shrill cry insinuated itself into his consciousness, intruded itself upon his joyful malice, demanding attention. For a second, he ignored it, intent as leopard upon finishing his kill.

But there it was again. A voice. A voice that recalled the image of Molly. Her smiling eyes. Red, flowing hair, like wind in ripe winter wheat. Waving. Inviting. He thought he was passing out, but the voice clarified.

"Help!"

*Kopi?* "Damn it, kid!" he yelled, not wanting to break the narcotic spell of his revenge. Suddenly he felt a presence behind him, a benevolence of unconscious recognition, not a threat; nevertheless reflexively he jerked his head around. No one. Was he losing his mind? He didn't want to know anyway. He only wanted to take what was rightfully his, for himself and for Molly. *'The justice we make,' wasn't that it, Father*

*Mike?* He looked down at Bliss, whose face now had a bluish sheen. A crazy thought darted through his mind: *Lilacs.*

"No," he screamed defiantly. But in defiance of what? Who? Harder and harder he squeezed, feeling a surge of energy tapped from unknown reservoirs. He hoped Bliss's eyes would pop from their sockets, but instead they rolled back under his lids, showing only the whites, gargoyle like and frightening.

"Help!"

"Goddamnit!" Peter shrieked. "I'm not finished with you, Bliss."

But a strange voice in his head told him, "Yes, you are."

Leaving Bliss choking for air, he ran to the ledge and crawled over as far as he could and looked down. "Hold on, kid!" Wrapping his leg around a small tree as an anchor, he could just reach the frantically outstretched little hand. Kopi's full weight yanked him down, his anchor leg loosened and he slid past the edge, almost going over before locking onto an exposed tree root. He re-braced himself by digging in with the heel of his left hand and finding a rock just under the soft dirt. As he looked into Kopi's face, a perfect portrait against the white rushing water, he couldn't avoid the feeling of being sucked over the edge and sent crashing into the river below. Dizziness overtook him. He closed his eyes for a moment, but still his head spun. He knew if he didn't get the kid up soon, they'd both succumb to his vertigo. He pulled harder. Kopi began to rise and he took a better handhold. One more heave and he'd be able to roll back over the lip of the precipice. A wave of relief washed over him, only to be abruptly replaced with a gush of fear as he felt a push from behind—

"It's not over, *Mister Pete!*" Bliss roared, planting his boot squarely on Peter's buttocks. "I blow the whistles in this game."

Over the edge they went again, with Kopi s little fingernails digging painfully into the flesh of his forearm. He flailed his other arm in a wild effort to grab anything and break their fall. Miraculously, he caught a piece of scraggy vine. Yet instantly he knew it wouldn't long delay the inevitable, for with Kopi hanging on, his strength would quickly fade. He looked up into Bliss's raging eyes—then saw only the sole of his boot, which crushed his nose and face with agonizing force.

"Great Peter! Save me!"

*Boom!*

An explosion of splintered wood and rock shards sent Bliss stumbling backwards, where he fell to the ground with a loud *huff.*

"You bloody beast!"

Bell's terrifying roar energized Peter. With all his reserves, he pulled himself up enough to see Bell struggling to operate the bolt action of his rifle and fire again as Bliss disappeared into the dense underbrush. Then his handhold gave way, dropping them another foot below the ledge, where he claimed a better grip on nipple of rock. But Bell was now out of sight.

"Reggie! Throw us a branch! Reggie!" He strained to hear a reply over the jet like roar of the falls. *He must have died. Or passed out.*

Little rivulets of blood, slick and syrupy, trickled down his arm around Kopi's hands. Suddenly, he felt the child's grip release; she slipped to his waist, hanging from his belt, which burned into his skin like a hot iron. He felt his strength slinking away. He wondered if the fall, now only moments away, would be enough to kill them. Or would they just drown? One rock broke loose, but he managed to transfer both hands to the smaller one next to it. It wouldn't be long now. Looking up for the last time, he beheld the splendid sky, with mountainous white clouds and—*vultures!* Wheeling lazily through the blueness a hundred feet above, they waited. "You'll have to fight the crocks," he moaned, flopping his head down between his outstretched arms.

"Great Peter!"

"Sorry, kid," he yelled, unable to see Kopi's face. He laughed out loud. "Who'd have ever guessed," he said, thinking for the first time of God. "I always thought I'd die flying." He heard himself laugh again, a sick, psychotic laugh, as if he already no longer inhabited his body. *I guess falling* is *flying. Wonder what it's like to* die, *to be dead?* Then, as his fingers capitulated to fatigue and the oily properties of blood, he relaxed in a strange resignation. "Guess I'm about to find out—"

Suddenly something powerful clamped down on his wrists. First he saw the tawny fingers, long and sinuous; then, moving quickly up the muscular arms, his eyes met a face of recent acquaintance, little known but instantly recognizable. The man from the plane who'd followed him and Molly all the way from Frederick, Maryland, to Tel Aviv.

*Mister Madras?*

## CHAPTER 34

"Mister Madras!" Peter gasped, breathless from fatigue, his feet once again happily planted on terra firma. He had a million questions, but before he could ask the first, a man in an odd-looking black and gold uniform called to Madras. "What are we to do with the girl?"

"Girl? What girl?" They couldn't be talking about Molly, could they? But his confusion evaporated when, for the first time, Kopi pulled back the hood of her burnoose, revealing sheaths of raven-black, wavy hair, which, together with the dark, clear eyes of youth and the velvet skin, painted for Peter the complete portrait of an visage now clearly female. "I should've known," he laughed. "Only a girl could be that much trouble."

Kopi scowled. Madras patted her head tenderly, "Go with them, child. No one will harm you." Oddly, Kopi displayed none of her usual defiance, but obediently joined the two men who were lifting Bell onto a litter.

"Is he…?" Though his feelings for Bell were mixed, Peter didn't want to be denied the chance to thank the man for saving his life, nor did he want to lose what may have been his last ally.

"He has a chance."

"Where are you taking them?"

"Kampala," Madras said. "They'll be well cared for."

"I don't mean to sound ungrateful, but what the hell are you doing here? You CIA too?"

"No."

"Then who are you with?"

"Perhaps it would be better to show you." Madras walked over to the large boulder with Martian markings, where Roscha had said he'd hidden the book, stopped and looked back. "Coming?"

Peter's mind raced. He was weak and wasted; his muscles shook from over-exertion. He knew he wasn't thinking clearly. "They killed Molly. I have to go back for her, give her a decent burial."

Madras retraced his steps. "We'll take care of her," he assured him, putting his hand on Peter's shoulder. The man's touch was oddly soothing; it warmed him like an embrace.

"Take care of her how, exactly?"

"Your distrust is understandable, Peter. I know what you've been through in the last several weeks. You and Molly and Kopi. All of it."

"That's the problem," Peter said accusingly. "How do you know? If you're not CIA, why have you been following us? Maybe you're with—"

"Ambassador Bliss?" Madras raised an eyebrow. "No. But I know all about him, and believe me, he will be dealt with at the appointed time. I promise you—"

"Yeah! He'll be dealt with. By me! Now!"

"No!"

"You mean you're going to stop me?" Peter's challenge was calculated; he wanted to know just how far Madras was prepared to go.

Madras hesitated. "For now, I'm just asking you to trust me. He will be punished. You have my word."

"By who, then?"

"By the fruits of his own choices, as will we all."

Peter reached into his pocket and felt the silken red tresses. "I should've killed the pig when I had the chance." He clenched his fists. He could still feel Bliss's throat in his hands, see his bulging eyes.

"Though it's difficult to see at this moment," Madras said with a somewhat condescending tone, "you did the right thing—"

"No! I was a fool." Peter grabbed Madras's arm. "Help me go after him, while there's still time. Do that for me and I'll do whatever you want."

"I can't do that," Madras answered sternly. "And Molly wouldn't want it that way."

"What would you know about Molly?" he shot back rudely, brushing off Madras's hand, turning away and suddenly feeling very cold.

"I worked for her father just before his death. And, you might say, we—Molly and I—are on the same side."

"Look, I'm going back for Molly. Then I'll take care of Bliss. Either help me or get out of my way." He started to edge past Madras, who at first stiffened but then relaxed and stepped aside.

"Very well, Peter. The choice is yours, just as it was a few moments ago when you chose to save an innocent child. When you chose life over revenge and death."

"Innocent?" he snorted. "You don't know Kopi."

Around them, approaching night dissolved shadows, turning the shimmering green to funereal black. He had to acknowledge two facts: this man had just saved his life, and there was nothing he could do for Molly now, nothing but keep himself—and the memory of her—alive. He could get Bliss later, after he'd rested. Besides, his gut told him he had to find out what Madras was up to, so he followed Madras back to the huge cleft stone with the ankh, where he pointed a small black device at its base. Silently, the boulder rose about six inches off the ground and yawned open at the cleft, revealing an entranceway to an underground grotto.

Madras gestured toward the opening. "What have you decided?"

Peter took a deep breath and stepped onto the platform of an escalator, which began a slow, silent descent through a rocky shaft into the bowels of the earth beneath Lake Victoria. Water, seeping through bedrock, splashed his face, trickling like tears down his cheek, recalling images of Molly, with her tears of joy the day he proposed to her, only steps away from where he now stood but seemingly a half a lifetime ago. Promptly, light from below began to shimmer off the wet walls, creating kaleidoscopic images, like desert mirages, along the length of the tube. A damp mustiness mixed with odors that drifted up the shaft from below, smells both familiar and comforting: the appetizing smell of cooking food, occasional whiffs of gasoline fumes, pungent ozone, even the perfume of flowers, or so he thought.

Soon the thunderous rumble of the great waterfall failed to penetrate the solid bedrock, being replaced by a low, persistent humming, like that of a giant dynamo. Other sounds permeated the background: voices of people and the movement of machines and strange, distant music echoing from the cavern below. Then, nearing the bottom, he saw what appeared to be the supporting part of a giant superstructure, which alternated chameleonlike between a flat stealthy black and a highly polished metallic sheen. Seconds later, the bottom half of an enormous companionway revealed itself, and a short way farther, another supporting column came into view. Suddenly the hidden image in the giant jigsaw puzzle leapt out at him: a bright and shiny, now dark and menacing, metallic monster. Jumping off the escalator even before it had reached bottom, he raced to examine it, and stood staring, entranced in silent awe for an eternal moment, before blurting, "They do exist." The satellites had not lied. *UMLOs,* Unidentified Metallic- Looking Objects from the satellite pictures—UFOs—were a reality.

Walking the craft's circumference, which he estimated to be better than one thousand feet, he at last encountered Madras, who had been waiting patiently for him right where he'd started. Warily, he surveyed the man with new eyes, and all he could think to say was, "How long?"

"It's about three hundred feet across—"

"No. This place. How long has it been here?"

"As long as you have," Madras replied.

"Forty years?"

Madras chuckled. It was the first time Peter had seen the stony-faced man smile, much less laugh.

"Our conversation seems to be one beat out of sync. No. I mean since *all* of you—your ancestors—have been here. About a hundred thousand years."

A flutter of fear knotted Peter's stomach; his chest shook with each thump of his heart. He calmed himself before challenging the weird notion, "But we've been around for millions of years, not just thousands."

"What you call modern man—people just like you—have only been here roughly one hundred thousand years. Not coincidentally, the Neanderthal community began disappearing about this same time," he added in an accusatory tone. "Along with many other untoward changes. No, your anthropology still can't explain the very sudden appearance of people fully as capable as you. There is a good reason for that mystery, but you'll soon know the answer."

"Who are you people, anyway?"

Madras waved his hand as if to erase the question. "All in good time, Peter."

Just then a loud claxon sounded, followed by a rumbling, then screeching noise. Above him, a huge partition began to descend from the ceiling, which he estimated to have been at least a hundred feet high. It soon became apparent that the partition separated the spacecraft servicing area from the rest of the mammoth underground complex, which was expansive, at least as big as a four-and-a-half-acre aircraft carrier deck, or so he thought.

"Time to go," Madras said, pointing up the steps of the gangway leading to the spacecraft's cabin.

"Go? Go where?"

"You want your questions answered, don't you?"

"What if I don't? What if I want to walk out of here right now?"

"Go ahead." Madras smiled again, but didn't laugh. "You're free to leave if you wish. You won't be harmed. Not by us."

"What's that supposed to mean?"

Madras didn't answer.

Blalock must have been right. This clearly was as big a threat to national security as they come. Perhaps by going along, he would discover a way to make his own life a worthy sacrifice for something greater than himself. He would go, and with that decision, he recalled his many conversations with Bo about how he'd regretted that he'd never "bloodied his sword," never shot down another fighter airplane in a dogfight, never been truly tested in combat one-on-one. *Take out your pens and pencils.*

He stepped onto the gangway. Every sense bristled with anticipation. Whether from stress or fatigue or his awe at seeing the unthinkable, he had, for the moment, completely forgotten about Molly, Roscha, Reggie and the rest—until he saw the ankh image on the carpet of the stairway. He stopped cold, as if hitting a wall of rock, but it was the realization that had paralyzed him: *Martians.* With a loud thump, the partition fully closed behind them, and for the first time, he sensed the finality of his decision to go. Could he have left?

"Peter," Madras called impatiently from the doorway. "We must hurry."

Now the lights gradually dimmed until the hangar was completely dark, except for the light from within the spacecraft at the top of the stairs. Still, he lingered, halfway up the steps of the gangway. Looking around, he felt a splash of panic and wondered again if he could escape. No, he counseled himself, he would bide his time, gather intelligence, look for the right moment.

Another clanking noise reverberated in the hangar, a sound like massive locks disengaging. More humming servos—instantly drowned out by the return of the thunderous falls, which were just beginning to appear under the giant hangar door and which hid the whole complex behind a heavy wall of raging water.

"We can wait no longer," Madras cautioned him.

"Strange," he thought out loud as he trudged up the steps, "the weirdest part is that it doesn't seem weird at all." Crossing the threshold of the entryway into the spacecraft, the door closed behind him with a muted *shusssh!* and it was quiet again. *Where are all the little green men?* If Madras was an alien, he sure didn't look the part. By all appearances, he was fully human. Even the spacecraft's interior was largely unremarkable: the passengers' compartment was little different from that of many jumbo jets, albeit a lot roomier and more elegant. He sat beside Madras in front of a portal. A very low humming sound—felt more than heard—emanated from below their feet, but aside from that there was no sound as they began to move slowly out of the hangar, until the raging fury of the falls hammered the hull of the craft like hail stones on a corrugated tin roof. Seconds later, a reassuring silence returned.

"That scared the hell out of me." Somewhat embarrassed, he realized he had a veritable deathgrip on Madras' arm and he quickly released it. "I can see why nobody's ever found this place. You always operate after dark?"

"On moonless nights... unless it's an emergency."

"Then this thing gives no radar return."

"We have systems that bend light around the ship. Takes an enormous amount of energy. We use it only when necessary."

"Why not all the time? Aren't you afraid of being discovered?"

"No."

"You've got to be kidding."

"Good evidence for extraterrestrial technology exists—both within and outside your government—and has for years. Though not about this place or this ship in particular. And I know that you know that. But even if a real ship were produced, it wouldn't matter, because there are always ambiguities, alternative theories, political agendas. You see, Peter, as a rule, people believe what they choose to believe. And what they believe about the outside world is always based on incomplete information."

Madras looked at him the way a parent looks at a child: with patience and caring but also with certain, determined superiority. "You mean like what I believe right now—about you? And all this?"

Madras sighed. "A moment's thought will confirm what I'm telling you, which is that we all make decisions based largely on probabilities. Worse, actually. We make them on *assumptions* about probabilities. And we assign very low probabilities to things outside our personal experience. That's why nineteenth-century Europeans didn't believe in zebras, and other unfamiliar African animals, until actual specimens were not just produced but produced in large numbers.

"Ideas are no different than animals. New ideas are awfully difficult to accept. They have a sense of unreality about them. Rest assured, there's a whole spectrum of reality beyond your current awareness—just as the visible portion of the electromagnetic spectrum is but a small part of light energy."

"After seeing this ship, I'm inclined to believe you." He shook his head. "Most of us just pooh-poohed the idea of UFOs. No scientists thought it was feasible to travel between stars—"

"An assumption that ignores possibilities much closer to home. The moon, for example. Even so, travel between stars is feasible."

"Just who are you, Mister Madras? Where'd you—and this ship—come from?"

"When we reach our destination, all your questions will be answered. For now, consider the fish whose world was the sea until he was plucked into the realm of the air by a fisherman. Startled, seeing the strangeness of this new reality, he thinks to himself: *All this while, just inches away, there was another universe.*

# CHAPTER 35

On a split-screen monitor that displayed views both fore and aft, Peter watched Earth recede into the black sea of timeless space even as the moon burgeoned like a smiling balloon before them. With growing size, the moon's surface grew paler, finally fading to a drab light gray with subtler shadings of ginger browns and pallid yellows. Images became crisper as the void between the ship and the moon rapidly shrank, while craters blossomed like inverted mushrooms on the viewscreen, their jagged mountainous rim lines guarding the lifeless expanses within.

Peter perceived a deceleration, but only visually, for there was no sensation of any movement within the craft itself because, Madras had explained, of its mastery over gravitational field forces. Now slowly moving across the surface at a stabilized altitude and rate, the ship entered the shadows cast by the interposition of the Earth between the sun and the moon, deeper and deeper into the darkness of the far side, until the image of the Earth faded completely, settling like the sun behind the imposing lunar landscape. Now they entered mysterious territory, the hidden face of the moon, the hemisphere forever turned away from Earth's prying eyes because of the moon's peculiar orbit.

*What a perfect hiding place: The dark side of the moon.*

A brilliant spotlight from the spacecraft lit up the surface with an acres-wide circle of light that strolled across the undulating terrain beneath them. Nothing could have prepared him for the bleakness of the place, the barren hostility. He thought how lucky the *Apollo* astronauts had been to make it back to Earth alive. He wondered if he ever would. He followed the light as it rippled and jumped over the rugged lunar surface, watched it crawl up the side of a steep mountain, cross its saw-toothed rim, and spill like a luminous waterfall over the other side and down into an enormous plain. Here it stopped a moment, apparently finding a checkpoint, before proceeding until it reached the foot of another mountain, where it stopped again. They had, he realized, traversed the basin of a huge crater.

Descending into the spotlight, which illuminated an area at the base of the crater's mountain, the ship appeared to want to crash into the rising terrain. Suddenly he saw a large section of the mountain separate and move aside. A gigantic, perfectly camouflaged hangar door, it neatly hid the entire underground facility. Shortly they came to rest in the center of the landing zone, a bull's-eye of blue light within concentric circles of flashing yellow lights around it, and the humming sound that had been with them all along subsided.

"Are you ready, Peter?" Madras asked.

"For some answers? Yeah, I'm ready." Just then there was an audible bump, and the doorway automatically opened. Outside he could hear the din of voices, of people going about their jobs, of machinery and soothing background music, much as it had been in the hangar on Earth. "Where're we going?"

"To see a friend of yours," Madras replied, walking toward a black doorway framed with yellow and black striping. "This way."

"A friend of mine?" He was certain no one he knew would be here.

"You'll see. It's just a short walk. Or we could take a mover." Madras pointed to an off-white vehicle that looked like a golf cart and seemed to glow with a creepy iridescence, which must have been the preferred mode of transportation, for all about them the small contraptions skittered to and fro like albino cockroaches.

"A what?"

"Mover. Short for motorized vehicle. But we just call them gobuggies."

"Why do they glow? They radioactive?" One cruised silently by as they talked.

"See? The have no headlights that would scatter light off the damp corridor walls in some areas and create a traffic hazard. These just glow enough so they can be seen coming."

"Maybe you ought to call them globuggies. Or better yet, globugs. Let's walk." Peter followed Madras down a long, dimly lit corridor, which stretched on for several hundred yards. On each side was module after module containing animals, some familiar, some not. Their collective howls, hisses, barks, squeals, and screams, only partially muted by thick Plexiglas, rose to frenzy as they passed, reminding him of the monkey house at the zoo at feeding time. None seemed of the domesticated kind that would be used for food. "Why all the animals?"

"This is part of our endangered species rehabilitation program. Every species here is either extinct on Earth or soon will be."

"Noah's Ark." Peter muttered to himself and wondered what possible national security implications animal husbandry could have.

"You could say that."

"Got any dinosaurs?" he asked, only half in jest.

"No dinosaurs," Madras answered matter-of-factly. "Only animals endangered or extinct by man's activities. The dinosaurs' departure was a part of the natural plan."

"What are you going to do with them?"

"They'll be resettled, either back on Earth or some other well-suited place. They—"

"Whoa!" Peter nearly jumped out of his skin as a midget-sized creature with a huge head and over-sized pitch black eyes skittered by. With skin a pale, deathly gray, mere slits formed its mouth, ears and nose. Suddenly he realized: This was the creature supposed UFO abductees had described for years, the "grays," the aliens everyone first imagined when one spoke of beings from other worlds.

"What was that?" Peter cringed and shook himself like a wet dog.

"A sentient being—just like you and me. They're harmless." As the creature passed them, close enough to touch, Madras nodded and smiled. The creature bowed slightly in acknowledgment but made no sound, then went about its business.

Walking quickly along, they passed an entranceway above which was an odd name: AREOPAGITE EXPERIMENTAL BIOLOGY LABORATORY. The name set off some kind of alarm, though he wasn't sure why, except that it sounded familiar. Next to the doorway was a flashing a red light and biohazard symbol. A sign in several languages, including English, warned of unauthorized entry, something about experimental infectious biological agents and the need for strict sterile procedure, but a globug pulling a trailer interposed itself as they passed, so he couldn't read the whole thing. But he made a mental note to check it out later. Then, turning a corner, his heart began to race; sweat jumped out of his pores, gathering quickly into cold streamers that ran down his face and neck. He nearly fainted and closed his eyes, falling against the wall, trying to steady himself.

"It's probably the lower gravity. Let's rest a moment," Madras suggested.

"No. I'm okay." But he knew it wasn't the low gravity, and he wasn't okay. Down the end of the corridor was a door outlined with yellow light. He forced himself to turn toward it, but his eyes slammed shut again, unconsciously knowing better than he how to protect him from the unpleasantness of the image, the image of Lilah with the ankh-decorated cheerleader's sweater, the image from his dream at the mission the day Molly died. *My God! That was today*. "Let's go," he said stoically.

But to his surprise—and relief—Madras stopped short of the door at the end. "Here we are, Peter."

Still trying to catch his breath, he walked into the room, a warm and friendly space, unlike the stark and dank corridor outside. Only one person occupied the room, and he immediately jumped up and glided over to greet him with a huge smile and outstretched hand.

"Hello, Pete!" the young man said, beaming. "Remember me?" Peter studied his face carefully. Slowly, frustratingly, his fatigued brain assembled the pieces: young man of about thirty years, tall, blond, athletic, and dressed in the same smart, yellow-trimmed black uniform as the spacecraft's crew. Most familiar, however, was his charismatic smile—and those ocean-from-space blue eyes with tiny golden flecks. He searched the archives of memory, building up the picture, piece by piece, until— "You're the bartender," he said with fair certainty. "The bartender at the New Stanley...in Nairobi. Right?"

The young man smiled even more broadly and took Peter's hand in a firm handshake. "Well, yes.... And no."

"I don't understand."

"Don't you remember? I said I'd be seeing you sooner than you think."

Peter shrugged. Not a single bell went off.

"Pete, it's me. Cap. Captain Bob Donaldson."

* * *

"I don't know who *you* are," Peter said, "but the Bob Donaldson I knew was eighty years old." He cocked his head and eyed the man head to toe, so as to emphasize the difference between what he'd just described and the hale and hardy young man who sat before him. "Besides, Cap's dead."

The man moved to the bar. "Would you care for something to drink?"

"Got any Jack Daniels? I could use a double."

"I'm afraid not. Perhaps—"

Frustrated, Peter shook his head. "What I really want are some answers. Who are you? Who are these people? What's going on here? Why am *I* here? What's *anyone* doing here? On the moon, for God's sake!"

"Settle down, settle down," the still-smiling man said, moving his hands up and down in a calming motion.

"No, you settle down! Is this fortress Martian? Because it can't be CIA. They're hunting for *you.* And I know all about the Martian book. The ankh is all over the spacecraft." He laughed in small, chaotic bursts and sounded to himself like a mad man, but he had to ratchet down volume, for the pain in his head had returned. "What Blalock said explains a lot," he thought out loud. "Hell, you could launch any manner of attacks from a base like this. No wonder they'd kill to get the book. Explains why you would, too. To keep this secret. "

"Yep. It is that, Pete—a well-kept secret, I mean."

Peter tried to scrub the fatigue from his face with both hands; his scar tingled maddeningly. Exhaustion was at last defeating the effects of the adrenaline he'd been running on for what seemed like days.

Settling back in the soft, crushed velvet recliner, he focused on the surroundings and again noticed the banality of it all. The place could have been anyone's living room, though the decor was right out of the fifties, with an air of comforting familiarity and easy-chair charm. All very human. "Madras said someone was going to tell me what's going on. How 'bout it?" He stared at the man, not really expecting an answer.

"Pete, you don't believe... Don't believe what you're seeing. Heck, I'd be the same way." The man sipped a glass of claret as he seemed to collect his thoughts. "Imagine how *I* feel. One minute I was there in the hospital bed—you remember, we were talkin' baseball, the Babe, Ted Williams and all. Then I was coughing, choking on phlegm, fighting for air. Horrible." He shook his head sadly.

Peter thought he detected genuine pain in the man's face.

"The next minute," he continued, "I was traveling in this dark tunnel—toward the light you so often heard people who'd had near-death experiences talk about. Well I'm a monkey's uncle if it didn't happen just that way."

"Then what happened?"

"Three beings met me—souls, no different really from you or me. Good people. Very warm. Friendly. They told me about some coming events on Earth. Offered me the chance to return. Under better circumstances, they said. Yep, it's true.

"They said it was a chance for me to help in the fulfillment of a vast and very important project. That it would enhance my opportunities for growth—in the spiritual sense, they meant. I wasn't forced at all, either—not in any way. There were other, maybe easier assignments—that's what they called them, assignments. They explained each one carefully. Showed me scenes of what the other assignments would be like.

"And that was the neat part. I actually was *in* the scene with others, others who were not aware I was there—"

"Where was there?" Peter asked, beginning to wonder if it were possible for the story to get even more bizarre than it already was. Although he had to admit, the man spoke with a certain innocent sincerity that begged respect.

"On Earth. It...." The man broke off abruptly, as if he'd caught himself divulging too much, but just as abruptly he picked up the tale. "As I was saying, I was just an observer. The way everyone is observed on Earth."

"Observed?"

"Don't we all observe each other, all the time? Just listen, Pete. I decided to go back. To accept the assignment back on Earth. Yep. Nostalgia, I guess. You see, because of some very special circumstances, I still have all the memories of my past life on Earth. Most people who went back on Earth don't remem—" He again cut himself off again. Or someone did. "My body is still mine, still the same—just forty-six years younger. Well, not *exactly* the same."

"What do you mean not exactly?"

"My body is slightly different from yours. But I'll explain that later.... Yep, it's unbelievable, Pete. Still is, when I stop to think about it."

*God I'm tired.* "Tell me more. What happened next?"

"Still don't believe me, do ya?" he said, chuckling with that puppy-dog friendly smile. "I don't expect you to. Not yet, anyway." He sipped his drink. "Remember what we talked about that day? The day I died. Other than baseball, I mean?"

"Lots of things," he said warily. "But why don't you refresh my memory." *He certainly has Cap's mannerisms down pat.* Brusquely, he jumped up from his chair and walked over to a window, from which he could see a lush botanical garden, bursting in bloom with every imaginable flower, radiating a rainbow of colors under a beautifully bright and soothing artificial daylight. Suddenly he felt the warmth of the man's hand on his shoulder.

"I told you something that day, Pete. Something I'd never told anyone before in my whole life. Course, you'd have to believe me on that, too. But since I died the same day, I never had the chance to tell anyone else." He gave a small laugh. "Remember?"

Peter turned slightly, enough to see the man out the corner of his stinging eye. He could see pain creep into the man's face, the man whose eyes now dropped a bit, losing some of their sparkle, eyes heavy with an obvious and profound sadness.

"I told you a story about a friend of mine in the war, my best friend, Bernie. Do you remember?"

He turned another notch, lifted his eyebrow in disbelief and anticipation of yet another revelation bringing back the unreality, the strangeness of the moment, making him to want to flee, to disappear into the comforting past, for only in his past did Molly now exist. How he wanted her, his almost wife.

"Oh yeah, I remember what Cap told me. But, you know, I can't be sure old Cap didn't tell someone else that. Now can I?"

The man's expression turned glum.

"All right," Peter said. "I'll play your little game. But on my terms. So here's a question for you. Cap used to give me baseball cards. I collected them my whole life. We talked about it a lot. Especially his favorite card, one his father gave to him. I've got that card right here in my back pocket." He tapped his wallet, as much to reassure himself it was still there, that his whole vast memory wasn't a fraud. "What card is it?"

The man's face brightened, as if illuminated by a supernatural incandescence within. Now Peter didn't know if he could bear to hear the words he somehow knew would flow from the man's mouth; not because he thought it would be a lie, but because he feared it would be the truth. And all that that implied. He faced the man, who grabbed him by the arms, grinning like Alice's Cheshire and said: "Honus Wagner!"

* * *

Peter opened his eyes. He'd slept the sleep of the dead, with no sense of missing time or awareness of place. Until he saw the ankh-patterned carpet. *It wasn't just a bad dream.* He sat in the same crushed-velvet chair where unknown hours before Captain Donaldson had told him an bewildering story that had, for the most part, convinced him of an impossibility. After which, one glass of wine, aided by his utter exhaustion, had knocked him senseless, like a fast-acting anesthetic.

"Mornin', Pete," Bob Donaldson chirped, jauntily striding through the door carrying some clean clothes, his face a beacon of goodwill. "Sleep well?"

"Fine...I think." His neck was stiff, grinding like sanded gears whenever he moved his head, which throbbed with every surge of his heart.

"Don't know how you could've slept much in that chair. But you nodded off so fast; I didn't want to move you." Bob handed him the clothes. "You can change in there."

In the tiny, cramped bathroom, Peter took off his tattered clothes, which had become putrid with dried blood and mud. His heart tore when he found Molly's lock of hair. He nuzzled it, inhaling a fragrant memory before transferring it to the pocket of his new pants. Outside, the man call to him.

"You hungry?"

"Yeah." His stomach growled furiously. "Haven't eaten in a couple of days...seems like anyway."

"Cafeteria's on the other side of the garden." He pointed to the window overlooking the lush botanical garden, which Peter now remembered from the previous evening.

"Don't have any Cracker Jacks, do they?"

"Don't think so. After you eat, I'll show you around. This place is really neat; you'll like it. Then there's someone else wants to meet you."

"Molly?"

"Sorry."

Peter went to sink for some water. "Got any aspirin?"

"Cabinet above you."

"So, who wants to meet me now?"

"The man who runs the whole shebang."

"He gonna tell me why I'm here? And what this moon base is for? Obviously you're not going to."

"Don't be mad at me, Pete. It's just not my place to say."

Peter moved close to the man's face, close enough to study those aquamarine eyes with their unmistakable yellow flecks, looking for some hint of deception, something to trigger a certainty of recognition or outright denial. "Is what's going on here evil? Just answer me that, Cap."

Never breaking his gaze, the man replied in the even, sure tones of an apostle, "No, Pete. It isn't." He walked to the door, easing it open before looking back. "As to why you're here, well, as I understand it, you came willingly."

"That's an open question, Cap."

Just outside the door, Peter heard a familiar chattering sound coming from behind the wall across the corridor, which rose and fell in volume several times in succession, like the voices of children riding one side of a carousel, with the sound rising and falling rhythmically. "What's that noise?"

"Here, I'll just show you." He pressed a button on the sill. Responding instantly, the velvet drapery drew into gathers section by section, revealing a vast lake, covering perhaps twenty-five or thirty acres. A huge flock of waterfowl flew in great circles around the shoreline. Several thousand more huddled in tight bunches around a central island, happily preening and dipping for food, as content in this alien setting as they would have been on the Chesapeake Bay. A dozen or so of the "Grays" rode the edges of the lake in the motorized globugs throwing feed around the shoreline. Two more in a dinghy headed for the island, sending another enormous swarm into the air, squawking, flapping, quacking, creating a cacophonous din as they circled, waiting for the keepers to leave.

"They for food?"

"Some are. But mainly they're for the Reconciliation Project."

Peter threw up his hands in frustration. "What the hell's this project you keep talking about? Come on, Cap. Who am I going to tell?" He grabbed the man by both arms, feeling him grow rigid as a frightened animal. "If you're truly my friend, you'll tell me."

But the man's expression turned sad, and he looked away. "I *am* your friend, Pete. Believe that. But it's not my place—"

"Does everyone here except me know about it?"

"Yep. Except you."

* * *

Traveling by globug, Bob Donaldson had taken Peter through the immense botanical gardens, covering over a hundred acres, but which, he'd learned, was only a small part of the entire ten-square-mile complex. A cornucopia of flowering plants and fruit bearing trees perfumed the air with seductive fragrances. Each variety of plant life seemed to glow with healthy vigor in the artificial sunlight, which was somehow subtly different from any light he'd ever experienced, for its effect was soothing, almost tranquilizing in its unchanging intensity and warmth.

Throughout the complex were people of every Earthly shape, sex and hue; people who seemed to radiate an inner joy, an exuberance for living and doing; busy people; smiling people; people whose purpose seemed well known to them—and well chosen.

Strangely, Peter had seen no children. Most residents appeared to be in their late twenties or early thirties, though some few appeared middle aged. Mingled here and there were the beings that did look alien—the Grays. But even they, despite their grossly different anatomy, seemed to fit in easily with the flow of daily life, being totally—and remarkably—accepted as equals.

After the garden, they'd gone by elevator into the bowels of the fortress. Ten stories down, directly underneath the large lake where he'd seen the ducks and the deepest part of the complex, was a huge electrolysis apparatus, which took water from the lake through feeders in the bedrock and electrically split it into hydrogen and oxygen gas. The dangerously explosive hydrogen was vented immediately to the vacuum of space through huge chimneys; the oxygen was used to supplement that produced by the plant life. All the air in the artificial atmosphere was recirculated using gargantuan fans, passing it first through carbon dioxide scrubbers that, along with the plant life, regulated the atmosphere within precise parameters.

According to Cap, some of the manufactured atmosphere had to be allowed to escape from the experimental biology lab in order to guarantee safety there, but he'd failed to elaborate on why that was necessary or what, exactly, the lab did.

Back on the main level, they'd taken up their globug again and continued the tour of the vast underground city, traveling past another great menagerie containing animals of every description, past a many-stories-high living area, which, he'd been told, were apartments for both long-and short-term residents, but about whom little else was said, except that there were many thousands who passed through every year.

Peter saw minifactories where staples were manufactured, shops in which no money was required, entertainment and recreational centers, places of higher learning. He was reminded of an aircraft carrier, complete and self-sufficient, well prepared for the long haul. Well prepared for battle. As the globug whisked them along the rocky corridors, on their way to meet a man named Pheras, Peter couldn't help but wonder if the mission of this moon base was similarly menacing. Because of Cap's reticence—and that of the others—he'd begun to form that conclusion.

"What can you tell me about Pheras?" he asked, expecting no answer.

Bob Donaldson's blue eyes lit up. "You're very lucky to meet him, Pete. You should feel honored. Yep. He's a very great—" He laughed. "I almost said, 'a great man,' but he's not a man, per se. Well, he is, and yet he isn't."

"Well, which is it?"

"He's an angel," he replied with a grin.

"Ohhh boy. Here we go...." But then he remembered Christmas Eve with Bo—and Apollyon.

"Laugh all you want, but he's an angel. He's—"

"Wait a minute! Just what do you mean by 'angel'? Is he an alien? Like the little Grays?"

"Nope.... Actually he's an Archangel, way up in the hierarchy."

"He have wings?"

"No wings," he said evenly, seeming unperturbed by the weirdness of the question. "But some angels have them." He stared blankly at Peter, as if to gauge his reaction.

Suddenly, a shiver caused his body to twitch. He felt a gush of fear as old as original sin race through him. Molly had been right about Lilah's prophecy after all, and this was somehow part of it. "Nothing seems crazy anymore."

Rounding a corner a bit too sharply, the globug's wheels squealed in protest. "You know, Pete, labels aren't really important."

"A rose by any other name?"

"You and I come from the same tradition—a Christian tradition—so I say he's an Archangel. To a Muslim, ah...ah...I don't know...to a

Hindu, they'd have a different name, too, I suppose, but they'd *have* a name. American Indians might call him a Great Eagle Spirit—or some such—and that's probably the most appropriate because that is just what he is, a Great Spirit."

"You say he's not exactly human. How's he different?"

The smiling blue eyes seemed to chuckle as he shook his head. "Spiritually he's no different. Not in any fundamental way. I mean.... Neither am I. Nope, he's just more accomplished. More advanced. Ask him yourself."

Just then they passed a set of large windowless doors with a word over the lintel he'd never seen: EDENIC GEORGIC AREA.

"Stop, Cap."

The man veered to the side, bouncing up against the stone wall with a shriek of scrapping metal. "Never gonna get used to these darn things."

"Georgic? What the hell's that?"

"That's where I came from," he said with satisfaction. "And everybody else here who came from Earth. Everyone that is, except you, Pete."

"Except me?"

"That's where they grow our new bodies. You, though, my friend, are the only one who didn't die first to get here. The only one from Earth, anyway. Yep. The only one. Ha!"

"Can we go in?"

"Sorry."

# CHAPTER 36

Bob Donaldson pulled the globug to a stop in front of an ornate portico marked HARMONY THEATER, and Peter jumped out when he saw Madras emerge from a side door. Quickly scanning the area, Peter's focus rested finally on the doorway through which Madras had just come. "Where's your winged friend?" he asked in a childish pique of sarcasm, more than a little nervous about the man—if such he was—that he was about to meet.

"I'm glad you've had a chance to renew an old friendship," Madras said with his usual poise and courtesy.

"Patience, Pete!" Bob Donaldson chided. "And remember, Pheras is an Archangel—no wings."

"Thank you, Bob. I'll take it from here."

"Have fun," Bob said gaily, his blue eyes twinkling as he sped off.

"Well, where is he?"

"Pheras will be here momentarily," Madras said. "Follow me." He escorted Peter through large baroque doors, at least twelve feet high, crafted with exquisite designs of what must have been historical scenes from some alien world, for they contained figures of surpassingly strange beings, animals and settings, all decorated in gold filigree and inlays of sundry precious stones, the rival of any in Versailles, the Vatican or the Hermitage Museum in Saint Petersburg. "We'll go down front. Near the podium. You will get the best view from there."

"View?"

"Yes. Though perhaps experience is a better word. You'll be fine. And I'll answer any questions you have after your remembrance."

*Remembrance?* He sat on a purple velvet seat with gold Martian ankh patterns inside a huge indoor auditorium. The stark white domed ceiling was a screen designed to show a 360-degree panorama that totally involved the viewer, immersing him in the scene, making him a participant as well as an observer. He looked around anxiously and wondered if this would be his last "experience." As far as he could tell, other than himself and Madras, the theater was empty. Then, silently, his seat started to recline. Soon he was looking almost straight up, so that nothing but screen intruded upon his peripheral vision.

"Look straight ahead," Madras told him. "Now relax. Open your mind. You've asked why you are here—"

"On the moon?"

"No. Here as Peter MacKenzie. Here in consciousness. But you'll soon see."

What seemed like an eternity passed without anything happening. Anxiety exploded in him like a grenade, raising the hair on his neck and causing his head to pound with each crashing thud of his heart. He tried to relax, but his prickling chin distracted him. *Funny, that's the first time since I've been here.* He could resist no longer and reached up to scratch it. It felt good—until he glanced down to see his hand had not moved from the armrest of his seat. Reflexively, he jumped, but nothing happened; he was paralyzed and seized with fear.

Then he felt Madras touch his arm. "Too much tension," the man said in kindly voice. "It won't allow the experience. You must relax. Think of something soothing, something you find pleasant."

So he thought of Molly. As the beauty of her face formed in his mind's eye, the pain dissipated. He breathed deeply, inhaling, holding it, then slowly exhaling, calming his storming heart. Suddenly her fragrance filled his nostrils, and he felt the silken texture of her red hair between his fingers. But he hadn't put his hand into his pocket, had he? No, he couldn't move his hand; it was on the arm of the chair, in the same position as before.

Almost imperceptibly, the lights began to dim, and with the fading light, he sensed a growing warmth at his back, not a warmth of temperature but an inner warmth, like that of a joyous emotion. He fell deeper into a relaxed state. Yet strangely, his awareness sharpened; his every sense vibrated at a new, higher level. He tried to turn and look, but couldn't. A subtle pressure on his shoulder induced an even deeper descent into an embryonic, fluidic place of peace.

Then a gentle, silent voice spoke directly to his consciousness. "Greetings and welcome, Peter. I am Pheras. If you will permit me, I am going to open your memory now and show you your past, a past you shared with everyone on Earth. May I do so?"

His thoughts answered in the affirmative. Yet he did not feel compelled to do so. He could have said no, couldn't he?

The screen sprang to life, lit up with a maelstrom of blurred images and multicolored stroboscopic flashes. With no peripheral vision, he was sucked into this swirling world, becoming part of its frightful force. He moved rapidly with hellacious noise and fury until he was nearly ill. Suddenly, the motion slowed to a normal pace; the images congealed into clarity; his consciousness reconstituted. Now he was there—*in the scene.*

"Where am I?" he blurted out loud. There was no response, and suddenly he realized: This was no film! These were his *memories,* which he now relived with a supernatural detachment, both as spectator and participant: He felt every searing emotion, saw every sight, heard every sound, savored every taste, delighted—or recoiled from—every tingling or lacerating touch. Memories long buried, not just from his current life's unconscious archives but from the shadowy long, long ago, resurrected themselves with an immediacy, a heart-known reality that left no doubt as to their authenticity. Events replayed at high velocity. In this dimension, time had no meaning; events did not succeed events but overlapped, layer upon layer, allowing everything to be experienced at once yet with a distinct separateness.

First he saw a surpassingly beautiful planet as viewed from space, a planet not unlike Earth—but not Earth. Breathless blue oceans reflected crystalline skies; fluttering clouds hovered like guardian angels over emerald continents.

Suddenly, he zoomed downward to the planet's surface, where life, with its boundless expression of variety, swarmed about him. There, towering mountains surveyed happy rivers, hills and valleys, all studded with prim villages, bustling with life, *human* life. He remembered this place. *Home. Mars!*

With dizzying speed, images upon images poured forth, bathing him in every imaginable emotion. Now he remembered, felt, *lived* the harmony of the early ages, days in which he and all humans were of a single kind, alike in every respect—no races, no ethnicity. All were physically as well as spiritually pure. All knew it, knew the legacy of their brotherhood and sisterhood—their oneness of spirit. Their purpose was plain and pure: They lived to learn and grow, their bodies providing the vehicle, the opportunity. Spiritual advancement came through discipline and mastery of the challenges of the flesh. All life was a sacred trust, to be husbanded, cultivated, and only judiciously used. For then as now death marked the end of life's chapters, but there was understanding of its timeless role in creation, growth and renewal.

Events fast-forwarded. Overwhelmed, he sickened from the rush, struggled to swim against the raging currents of timeless memory, but could not stop the flow nor blunt the dismaying emotions.

Zooming outward for a broader view, he saw many cities, like gargantuan anthills, swarming with the varied racial forms he knew from Earth. Now he saw—*was living in*—a great city. Images blurred, blended, merged and then refocused. In rapid succession he read a litany of newspaper headlines proclaiming the great discoveries of those days in genetics and heard the boastful pride of the scientists who had produced the races through genetic tampering in their heady quest for power, the power to create as the Creator had created. He felt their hubris, felt his own. But the power to create new sentient forms became a power of tyranny. Their differences now divided them, pitted one against the other, and the beautiful existence they had known together on Mars began to putrefy like a rotting carcass.

And a subtler change crept insidiously into their life ethic. Controlling the lusts of their own animal nature, formerly a mark of high accomplishment, gave way to a new ethic of hedonism, then unchained animalism. Timeless tradition and its supporting rituals—including those for marriage of men and women, within whose covenants the judicious nurturing of children could be effected—were discarded in a willing slavery to all animal urges.

Breeding programs that produced the races yielded other bitter fruit: chimeras, forms of beastly countenance and vicious disposition that roamed the lands spreading havoc. Ultimately, breeding without restraint produced too many bodies for those of proper spiritual attainment and rank to occupy. But the living vessels had to be filled. So, according to higher law, less accomplished spirits awaiting stations as different forms, on other planets, were forced to occupy the surplus forms. Unprepared for the challenge, they added to the friction among the peoples whose collective temperature rose to an ever higher degree. Nation fell against nation. A horrid estrangement overtook them as they wandered farther and farther from their path, their purpose. They had forgotten who they were. Oh, yes! The emotion came clear, the memory pure: losing humility was nothing compared to this: They had outsmarted themselves and lost their identity! Forgetting their spiritual nature, they worshipped the vessel rather than the divine nectar it contained.

Fast-forward again, at blurring, nauseating speeds. But suddenly something had changed. He was back on Earth. Present day. He shuddered. Some laughing, wicked presence accompanied him, and he felt impending calamity. Another image superimposed itself: the pulsating, bulging, frightened eyes of Bliss as Peter's hands closed fiercely around his throat. *What's this?*

Before he had time to consider further, like a yo-yo, he snapped back to the past on Mars.

Creating a world ruled by computers, they lived digital lives of perpetual electronic delusion, isolated by hatred and mistrust, cloistered, pathetic lives, avoiding face-to-face relationships, preferring instead to live off images, digitally created, malleable, mutable, lying images. Their estrangement was complete, from each other and from themselves. Actions became disengaged from effect, for who ever knew if any result was real? Allying themselves according to skin color, knowledge of technical exotica, sexual orientation, or idiosyncratic ideologies, they formed groups with the characteristics of primitive tribes, further splintering the structure of a magnificent civilization. Denying the congeniality of the common good, they fought endless, useless wars.

Martian Potentates no one had ever seen in the flesh, and who may never have existed—except as illusory fictional personas, arrays of electrons—ruled their lives. Finally, they lost the ability to know truth. And with it, they lost the knowledge of their divineness and its greatest gift—the gift of individual free will. Dangerous spiritual renegades, abnegating responsibility, denying agency, forgetting ultimate accountability, they lived a miserable animal existence. Wars of surpassing violence ensued, and with them war's cohorts: pestilence, famine, plague.

Suddenly, his very soul was shaken to the core by an enormous explosion. One horrible supernova image, all brilliant and colorful light, consumed him—everyone!—with a terrifying emotion, as a final, screaming conflagration ripped the atmosphere from his beautiful home, Mars, stealing forever her grandeur, and leaving them all homeless spiritual vagabonds.

"Peace be unto to you, Peter MacKenzie," Pheras said lovingly.

And then Peter felt cold. The lights came up. Drained and confused, he let his head float back to rest on the chair back, but then jerked it forward and swung around to try and catch a glimpse of Pheras. Nothing.

"Where is he? Was he even here?"

Madras nodded. "How do you feel?"

"Like I just fought a war. Or hung-over, I'm not sure which."

"Maybe a little of both."

"What did he—you—do to me?"

"Pheras allowed you to view your life memory—your *whole* life's memory. Or nearly all."

"So, we were all on Mars before Earth?"

Again Madras nodded.

"We blew ourselves up," he mumbled under his breath. "Damn! Why doesn't that surprise me? No wonder Roscha was freaked out. He deciphered the book, and the book explained this?"

Madras nodded. "Partly that—"

"And we're still…*alive?"*

"Eternally so."

"All of us?"

"All."

"Then where's Molly?"

Madras seemed to look straight through him. "Surely you must be tired. You were gone for quite some time."

Yes, he was tired and also, perhaps, hung-over. Had they drugged him, he wondered? He looked at his watch. Eight hours. The hammer inside his head was still hard at work. Was it from a drug? Or just the lingering effects of a rifle butt? He tried to review his situation, assess his intelligence to date, but his mind was a muddle. His most dire concern remained unanswered: What were these people—if such they were—doing here now, on the dark side of the moon?

Boarding the globug to leave the amphitheater, Peter struggled to comprehend the meaning of his experience. But now, only moments later, the images were fading, assuming a more dream-like quality. Oh, he still remembered what he'd just seen, but now it was more like an old recollection, rather than having the primacy of intense recent experience. "Why can't I remember it now?" he blurted. "Experience it I mean, like a moment ago?"

"You were given a gift," Madras replied. "You were allowed to see your past by special dispensation because of your involvement with the *Book of the Martian Covenant* and because of a special request from a powerful friend."

"You mean Bob?"

"No, though Bob is your friend. But you asked about your experience. Your memories are already dimming because you're still incarnate. Recall of past incarnations will fade quickly."

"Okay. But why can Bob Donaldson remember his life on Earth? He died, but he still remembers."

"Bob has been reconciled."

"Reconciled? The Reconciliation Project stuff? Wasn't Pheras supposed to explain all that to me?"

"In good time."

"Now is a good time."

"I can tell you this much, it means he's moved to a higher state of existence. In a very real sense, it means he's graduated." Madras stopped the globug. He turned to Peter and said in a solemn voice: "Beyond whatever else you wish to take from this experience. Above it all, be grateful."

"Grateful? For what? For having the only woman I've ever loved ripped away from me? On our wedding day?" He could feel his face contort with the memory of her dying smile. "She was my last chance for salvation, Mister Madras."

"Gratitude is an exalted virtue, Peter." After a pause, he added, "And there's no such thing as a last chance."

* * *

As Madras drove the globug, snaking its way through the seemingly endless subterranean tubes, nearly all teeming with a lunar society intent upon some great undertaking called the Reconciliation Project, which Madras, Cap and the others seemed afraid to discuss, Peter contemplated his next move. Suddenly the sign for the Edenic Georgic Area and flashed by. "Stop here," he yelled.

With a plaintive squeal, the globug came to an abrupt halt. "What's the matter?"

Peter pointed to the red sign. "Can we go in?"

"It's been a long day, Peter," Madras answered stiffly. "Perhaps tomorrow—"

"Come on," he pleaded. "Bob wouldn't take me. He said you would. Said I'd be told about the Reconciliation Project, too. So far I haven't been told much of anything. Hey, aren't we all just one big happy Martian family?"

"You joke," Madras said, as he started the globug moving again, "but in a very real sense, it is true."

"So why can't I know? What's the harm, if you people really have nothing to hide?"

"Perhaps tomorrow," Madras repeated, coming to a stop, as their path was blocked by a lorry. Two men dressed in white laboratory suits, including helmet, breathing apparatus and boots, maneuvered the large motorized flatbed in a sharp turn to line up with the double doors marked BIOHAZARD and came to a stop.

One man jumped off and went to the rear of the lorry to rearrange the cargo, which had shifted in the turn. As he did, he lifted the canvas cover, revealing cages stacked four high, each containing half a dozen gray mallards. Exposed to the hubbub of the corridor, the frightened ducks began a chorus of reedy squawking, which continued even after he lowered the tarp.

"Sorry, sir," the driver called to Madras, who nodded politely and then, it seemed, waited just long enough for the lorry to be safely out of view behind closed doors before he proceeded.

Watching the lorry disappear, Peter had an unexpected chill and sensed that the key to unlocking all his remaining questions lay behind those slowly closing doors. "Where're we going now?"

"Bob said he wanted to have dinner with you. If you have no objection?"

"Would it matter?" he asked coldly.

"You always have a choice, Peter. That's what life's all about. Choices. And for your safety, it's best that you are escorted about the complex. At least for the time being. That's why I've asked Bob to meet you and instruct you on some choices you will be facing shortly."

* * *

Peter sat with Bob Donaldson on a cushioned bench and inhaled the sweet, utterly distinctive aroma of lilacs, recalling a world lost forever. He thought about Madras's fish story and then of his mother and Clancey and the billions back on Earth. *If they only knew.*

He stared at a magnolia blossom, as large as a sombrero, which unfolded before his eyes as if it were showing off for him. Suddenly the feeling that it really *was* showing off for him, eager to please him, to communicate with him, caused a frightening sensation. He took another deep breath and drank in the fragrant air. His anxiety eased but did not pass. Everything here, from plants to people, seemed so blessed beautiful, so harmonious, so perfect. But, he thought, the operative word was "seem." Appearances could be oh so deceiving. Could he even believe his own senses anymore?

"Will I ever see Molly again?"

"Pete, you keep asking me things you should be asking Madras. Just be patient a little longer."

"Why, Cap? Give me a reason, a clue, as to what this is all about."

"All I can tell you"—he scanned the area warily and lowered his voice—"is that people are prepared here to be sent back to Earth. People like me who died. You know I love you like a son, Pete." His eyes twinkled like lapis in the bright light. "I know that must seem strange to you, since I'm now younger than you physically. But you've got to believe I want to help you. I just can't tell you much more until you—"

"Until I what?"

"Until you're better prepared to hear it." He glanced furtively about the garden, nodding and smiling every now and then to passersby.

Deciding this line of questioning was futile, he tried a different approach. "Today I had a vision of my past—our past—right?"

"I don't know, Pete; you'll have to tell me."

"Pheras allowed me to remember my past on Mars. That's what he said it was. And, by the way, I never saw him."

The man chuckled. "Believe me, if that's what Pheras told you; take it as the gospel truth. Yep. Tell me what you remembered. Because I only know the general history; I don't have any memory of it now."

"What? I thought you told me you remembered your past life."

"That's right. My immediate past life. Nothing more. And that's only because I'll need it. Because I'm going back there soo—"

"Going back? Am I going back too? What about the others?"

"Did Madras or Pheras tell you what happened to everyone after Mars was destroyed?"

"No, they didn't." Peter sensed the man was angling for an acceptable way of telling something he was not supposed to tell.

"Don't you see what this means, Pete? Don't you at least believe what *I've* told you? Don't you believe in me?" He leaned back and threw both arms over the back of the bench, shaking his head. "Nope, I can see you still haven't accepted the truth."

"What truth? What the hell are you talking about?"

"About who you are. That you—we, all of us—are spirits! First. Foremost. And forever. Not just in human forms, either, but in other forms and in other places. And that things are exactly the way they're supposed to be."

"You know, Cap, I'd really, really like to believe that. Who wouldn't? But there's this little problem of personal experience."

"Believe it, then. *Choose to.* You're still incarnate, so it's natural for you to not remember anything except your present life, even though you were allowed to remember other lives today. Yep. Those memories are fading now, aren't they?"

The comment surprised him. "Maybe they weren't really my memories after all. How do I know I wasn't given some hallucinogenic drug? LSD or something?"

"The memories were real. Every experience we've had from our creation day is remembered by the soul. That's the first thing they taught me."

"What the hell good is it if you can't recall it?"

"Trust me, it all matters. Every experience you've had has allowed you to change. Yep. That's the key word: *Allowed.* You see, experience gives us the opportunity to change—to grow in the spirit. Good or bad, positive or negative. All experience does is allow us to choose."

"What if I choose to leave now? Go back to Earth?"

"Last I checked, there was no frequent flyer program for ol' Gus," he chuckled.

"Gus?"

"That's what we call the ship you came in on. It's short for *Areopagus*."

"That's what the Mars lander that brought back your Martian book was called."

"I know. That's an irony, isn't it? But you know, both names fit to a tee."

"Just what I thought," he sighed, "I couldn't leave even if I wanted to."

"Cheer up, Pete! Even though we can't always choose our circumstances, we can still choose our attitude. Yep, Pete, that's the greatest thing. We get to choose. Animals don't. Nothing else does. That's why attitude really is everything, because, in the end, it's our attitudes that determine our choices and how we grow.

"And here's something else you should know. We are not all the same anymore. Nope. Even though we all started out the same. We haven't all developed at the same rate because we haven't all made the same choices. And that's not surprising, is it?"

"It's *all* surprising. And hard to swallow."

"Look, Madras wants me to tell you this stuff. Pheras too. It's important for you to know."

"For what?"

"Now listen, what would be 'hard to swallow,' as you say, is if every free-choosing spirit chose the same way over time. But we don't. Over vast time some of us attain advanced degrees, so to speak, like Madras and Pheras, and some of us have been held back. Some have even regressed. Yep. Some people will consistently choose badly. That's what you get when you have free will.

"Now the reason you can't remember your past incarnation is because it would interfere with the opportunities for growth that your current life offers. It's really a marvelous system when you understand it."

"Cap, all I want is to have Molly back, for none of this to have happened."

"When you're *in* life—*in*carnate—nothing seems fair. No justice, right?"

"No, Cap. That much I know: There's no justice."

"Most folks think like you. But that's not right. That would mean God is unjust. And he's not. I know, I know. Some people die young and we think life isn't fair, as if life was a drink and some only got half a cup. They think fairness is about time. But in reality, time is our fabrication; it doesn't matter. Eventually we'll all make it—no matter how many lifetimes it takes—because life's not like a box of chocolates; it's like a circle: no matter where you start your journey and no matter which way you go, you always end up home—back where you started. Just some circles are bigger than others, depending on choices. But in the meantime, we're all accountable for those choices. Accountability's what guides us. It's like a feedback system. Without it, we'd go nowhere fast. So some choices lead to bad experiences."

"You mean if a rat doesn't bump into some walls, he'll never get out of the maze?"

Bob chuckled. "Somethin' like that. But it's not easy. Nope. Never said it was easy."

Peter took out the tattered last letter from his father, which he always signed: Your wingman, Dad. He remembered how his father had told him the fighter pilot's first creed: You never leave your wingman. And how he'd promised never to leave him.

"Remember when Dad was killed in Vietnam, Cap?"

"I do."

"Before he left on that last cruise, he and Mom had an awful fight. They didn't think I heard it. He told her he wasn't coming back. He was divorcing her. He told her she could have custody of me—" His heart sank with his head and his tired eyes welled. "That's the part I'd forgotten until this very moment. That he gave me away. And all these years I've hated my mother for chasing him away. But he *gave* me away. Abandoned me. I guess I just didn't want to accept that he didn't want me."

"I'm sorry, Pete."

"You knew, didn't you?

He nodded. "Don't hate him too much, though. I'm sure he regretted what he said, and I think he would've come back for you if he could've. But you know what? I'm glad he didn't. Without you, I'd never have known what it was to have a son."

"I'm just tired of losing people I love."

"I know you didn't exactly ask for these painful experiences," Bob said, rubbing Peter's shoulder. "But all experiences are necessary. Even the bad ones. Your choice now—as always—is what you decide to do with the things that happen to you. I hope this helps you, Pete, 'cause you have some tough choices to make. I'm just tryin' to prepare you."

* * *

Peter tossed and turned, unable to sleep. Next door, Cap snored loudly. It was three-thirty A.M. by Earth time. But here on the moon there was no night or day; people worked and lived in shifts around the clock. It reminded him of his navy friends who lived out their careers on submarines, where biological clocks had to be reset to meet the demands of twenty-four-hour operations in a windowless metal cocoon, sometimes for many months at a time.

He had been on the moon nearly three days, and he couldn't make up his mind about what his experience so far had meant. Never before had life been so confusing, nor he so conflicted—both emotionally and intellectually. On the one hand, Bob seemed to be the genuine article, and all of the people he'd met so far seemed happy, enthusiastic and committed—to whatever they were doing. But that's what bothered him. What *were* they doing? What was this Reconciliation Project? And if it was for the worldly good, why were they so secretive about their plans? Why couldn't he be trusted to know? If it were true that people were being replaced on Earth, was this the end of the world that Molly believed Lilah was talking about? And what the hell was going on in that lab? And the…what was it called? Something Georgic Area?

Too many questions. Not enough answers. In his experience, it was a scenario that usually made for unhappy outcomes. So far as he could tell, nothing was kept locked, not offices, shops or even apartments. Nothing but those two areas. Also, he had noticed there were no weapons, at least none that he could see and, remarkably, no surveillance cameras. *That's because I'm the only alien here.* He decided to find out once and for all what was going on in the restricted laboratory.

"No surveillance cameras," he whispered to himself as he rolled out of bed. "That'll make it easier."

# CHAPTER 37

The corridor around the Areopagite Experimental Biology Lab buzzed with activity as Peter watched several people approach the entrance, pause at the threshold, assume a rigid posture, then say something. Only seconds later, the door would open.

*Voice printing at least. Maybe retinal scanning. It's not going to be so easy.*

A globug and lorry with the same configuration of cargo he'd seen earlier that day with Madras slowed as it rounded the corner past him. A soft chattering and an occasional muted quack emanated from under the tarpaulin. Only one man rode the lorry this time. Quickly, Peter hopped on, covering himself with the canvas. A short ways on, the globug stopped.

"Fleming!" the driver called.

For a moment, nothing happened. Peter lay still, but his face was pressed up against a cage, where he was eye-to-eye with a shiny green-headed mallard with a troubled look. *Please don't—*

*Quack!*

Then the other ducks started quacking. He felt the man get off the globug and heard him start to walk toward the back of the lorry. Lifting the cover on the opposite side, Peter saw another globug parked nearby. If he could get behind it quickly.... He had one foot on the floor when the sound of the man's footsteps stopped, then moved away from him, toward the laboratory door. He got back under cover.

"Fleming," the driver said again in a more normal volume, and small servos began to whine. The door was opening; the lorry started moving.

Just inside the lab entrance the lorry stopped again. A rush of air fluttered the tarp, which sucked up against his face. His ears popped, telling him there was a lower pressure in the chamber, enough to prevent the escape of anything toxic—or contagious. Through these doors the globug stopped again. A computerized androgynous voice droned, "Beginning decontamination."

After several seconds of a modulating, low-frequency tone and a blue light so intense it hurt his closed eyes even through the canvas, the computer announced: "Decontamination complete." Another rush of air. More doors whined open. It smelled like a hospital. With a jerk, the globug started again. Lifting the edge of the tarp he saw row upon row of numbered laboratory cubicles and offices but only one other person, far back in a corner lab. The globug went straight a few more seconds, then turned right and stopped.

"Hey, Wally," a man wearing a small headphone but no helmet said. "How's it goin'?"

"It's a beautiful day in the neighborhood. How you been, Don?"

"Ehhh, can't complain."

"This the last load of NAV?"

The man without a helmet checked his digital clipboard. "Uh-huh. All North American virus mixture. Ebola-BRQ."

"Bravo, Romeo, Quebec," Wally repeated in confirmation. "Makes me shiver just to say it."

"Just sit tight a minute while I set it up. Then you can drive 'em in."

"Oakey Doakey."

The man with no helmet entered a walk-in freezer and returned with a canister the size of a gallon milk jug marked with the biohazard symbol and the words "Extreme Danger-Airborne Viral Agent" in large red letters.

"You know, Don, you really should be wearing your hood in here. At least when you handle *that* stuff." He nodded at the container. "Just because we're immune to the Ebola series doesn't mean we're immune to everything in here."

"Ahh, go on. You sound like my Jewish mother."

"Can't be too careful. What if you grab a can of Eblis-A by accident one time and drop it? Then what?"

"Okay, what?" he said dismissively. "You mean I'd end up back with them?" He jerked his head around, gesturing.

*Is he talking about Earth?*

"Maybe. And from what I hear, you don't want to go where they're going, starting, what? Day after tomorrow? *I* sure as heck don't."

"Holy cow! Two more days? I thought dispersal wasn't due to start 'til next week."

"All I know is what I'm told. Dispersal starts in—" He looked at his watch. "—about forty-eight hours. Somewhere in China."

"You sure?"

He shrugged. "Maybe I'm just excited to go back home."

*Back home! That's what Cap said.*

"It's gotta be soon, or they wouldn't be loading the ship."

"Poor buggers. I feel sorry for 'em."

"Pity *us,* huh? We're the ones who have to bury them all."

"Yeah, that's going to be a helluva mess to contend with."

"Beats the alternative."

"Yeah, I suppose so. Where they're going is no paradise. Not like Earth will be again."

Peter watched the man named Don remove what must have been a safety pin from the top of the canister, after which he used a tool about the size of a fingernail clipper to release a securing ring around the lid. He shoved the canister into a cannonlike breech in the center of the control console and gave it a firm half-turn with a large wrench.

Peter gingerly stepped off the back of the globug. The ducks began quacking. *Damn!* Quickly, he crawled back under the lorry, behind one of its wheels.

"Hey, you guys," Wally quipped, "pipe down back there! This ain't goin' to hurt a bit."

From under the lorry Peter scanned the area, looking for a place to hide, but the area around him was open and well lit, except for—*There!*

A short distance behind him was a small alcove next to the men's room. With the cages stacked four high on the lorry, the two men's view down the hall was partially blocked. If he were fast, he just might make it. Slipping off his shoes and tucking them under the tarp, he took four or five giant steps to a standpipe with a fire extinguisher, which was recessed about two feet into the wall and into whose small space he squeezed his body back out of sight.

"I'm about ready here," Don said, "so whenever you are." He made some final settings on the console. "These going straight to the hangar?"

"Yeah. Straight to the ship."

"See ya, Wally."

"Later gator," he said and drove the lorry with the ducks into a large treatment chamber.

From his standpipe retreat, Peter had a clear view of the chamber, the top half of which was Plexiglas. After removing the canvas tarpaulin, Wally left the globug and lorry, entered an adjoining room through airtight doors, where he then waited, giving his companion the thumbs-up signal.

Don fired the canister with a soft *pop,* releasing a greenish cloud of virus into the compartment. A red sign above the Plexiglas window flashed, "Contamination Alert!" A warning claxon sounded, *Ahooogah! Ahooogah! Ahooogah!* Only a moment later, the claxon stopped, replaced by the sound of rushing air. The green fog quickly cleared, followed by the low-frequency tone and the harsh blue light. Then the sign flashed: "Decontamination Complete." Wally re-entered the chamber, replaced the tarpaulin, mounted the globug and began to drive the lorry straight through to what Peter guessed was a parallel corridor leading to the hangar area.

An icy chill shuddered through his body. He tried to persuade himself he hadn't heard what he'd manifestly just heard. But no matter how hard he fought the tragic notion, the words of Wally and Don were inescapable. This was no dream or memory, but the here and now. With each passing second, the conclusion assumed an ever more frightening dimension. Could it be true? That Lilah was right? That this was the end of the world? To his weary mind, the answer was yes, and it was an end with a malevolent twist. Though some doubts remained—there was the matter of the utter benevolence of the people he'd met, their undisguised gaiety, their passion—the consequences of his being wrong seemed far outweighed by the enormity of the other calculated outcome. Something had to be done to stop it. But how? And who would help? Time was short.

Quickly formulating a plan, he decided that hitching a ride out the way he'd come in would be impossible. *But I'm already inside. There's no security to get out.* All he had to do was walk out. But not before he had the only thing he could use that might stop what was happening. What did the man call it? Eblis something or other. He had to get back into the walk-in freezer.

He peered down the corridor. All clear. *No!* He jumped back, catching a glimpse of a white suit through the glass inoculation chamber. Don was rounding the corner, heading his way. He jerked himself violently back into the alcove, back so hard it hurt, trying to melt into the wall out of view. The prongs on the standpipe bit like teeth into his side and thigh. Footsteps got louder. *Become invisible!* he told himself. Closer now. Into view.

His heart nearly exploded from his chest and he was fully prepared for the hand-to-hand combat that would surely ensue. But miraculously, the white shrouded figure floated past. Don had taken his comrade's advice and put on his hood, obscuring his peripheral vision.

Quietly, he allowed himself to exhale, as he heard the door to the men's room. Knowing he wouldn't have long before Don reappeared, Peter bounded down the hall to the freezer in gazellelike leaps on shoeless feet. Inside, shelf upon shelf of canisters lined the walls, each with a different group marking: North American, Asian, Eastern European, Indian Sub-Continent. Some were simply marked "Experimental." Within each group were countless canisters: Ebola-B, Ebola-BRQ, Hanta-S, Dengue Q, HIV-Sub-Saharan. But only different variants of the Ebola virus were on shelves with geographic markings. He focused on the experimental shelves. "Eblis, Eblis," he kept repeating, as if in his bleary fatigue he could forget, until at last he saw it. *There!* On a shelf by itself. A metal case marked Eblis-A.

Only one canister was inside the case. A different kind of canister—hard, clear plastic. It contained an ugly greenish-black mass, like a storm cloud, the ones that spawn tornadoes. He read the label:

WARNING! Virulently antithetical to a broad spectrum of animal life. Rabidly contagious. Multiple vectored airborne variant. Fast-acting. Produces debilitating muscular and respiratory symptoms in twenty-four hours, followed by coma and death (usually within forty-eight hours). Mortality rates exceed 98 percent in primates; 100 percent in humanoids, anthropoids. No known vaccine. No effective treatment. Experimental purposes only. Exercise extreme caution: P-4Q-Extreme Protocols only!

Taking off his shirt, he wrapped the canister in it and started down the corridor, past the men's room, toward the doors he had come in through on the lorry. *Damnit!* He heard the servos whining as the doors of the outer chamber opened; soon someone would emerge through the inner doorway.

*Now where?* He took a deep breath and held it, then he walked nonchalantly into the men's room, fully expecting to meet Don on his way out. But the man was still in a stall. All Peter needed was the man's suit. With it he could walk out unnoticed. He took the hood and upper-torso pullover off the rack. *No pants.* He peeked under the stall door. They were slung down around Don's knees.

Back to the corridor. Doors whirring, whining. *Think!* He ran back to the inoculation chamber. If he could just get in, he'd be able to escape to the hangar deck. "Door? Door? Where the hell's the door switch?" Found it. He pushed the button. Nothing happened. Frantically, he pushed every button and threw every switch he could reach.

*Why isn't anything happening?*

Finally he saw the manual safety latch. "Come onnn..." The chamber door opened. He glanced down the hallway one final time, where the door lights were flashing. Another lorry load of waterfowl was headed in. Don would be out soon. It was now or never.

Inside the chamber, he closed the door behind him, but then could not open the door at the other side, the door leading to the safe room, where the man named Wally had waited for the inoculation to be completed. *Ahooogah! Ahooogah! Ahooogah!* He'd pushed too many buttons. A contamination-decontamination cycle had started, and he was going to be exposed with whatever was left in the canister, just like the ducks. *Way to go, MacKenzie!*

A muted pop from the cannon dispenser signaled the beginning of the inoculation phase, with its greenish fog, which rapidly enveloped him, filling his nostrils with a deathly stench. After a few seconds' delay, there followed a sudden pressure change and a rush of fresh air. Then the low-frequency tone started, much harsher and more penetrating than before, like nothing he could have imagined. He covered his ears—it didn't help. He fell helplessly to his knees, pain screaming inside his head, dropping the viral canister, which unwrapped from his shirt and rolled freely across the floor. Then the blinding blue light flashed on, sending him into new realms of pain. Eyes clamped shut and writhing in agony, he descended momentarily into a deathly black silence. Only seconds later, he opened his eyes and realized that the star-bright light had blinded him. He groped the floor, desperately feeling for the canister of Eblis-A. Slowly, his vision improved, first with shadowy grays and indistinct forms, but quickly images clarified as he pulled himself up to peer over the edge of the low wall, just as a globug came into view at the far end of the hall and the door to the men's room swung open. Dazed, he struggled to focus his mind; he had only seconds. The chamber's exit doors! They'd opened automatically at the end of the cycle while he was blacked out, and now they were swinging shut, closing off his escape route.

*God help me!*

With one audacious long-jump, he managed to stretch an arm into the closing jaws of the door, prying them open just enough to squeeze his beaten body through to the other side, where he got to his feet, Eblis-A under his arm, and sprinted down the long corridor that led to the hangar bay.

* * *

"Are we on schedule?" Pheras asked.

"Yes," Madras replied sadly. "All preparations are complete. We're ready to start the dispersal tomorrow in.... Let me see." He glanced down at the digital device he wore like a wrist watch, repeatedly pressing a key with the nub of gold metal that formed the arm of a Martian ankh on his pinky ring, scrolling through a list of geographic names. "The Yangtze and Hwang Ho river basins, between Peking and Nanking. We'll release five thousand fowl over the first twenty-four hours." He looked up at Pheras, hoping for some signal of approval, some vestige of hope, anything to make him feel better about this unpleasant task.

Pheras gave no sign, but his usually bright aura dimmed. "It distresses me still, Madras. Horribly." His luminous eyes slipped behind silvered lids.

"It's hard to believe it came to this," Madras said with disappointment. "Despite everything. The Covenant. Our experience with Mars. All the warning signs."

Pheras sighed. "It is a bitter pill, my friend. But dire situations themselves dictate desperate measures. Lo all these years, I had such high hopes for them all."

"Unconquerable hope," Madras muttered, trying to console himself.

"Is with us always," Pheras concluded. "But the Covenant demands—"

"Yes, yes, I know...."

"Sometimes there is but one way. The Covenant must be honored. And there must be no shrinking from that. Further delay is impossible.

*Lord, it's finally come,* Madras thought. How long had it been? Over a hundred and fifty years since the beginning preparations, over fifty since the replacements had begun. Hope that changes would be made, reprieves or special dispensations negotiated, had kept his heart light, but the reality was breaking all around him now. *It is time.*

"As to the means, you have followed the directive to the letter?"

"Scrupulously. There will be no suffering in their passing. As you know, we engineered the viruses to be as humane as possible. No one will feel any pain, just a profound lethargy, which will be followed within a few hours by a sensation of normal sleepiness. A coma with respiratory and cardiac arrest will ensue within forty-eight hours of infection. The experience will in no way be uncomfortable, no different really than going to sleep in the usual way."

"What is your estimate of the total time to completion?"

"To disperse all the waterfowl? Or for the viruses to fully disseminate?"

"For the dying to be done."

Madras picked up the thread of his grim analysis. "It will start fairly slowly, spreading outward from each locus of infestation as the birds migrate...and people travel, mingle. But though the virus is multiple-vectored, the principle means of spread will be airborne droplets, person to person, so over all the spread will be very rapid. The conclusion will depend somewhat on the temporary countermeasures they may conceive. But the end result is assured: There will be no more unreconstructed Homo sapiens on Earth within eight to twelve months."

"Anyone left at Lake Vic—?" An urgent knock on the door. "Enter," Pheras commanded. "Hello, Bob. What can I do for you?"

Bob Donaldson dipped his head reverently. "Peter MacKenzie has been in the lab. He left while I was sleeping—"

"Never mind, my son. Your assurances about your friend were heartfelt and well intended."

Bob gulped out the words: "He's taken the Eblis-A."

Madras's jaw dropped. He looked at Pheras, whose countenance varied not at all as he spoke calmly, "It would seem Mr. MacKenzie has made his choice."

"This could change everything," Madras declared gravely, thinking how ugly the outcome might be if MacKenzie weren't soon stopped, for his replacement body could indeed die again, and being familiar with the Eblis-A research, he had no desire to experience a profoundly unpleasant and unnecessary death.

"We must not panic everyone," Pheras commanded.

Madras nodded to Bob, who left on a run.

* * *

"Something's wrong with this picture," Peter muttered to himself as he stepped onto the elevator that would take him to the main ventilation area beneath the lake. What was it about this place? No one had tried to stop him. Yet surely they knew by now what he was up to. He'd made his way easily, without disguise or subterfuge, through the hangar area, where workers loaded cage after cage of infected waterfowl onto the spacecraft, past the fabulous botanical garden, past the two menageries with their exotic complement of animals, past the aviary and into the elevator. *My God, it's almost a party atmosphere.*

All along the way he passed happy people, people busy about their daily activities, seemingly unconcerned about the debacle about to befall their brethren back on Earth. Had they no awareness of the plan? Were they hapless pawns in an impending cosmic holocaust? Or was their joyousness a manifestation of their enslavement to some exotic drug or brainwashing technique? Perhaps they were just soulless trolls, in the thrall of some charismatic leader? Nazis soldiers in blind obedience to a Hitlerian Pheras?

"I guess it really doesn't matter," he said in a normal voice, oblivious to the lovely young woman who now shared the elevator, which, unnoticed, had stopped.

"Excuse me?" she said innocently. "But were you talking to me?"

"No," he said, forcing a tiny smile as the elevator continued its descent. "I have a lot on my mind. Guess I was talking to myself out loud."

Her sunny countenance turned cloudy. "You're concerned about someone you left back there, aren't you? Someone who didn't make it?"

His mind and heart clashed, wrenched by the horrible truth of the "Project" and the genuine empathy of this warm-hearted stranger with big green eyes. "I guess you caught me." Just then the elevator stopped again, its doors opening with a muted swish.

She smiled at him and said, "This is my floor." Stepping out of the elevator, she turned to him. "Try to keep in mind that we are each the agent of our own destiny. You can't live another's life for them, any more than they could live yours."

The doors closed. His stomach lurched with the drop of the elevator. She was gone, but her image lingered, reminding him of Molly and accentuating his profound confusion. It didn't help that he'd never felt so utterly used up, so spent. His mind struggled to balance the sacrifice he was about to make—including his own life and the lives of possibly innocent people—against the lives he might conceivably save on Earth. Then it occurred to him that maybe there wasn't much worth saving on Earth: the injustice, the wars, the violence to mind and body and environment. But the alternative was unthinkable. His stomach sank, along with the relentlessly plunge of the elevator. *Down into hell.*

Now in the atmospheric regeneration area, making his way along the catwalk on the periphery of the dome-shaped chamber, he felt a chill as the cold air gushed past him, dumping into the abyss that surrounded the central electrolysis pond like a moat. As Cap had told him, fresh oxygen from electrolysis, after being separated from free hydrogen, mixed with this surging ocean of returning air, renewing it, before being sucked up in windy volumes by colossal fan blades the size of helicopter rotors and being sent to aerate the complex.

Except for two people working in a control room two stories above him, he was alone. He crossed to the inner circular catwalk that surrounded the electrode pond, with its water boiling and churning, creating a fog of humid air above the turbulent surface and dampening everything in the chamber. Lightning bolts of arcing electricity bathed the atmosphere in a pale blue glow, which now and then winked brighter with flashes of blinding white light. The acrid smell of ozone stung his nostrils. His hair stood on end from the gale force current of air rushing up from below as he stood on the catwalk over the moat. *Here should do the trick.*

Sitting down on the catwalk, he took out the screwdriver he had taken from the walk-in freezer and scratched his itching chin with its blade, and for the last time considered the action he was about to take. Calmly, he took a deep breath, then, reflecting again on images of Earth, teeming with life—human life—he thought of his mother and Clancey, and of Beth and of how he'd failed Bo. He'd been a traitor to his friend, he knew—and a coward. For that, he feared, there would be no redemption. Not now that Molly was gone.

Still doubts vexed him. He remembered the war he'd taken part in, the wars of his father and his father's father, the carnage and the savagery down through the ages, the human suffering it had spawned. Were we fatally flawed somehow? As a species? Spiritually? *Earth has become Mars!*

So he *did* remember the Martian re-visitation. But visions of a new worldwide calamity pushed his doubts aside. *"Yes!"* he shouted into the raging wind with little danger of being heard, as he pulled the grenadelike safety pin from the canister. He tried to insert the screwdriver blade into the hole meant for the special tool he'd seen the man use in the laboratory, but it wasn't working, so he tried to pry the lid. "Damnit!" The blade slipped, penetrating the flesh between his thumb and forefinger and causing blood to spurt all over him, as the canister nearly rolled off the catwalk into the abyss before he could grab it.

"Pete, don't do it!" Bob Donaldson yelled from the edge of the moat. "I'm beggin' you. Give me the canister. Please!"

"Stay away, Cap!"

Bob ran to the ladder for the control room and started to climb.

*Hurry! Before he shuts down the fans.*

Feverishly, he rubbed the screwdriver blade against the stone piling, desperately trying to file it down enough so it would insert into the recessed fitting. *Got it!* He wrenched it around with all his might. The security ring broke free. All he had to do now was unscrew the lid and scatter the virus into the wind. He twisted the lid, but frustratingly, blood from his injured hand made the canister slimy, so he tore off his shirt and tried to wipe it clean for a better grip. No good.

"Peter! Don't do it!" As if from a dream, a familiar voice, though muted by the roar of the wind, called to him. *"Peter!"* the voice rang out again, more urgently.

No dream, this voice had a body, though as yet not clearly discernable in the flashing blue lights, which teased him with stroboscopic snatches of images. He strained his eyes, flicking them right and left, blinking wildly, aching for a clearer view. Then the form moved closer. A female body, hair lofting in the rushing air, flaring about her head like a flame. She called out again, stepping closer. Now the face etched a pattern that resonated with growing intensity like the thunderous wind that roared about him. The woman stepped into full view. She spoke again, this time in a more normal volume, which, due to the howling wind, he could barely hear. Nevertheless, he saw her lips form the words.

"Peter, darling."

"Molly?"

# CHAPTER 38

"I'll handle Mister MacKenzie personally," Madras vowed as he headed for the dark gray door through which Bob Donaldson had just departed.

"One moment, Madras," Pheras commanded. "Lake Victoria Base. Has everyone been safely evacuated?"

"Yes," he replied, barely able to concentrate on the question. "We have no further need of it anyway." His hand quivered on the doorknob. One word kept repeating in his brain: *Eblis-A*. He knew Peter MacKenzie could, indeed, be a major problem, an incitement to disaster, and he wondered if Pheras had foreseen this unplanned outcome.

"No, Madras, I didn't."

How he hated having his thoughts read back to him, for he never knew when, or under what circumstances, Pheras would do it.

"You forget," the archangel chided, pinching the skin on his own arm as if to emphasize the point. "Even angels must have both feet in only one world at a time. Only the Source of All Things resides in every realm at once."

"Sorry."

Pheras waved his hand and shook his head. "As far as the Reconciliation is concerned, I can do no more than you to affect its outcome."

Madras detected something he'd never before seen: a subtle but distinct wrinkle in Pheras's imperturbable expression.

"By law," Pheras added, turning away, as if to hide his alarm, "my influence is no more nor less than Peter MacKenzie's while I'm in this body, and his actions, as well as yours, had—and will have—consequences I didn't ask to see. Even if I'd possessed that knowledge, I couldn't have shared it with you. And should you think my attitude cavalier—" He turned to face Madras again, his radiance restored, and beaming a grin. "I, too, will be held accountable for the success or failure of this project." The angel's smile created shafts of multicolored light that Madras could feel on his face like tiny kisses. "But you know these things, Madras."

Yes, he knew Pheras had superhuman abilities, but he also knew Pheras had corporeal limitations, though at times like this he wished it were otherwise. What he wasn't quite clear on, was just when and how Pheras turned his abilities on or off, just when and how he decided to use them.

The aura that framed Pheras's head brightened. "You blame yourself for Peter MacKenzie?"

"She chose him," Madras replied. For a split second he *was* sorry that he'd brought MacKenzie here, forgetting for the moment why he had.

"And has she failed in any way? Was her love somehow flawed? Her mission tainted?"

A twinkling of resentment remained, as slowly, grudgingly he shook his head. "No. There is such power in them. All of them. If only they would see it."

"What then? Their choices would be better?"

"I guess that's what I meant." His shoulders sank.

"Ah, yes. The wish is ever on one's lips. But another's life is not our ship to sail."

"Sometimes," Madras said, feeling his pulse against the collar of his tunic. *Eblis-A!* "I think one life is far too much to deal with."

"And if life were easy?"

"Oh," he breathed heavily, "I don't know.... You're right. I complain too much."

"Madras, Madras, you've misunderstood me. My only point was this: Without struggle, where's the sweetness of victory? The zest in achievement and its reward? The passion?"

Madras thought of Molly, her reverence for life, love and family, and her love for Peter. *If not for love, why do anything?*

"I knew you'd see it." Pheras patted him on the shoulder, a touch as calming as a mother's kiss. "Love's unbounded power is ALL. Don't let a minor setback spoil your faith, my friend. Let the brightness of your future—our collective futures—chase the shadows of your doubt away."

"Then *you* will stop him?"

"No, we will just have to do our best to convince Mr. MacKenzie to do the right thing."

"Will you come with me, then?"

Pheras put his hand over Madras's on the door handle, raised his bushy silver eyebrows and said, "If not for love?"

# CHAPTER 39

*"Molly?"* Peter hollered with every farthing of his strength, but the sound died in his throat, suppressed by fatigue and the thronging winds. The woman stepped closer, rounding the edge of the moat, coming into full view near one of the four narrow walkways that crossed the deep crevasse of the moat like spokes of a wheel and connected with the main island and the inner circular catwalk, on whose deathly cold stone he now sat, growing ever number as it sapped his body heat.

Suddenly the whine of the huge fans began to die. The wind receded swiftly until it was no more than a mere whisper of a breeze. Soon a morguelike stillness settled over the chamber, yet he knew they couldn't keep those fans off very long.

"Molly?" His echo reverberated in the chamber, interrupted only by the intermittent buzzing and crackling of the arching electrical charges, which leapt and undulated like blue semaphores between the giant electrodes. "Molly?" he called again, softly this time, and with profound disbelief.

"Yes, Peter!" she said again, moving slowly, cautiously nearer. "It really is me. Your Ingrid, remember?"

"But Molly's dead."

"No, my darling, Bogie," she called with a laughing, loving color to her voice, almost childlike in its comic enthusiasm. "How I've wanted to say that to you again."

Out of the corner of his eye, he saw Cap descend the control room ladder, using only his hands, as if rappelling, and run toward him.

"Pete, listen to me," Bob Donaldson said urgently, skidding to the woman's side on the polished bedrock. "What you're trying to do is admirable, son." Then he looked down at himself. "Sorry about the 'son' part. I can't get used to the fact I'm forty years younger than I was."

"That's the problem, Cap. I can't either."

Shaking his fashion-model head, Bob said: "You're thinking that by killing yourself and everyone here that you'll save so many on Earth...." He started out on the catwalk.

"Don't, Cap. Please don't."

"But Pete, nothing can stop the Reconciliation—"

"The worst thing for me now would be to watch you die again." He laughed at himself. "Guess you did have me convinced. For a while anyway." He tried harder to remove the top, twisting until his wrist bones cried with pain; still the stubborn lid resisted.

"Sorry, Pete. But I can't let you."

"Stop right there, Cap! I *know* what Reconciliation means. I don't know how they turned you.... Hell, I don't even know what you are, really. Or who she is."

"I beg you, Peter," Molly cried. "Don't do this. If it would convince you, I'd fling myself into this dark hole right now."

"If it would make you happy." She inched closer to the edge. Terrified by regret, he yelled, "No, don't!"

She stepped closer, next to the short-post railing. "Nothing but being with you again—being your wife—would make me truly happy."

"Don't!" Peter warned. "Please!" The truth was, he couldn't bear to see either of them die again—even if they were imposters.

Bob Donaldson crept closer still. "It's just that you don't understand about the Reconciliation. Don't know the whole story. Let Madras explain—"

"Explain? I *saw*, Cap. With my own eyes. Heard with my own ears. I know what the plan is. I know all about the virus." Glancing down for an instant, he rapped the edge of the lid on the stone platform and felt a rush of air. *No, Cap!*

A crushing blow from Bob Donaldson's right hand landed squarely on Peter's scarred chin, stunning him and knocking him half over the edge of the black abyss and the canister out of his hand. It rolled away, teetering on a sharp angle of stone several feet away. For an instant, they froze in a standoff, staring at each other in shocked and sorrowed amazement.

"Not bad for an old man!" Peter dove for the canister just as Bob grabbed it. Struggling ferociously, Peter managed to wrest the canister from Bob's younger, stronger hands. But not for long, as Bob returned blow for blow. Another. And another until he again had the viral container.

*Got it back!*

But the canister quickly passed back into Bob's hands, then back again to Peter's. Two times. Three times the canister traded hands, as each gave as good as he got, blow for stunning blow. Until finally, Peter, with a well-placed thrust of his aching legs, sent Bob crashing hard onto his back, his head whiplashing to the stone floor with a mushy thud, where he lay motionless on the catwalk's margin, one leg draped precariously over the ledge, a slender rail post the only thing between him and certain death.

*Ahhhh!* Peter strained against the canister lid until he heard his wrist crack with under the effort.

"Peter, for the love of God!" Molly screamed.

*Damnit! If there is a God...* He banged the canister's lid. Twisted it. Cursed it. Time after time his grip slipped and his wrists weakened. It wouldn't give. A sudden flash caught in his eye. "Cap!" he yelled, quickly rolling aside, but then, almost unconsciously, he thrust out his hand as Bob flew past him, falling head first over the edge, managing at the last instant to latch onto Peter's outstretched hand.

*"Pete! Help me!"*

"I've got you!" Without thinking, he let go of the feeble railing and stretched out his other hand to grasp Bob's wrist at the same time he slung his leg around the rail post. Now this was all that kept both from freefalling into the dark void. "Cap!" Peering into the blackness, he was unable to see the face of the man who claimed to be his surrogate father, until a bolt of arching electricity illuminated his eerily disfigured face, blue and black with shadow, light and pain.

*Roy Corbett!* Suddenly Bob Donaldson's face morphed into Roy's and back again. His F-14 fighter's backseat crewman, and one-time good friend, was again slipping beneath the waves before his terrified eyes.

Everything he'd ever cared about was lost, or being lost. In staccato bursts, scenes jumped one upon another from memory. His father's funeral. Taps being played. The firing of the Honor Guard's guns. The missing-man formation of F-4 Phantoms. A neatly folded American flag on his mother's quiet lap. Out of the corner of his eye, he caught a glimpse of Molly. No, she was lost too.

"Cap! I can't hold—" He wanted to save Cap more than himself, more at this moment than the World. But his bloody fingers failed, and as Cap slipped away, never diverting his eyes, his faint image disappeared like stars in a cloudy night sky. The last thing Peter heard was "I love you, Pete," the sound fading into black nothingness like a dying scream, until the awful muted sound of impact reached up through the lightless void and slapped him like an open hand.

"Oh, my God! Peter!" Molly cried and started onto the catwalk. "I'm coming."

"Stay there!" Peter warned. "You saw what just happened." He wanted more than anything to cry, but couldn't. Swampy and dank, the atmosphere hung heavy with the smell of ozone and without circulating air, the temperature had risen twenty degrees in only minutes, sapping what was left of his strength. He forced his mind back to his duty, but drenching sweat made dealing with the canister even more difficult than before.

"I know how much Captain Donaldson meant to you," Molly said with quavering voice. "With what you've been through, it's hard to have faith. But at some point you have to trust—"

"How do I know you're really Molly? How? Any more than I know he was the real Bob Donaldson? How do I know who any of you are? Can you tell me?"

"If you can't believe your eyes," she said with an undeniable sadness, "then believe your heart. What's your heart telling you?"

That had always been his problem: an uncertain heart. "Oh, I believe you are all Martians. Too bad Orson Welles didn't live to see this. This is the real 'War of the Worlds.'"

Molly's shoulders dropped. She edged closer, seeming more confident, less afraid.

"Stay back!" *God knows I don't want to hurt you.* He held up the canister. "You know what this is, don't you?"

"We know," Madras answered, joining Molly on the bleak rim of the moat.

"Peter, darling. My heart tells me that you still love me. And if I'm right, you mustn't do this."

Madras looked at the woman. "Bob?"

She shook her head gravely, then turned back to Peter. "What you're trying to do is heroic. Just as Bob said. Just as when you saved my life so many times. And Kopi's. Yes, I saw it all. You were only thinking of me—"

"How?" Peter's head swirled. "You were dead. Cap, too. How do I know you aren't somehow tapping into my memory or—?" His reserves of energy were rapidly deleting, yet determined, he drew himself up, forced himself to focus. "No, Molly. There's too much at stake." God how he wanted it to be her. *It can't be her!*

Madras stepped out onto the catwalk, not ten feet away.

"I'm warning you for the last time," he said with voice so hoarse it barely registered. "Give me room to think." Droplets of sweat ran into his eyes, his ears, his mouth, all salty and bitter. He tried again to get a good grip on the canister lid, but the blood and sweat denied him.

"Peter," Madras said calmly, like the Madras of old, cool and collected, "I will do as you wish. We all will. And you will do what you must. But before you do anything I ask that you hear me out."

Desperately, Peter banged the canister on the catwalk, almost crying from frustration. "Make it fast."

"Just stop what you're doing for a minute," Madras urged. "Do you remember what happened on Mars? Don't you believe your own experience?"

"Most of it...I think. It's getting pretty vague. Besides, I don't know if I believe any of it anymore. Especially now that I know what you're planning. It's all some kind of mind game or...or drugs or something."

"No, Peter. Listen to him," Molly implored. "Don't destroy our chance to be together again."

"Did you know they're going to kill everyone in the world with some God-awful virus?"

Molly looked at him with an expression both adoring and apprehensive, as that of a mother as she beholds her newborn baby's first tentative, trembling steps. "I do know, Peter. And as difficult as it may be to believe, it's for the best. Put down the canister. For your sake. *For us!*"

"How could destroying all human life be for the best?"

"Even if you kill us all, it won't stop the Reconciliation," Madras assured him. "You would only delay it. Because the Reconciliation is about an accounting of souls not bodies. But if you persist in doing this, you will be responsible for the final destruction of life on Earth. All life on Earth. Forever. Despite the theories of your astronomers, there aren't many places like it. And because of natural law, it cannot be re-created with the utterance of a few magical words. Perhaps more important for you to know is that even without the Reconciliation, those on Earth will not see another generation in flesh and blood."

Out of the flickering shadows a different man emerged, a man whose face bespoke an unutterable peace. In appearance about sixty years old, with the white hair of age but possessing a fresh-as-dawn complexion harboring no detectable wrinkles, Pheras stood silently for a moment with his arm around Molly, before speaking in a voice strangely soothing—and familiar. "Some things are irrevocable, Peter. Some things once broken cannot be fixed."

*I know this voice.* "Pheras? Is this your idea of reinforcements, Mister Madras? You're going to have to do better than that." He sat on the canister's lid, hoping the heat of his body would make the metal expand, loosening it, so he could be done with it all. "The CIA knew about you and this moon base, didn't they? They were planning to destroy all this."

"They don't have the means," Madras said with assurance. "But no matter. Bigger plans are under way on Earth right now by terrorist forces that will accomplish the final destruction of the paradise that was Earth—"

"Allow me, my son," Pheras said calmly, addressing Madras.

"Peter, do you know what DNA is?"

"I know it's the basis of life."

"Indeed. DNA is the celestial jewel of life, a divinely felicitous combination of primordial elements with the ability to carry information. But more importantly for life, it can duplicate itself, without which capability it could not communicate the information it sacredly harbors. Let me tell you a story. It's about DNA and Earth's immediate future—"

"I don't want to hear another cockamamie story."

"I'm afraid you must, Peter. Right now there is a bioengineering company called the Aquarian Genomic Research Center, a private research organization purportedly funded by a large American foundation. Openly, they are pursuing human cloning and the production of stem cells for compassionate medical purposes, to grow replacement organs for transplantation and the like. A noble cause if true. But in reality, they are funded by wealthy Islamic terrorists, and they are pursuing more nefarious ends. Two programs are well advanced. One aims to create genetically engineered monsters, creatures indistinguishable from human to the uninitiated but who nonetheless lack free will. They are to be trained in special madrasas, or Islamic schools, where they will be taught blind obedience to their masters. And their sole purpose in life will be to die in the service of death, to carry bombs or disease or toxins, spreading carnage and mayhem in endless supply.

But it is the second Aquarian Genomic Research Center program that will, though quite by accident, spell doom for all DNA-based life on Earth. Viruses come in two forms, Peter. One form is itself based on DNA but the other is based on a related molecule, also necessary for life, RNA. While the Aquarian Center's current pursuit of a viral weapon unlike any other in its lethality and its cruelty to human flesh will fail, the project's unwitting byproduct, an RNA virus that attacks the molecules necessary for DNA to replicate itself—will be flushed down the drain during routine housekeeping, ending up in the Potomac river, then the Chesapeake Bay, then the Atlantic Ocean, where, as it travels by currents to every other ocean, it will destroy first the phytoplankton and zooplankton, then the sea life that depends upon them. Finding its way up the food chain, it will begin to claim human lives with a disease the course of which is excruciating, tortured and ugly. Imagine your body without the ability to replace or repair cells. No replacement of blood cells or skin cells. Hairless bodies erupt in suppurating sores both inside and out. Death comes only after a long and agonizing process of living decay. But the virus does not stop there. Slowly but surely, it will infect all DNA-based life forms, even unto the lowly bacteria. Before twenty five years are gone, the fate of all life on Earth will be sealed. Before one hundred years, the Earth will be a lifeless brown and blue orb, not unlike Mars is today, lifeless and forlorn."

Just then the huge fans slowly began to turn. Peter drank in the bracing cool air, though it did little to clarify his thinking. He looked at Molly and thought of her last kiss, her fragrance, her warmth. He saw the air loft her magnificent red hair, flashing purple highlights in the electric discharges, perfect strawberry tresses, just as he'd remembered them; her green eyes shone a curious purple in the blue bursts of light, causing him to remember. "Where's your locket?"

She hesitated, put her hand to her breast, and looked at Madras and Pheras. Then, with a pained expression, she said: "It was lost."

"Figures." Peter pushed his hand into his pocket and pulled out the silken red strands Kufu had stolen. *This is what's real. As God is my witness, Molly. Wherever you are. I love you.* He dried his hand in the current of air. Just enough so that he could break the lid's seal at last. Slowly he unscrewed it a turn, never taking his eyes off Madras, who was closest to him and who appeared ready to spring.

*And it's too late now. For all of us.*

"Peter," Pheras said without a hint of concern, "I want you to look at me." He motioned for Molly and Madras to come over to his side. He then lay down on his back, Molly on one side, Madras on the other, and he closed his eyes and began to breathe ever more slowly, ever more shallowly. To all appearances he was sleeping, until soon his chest ceased to rise and fall.

"He's not breathing," Peter uttered unconsciously.

Madras and Molly did not react, but stabilized his body, like two bookends, as if trying to prevent Pheras from falling into the chasm.

Out of Pheras's reclining physical body there arose a shimmering body of glorious, silver light brighter than the sun itself; yet gazing into it caused no discomfort. To the contrary, to look upon it elicited a soothing, peaceful calm. Fully erect now, the body of light, though resembling the physical body of Pheras was somewhat transformed, still human but a form indescribably more beautiful.

As it flowed across the chasm toward him, Peter knew he was finished, for this was truly an irresistible force. Now somehow the lid between his fingers moved easily. The top of the canister rolled to the edge of the catwalk and fell into the void. Several seconds later he heard the faint clink as it hit bottom. The bright light almost upon him, he quickly tapped the contents of the canister out onto the catwalk and did his best to scatter the deadly dust into the rising column of air. *There! It's done.*

At that moment the bright body of light settled over Peter like a twinkling veil. But instead of the horror he'd expected, a feeling of complete serenity, devoid of even the most trivial anxiety, unfolded within him, and then, just as he had in his Martian memories, Pheras spoke directly to his mind.

*Peter, do not be troubled, for everything is as it should be. Madras spoke the truth: Those whose bodies will die in the Reconciliation will live on, as will we all—by divine grace. But we all must face the consequences of our own choices. We are all accountable. Our powers are grand, but so, too, are our responsibilities.*

*And it is only fitting that those whose heavy labors have brought them far along the road to enlightenment should be justly rewarded for their accomplishments, as it is now fitting that you, too, be rewarded for the difficult choices you have made here and in the recent past.*

Peter thought, *But I've just committed a grievous act. And now I'm sorry. Poor Cap.* His eyes ached with tears that somehow would not flow.

*You acted,* Pheras said, *from the heart of goodness, Peter. It was a worthy, unselfish sacrifice.... And no harm was done.*

*What?* Peter felt a combination of relief and disappointment.

*When you dropped the canister in the inoculation chamber, the virus was deactivated by the prophylactic light; there was never any danger. Oh, no one knew that, not even I until this moment when I left my corporeal form.*

*Then what's to become of me?* Peter asked. *Why was I brought here in the first place?*

*You were brought here by special dispensation. Because of the great love of a great and good heart—*

*Molly?*

*And the kindness of a Good Samaritan—*

*Madras?*

*Yes, but it was she who interceded on your behalf in a most vigorous way. Make no mistake, though, Peter: It was your own acts that earned you the privilege of helping to reestablish a harmony on Earth. Your own acts transformed you. Your decision to forgo your own revenge, to put aside your hatred of Bandar Bliss in order to save the life of a young girl was a most difficult achievement, as was your willingness to sacrifice yourself for those nameless billions you left behind on Earth. And, while thanks must go to Molly for her positive influence, be gratified: For the true accomplishment is yours alone.*

*I leave you now in the company of your friends and your betrothed. Be of good cheer, Peter. For know this: You are loved.*

With those words, Peter spun into a vortex of light and shadow until, gradually, his awareness faded into the blissful nothingness of deep sleep.

# CHAPTER 40

Peter awoke to a dreamy visage: smiling green eyes; sunny, freckle-dappled complexion; full, pouty pink lips; and warm, silken red hair that fell about the woman's face and shoulders like a sacred robe, and the vision—so close, so touchable, so like Molly—drew him upright in bed. He blinked hard several times and shook his head to be sure. Yes, the pain was still there; he was truly awake and aware.

"Molly!" The word spurted out of him in reflex. "So it wasn't all a dream."

"No, Peter, it's not a dream. I'm here. Now lie back awhile," she told him, gently pushing him back onto the bed.

"How long have I—"

"You've been out for nearly forty-eight hours." Her warm hands with their delicate, slender fingers lovingly stroked his brow. Then he saw the silvery plastic band with its faux diamonds and took her hand.

"But you didn't have this on when—"

"No, I didn't. Madras, the old sweetheart, went back for it." Suddenly her bright smile withered. "But he couldn't find my locket."

"Then Pheras? Everything?" He felt the short hairs on his neck stiffen and his chin began to tingle. *Earth!*

"There will be plenty of time for questions, my love. In fact, we've got all the time in the world—in the universe. Nothing can separate us now."

"Really?" He tapped on the petite piece of plastic. "And the ring? Does this mean you'll still marry me?"

"Of course silly. Besides, have you forgotten the Chinese proverb, 'You own the life you save?' Well, I belong to you. Have for some time." She kissed him full on his lips. "Emmm...You know how they say the anticipation of a thing is better than the reality? Well, whoever *they* are—they're wrong."

Her obvious joy touched him like warm sunlight, and he pulled her down, kissing her with heart, soul and mind. How he loved the taste of her, the satiny feel of her as he nuzzled her neck, the scent of her. "Lilacs?"

"Uh-huh. Bob told me it was your favorite."

*Cap. I'm sorry.*

"Your nose is cold."

"Does that mean I'll have to sit up and beg for another kiss?"

She angled her head. Her mouth turned up in a jolly smile. "Very funny."

"Just don't ask me to play dead."

"Ruff, ruff," she teased. "Your blood sugar's low."

"Huh?"

"That's why your nose is cold. Hungry?"

"Got any Cracker Jacks?" he said in point of habit, expecting the usual shaking head or curt reply in the negative. But to his surprise, she reached into a large travel bag beside his bed and flipped a small box onto his lap. "Cracker Jacks!"

"You can thank Madras for these too."

"No, I thank *you* for remembering," he said, gratefully ripping into the package and popping a piece of the caramel popcorn into his mouth. "And you too, Madras, wherever you are. Just put it on my tab."

"You certainly haven't changed," she giggled.

"And what about you?" he said somberly. "Have you changed?" He remembered his talks with Cap about how their bodies—spirits?—had been somehow changed.

"Not my love for you." She touched his nose with her finger.

"What about my Mom?" he asked, afraid of what he'd hear. "What about Clancey? What about—"

She shook her head. "I honestly don't know, Peter.... It's different for you. You didn't die."

*Not Yet!* He ran his fingertip over the length of his scar, his infallible trouble detector, which suddenly screamed for attention—thank God she was right, he hadn't changed.

She looked at him with a more thoughtful expression, crinkling up her brow as if conflicting ideas had collided inside her with devastating effect. "You asked if I'd changed. Well, yes, in some ways. We have a new realization, a higher awareness. A new respect for the individual paths people take. And though I still have fond memories—"

"Like AJ?"

"Yes, even for AJ."

"And your father?"

She looked away for a moment. "Now I see those biological relationships in a new light. We've all been fathers and mothers, brothers and sisters over the expanse of our being."

"So they're all dead? Like AJ?"

"I wouldn't lie to you, Peter. Not any more—"

"Any more? When did you ever?"

Looking somewhat mortified, she sighed, but he noticed she didn't blush, as she was so quick to in the past. "Remember the night in Jerusalem when I got drunk? When you tried to make love to me and I started snoring?"

"What about it?"

"I wasn't really sleeping."

"Why you rascal, you!"

"And, my love," she said softly with a look of mock indignation, "I know about the Palestinian boy. You were sweet to lie for me. But I really did kill him." Then, with a brighter voice, "Are you feeling up to seeing an old friend?"

Peter's heart leaped. Almost as much as wanting Molly back, he wanted Cap. Before he knew it, he heard himself say, "Okay."

"Come in, Bo!"

*"Bo?"* He sat up so fast he nearly blacked out and fell helplessly back onto the bed, his heart fluttering, his head swimming. Yet he managed to keep his eyes on the doorway. *It can't be!*

But it was. Looking as hale and hardy as the last time Peter had seen him, Bo sauntered in, his face ablaze with a welcoming smile, his big dark eyes twinkled under his heavy eyebrows and— "You've got hair!"

"Good to see you again, old buddy." Bo grasped Peter's hand with his signature vice-grip handshake and ran his other hand over his lush head of brown hair. "Like it?"

"Bo, I.... I…" Unable to speak, he wondered why Bo just stared at him with this look of wonderment. Why didn't he say something about Beth? All the things Peter had left unsaid back on Earth, eons ago it now seemed, flooded back. Now if only he could find the courage— "Bo, there's something I've got to say. Last Christmas Eve—"

"Molly," Bo said, cutting him off, "would you bring him in please?"

"Bring who?" Peter said impatiently. "Bo this can't wait. It's eating me alive." Molly was gone only seconds before he heard the tiny, plaintive cries.

"It's a boy," Molly said joyfully, carrying the brightly bundled infant to his bedside, tickling the baby's wrinkled pink face, nuzzling him and cooing as she displayed him like a trophy. "Look like anyone you know?" She pointed to the tiny dimple at the peak of its jaw. "See the chin?

"My God!" Peter exclaimed. "Mine?"

"And Beth's," Bo said in a strangely happy voice.

"I'm so sorry, Bo." He didn't know if he'd be able to stop the tears. He coughed, cleared his throat, trying to compose himself. "What I did to you...." His head sank to his chest, shaking. "I'm more ashamed of it than anything else. It's unforgivable."

"Nothing is unforgivable," Bo told him. "And I do forgive you. For this and for anything else you may have done. It's a new beginning, Pete."

"But what about Beth?"

"Beth died in childbirth."

"Is she here?" Peter asked.

Bo and Molly looked at each other, but said nothing.

The infant clung desperately to Peter's little finger, cooing and gurgling, alternately smiling and frowning. "Does my little wingman have a name?"

"We'd picked the name Abel," Bo said. "After my father."

"It's perfect," Molly declared. "Perfect for our first child." She kissed Peter and looked at him expectantly.

"Good luck to you both," Bo said, backing out of the room.

Knowing his business with Bo was unfinished, he called to him, "Can I see you later, Bo?" "You bet your life," Bo said with a sly grin. And he was gone.

*You bet your life?* He shuddered.

"Knock, knock?" It was Madras, who now stuck his head around the door's edge.

"Come in, Madras." Peter was truly glad to see the man. "I guess I owe you another one." He nodded toward the baby and Molly while holding up the box of Jacks.

"Well, don't thank me yet." Madras curled his finger at someone in the hallway.

"Kopi!" Peter blurted.

"Actually, it's Kopilla," Madras corrected. "Come in, child. Come, come."

"But how?" Molly asked with obvious astonishment.

"Don't tell me," Peter said. "She stowed away."

"We found her in the Botanical Gardens," Madras said, vigorously nodding his as he spoke, "living happily off the low-hanging fruit. We managed to find her records. Her birth certificate says Kopilla, but she had a fraternal twin, a boy named Kopi. Unfortunately, he was lost in the war. Whether out of respect or denial, now she insists on using his name. I guess it's a hard habit to break."

Molly opened her arms invitingly. "Come here, sweetheart."

With small, tentative steps, the young woman moved closer to Peter's bedside and curtsied in a surprisingly well-mannered and feminine display as she greeted him. "Hello, Great Peter."

"My, my but you're unbelievable, kid." Peter laughed. "I like the dress, though; it suits you. But you can drop the 'Great' stuff. Peter will do just fine."

"How about 'Dad'?" Molly said with lifted brow and pulled the child to her side. She kissed the top of her head while looking impishly at Peter. "I want Kopi to be with us, too."

"What's one more," he said uneasily, wondering where this was all leading to, when Kopi jumped on him and peppered his cheek with kisses.

"Thank you, Grea— I mean Peter." But then she started to cry.

"What's the matter, honey?" Molly asked consolingly.

"Nobody mentioned school," Peter joked.

Sobbing, Kopi reached into the large, embroidered pocket of her blue and yellow floral-print dress and withdrew Molly's locket.

"My locket!"

"Kopi took, the day you die."

"Why didn't you take the ring too?" Molly asked, but the girl said nothing, just rocked side to side, staring at her feet.

"I guess the kid has an eye for value," Peter quipped.

They all laughed.

"Well, thank you," Molly said. "I'll cherish it even more now. But would you do me favor?"

"Oh, yes! Kopi do anything!"

Then Molly put the necklace around the girl's neck. "Will you wear it for me?"

"Thank you Great Molly."

"I suspect saying 'Great' will be another hard habit to break," Madras said.

Molly stood up and brushed the wrinkles out of her black slacks, part of the black and yellow moonbase uniform. ""Sorry, darling, but I have to go. Madras needs to speak with you and I have some arrangements to make. Back in about an hour." She kissed him goodbye, got up and walked to the door.

"Hey, good looking," Peter called after her. "I do see a difference in you."

"What?"

"No limp!"

"Ohhh, that's right. My new body's perfect. No more limp." She patted herself on the leg. "No stuttering either." She blew him another kiss. "Just get ready for a surprise when I get back."

"Another surprise?" he said, only half joking. "I'm not sure my heart can take it."

"Wait a minute." Molly returned to his bedside and thrust out her open hand. "Speaking of surprises, where's mine?" She dipped her head to the Cracker Jacks box.

"Oh yeah, I forgot." He handed her the paper-wrapped toy, which she enthusiastically extracted. "Well, what is it?"

She held up a tiny plastic Martian ankh.

* * *

As Peter lay in bed, still weak and woozy from what Molly had determined was a mild concussion, he listened to Madras drone on about the history of Mars, the next phase of human evolution and the realm of the spirit. While it was all very interesting, it did little to untangle his hopelessly conflicted emotions.

"You remember what we did to Mars?" Madras asked the obviously rhetorical question while nudging the side of the bed. "Peter? Are you listening?"

"Yeah, yeah. Listening." But he wasn't. He thought of the hangar bay, the spacecraft and home.

"We destroyed it." Madras said sternly, resuming his dissertation. "We destroyed each other—each other's form—and created maelstroms of pain and suffering—all unnecessary. We had become powerful in the material realm. And prideful. We exercised our power devoid of love. Hubris destroyed us then, Peter. And it has again.

"But why kill all the people, Madras? I still don't get that part."

"Have you forgotten what Pheras said about the terrorists?"

He shook his head.

"Because of divine grace and because we need a physical world to advance spiritually, to return to a state of perfection, we were given another world—Earth. But not before a long time had passed—a time of limbo—and not without conditions. These conditions were spelled out in a book: *The Book of the Martian Covenant*. Also called *The First Covenant*, it is a most solemn contract, a Holy Text.

"We had been given a second chance; we were permitted to take up human form again on Earth, but not as it had been in the beginning on Mars. We were allowed only those forms we had changed to with our genetic engineering on Mars. Every racial variety was retained. Every fruit of our own misguided labors. Groups of each racial variety were set down in a different part of the planet. Each was given a copy of *The First Covenant*. Those few who remained on Mars after the holocaust, those who had to live out their last lives as Martian citizens on a devastated planet were also given the sacred book. It was one of these that your Martian explorer spacecraft—your *aptly* named *Areopagus*—found and returned to Earth, the one Professor Venable deciphered. He knew what was coming. He knew that each individual soul had signed on to that agreement, including him; that each would be held to account for his or her choices.

"So we were allowed to start again, but aside from some few personal mementos of the past, we were permitted very little from the former world. No computers. No written material. No means of artificial memory whatsoever. We were like Robinson Crusoe's in a Second Eden.

"Without the technology, without the books, without writing implements, without easily accessible power, it took only a couple of generations before most of the old knowledge had been lost. Even the old language. Humanity reverted to a primitive state. Day-to-day survival took precedence over everything else. Luxuries of civilized culture that we had so taken for granted were but a vestigial memory."

"And the books," Peter wondered. "Why hasn't anyone ever found a copy of The Covenant before?"

"Our reverence for the Covenant, and all it stood for, diminished over time like an unwatched flame. Eventually all—save one—of the Earthly copies were destroyed."

"There's one left on Earth?"

"Not anymore. It's here. With the only other remaining Martian copy—the one we recovered from Mister Venable. We've placed it in its Holy place. Beside its sister in the Ark of the Covenant."

"The one Moses—?"

"The same. We brought it here centuries ago. To guarantee its preservation."

"So the Ark isn't lost in a warehouse somewhere," Peter mused, thinking of the Indiana Jones movie.

Madras looked puzzled.

"Never mind," Peter told him. "It would be too hard to explain. What happened next?"

"Soon we fragmented into vagrant tribes, scattering throughout the globe. It took a hundred thousand years to get it all back. But as a people we had learned little of true value. Some, yes. But not many. The terms of the Covenant provided quite simply that we not be allowed to destroy another world. That if it came to that again, a reconciliation would be made. Each of us would be held to account.

"And the time has come?"

Madras nodded grimly.

"I still don't get it. You and Molly and Bob—"

"Some—the few—have grown spiritually through the dint of their own effort, through wise but often difficult choices. For make no mistake, growth is never easy for anyone. Though in terms of pain of effort, the difficulty is the same for each one of us at his level of achievement. The next step is always just as hard as the one below it and the one above it. This way, in the end, the experience of life in all its complexity is completely fair and equal. Molly and Bob have, as it were, graduated through their own work to another level of being and awareness. They, and all the others here, as well as a multitude on Earth, have been given new and different bodies—"

"So Molly isn't really Molly at all, not the same one I knew."

"She is exactly the same, in every respect that matters—her spiritual nature. Only our bodies are slightly different."

"Different how?"

"For one thing, we are immune to the viruses that are going to be used in the Reconciliation. But simply put: Our capacities for pleasure are enhanced; our propensity to pain reduced. Rather than being the slave of our appetites, we will be their masters, able to summon them at will and slake them with keener satisfaction. But our physical bodies, our forms, are not who we are. Bodies are vessels of the spirit. Nothing more. Nothing less. They are important, yes. But they are not who we are. You must believe that—"

"So what's going to happen to them all? After the virus, after God annihilates all his bad boys and girls?"

Madras looked mortified. "Never, Peter! You have misjudged Him. He is ever the Creator, not the Destroyer. Would you kill even one of your children just because he had failed to meet your expectations? Because they failed geometry? Or social studies? Of course not! But neither would you lie to them and tell them that they had done well when you knew that they had not. You would hold them accountable, would you not? They would have to take geometry again and again, as many times as it took until they passed. Excellence, indeed perfection, lies on that path, does it not?

Madras reached around his neck and pulled out a golden Martian ankh on a chain. "Look at it another way. Imagine that we were gold, like the gold in this pendant. We all start with the same amount; we never lose as much as one atom of our share no matter what happens. But look again at this ankh. It is a thing of great beauty because it is fashioned by the creative efforts of Free Will. If you—or anyone—could choose between equal amounts of gold, one in the form of an undisturbed nugget and one sculpted with the divine spark of Will, which would you take? You see, we make all that's meaningful in this world; we are the makers of meaning. The ankh is an expression of the yearning for loving perfection through choice and action, yet it is at base no more valuable than the nugget. I tell you truly, Peter, that in the end, we will all shine as this ankh—as perfect expressions of God."

"You still haven't said what happens to them after you kill them."

"First, remember that we all must experience death of the physical body. It is necessary and cannot be avoided. Why that is so is a mystery known only to the Father of all things—or the Mother, if you prefer; the concept of male and female means nothing in the transcendent reality of the Creator." Madras sighed heavily, as if he, too, at that moment felt the burden of his own mortality. "But to answer your question directly, they will be moved to another place. Another planet in a distant galaxy. The conditions they will find there are less hospitable than the Edens of Earth or Mars. For these are unique. From their new home they will have to start over yet again. But make no mistake; it will be a much more difficult existence than that which was known on Earth. They will be monitored and helped when they ask—as individuals. But they must make their own world better, through their own choices, individually and collectively.

"This is not a curse or a punishment but a natural consequence of who we are and the choices we have made. For we are Children of God. Not just godlike. True gods!"

All well and good, he thought, yet his mind played incessant ping-pong with the paradoxical notions of death and salvation being necessary halves of the same completeness. Was this truly the fabled Judgment Day Madras now spoke of, the one predicted by every people of every time, by every religious tradition? Or the final battle for Earth against some alien horde?

But then he thought about his session with Pheras—all loving and harmonious, in a way he had never before experienced? That was more convincing than mere words; those thoughts, those feelings, targeted his heart. Even so, the idea that most of human life—his mother, Clancy—would soon be eradicated rattled him. His mind exploded with the staggering awareness. Despite his love for Molly, despite his growing belief and all his discordant feelings to the contrary, the proposed action—the Reconciliation—could not go forward unopposed. He was by instinct, after all, a warrior. Now he couldn't help but recall the conversation he'd overheard between Don and Wally, the men in the lab preparing for the dispersal of the penultimate virus. *Day after tomorrow, they'd said.* And Molly had told him he'd been out for two days. *That means today is the day! The ship hasn't left yet. There still may be time.*

***

Peter couldn't take his eyes off Molly or his mind off his plan as they raced down the dark-walled corridor in a globug. He kept trying to see if he could detect any difference in her, any physical change in the "new" Molly, the replacement body. But he couldn't. She was, if anything, even more beautiful than ever to his yearning eyes. Leaving her again would be the hardest thing he'd ever do. But then with all Madras and Pheras had told him, neither had reassured him as to where *he* was going. After all, his body had not been replaced; maybe he was slated for some "distant galaxy" with the others anyway. He was still an outsider, someone who had not passed some unspoken initiation.

She tilted her head against his, cooed lovingly. He'd wanted to drive, but she'd insisted, saying he still hadn't recovered from his concussion.

"Where're we going?"

"You'll see," she smiled. We're almost there. Besides, it's a surprise, remember?"

He didn't really want to meet any new people today; he just wanted to be with her a short while longer. Then he'd go to the hangar, the ship, and somehow find a way to throw a monkey wrench into their plans. If nothing else, he'd make his way back home. Back to Earth. *Beautiful Earth!*

"So where's Bo gone to?" he asked, still feeling guilty over their shared and sordid past.

"Working," she said casually.

"What's work here?"

"Oh, different things. Whatever's needed. Today I think he's helping to load the ship with the waterfowl," she said, bending over to kiss his cheek. The globug swerved.

"Better keep your eyes on the road," he advised, straining a chuckle. "You wouldn't want to kill the last remaining original person on the moon, would you?" *Maybe Bo can get me on the ship.*

"Don't forget Kopi," she corrected. "And Abel. Our family. Goodness! It feels almost unbearably wonderful just to say it. Family."

*My God! I can't leave them here.* But he forced himself to keep his mind on the mission, so he kept the tone of their conversation light and airy and continued the joke. "Now I know what the last dinosaur felt like."

She nudged him playfully. "You're so funny. That's one of the things I love about you. But no, today *you* are my lucky assignment. Just you."

"You know, something's puzzled me ever since I got here. Why all these ducks?"

"The ducks are the principal way the viruses are going to be introduced back on Earth."

"Don't the viruses kill the ducks?"

"These don't. It's really not unusual. Ducks make great homes for viruses. All of them are carriers of some virus or other. Of course most are harmless to humans. But sometimes they mutate while the ducks carry them. They change into bad ones that make people sick."

Driving with one hand, she used her other to finger the collar of his shirt, curling the hair around his ears with her deft fingers. It was a gesture that under better circumstances would have aroused and excited him but now it passed just above his level of consciousness, for he knew time was growing ever shorter. "But why not just throw a bunch of it into the water supply or something? Like Pheras said the terrorists were doing."

"Because this is a very natural—and efficient—way to get the job done. Remember the Hong Kong flu? Or Fujian flu? Or SARS? Practically every year a new flu virus gets started overseas, usually Asia. So many people there keep ducks, especially in China. Pigs too. But ducks are better for this project because many of them migrate, or they associate with other migratory species. So they made a better agent for spreading the viruses."

He thought her face saddened somewhat as she spoke. He hoped he was right about that; it mattered. "Hey!" His eyes locked onto the big red letters. "Stop here for a minute, will you?" They stopped at the Edenic Georgic Area entrance.

"What wrong?"

"This Georgic Area. That's where you came from, isn't it? The new you, I mean."

She nodded.

"Can we go in?"

"I don't see why not."

Her ready affirmative reply surprised him, caused him to shudder.

"But we can't take too much time," she cautioned. "We don't want to be—"

"I know, I know. Late. I just want a peek. See how it's done. You can give me the professional tour later." The globug whisked them through automatic doors, where inside assiduous technicians wandered about what looked like an empty warehouse talking to their Dick Tracy wrist-watch computers like the one Madras wore, speaking commands and receiving replies in a soothing female computer voice, seemingly oblivious to each other's presence—or theirs. "What's this?" He pointed to the only appliance in the large void of space, a small screen on a pedestal resembling a rather stylish ATM machine, except that it glowed with a weird bluish light.

"That's the main computer," she told him. "Amazing isn't it? Because it takes enormous computing power to deal with the genetics of farming new bodies. That's one thing we were right about—nanotechnology"

"Farming?" he asked, stunned.

"Yes. That's basically what georgic means: farming. All the genetic data for a given individual is manipulated here. Everything in that small computer is linked to the wrist computers and every other computer on the base. I'll show it to you in more detail another time, because—"

"We're running late. Okay, I've seen enough anyway." Strangely, he was beginning to feel at home here. The thought both frightened and amused him. Perhaps being with Molly again comforted him. Too bad it had to end. Somehow he'd have to get to the spacecraft, stow away like Kopilla did, and make it back to Earth. But for now he couldn't resist the pleasure of her company. He patted her lovingly on her back, ran his hand up between her shoulders, lifting her splendid red locks, exposing the milky nape of her neck and her baby-pink ear. She touched his thigh warmly.

"Hey! What's this?" he said, bending back the curve of her ear to expose a deep purple-pink scar. "Now where have I seen that before?"

"Oh, the ankh, the Martian symbol. It's really the only way you can tell our new bodies. It's a permanent scar from where the monitoring umbilical attached. We all have it. I'll show you in a minute."

The globug slowed to a crawl as Molly gave the automatic door opener time to operate. "We're entering the main cultivation area now," she said matter-of-factly, as if she were a docent on a museum tour.

"My God!" he gasped. The air filled his lungs and nostrils with a syrupy-sweet almost honeylike smell that nauseated him. There, on either side of the central concourse, running on for what looked like miles, were row upon row of large, clear, cylindrical tanks, each filled with a translucent liquid—and a developing human body! In various stages of development, from fertilized egg up through thirty-year-old men and women, every race of human being was represented. All were bathed in a soft bluish light, and all were connected through a wiring harness that ran up to a large conduit, which coursed back toward the main computer.

"The growth process is speeded up over two thousand times," Molly lectured. "From conception, which is done parthenogenically in that lab area over there, to mature adult takes place in only two to four days, depending..."

"That why I couldn't see you when I got here?"

"Partly," she nodded. "Oh, and look there, see? See that one?" She pointed to beautiful young woman of about eighteen years just beside the globug. The letters EVE in big red letters ran across the top of the cylinder. "She's an EVE.... Like me." She looked at him and smiled proudly. "There's the electrode attached behind her left ear. You can see it clearly there."

"Eve? I don't see that many." He looked down the rows of cylinders as far as he could but saw only one or two others so marked.

"I'm an Eve because I've been selected to be a mother. Not many of us will be. It's a truly a great honor here."

"Congratulations!" he said with all sincerity. "You finally got what you wanted."

"Only if I have you, too, Peter," she said with what seemed a twinge of sadness.

He stared at the massive underground people farm. *On the moon!* He was reminded again of Madras's fish story. "We all thought we were so smart," he muttered, remembering the hubris Madras had mentioned over and over again. "But we weren't so smart after all." He motioned to her, signaling that he'd seen enough, and so they left.

"Ho, hum," Molly sighed only moments later, as the globug bucked and jitterbugged to a stop. "It's still not a perfect world, is it?"

"Our stallion must need some grass and water," Peter joked. *Time to say goodbye, Molly.*

"Guess so," she smiled. "Well, it's not that far. Feel up to a walk?"

"Suits me." He jumped off the globug and nearly fell over from the sharp knifelike pain of a shin splint. Rubbing his leg, he hobbled alongside her. Gaily, she put his arm over her shoulder to help support him.

"Poor old man," she consoled. "You're going to feel a lot better real soon."

He laughed. But suddenly, his scar began to itch dreadfully. He spotted a bathroom in an alcove between two corridors, one of which he knew led to the hangar. "Wait," he said, pointing. "When you gotta go, you gotta go."

"I'll be here for you," she said, and kissed him.

But as soon as she had turned away, he bolted for the hangar and instantly he was lost and confused. He couldn't remember the right way. He turned the corner, kept walking. Faster. Past the animals cages, one upon another, row after row. Frighteningly, some lunged at him, being stopped only by the thick Plexiglas; some growled menacingly; some just paced relentlessly back and forth and greeted him with vacant stares. A colossal king cobra reared its hooded head, and though he could not hear it, he could see and feel it hiss at him; its eyes seeming to convey a lethal warning.

Big-headed, big-eyed Grays skittered this way and that, going about their duties with focused determination. Then, without waning, the corridor grew darker than before. Only the indirect light from the animal cages illuminated the way. Or was he growing faint? *My eyes?*

Suddenly, he bumped into—*Molly!*

"Peter. What happened?"

"I-I don't know," he stuttered, thinking of the old Molly, the real Molly.

"You must've gotten turned around; it's easy to do in this place. And you're not over that concussion either. Come on, this way."

She dragged him along by his cold wet hand, but her touch no longer soothed his dread. They passed the door where only a couple of days before Madras had mercifully stopped and introduced him to Bob. Beyond it, now only twenty or thirty steps away, outlined in a supernatural yellow light, was the door of his ghastly dream at the mission. The day Molly died. A door behind which he'd felt an indeterminate evil, or so he'd thought. But just like Molly and Pheras and the rest, this was no dream. And his fear was real. Palpable. Hair stiffened on his neck. His heart pounded. Sweat ran in torrents. His whole body tensed reflexively, sensing a corporeal danger, making it difficult to put one foot after the other. *It's just my body,* he told himself, over and over. Not something ultimately important. His real self, his soul would survive any encounter, wouldn't it? Still—?

Molly! His rock. She was beside him. Holding his hand tightly, tighter even as they approached the door, now only a brief few paces away. Now at last he knew. The phantom in his dream at Father Easterbrook's mission. The phantom that his dream paralysis prevented him from seeing as he approached that awful door outlined in yellow light.

*Molly!*

His terror now blended with a sudden and buoyant elation. Fear of extinction transformed itself into a feeling of eager anticipation, of wondrous surprise, of a gift-giving ceremony. *Like Christmas morning.*

Compelled, he reached for the doorknob, but she stepped in front of him, grabbed it for him, smiling radiantly, lovingly. In one easy motion, she flung the door open wide.

*Cap!*

Bob Donaldson stood with Madras on either side of a man in a wheel chair who faced away from him. And there was the man called Apollyon, whose ankh Peter still wore.

*My God! He does have wings!*

Out of the corner of his eye, entering through a side door, he glimpsed another figure who looked familiar in some strange way, but who—*Reggie! Without the mustache.*

And there was Molly's uncle Malcolm. And Kopilla. And Lilah toasting drinks with Bo. All smiling. Welcoming. Joyous. They clapped their hands in enthusiastic ovation and as a chorus said, "Congratulations, Peter!" As they cheered, Madras gleefully spun the wheelchair around.

*Ouch!*

He felt a sting on his neck. Reflexively, he slapped at it, as if it were a mosquito and hit Molly's hand. A creeping numbness washed over him Just before his vision faded completely away, he at last recognized the man in the chair.

*It's me!*

# EPILOGUE: COMMENCEMENT

"Now what?" Li Kwan Lo bellowed.

"He says it's still not fresh," the boyish-looking waiter replied. "He says he'll have your job. He says—"

"Fool!" He sunk the blade of his meat cleaver deep into the hard oak chopping block. As head chef at the Grand Hotel Beijing, he was normally a sedate and reasonable man, but this was an outrage. For the second time, the grumpy patron had sent back his renowned Orange Duck, the flagship entree on his laudable menu, complaining that the duck was not fresh. Such a craven allegation had never before been leveled at the kitchen of the mighty Grand, nor had he, personally, ever before been so maligned. Much less threatened.

"What should I tell him?" the intimidated young waiter asked, stepping out of range of the fulminating chef, who seemed to be looking for something else to grab.

"Tell him...tell him to go to hell. Or at least to go some other place to eat."

"But sir!"

"All right! All right!" Li Kwan calmed himself as much as he could given the circumstances. He pounded the chopping block with his fist and thought what to do. "I know. Come with me."

The obedient young waiter followed Li Kwan out the back door of the kitchen, past the loading dock, down the steps to the fowl yard, where hundreds of hapless ducks, chickens, pheasants, quail, and pigeons spent the last moments of their wretched lives in wicker cages, awaiting the dubious honor of becoming the centerpiece of one of Li Kwan's famous dishes and the pinnacle of some rich patron's quest for epicurean adventure.

Li Kwan pointed to a cage. "Take that mallard. Quickly." He brushed the air with his hand like a flapping wing. "Come on! Come on!"

Hunched over with his head down like a scolded child, the young waiter grabbed the yellow wicker cage and quickly tried to catch up with Li Kwan, who was already half way back to the kitchen. Inside, the waiter looked expectantly at his boss.

"Bind his wings and bill," the chef ordered.

"But I—"

"Never mind," Li Kwan growled, snatching the cage. The duck squawked loudly in protest, as if it knew its ineludible fate. A wooden clothespin secured the duck's bill and ended its squawking; a thin rubber band bound its already flightless wings. On his way through the kitchen, Li Kwan stopped, uttered some unrepeatable curse, and grabbed a pair of pliers from a small tool kit kept in the top drawer of a file cabinet. "Take me to his table," he commanded his young assistant.

Startled patrons gasped and stared in stunned disbelief as the two brushed by, duck in hand. Some muttered rude remarks concerning the advisability of such an unsanitary practice in any restaurant, much less the mighty Grand; some declared they'd never come again. At that moment, Li Kwan could not have cared less.

At last the two arrived at the finicky guest's VIP alcove, an ornate faux pagoda, one of which was built into each corner of the fabulous dining hall. Made from the finest polished ebony, with two real elephant's tusks accenting the entranceway, each pagoda was artfully adorned with ivory figurines and gold leaf, affording the ultimate in sedate private dining for a select few of the Grand's wealthiest dinner guests.

Up the plush carpeted steps Li Kwan strode, pausing at the top to compose himself, for in his present stormy state of mind he feared he'd speak too coarsely. Through the pellucid rice-paper swinging doors he could see the table where his fastidious patron, a corpulent man of what he guessed was Middle Eastern descent, sat with a female companion close by, a young woman who appeared half his middle-age and only half interested in being there. Across from them was a large-framed man with blond-streaked white hair to match his starched white shirt and a navy blue- and blood red-striped tie. From his accent, Li Kwan pegged him as American. He listened for a moment to the self-important fusillades of overblown rhetoric, a preview of what he would momentarily confront.

"With all respect, Admiral," the dark-complexioned man said with what sounded to Li Kwan like a mocking, superior tone, "Blalock was your biggest handicap from the beginning. If you'd only consulted me, I could've told you he wasn't to be trusted."

"So, you're telling me Reggie Bell went rogue, killed Blalock and his men, then took off with Venable and the book?"

"That, as you Americans say, is the long and the short of it."

"Ah, it doesn't matter now anyway. We found their scummy little alien base in Uganda and kicked their little green asses into the next galaxy."

"Green? Is that what they really looked like?"

"Actually, we don't know. We weren't able to capture any of them."

"But you're sure they're all gone?"

"Sure as we need to be. It was obvious the base had been there a long, long while. If they'd had the capability to do us any harm, they would've by now. No, our invaders from Mars—or wherever the little bastards came from—won't be a concern going forward. At least not this bunch. Now, about the Homeland Security contract for your research center—what's it called again?"

"Aquarian Genomic Research Center. Just think AGRC. We have some excellent scientists with us. The best. We can handle anything in the biotechnology area for you."

Li Kwan could abide the schizoid conversation—and the now frantically squirming mallard—no longer. "Sir," he said, restraining his urge to say something less civil as he entered the swank retreat. "I am Li Kwan Lo, your chef. I understand the duck was not to your liking."

"When I pay top price," the man said snidely, "I expect the best. I'll accept nothing less. The duck you gave me was older than my grandmother, and about as tough an old bird as she was. If you can't do better—"

Li Kwan raised his hand to stem the ugly screed and bowed. In a flash, he thought of his wife and children. It was not, after all, entirely out of the question that this man could cause him difficulty. Such positions as his required not only talent but also political connections; someone better connected might be given an opening by just such an unpleasant incident as this. He managed to calm his rage. Through gritted-teeth smile he said, "If you would be so kind." He bowed again and presented the mallard. "As you can see, I have here a live mallard."

"You show me a live one now," the patron grumbled, "but you'll just bring back the same one you gave me the last two times. I want to see your—"

"But, sir," Li Kwan interrupted, "if you will permit me. May I see your room key?"

The dark-eyed man, whose pockmarked complexion shown with a slick sheen even in the low light, groaned as he reached into his white dinner jacket pocket and produced the requested room key.

"Thank you, kind sir." He bowed once more, still lower in mocking deference. He handed the mallard, with its beautifully shimmering green head, to the young waiter and with all the crispness of a drill sergeant, sternly commanded, "Hold him."

Taking the pliers, he bent the metal ring that held the key to the Grand's emblem, a golden pagoda, separating them and allowing him to remove the key, which he then handed back to his testy patron. Next he positioned the ring so that its two open ends straddled the web of the duck's foot and pinched it closed, securing the pagoda with its room number to the duck. The injured duck lurched violently, breaking the rubber band that had immobilized its wings. For a second or two, its beautiful iridescent blue wing chevrons flashed stroboscopically, producing a flurry of downy fluff, which mingled with the invisible dust to create a haze of prickly air.

"My apologies," Li Kwan said, bowing more deeply than ever. "*This* is *your* duck. Please accept with my compliments and that of the Grand Beijing Hotel, Mister?"

"Bliss...Bandar Bliss," said the troublemaker. "And you'd best remember it—" He put his chubby finger to his nose, rubbing it furiously. *"Ahhh. Ahhh. Ahhhchooo!"*

# THE END

Milton Keynes UK
Ingram Content Group UK Ltd.
UKHW040659021124
450602UK00003B/25

9 798895 311172